Hiding Behind The Couch

Those
Jeffries Boys

by
Debbie McGowan

Beaten Track
www.beatentrackpublishing.com

I0630974

Those Jeffries Boys

First published 2016 by Beaten Track Publishing
Copyright © 2016, 2018 Debbie McGowan

All rights reserved.
No part of this publication may be reproduced, stored in a retrieval system, or transmitted, in any form or by any means, without the prior permission of the publisher, nor be otherwise circulated without the publisher's prior consent in any form of binding or cover other than that in which it is published and without a similar condition including this condition being imposed on the subsequent publisher.

The moral right of the author has been asserted.

ISBN: 978 1 78645 044 9

Cover Design: Decorous Anarchy Studios
decorousanarchystudios.wordpress.com

Beaten Track Publishing,
Burscough, Lancashire.
www.beatentrackpublishing.com

For Andrea…

This is but a token of my appreciation for all that you are, and all that you do for me.

(A ludicrously) Belated Happy Birthday, mate. Love ya. (Think we can skip the hearts and flowers, though.)

Deb x

Contents

1: Double Hit
Tuesday, 25th September

"Night, night, baby girl." Mike Jeffries blew a kiss to his daughter, gave the dimmer a half turn, and backed out of the tiny space that served as their bedroom. Bethan had only recently started sleeping through the night, and Mike was grateful for the brief few hours' reprieve from six months of sheer exhaustion, although with it came a new set of worries, about whether she had rolled over and suffocated, or wriggled down past the cot bumper and knocked herself unconscious on the hard wooden bars of her cot, or…

He imagined too many awful things, and his brothers, sisters-in-law, mum, dad—even his mum's husband—all said exactly the same. He was worrying over nothing, but it was perfectly natural. These were the wonders of parenthood, of which he was effectively taking a double hit. Being a single parent was the toughest challenge he had ever faced, and it was unending. Yet for the first time in his life, he knew he would never stop trying to get it right; he would never give up.

Bethan was his reason for getting out of bed every morning, his motivation for long hours of hard slog. Just one glimpse of her smile could take away the aches and pains of the day, and her giggles made his heart swell with love. Through teething, terrible colds and poorly tummies, he had matched her tear for tear, powerless to ease her suffering. And if someone had made the offer—your life for her well-being—he would have taken it without a second thought. She was his everything.

But for all of this, Mike looked forward to the hour or so he got to himself after Bethan had gone to sleep. As usual, he made a coffee and lay full stretch on the sofa, listening with eyes closed to the TV's murmur, the heater's hum. In a minute, he'd get his phone and see what was happening online—it was still early evening, so there should be a few people around. He'd never been the sociable type—thinking back, there was no-one from his past he would even have called a friend. Drinking buddies, teammates, people he worked with—he'd always had plenty of company if he'd wanted it, and he *had* wanted it.

Now, he didn't know what he wanted. As a painter and decorator, he spent most days working on his own. Sometimes, on the bigger jobs, he'd be part of a crew, but the mainstay of his work came from private houses, where the occupants left him to get on with the job unhindered, give or take a household pet or two. It was tough going—long hours and lots of physical exertion—but he was good at it, and if nothing else, it kept him fit, which was as well. He hardly got out for a run these days, and his daily trips to the gym were a thing of the distant past. His mum said he was welcome to use the gym in the house anytime—she'd even come and sit with Bethan—but Mike had imposed enough.

Bethan was three days old when Rachel walked out on them, and Mike had panicked. He could barely look after himself, never mind a newborn baby. He'd focused on what he could do—get them both away from the flat, to somewhere safe—but he'd caused so much trouble that Len—his mum's fourth husband—had threatened to do him over if he came anywhere near them again. In desperation, he'd turned up on his brother's doorstep—not Dan's, but Andy's. He'd begged for asylum, and Andy had granted it without question.

Even now, Mike was amazed—and profoundly grateful—that Andy had taken them in. They'd never got on. Back when they were kids, their mum used to say 'two's company, three's a crowd' to explain why one of them was always left out, and the one that was left out was usually Mike. But then, there was only a year between Andy and Dan; they were more than brothers, they were friends, whereas Mike was just the loser who couldn't keep a job or a relationship. He might've been the eldest, but it didn't guarantee their respect, because respect was earned. He knew that now. And he'd done nothing to earn theirs.

When Mike had first met Rachel, he was newly divorced, and he was man enough to hold his hands up and admit it was his fault the marriage had failed. Anne had put up with a lot of crap over the years, of him flitting from job to job, the drinking, the mood swings—he'd done everything he could to annihilate their marriage, although not intentionally. He'd been an idiot, too caught up in feeling sorry for himself to care about the damage he was doing to other people—his mum and brothers included.

He was disgusted and remorseful, and Anne was still too angry to accept his apologies. He didn't blame her. She'd wasted seventeen years of her life trying to make their marriage work, and she was doing great without him. After she'd kicked him out, she'd sold the house and moved down south—new town, new job… Without him dragging her down, she was happy and successful. She deserved it. She was getting a second chance while she was still young enough to make the most of it.

Mike realised he had also been given a second chance. If Bethan hadn't come into his life, he'd still have been making those same mistakes. He was a long way from finding happiness, or success—forty-four, single and living in his mum's converted summerhouse—but he was finally on the right track, and he was determined to give Bethan the best start he could. In the new year, he was going to find them a house, where she would have her own room with the most beautiful wallpaper he could find, a soft, thick carpet, and more toys than she knew what to do with.

Whatever Bethan wanted—a bike, her own playground in the garden, anything—he would provide. He had to get it right, make sure she knew how much he loved her, how much he'd wanted her, that she wasn't a mistake. Because one day, she'd want to know about her mum, and he was dreading telling her.

Some mummies find it very hard to look after their babies…

Sometimes having a baby makes the mummy sick…

Your mother is serving a life sentence for murder.

He didn't want to think about it. He picked up his phone, unlocked it, wasted five minutes waiting for his newsfeed to load, and decided he didn't want to be sociable, either. Instead, he drank his coffee and switched the TV over to the football, although he saw five minutes of the game at most before his thoughts drifted back to Rachel. He didn't love her. He'd never loved her. He'd tried to do the right thing, to stand by her. Preventing Bethan's conception had been his responsibility as much as Rachel's, and the truth was he couldn't remember if they'd used a condom. There was too much crap in the way, and he couldn't think clearly. It made him frustrated and angry and reminded him of how utterly powerless he had been, how powerless he *was*…

He awoke in the middle of the night, got his duvet from his bed, and slept on the couch.

When his phone alarm sounded at six-thirty, Bethan was already awake and chattering to herself. Mike listened and smiled. She was such a happy baby, hardly any bother, really, even if she didn't sleep as much as he would have liked. Wrapping the duvet around him, he went to the bedroom and watched his daughter, sitting in the centre of her cot, the telltale dark patches around her middle a good indication of another nappy failure.

"Come on, monster. Let's have a shower." He dumped the duvet and lifted Bethan out, dangling her at arm's length and breathing through his mouth as he set the shower running and put her down on the bathmat.

"Ready?" he said. She giggled as he grabbed the top of her Babygro and tugged. The press-studs popped one after the other in rapid succession, like popcorn in a pan. "Ew. Stinky." With a wad of toilet paper at the ready, Mike removed the full, wet nappy and as much of the poo from her skin as he could. He quickly undressed, scooped up his daughter, and stepped under the shower with her. There wasn't time in the mornings to wash and feed her and then wash and feed himself, and she loved the shower. She tilted her little head back and half-closed her eyes, shaky gasps of excitement escaping her as the water sprayed over her face, making her skin sparkle under the bathroom light.

One-handed, Mike squeezed shower gel onto the sponge—he was used to smelling like InfaCare these days—gave Bethan a good clean and then himself. He squirted a tiny blob of shampoo onto his palm and another onto his head, knowing she would copy his actions as he washed her hair. Rachel was blonde and fair skinned, but Bethan's complexion was dark, with thick deep-brown wavy hair—'the Jeffries genes', as their family called them, even though it came from their mum's side, not their dad's.

Bethan cooed and giggled as Mike screwed up his eyes against the sting-free shampoo. He had suds dripping off his nose and into his mouth, and he stuck his head right under the water to rinse off, shaking like a wet dog before repeating the rinse-off process more gently with his daughter.

Back to the bedroom to dry off and dust with talc, a moment of panic flashed through Mike's mind, as it did every morning. *I have no bloody idea what I'm doing!* Six months of muddling through, learning new skills that were nothing like he'd ever done before—fastening nappies, picking tiny pink outfits, getting little woolly tights the right way around. What had his life become, that one of his greatest delights was no longer having to sterilise bottles, teats, bowls and spoons?

He set Bethan down in the middle of the bed while he dressed, gave her hair a quick blow with the hairdryer on a cool setting, and then it was onwards to the kitchen.

"Meeeeaaaaaawwwww…" He zoomed her, Supergirl style, across their small open-plan room to her high chair. He settled her in it and got the kettle on.

"Weetabix?" he asked, even though any suggestion would have resulted in the same response of 'Esss!' He put a jug of milk in the microwave to warm, two slices of bread in the toaster, prepared a feeder cup of no-added-sugar strawberry squash, stuck a teabag in a mug, added the milk to the Weetabix in the sucker-bottomed bowl, found a spoon, filled his cup…

The toast popped as he stuck the bowl to the high-chair tray. He congratulated himself on his expert multitasking, handed Bethan her spoon and set about buttering his toast.

"Mmmm," Bethan said.

"Is that yummy?" he asked, glancing her way. "Ah, crap." He started to laugh, because if he didn't…well, he tried only to laugh these days. It had taken less than ten seconds and one spoonful of breakfast cereal—specifically, the one cereal he could have used to affix dado rails and cornices—to ruin a clean outfit in the absence of a bib. Still, if he'd been rating his performance out of ten, it would have been around an eight. The dress would wash, as would his daughter, who by this point was almost entirely covered in Weetabix.

"I'll help you," he said, taking a bite of toast and advancing on Bethan, who shook her head rapidly. "Come on, sweetheart. Nana's waiting."

"Nnnn."

"Yep. Daddy's gotta go work."

"Mm…mm…mm…mah!"

A few seconds of trying to wrestle the spoon from Bethan's clutches and Mike gave up and got a second spoon. Another bite of toast, another spoonful of Weetabix down the hatch. If he hadn't forgotten the bib, they'd have been done in record time, but there was always something. When Bethan was done eating, he gave her the cup of juice. She couldn't make any more mess, and it might loosen up some of the dried-on cereal. He left her with her drink while he went to find her a clean dress and returned with a little peach skirt and cream jumper—

He stopped in the middle of the room, breathing out heavily through his nose. *Count to ten…one, two, three…*

"How, madam, did you get that lid off?"

She gave him a grin, showing off her two new front teeth through the dribbly waterfall of strawberry squash dripping from her hair and running all down her face. It would have to be a baby-wipe cleanup; time was running out. He quickly whipped the dress off, using it to soak up as much of the juice as possible, gave Bethan's face a good polish with a handful of baby wipes, put on her clean clothes, scooped her out of the chair, downed as much of his tea as he could in one gulp, grabbed the remaining piece of now cold toast and his keys, and set off across the garden to the house.

It was a drizzly morning, still a little dark, making the not-so-distant glow of the kitchen lights warm and welcoming. His mum would have been up an hour already, making breakfast for Len and taking a quick early morning swim ahead of a day of minding whichever grandchildren came her way. Mike entered through the conservatory doors, inhaling the familiar chlorine-humid air as he walked along the edge of the pool.

"Morning," he called, stepping into the big airy kitchen, where his mum was sitting at the table, reading a magazine and drinking coffee.

"Morning, love. Is it raining?"

"A bit," Mike confirmed and pointed at Bethan. "This one's wet because she just tipped her juice over her head."

"Ah." His mum chuckled and rolled her eyes. "I don't know about you, missus." She took her granddaughter and gave her a kiss on the forehead. "Mmm. You taste lovely." Bethan cooed in response. "Busy day?" she asked Mike.

"I've got to finish off one job and price up another. Should be done mid-afternoon. Is that all right?"

"I'm not going anywhere until five."

"I'll definitely be back by then. See you later."

With a kiss for Bethan and another for his mum, Mike went out to his van, checked everything he needed was in the back, and set off down the long gravel driveway. He stopped to open the gates; the postman arrived as he drove through them.

"Morning," Mike greeted as he moved to get out of the van to shut the gates again. The postie was in his usual attire of shorts and a short-sleeved shirt; he'd no doubt still be dressed like that come January.

"Morning," he said. "I'll shut them when I'm done."

"Cheers, mate." Mike closed his van door and set off for the Hunters' house. He'd been working on it for the past fortnight and needed to put the finishing touches to the hallway—a bit of architrave and a replacement skirting board. It was a big house, not unlike his mum's place, with high ceilings and heavy old doors, which had been stripped back to good, solid oak by the previous occupants, and the Hunters had asked him to paint them in white gloss. The bare-wood trend had passed long ago, which Mike thought was a shame, especially when the timber was in good condition. Still, they paid him for his wallpaper-hanging skills, not his opinion.

Pulling up outside the Hunters', he was surprised to see a car in the drive. Mrs. Hunter had given Mike a key to the back door; she'd normally left before he arrived and didn't get back until around four o'clock with the kids. Or not 'kids', really, seeing as the youngest was in sixth form, and the eldest was at university, doing the modern equivalent of Mike's degree. Back when he was at uni, it was called 'Computing, Information and Communication Technology'; now it was 'Computer Systems Engineering'.

When Mike was in his twenties, his knowledge of computers put him in hot demand. He'd entered the work force at the beginning of the home computer boom, when the first mass-produced PCs came onto the market. His first job had been working for a company that installed computers in people's homes and offered on-the-spot training to its customers, which was how he'd met Anne. Her dad had bought a top-of-the-range Apple Macintosh—the sort that sold for more now than it had then, and it had cost a pretty penny to start with. However, his ex-father-in-law's understanding of technology stopped at switching the kettle on, and in all the years Mike had known Alan, he hadn't got much beyond that.

While the rest of Mike's colleagues had kept their skills up to date, he hadn't. He had no excuses. He was just a lazy git who worked as little as possible. It wasn't long after he and Anne married that she had set her first ultimatum, and it was a fair one. They'd bought a house, and they had bills to pay. All she'd asked was that he earned enough to pay half, and it wasn't that much. He could have earned the month's bills in a week if he'd put his mind to it.

'Couldn't be arsed' was the story of his life, and in the end, Mike's IT skills had been about as much use as his father-in-law's, but he was working on it. He'd been saving up to buy a computer and catch up on all those years he'd wasted.

Mike didn't feel comfortable letting himself in the back door of the Hunters' house when there was obviously someone home, so he rang the doorbell and returned to his van to unload.

The door opened, and Mrs. Hunter peered out through the rain. "You're early today."

"Am I?" Mike knew different, but it wasn't in his interests to contradict the woman holding the purse strings.

She checked her watch. "Goodness. Is it that time already? Oh, well. They'll manage without me a little longer. I've got your money here. Coffee? It's fresh."

"Great, thanks." Mike followed her in, set his ladder against the hallway wall and went back to his van for the paint, brushes and adhesive. The aromas of coffee and perfume greeted him on his return, prompting a flashback to mornings with Anne. *The same perfume?* Whatever, it wasn't a bad memory. Shutting the front door behind him, Mike stopped to admire his work. He'd done a damned good job of it, even if he did say so himself. The colour scheme Mrs. Hunter had gone with was bright and neutral, and there were so many lights in the place that every seam had to be spot on.

"Milk and sugar?" she called from the kitchen.

"Please. One sugar." Mike went through to join her. The kitchen had the same neutral scheme as the rest of the house, with white porcelain tiles, which were a bugger to put up because they were heavy, and he couldn't get a decent key on the smooth plaster. In the end, he'd swallowed his pride and asked Andy for tips, which resulted in his brother coming to give him a hand in return for a pint. It was a deal that worked all in Mike's favour, and he felt both gratitude and guilt; he already owed Andy big time.

"You've done a wonderful job, Mike. I've been telling everyone."

"Thanks. I'm glad you're pleased with it."

"More than pleased. Delighted." She picked up an envelope from the counter and handed it over with Mike's coffee. "There's a letter of recommendation in with the payment," she said.

"Thanks very much." Mike was astounded. "That means a lot."

"Credit where it's due. You've no idea how many cowboys there are out there. Well, you probably do. I don't know if I told you, but when I asked you for an estimate, I'd already had one from Heysham's. They quoted five hundred pounds more than you, and when I requested references, they couldn't provide any. Instead, they sent me a link to a photo album of previous jobs. Well, anyone could put one of those together, couldn't they?"

Mike nodded in agreement. Heysham's were his only real competition—a family business that employed additional staff—but their reputation was appalling. Jobs left unfinished, shoddy workmanship, overshooting their completion dates. However, he wasn't going to actively bad-mouth them. It would only come back to get him later.

"I'll leave you to it," Mrs. Hunter said. She picked up her coffee cup and drained it at the same time as collecting her bag. She put the cup in the dishwasher and was almost at the door when she turned back. "Oh, before I forget, I've passed your number on to a friend of mine. She's got an apartment in Dovedale."

"Yeah? My brother lives there."

"Right, so you've seen the apartments. Not as big as this place, admittedly, but I think she wants the full works, and sooner rather than later. Anyway, much as I'd love to chat with you all day..."

"Have a good one," Mike said.

"I'll do my best." A few seconds later, he heard the front door close, but before he had a chance to relish the peace and solitude, his phone buzzed in his pocket. He took it out, his heart skipping a beat when he saw his mum's number displayed. *Oh shit, oh shit...*

"Hey, Mum."

"Michael. Sorry to disturb you when you've only just got to work. Before I go any further, Bethan's fine."

That was a relief, although it might be a while before he was steady enough to climb his ladder. "What's up?"

"A court letter has come for you."

"What for?"

"Do you want me to open it?"

"Please."

His mum put her phone on speaker, and he listened to the envelope being slit open, the paper being withdrawn. Then silence. "Mum?"

"Hold on, I'm reading."

He tried to think of any occasions in the past few months he'd parked where he shouldn't, or jumped a red light, or been flashed by a speed camera. His insurance was current, and he'd been making the IVA payments—

"It says you're required to attend a meeting at the family court at the request of Jacqueline Perry—is that Rachel's mother?"

"Yeah," Mike confirmed. He leaned back on the cupboard behind him and knocked over a vase but caught it before the flowers slid out. *Family court?* Rachel's mother had been there for the trial, but she'd made no attempts to contact Mike or see Bethan since. In fact, the only member of Rachel's family he'd seen was her younger brother, Pez, and only then, because he worked for Len. "Does it say why?" he asked.

"To discuss her intention to seek a special guardianship order."

"I don't understand. What does that mean?"

"She wants custody of Bethan."

Mike's blood pressure spiked. He felt like his head was going to burst. "Oh, no. No way."

"She's not going to get it, love."

He wanted to believe that, but his mother's certainty was overridden by the lies Rachel claimed she'd told her family, about him raping her and keeping her trapped in his flat. His mum was reassuring him based on what she knew, and she knew nothing about any of that. The courts would believe Rachel's mother over him. She was a deputy headteacher who had raised three children, and he was just a painter and decorator living in a glorified shed where he had to share a room with his daughter.

"Are you still there, Mike?"

"Err, yeah. When is it?"

"Next Wednesday. Do you want me to call the lawyer?"

"Better had."

"All right, love. Try not to worry. I'll see you later."

"Thanks, Mum. Bye."

2: The Whole of the Moon
Wednesday, 26th September

With Rosie on one hip and Sorsha lying on the changing mat and kicking her legs in the air, Andy attempted to keep his phone gripped between his chin and shoulder. Nappyless Sorsha gurgled and started to pee. Andy grabbed a wad of tissues to soak it up. His phone slipped and fell with a thunk and a splash, right into the puddle.

"Crap," he said, hoping his cursing wasn't a prediction of what was coming next. He retrieved his phone and set it to one side. "Dropped my phone," he said loudly by way of explaining to Shaunna on the other end of the line. "Give me a sec."

Andy grabbed a cushion off the couch, put it on the floor next to the changing mat and laid Rosie on it. Both sisters turned to look at each other and made cooing noises. Andy sighed contentedly—being a *real* dad had well and truly done for his pretentions of wanting to be free and independent forever—and gave his phone a quick once-over with a baby wipe. He put it to his ear again and felt a dribble run down his cheek. Could be pee, could be baby-wipe juice, he didn't care. Gazing at his three-month-old twin daughters, he returned to his conversation with their mummy.

"What were you saying again?"

"Dinner at Dan and Adele's on Saturday."

"Ah, yeah. I think she's bonkers."

"She's not sick, she's pregnant."

Andy chuckled. "I knew that, didn't I?" He was asking his daughters. They didn't offer an opinion.

"Why's she bonkers?" Shaunna asked. "Adele wants to have one last dinner party before the caesarean."

"That's what I mean. Why *before*? I mean, I get she's gonna be incapacitated for a couple of weeks, but you can still have dinner parties when you've got a baby."

"Ha. Just because you're Dad of the Year…"

"I wouldn't go that far." Andy grinned around his words. He was loving every minute of being a dad. Shaunna had been back at work for a month already, and she was more than happy for him to be the stay-at-home parent. Even so, her praise was an aphrodisiac, not that they needed any help in that department.

"So, I'll give Mike a call," she said.

"He won't come. I'll tell you that now."

"Yeah, he will," Shaunna asserted confidently. She had a trick up her sleeve, of that Andy was quite sure, especially when she added, "Just leave him to me and Adele." His poor brother stood no chance.

"OK, so if Mike comes, Mum's going to be looking after Bethan, yeah?"

"Yep. She's having all four of them."

Andy made a quick grab for Rosie as she rolled towards Sorsha and off the cushion. "Poor Len. Gotta feel sorry for the bloke."

"Poor Len nothing. He said he can't wait."

That was probably true. Andy's stepdad didn't look like the doting grandad type—he was a tough nut, with his many-times-broken nose and gruff voice that spoke of a history involving a bit more than dodgy business deals—but he loved having the grandkids over, including Krissi, although at almost twenty-five she didn't exactly need babysitting. No matter that they weren't Len's blood relatives; he would lay down his life for any one of them.

"So anyway," Shaunna continued, "I'm going to call Mike on my lunch break."

"You know he'll have a million excuses."

"And I've prepared a million comebacks, so we're all good."

"OK. I'll leave him in your capable hands, then."

"You'd better believe it. Love you."

"Love you, too. Bye." Andy hung up. "Right, girls. Let's get those nappies on, and we can go shopping for Mummy's dinner."

***

Had Shaunna known her boss was planning on redecorating the salon, she'd have suggested Mike for the job, but it was too late now. The guy Hayley had booked was due any moment, and Shaunna was trying to rationalise. Of course she wasn't going to sabotage the bloke's visit, and she definitely wasn't going to subtly suggest to Mike that he pop into the salon, or hint to Hayley that her brother-in-law was a painter and decorator. Joking aside, that really wasn't a good idea. It was bad enough that Hayley had 'the hods' for two Jeffries brothers. A third would probably see the place going up in flames.

Instead, Shaunna sent Mike a text message, to ask if he was free to talk at lunchtime, and then picked up the hairdryer, ready to dry her client's hair.

"I'll go and pud the keddle on, sweedie," Hayley announced and disappeared through the door to the salon storeroom.

"OK," Shaunna called, after the event.

Leah—her client—met her gaze in the mirror. "Are you all right?"

"Hm? Oh, yeah. I was just thinking." Shaunna smiled to cover her disgruntlement and quickly checked her phone to see if Mike had responded, which he hadn't. She switched on the dryer and lifted a section of hair with the brush. Her eyes lost focus, taking her thoughts with them.

She wasn't especially surprised Mike hadn't replied. Since he'd moved into the summerhouse at his mum and Len's place, he'd been taking on as much work as he could, trying to save up for a house for him and Bethan. Andy and Dan had offered to help him out with a loan for the down payment, but Mike refused, and not out of stubbornness. Out of pride.

Whilst the three brothers were similar in many ways—beyond their dark good looks and strong, muscular physiques—they were also starkly different in others. Mike was the eldest and the least confident of the three; Dan, the youngest, was more serious and intense than his older brothers. Andy, the middle child, was the most gregarious and impulsive, although they all shared the same competitive streak, and they were risk-takers.

However, where Dan and Andy made their own opportunities, Mike was reluctant to put himself out there, in both his personal and professional life, and Shaunna could understand why. He'd taken quite a few knocks in recent years. After he'd lost yet another job, Anne had ended their seventeen-year marriage, and Mike had gone to stay with his mum and Len. A few weeks later, Andy and Jess had fallen out, and Andy had also gone to stay at his mum's place.

By his own admission, Mike had intentionally stirred up trouble with Andy, and he'd since apologised, but at the time, he'd felt under attack, like everything was working against him. It was another of the Jeffries traits, to lash out in self-defence, which Andy avoided by walking away from the situation, although, since his yearlong stint in Dubai, he stayed closer to home and was gone for hours rather than months.

The last time he'd gone walkabout was before the twins were born, when Rachel had claimed Andy was Bethan's father, and to Shaunna's mind, Andy's method of dealing, or not dealing, had to be better than the way Dan went for Adele—verbally, not physically. The Jeffries men worshipped women and would never dream of laying a finger on them. Aside from which,

Adele gave as good as she got. Five foot two she might be, but only a fool—or the man who was in love with her—would take her on, and when it came to spitefulness, Dan and Adele were the world champions.

Mike would have put Anne through the wringer in much the same way, but Dan was successful and earned big bucks, and it was enough to keep Adele's affections when all else was lost. Mike had acted like a failure and owed a lot of money. There was nothing left to sustain his and Anne's marriage.

When the divorce had finalised, he'd gone on holiday to Greece, no doubt courtesy of a pay-day loan, and he'd met Rachel. As far as he was concerned, it was no more than a casual holiday fling, but when she'd contacted him a month later to say she was pregnant, he'd vowed to do the right thing. He'd stood by her, invited her to move in with him, taken whatever work he could find, taken the abuse—only verbal at first, but it quickly became emotional and then physical. Three days after she gave birth to Bethan, Rachel had walked out, leaving Mike with the baby.

In Shaunna's opinion—and everyone else's, for that matter—Bethan was the best thing that had ever happened to Mike. She gave him purpose and kept him from going under, because he was deeply hurt. But he was a Jeffries boy. They didn't talk about their feelings. They grunted and dealt with it in their own way. Dan worked out until he passed out, Andy jumped from planes, Mike shut down and withdrew into himself. Or that's what he'd done until Bethan came along. Now he had no choice but to keep going. He was a single dad with a six-month-old daughter. Shutting down was no longer an option.

So Mike didn't talk much about how he was feeling...to anyone other than Shaunna. He'd talk to her. And talk, and talk—sometimes she had to bite her tongue and remind herself of how lonely he was so she didn't tell him to shut up. He talked about Bethan, and football, and work, or more often the lack of it. Dan and Andy pushed jobs his way whenever they could—Dan even asked Mike if he would be his decorator on The Great Living Room Makeover, should it ever happen. Right at that moment, it was looking about as likely as Mike getting to be Dan's best man. Even so, it was a very thoughtful gesture, when Dan could just as easily have done the work himself. That said, Adele was much nicer to Mike than she was to Dan, so perhaps it was better all round—less chance of it ending in tears or bloodshed.

Shaunna switched off the hairdryer and put it back in the stand. "All done," she said.

"Wow!" Leah smiled at her reflection and shook her head. Her smooth, newly highlighted hair tumbled like flowing water, down onto her shoulders. "Thank you. It's fab!"

"You're very welcome." Shaunna removed the black cape from around Leah's shoulders, took it to the rail and exchanged it for her jacket. "This is lovely," she said, smoothing her palm over the soft purple felt.

"Thanks. I got it from a designer who makes clothes to order."

"I bet it cost a fair bit."

"Not really. It was a little more than off-the-peg, but it's worth it for the fit." Leah ran her fingers through her hair, admiring her reflection again. She turned back to Shaunna and gave her arm an affectionate squeeze. "You're a miracle worker."

Shaunna laughed bashfully. When her clients were happy, she was, and Leah's hair was quite a challenge. It was thick and heavy at the back but thinner at her temples, so it required cutting and tinting to draw attention away from the partially receded hairline.

Leah confirmed her appointment for the following week and left at the same time as Hayley came through from the storeroom with two cups of tea. She stopped dead and stared past Shaunna, out of the salon's front window.

"What?" Shaunna asked, slowly turning and wondering if Leah had taken a tumble.

"*Eurgh mah gad*. Sweedie! There really are three of them!"

Shaunna was too stunned by the appearance of her brother-in-law to tell Hayley she already knew there were three of them. She'd spent the better part of Leah's appointment thinking about them, none of which explained why Mike was now walking into the salon. He closed the door behind him, turned…and stayed right where he was. He looked as astonished as Shaunna felt.

"Mike? What…are…" One sideways glance at Hayley's delighted expression gave Shaunna her answer.

"Shaw?"

That was the other thing he did, along with the talk-and-talk. Shorten her name. Not that it was a bad thing, just that no-one had ever called her it before, which, now she thought on it, was quite amazing in itself when everyone else's name got shortened. Even she called Hayley 'Hayles'.

"I knew you were a hairdresser, but…" Mike scratched his head. "How long have you worked here?"

"Four years." Shaunna glanced at her boss again; Hayley nodded vaguely to confirm it was true.

Mike frowned, looking a little guilty, like he felt he should have known that, but it had never come up in conversation. Mike had no need for a stylist—or, at least, Shaunna would have loved to give him a makeover, but she doubted he'd go for it. So Mike was Hayley's painter and decorator, and with her soft spot for the Jeffries brothers, they could probably skip the formalities. Whether he could do the job or not, it was his already.

Hayley approached Mike and held out her hand. Nervously, he shook it and said, "Hi. I'm Mike Jeffries."

"Yah, sweedie. Andy's brother?"

"That's right." Mike's eyes flitted from Hayley to Shaunna.

"You OK?" Shaunna asked.

He nodded unconvincingly. "Nice place," he said, glancing around the salon walls. His eyes widened when they reached the full-size print of Andy and Shaunna. He cleared his throat and turned his attention back to Hayley. "What did you have in mind?"

"How about I make you a nice cup of tea, sweedie, and I'll tell you about whad I want." Hayley fluttered her eyelashes at him. "How d'you take it?"

"White, one sugar, cheers."

"OK, then. Be right back." Hayley tottered off to make another cup of tea. When she was out of sight, Mike looked to Shaunna in bewilderment.

"She's harmless," Shaunna whispered. "Just a flirt."

Mike nodded, a sigh of relief escaping. He looked around him again, properly this time, rather than merely to avoid Hayley's gaze. "That photo of you and our Andy is spectacular." He walked over to get a closer look.

"Aw, thanks, Mike. Haven't you seen it before?"

"Well, yeah, but it was Andy who showed me, and I felt a bit weird looking at the pair of you with no kit on while he was standing there."

Shaunna laughed. "I see your point."

Mike kept his back to her, continuing to stare at the photo as he spoke. "I enjoyed staying at your place. It was nice, you know? Seeing you together, happy, no arguments or fights. Not that I'm saying Mum and Len fight. They might—I'm too far away to hear them if they do." He turned to face her. "I miss the company."

Shaunna went over to join him and brushed her hand down his arm. "I know. Speaking of company, I need to sort out arrangements with you for Saturday."

"What's Saturday?"

"Did you get my text?"

Mike shook his head.

"Ah. Well, we're all invited to—" The salon door opened, and Shaunna's twelve-thirty client entered. A second later, Hayley returned from the storeroom. Shaunna noticed Mike immediately becoming agitated. "I'll talk to you after you're finished with Hayley," she suggested.

"There you go, sweedie." Hayley set the cup down on the counter. Mike nodded in thanks. "I was thinking…" She beckoned him over to the other side of the salon, away from Shaunna and her customer, and started to explain what she had in mind, which sounded straightforward enough to Shaunna, but she could see Mike was barely paying attention. It was astounding how much damage Rachel Perry had done, and in a relatively short space of time. For all of Mike's size and the way he came off as being quite aggressive, Rachel had made him afraid, of women. He glanced back fearfully at Shaunna. She smiled her reassurance and made mental notes of Hayley's requirements on Mike's behalf.

"Whaddaya say, sweedie?" Hayley asked.

Mike frowned thoughtfully and gave her his best tradesman's nod.

"About how much?" she prompted.

"Ah, oh, hm." Mike rubbed his chin. "I need to price up the tiles and get back to you," he said.

"OK. Yah, sure," Hayley agreed. "When will that be, d'you think. This week?"

"Yep. By Friday?"

"Perfect."

**

"Mmm, something smells good."

Andy leaned back so he could see Shaunna whilst continuing to stir the wok: red Thai chicken curry with a crazy amount of coconut, because she loved sweet stuff. Not too many chillies, though. Shaunna hung her coat and kicked off her shoes, exchanging them for flip-floppy fuzzy bunny slippers, and *still* she looked hot as all get-out.

"Any joy with Mike?" he asked.

"Sort of. He says he'll think about it." She put her arms around Andy's waist and leaned up for a kiss. "How's your day been, sexy?"

"Awesome. We went to the shops, then we watched *The Clangers* and the Foo Fighters, and then..." Shaunna was laughing and shaking her head. "What?"

"I love how you list the Foo Fighters like they're a kids' TV programme."

"The girls love a bit of Dave Grohl. I stuck on *In Your Honor*, and they were both out like a light."

"Only your daughters. So what's this delicious concoction?" She stood on tiptoes and peered into the pan.

Andy took a teaspoon from the drawer and dipped it in the sauce for her to try. "I even made the paste myself." He blew on the spoon and held it steady while she closed her mouth around it and slid her lips back, sucking the spoon clean.

"Oh, that is gorgeous."

"A woman in Prachuap showed me how to do gai prik gaeng ped."

Shaunna raised an eyebrow. "Sounds like some kind of three-in-a-bed sesh."

Andy laughed. "Not quite. It's chicken cooked in red curry paste."

"Shame." Shaunna kissed his cheek. "Have I got time for a bath?"

"Yep."

"OK. See you in a bit." She kissed him again and trailed her fingernails across his lower back as she left. It had the desired effect, and he wiggled his hips to make the necessary adjustments, in more than half a mind to abandon his curry and follow her. Another few minutes and it would be in a state where he could leave it without it spoiling. Above him, he heard the bathroom door open. He switched off the heat under the rice, stirred the sauce and sniffed at the sweetly aromatic steam. He'd got it exactly right, as the memories now flooding his mind testified.

He'd gone to Thailand the year after he'd graduated. It had been a hell of a trip in more ways than one, for it was in Thailand he'd learned to dive, through volunteering on a marine conservation project. It had meant paying for the diving certification and equipment, or, rather, his mum paid for it on the proviso he paid her back as soon as he came home, but that didn't happen, for various reasons, including illness and the fact that he'd packed up and buggered off again as soon as he was fit.

Eventually, Dan had given their mum the money, even though Andy had told him not to, but that's how it had been back then. Andy had never asked Dan to bail him out; he didn't want him to, which was precisely why Dan had done it, and not just the once. If it had been a simple case of one-upmanship, Andy would have let it ride, but he'd always known there was more to it. He'd paid Dan back since, as far as he could tell. Dan said Andy owed him nothing, but he wasn't convinced. Still, it was all water under the bridge. They were best buds again, back to how they had been as kids, and Andy regretted nothing, even if that trip to Thailand—and many of those that followed it— had more downs than ups. It kept things interesting if nothing else.

He'd stayed in Thailand for around two months—a week of diving lessons, followed by four weeks fixing and maintaining coral nurseries, after which he'd set off on the next leg of his journey. He'd ended up on Koh Phangan—one of the islands famed for its full moon parties—where he'd remained until the next full moon and then fled as soon as he could arrange transport, because the island was too touristy, and…there was a girl.

He was ashamed to say, in spite of spending almost his entire time on KPG with her, he couldn't recall her name. They were all perpetually exhausted, drunk, stoned, or any combination thereof, although Andy only did the first two. He had something of an aversion to drugs, since many of his old school 'friends' had been heavily into acid and ecstasy, and he preferred real trips. They were safer. Arguably. OK, not that much safer, but it wasn't his daring sense of adventure that had kept the girl of his dreams from him for all those years. It was his idiot mates.

He remembered that night, sitting on the beach on KPG, with the full moon somewhere behind the heavy clouds above him, the gentle tickle against his skin as a girl dotted luminous body paint over his shoulder and down his arm. He had been too drunk to know if it was the alcohol making the music distort and phase, and making him melancholy. He'd wished it wasn't a random girl at his side. He'd wished and he'd wondered what *she* would be up to. Two a.m. local time, eight p.m. back in England. Maybe she was reading her daughter a bedtime story. Or maybe she and he were cuddled up on the sofa, watching TV together.

Still, no regrets. At twenty-three, Andy had not been the man Shaunna needed.

After KPG, he'd gone trekking until he ran out of money and made it to Bangkok airport with the equivalent of about £1.50 in his pocket and a banging headache. It was his own stupid fault. He'd forgotten to take the antimalarial tablets, not just once or twice, but systematically. The risk was negligible, and they'd given him nightmares, so he'd essentially put them out of his mind.

The symptoms started in earnest when they stopped to refuel, and at first, he'd put it down to jet lag. Even now, eighteen years later, he could recall little more than getting back on the plane at Abu Dhabi. He certainly didn't remember landing in Heathrow, although apparently, he'd called Dan from the airport and said he thought he was dying. By all accounts, Dan had picked him up and tried to take him to hospital, but Andy had refused to go, so Dan had made the four-hour drive to deliver him to their mum's house, she'd called the emergency GP, and then she'd nursed him through the ordeal.

It was a few days before he'd been with it enough to realise where he was, and when he was finally well enough to go home, his mum had sent him away with a food package and a warning that next time the mosquitoes would be the least of his worries. She was right about that. Hypothermia, altitude sickness, a broken arm, almost a broken neck, a brush with a Portuguese man-of-war, a near-fatal car crash...

But it was all behind him. His daughters and their mother were all the adventure he needed, and right now, there was a sexy redhead waiting for him to pack in with the nostalgia and get his ass in that bathroom.

Andy gave his curry one last stir, switched off the flame and covered the wok. Hoping not to wake the babies—and also hoping to sneak up on Shaunna—he took off his shoes at the bottom of the stairs and crept upwards, slowly, stealthily, stepping over the creaking floorboard, which he kept meaning to fix, and along the landing.

The bathroom door was ajar; the pale-golden flicker of multiple candle flames reflected off the white tiles. Otherwise, the room was in darkness, opening his senses to the flowery aroma, the steady *swish-splash, swish-splash*, and the moist air condensing on his face and arms. Pushing the door open a little further, he peeked around it, at the deep, claw-footed bathtub that was easily big enough for two, and almost choked on the breath that caught in his throat. Not just a twitch in his boxer shorts; he was already fully good to go.

With her head resting on the end of the bath closest to the door, Shaunna lay with her knees raised out of the water, snow-capped peaks in a foaming ocean. Her hair, partly secured in a clip, cascaded over the lip of the bath, undulating like the tide as she arched her back and ran her palms up and down her sides, cupping the outer curves of her breasts, smoothing the dip of her waist, sliding inwards at her hips… Andy sucked the escaped saliva back into his mouth and swallowed. She leaned back and peered over her shoulder at him.

"Hi." She smiled, open-lipped, and then laughed at his expression.

"Hi," he replied, beyond that lost for words.

"I was wondering where you'd got to."

"Thailand."

Shaunna rolled onto her front. "Flying visit?"

Andy grinned. "Trip down Memory Lane. How's the water?"

Shaunna lifted on her arms, exposing her cleavage, her breasts hidden from view by the bath. She blinked up at him. "Why don't you come and find out?"

Andy looked away only for as long as it took to tug his t-shirt over his head. He unfastened his jeans and pushed them down, along with his boxers, and trampled out of them. He pulled his socks off on his way across the room and waited for Shaunna to move so there was space for him, but she was in no hurry to do so. She leaned on one arm, her other hand resting on her hip, her fingers just visible under the water, where they moved with a slow, deliberate rhythm. He watched her, watching him, and tensed his pelvic muscles. His erection bobbed up and down.

Shaunna smiled and licked her lips. "Let me help you with that."

He got one foot in the water, the other still on the bathmat, before she sat up and homed in on him, taking him into her mouth. Unable and unwilling to move, he tightened his glutes and hamstrings, glad he'd kept up his training, even on those days when the call for sleep proved almost irresistible. He held his position and followed with his eyes the smooth, firm motion of her lips over his skin, like being wrapped in hot silk. Her red ringlets tickled his thigh, and he reached down, combing his fingers through them, sandwiching the soft curls and slowly going out of his mind.

She eased back and released him with a gentle *pop*, smiling up at him. "You getting in?"

He lifted his other foot over the edge of the bath. She reclined, legs parted, so that he came down on top of her, although the bath wasn't long enough for him to straighten out. Instead, he knelt between her legs, his head bent to kiss a nipple, his fingers working their way along her inner thigh, exploring and delighting in the slipperiness her arousal created. The heat of her body, her scent, her breathy moans and the slap of the water against his skin as she writhed beneath him, had him taking matters into his own hand.

"Oh, no." She grabbed his arm, stilling it.

He nuzzled between her breasts and murmured, "You're driving me crazy, RHB."

"I can see that." Cupping his face, she pulled him closer and kissed him deeply, but their bodies were no longer in contact, and both of them were getting desperate for release. Shaunna broke the kiss. "Get up," she instructed.

Andy moved back and waited to see where she wanted him, although anywhere would have done. She clambered to her knees and turned away from him, leaning on the end of the bath.

He considered the logistics for a moment. "This isn't gonna work."

She wiggled her glorious round hips and stayed where she was. He was too far gone to protest. He shuffled through the water, getting as close up behind her as he could, unable to resist running his hands over her buttocks on the way to gripping her hips. It really wasn't going to work.

"Come on, big boy," she taunted, pushing back onto him. "You can do better than that."

He laughed, but the bath was too narrow. With all the will in the world—and a not-diminutive manhood at his disposal—there was no way he could get close enough. He shuffled back again and got out of the bath. She turned and scowled, still incredibly sexy, but he was starting to get cold, and his desire was at the point of do or die.

"When you're done in there—" he modestly cupped his unwaning erection "—I'll be in the bedroom." Still holding himself, he strolled towards the bathroom door, heard the plug being pulled, and pretended to make a dash for it. Shaunna rushed to catch up with him, slipped on the wet tiles and tumbled, right into Andy's arms.

"Lucky you were here," she panted. Her lips were pink, full and luscious. He leaned down to kiss them. Then, like a chivalrous knight, he scooped her up in both arms and carried her to their bedroom, or halfway to their bedroom, by which point their slippery wet skin had conspired against them. He kept hold of her whilst she hopped and giggled her way to the bed. Andy released her, and as she fell back onto the plush cotton duvet, he kissed his way up from her feet, caressing her sensitive spots with light-touch tongue and lips—her insteps, the insides of her ankles, the backs of her knees, her inner thighs, her outer labia, her clitoris... He stayed there for a while, relishing her taste, her scent, her writhing and groaning at his touch, before continuing his upward journey and sliding deep inside her.

No pretence of tenderness now, he thrust, piston-like, kissing her hard on the lips and swallowing her cries for *more, harder, faster*, until finally *she was, she was...* Her orgasm lifted him clear off the bed, and with one last thrust he joined her while she rutted against his pelvic bone, riding out the sensation to the last, her words echoing indecipherably in the din of throbbing in his head. He knew nothing beyond the wonder that never ceased.

"Is that curry ready?" she asked breathlessly.

Andy rolled onto the bed beside her. "Give me a minute."

"OK." She leaned over and kissed him, and then traced his lips with her finger. "Red hot curry..." she mused.

He grinned and lightly bit her fingertip. "Yep. Not as hot as you."

"Ready for another round?"

"I'll go check on that curry." With an effort, he hauled himself up off the bed. Behind him, she laughed.

"I was kidding," she said, already reaching for the breast pump to alleviate the inevitable post-orgasmic let-down reflex.

He pulled on a pair of sweatpants and turned back, leaning down to kiss her, his fingers trailing over her enlarged, moist nipple. "After dinner?" On cue came a tiny cry through the baby monitor. Shaunna sighed. Andy laughed and kissed her again. "You do that, and I'll deal with the girls. Who d'you want first?"

3: One for the Team
Thursday, 27th September

"All right, Mike? Didn't expect to see you today." Dan moved aside and waited for his eldest brother to wipe his feet and come in. The weather was appalling, although Mike was somewhat overplaying the whole dirty-boots routine. "Don't worry about a bit of mud."

"Mud's not so bad." Mike finally stepped inside and inspected the floor behind him. "Paint's a bugger to get out of an oak floor."

"Fair point," Dan conceded, but there was neither mud nor paint on boots or floor. "I thought you were working at... somewhere?"

"Park Lane, yeah. Finished it yesterday. I've just priced up a job in here." Mike thumbed upwards to indicate he was talking about Dan and Adele's apartment building.

"Oh, right. What number?"

"Thirty-five."

Dan pondered a moment and shook his head. He didn't know many of his neighbours. Dovedale wasn't that sort of building. "They're big houses on Park Lane. Did they pay up?" He led the way through to the living room, glancing behind him to check Mike was following, which he was.

"Yep. By cheque."

"Ah. I hate it when they do that. You staying for a drink?"

"Sure. Why not? You home alone?"

"Yeah. Adele's gone for a lunchtime soirée with the girls from the department store. Coffee or tea?"

Mike rotated on the spot, eyeing up the décor. "Either'll do me."

"Coffee, then," Dan decided. He'd been working in the Campion Trust office all week—with Alice—and it had involved a lot of tea drinking. He went through to the kitchen and set up the coffee filter.

"I'm not stopping you working, am I?" Mike asked from the other room.

"Not at all. I was about to take a break anyway." That wasn't entirely true; he'd hoped to finish the estimate he'd been working on before Shu finished preschool for the day, but it could wait.

"You had any more thoughts on when you want to get started on this place?"

Dan switched on the coffee machine and rejoined his brother, both standing side by side, with their eyes fixed on the wall behind the sofa. "Adele's still trying to decide on paper." Dan gave Mike a weary look. "She's narrowed it down to the last dozen."

Mike laughed, but it sounded a little forced.

"You strapped?" Dan asked.

"A bit. I'd have been all right if the Park Lane job was cash-in-hand."

"You paid the cheque in?"

"Yeah. This morning."

"I can transfer the money in the interim," Dan offered, already with his phone out to access his bank account.

"It's fine, really. Cheers, though." Mike turned away and rubbed hard at his head.

Dan knew better than to push it, but his offer, and Mike's rejection of it, had created an awkward pause, and the coffee wasn't done yet. He went for a change of subject. "You coming over on Saturday?"

"I'd love to…you know how it is."

Dan raised an eyebrow.

"I'm working."

"At seven in the evening?"

"Dunno yet. I'll see how much I get done. But I'm knackered by then."

It was all bull, Dan knew. Mike felt like an outsider, which he was in many respects, because it was about more than genetic association. Shaunna and Adele had been best friends since they were knee-high, and between that and Dan and Andy's business, they spent a lot of time as a foursome. They were also part of the same friendship group—'The Circle', as Dan's mate Tom Kerry had called them during his groom's speech on the occasion of his marriage to Adele…perhaps the less said about that the better.

They'd seen very little of Mike over the years. He'd left home to go to university, and whilst he and Anne had lived less than an hour's drive away, he'd visited only when he needed something, or if his presence was specifically requested, for Dan and Adele's engagement party, for instance, when Dan had asked him to be his best man. He felt bad now, for fobbing Mike off, because Adele had made it clear she wasn't going through the whole rigmarole of getting married again. But Mike had been an arrogant shit who blamed everyone else for his own failings.

Mike could've had a successful career in IT. He'd had a beautiful wife, a gorgeous house, and that chip on his shoulder had been costly. He'd lost everything. No matter what opportunities life threw Mike's way, he seemed determined to prove he was a loser, though it was never his fault, of course.

That held true until he became a dad, and while Bethan was to be celebrated for bringing about the small miracle of turning her father into a decent human being, there was another stopping block to Mike socialising with his brothers and their girlfriends: he was single, and they weren't.

The coffee machine stopped spluttering, and Dan went to pour the coffees. "How's my gorgeous niece doing?" he called through.

"Fine. Grumpy. Teething again." The words rolled into a yawn, and Mike came out of it laughing. "Plus she's learnt how to shout 'Da', which is awesome any time except half four in the morning, when I've only had three hours of shut-eye and I know it's all I'm getting."

Dan returned with two mugs and passed one to his brother, gesturing for him to sit down. Mike accepted and settled at one end of the sofa. He was back to looking around the walls. Dan decided to go for a different approach.

"No pressure at all, Mike, but Kris and Ade are coming on Saturday. I reckon between you and Ade, you could pin Adele down on the wallpaper."

"Dan…"

"Just pop in for a beer. That's all I'm suggesting. And you can bring Bethan with you, if that's what you're worried about."

Mike frowned into his steaming mug.

"The invitation's open, if you change your mind. I'll say no more." Dan sipped at his coffee and suppressed a sigh. They'd never been close, and there was a lot of crap in their shared past that they would never deal with. Navigating the debris was always going to be a challenge, and if Mike didn't want to do something, it wasn't up to Dan to talk him into it. Maybe Andy would have more joy, though he doubted it.

Dan couldn't think of anything else to say, so he turned the TV up—it was already tuned to a news channel—and watched the pictures, not listening to a word the bloke onscreen was saying. It bothered him that Mike was lonely, but there wasn't much he could do about it. Or there was one thing. Shaunna had mentioned it months ago, and Dan had put it on the back burner, waiting to see if Mike really had changed his ways. After all, there was no point bringing him in if he was going to bugger off midway through the season. However, it would mean putting someone else's nose out of joint. Still, family should come first, and they'd recoup their losses soon enough, if—

"Are you all set for next week?" Mike's question cut Dan off mid-thought, and to his shame, he'd almost asked 'Why? What's happening next week?' It had to be the first time it had slipped his mind—if anything, he'd been struggling *not* to think about it.

"I think so," he said. He felt himself smile, because he was happy, yet terrified in equal measure. "Adele's got it all in hand."

"Course she has. She's a woman."

Dan chuckled at Mike's remark. True, women did seem to have a knack for being prepared for any eventuality, but after what they'd been through with little Shaunna being born so early, and then the miscarriage, Dan was being over-cautious— not that he was in the least bit superstitious. He had no qualms about walking under ladders. He didn't worry about broken mirrors or lone magpies, but there was no point in tempting fate if it could be avoided. The only reason he'd agreed to being told the baby's sex was to bargain with Adele—yes to finding out the sex on the condition they didn't discuss names.

So he knew they were having a boy, and he had a name, which he was keeping to himself. He also had a whole wish list online—newborn-size replica kits, football booties, the smallest flying jacket ever—and still bigger purchases in mind, but until he'd seen his son arrive, safe and sound, he wasn't buying a thing.

"It'll be nice, though, hey?" Mike said.

"What's that?"

"Having a normal baby. Not that I'm saying Shaunna's abnormal." Mike fidgeted uncomfortably.

"It's all right, I know what you mean. And yeah, it will." Dan drank some more of his coffee and watched his brother out of the corner of his eye. "I was wondering if you're still up for joining our Sunday League team?"

"Yeah, definitely. I thought you had a full squad, though."

"We do, but it's about time we had a reshuffle. We're not doing well this season. Bloody Anchors are kicking our arses."

"Because they've recruited all Aitch's lot."

"Hm. I tell you what, Mike, they were filthy before…"

"What can you expect when they are *The* Filth?"

Dan turned and gave him a look, acting like he'd taken offence, when he was having to fight back the laugh. Being mates—and teammates—with Aitch meant Dan knew a lot of their local police force from nights out, and they were decent people, although The Blue Anchor landlord recruiting a load of them 'to clean up' his football team had taken the banter to a whole new level.

With Aitch playing for The Red Lions, he was coming in for a fair bit of flak at work. Dan thought it was pretty hard-faced, considering Aitch was a detective inspector, but it counted for nothing on the football pitch. Subordinates or not, with their new sponsor and swanky new kit, the Blue Anchors were the better team this season, and it was all the justification Dan needed for giving Mike a tryout.

"We haven't got a match this Sunday, so we're meeting up a bit later. Probably eleven-ish?"

"Sounds good to me."

"Bethan's welcome. The twins'll be there, and Libby usually looks after Shu. Unless Len and Pez come, then they…" At the mention of Pez, Mike had tensed. "He's a good kid."

"Yeah, so Len says."

"But he's Rachel's brother," Dan said on his behalf.

"It's not that." Mike focused on the TV. It was a few minutes before he said anything more, and then it was with a couple of false starts. "Rachel's mother is taking me to court."

"Rachel's mother?" Dan repeated. He tried to make the connection in his brain but came up blank. Rachel was serving a life sentence for causing a woman's death by tampering with the brakes on her Corvette. She hadn't known her victim, nor, apparently, shown remorse during the trial. Rachel Perry was a crazed psychopath, and like the woman in the Corvette, Mike was merely a means to an end—a way to get Andy's attention.

With Rachel behind bars, Dan had thought it was over. "Is she putting together an appeal?" he asked.

"Nope. She's applying for custody."

"She's—" Dan stopped himself from mouthing off in disbelief, but at the same time, he realised a child's grandmother stood a good chance against its father. If Rachel wasn't a murdering bitch, she'd probably have stood a chance of getting custody herself, and it was all wrong. "She's not gonna get it," Dan said firmly.

"Isn't she?"

"You're Bethan's dad."

"Yeah, look at me. I'm hardly the best thing for her, am I? Self-employed, if I can get work at all, still living with my mum…"

"That's bollocks, and you know it."

Mike coughed out a small, dry laugh.

"Seriously, bro. Kids Bethan's age are already bonded with whoever looks after them. The judge'll know that."

Mike turned and looked Dan in the eye. "I dunno what I'm gonna do. If I lose her…"

"It won't come to that."

Mike looked away. "It might."

"It won't come to that," Dan repeated forcefully. "We won't let it."

***

"Afternoon, ladies," Dan greeted the other parents—mostly mothers—waiting outside the preschool classroom door. He was usually more than happy to stand with them, engage in a little chitchat and lighthearted flirting. This afternoon, he made

37

a beeline for the two men standing a few feet from the mums. "Alright?"

"Alright," the younger of the two responded. The other nodded and continued watching the classroom door even though it was still a good five minutes before the children would be let out.

"Got any plans for the weekend?" Dan asked.

"Going down to Shropshire, visiting the in-laws," the younger man said.

"Yeah? It's nice down there."

"Yeah, it is. How about you?"

"Dinner party on Saturday. Shaunna's mum wanted a last hurrah before the birth."

"Ah, that's right. The baby's due next week, isn't it?"

"Monday, yeah."

There was movement inside the building, and Dan and the rest of the parents watched through the window as their offspring put on their coats. The door opened, and the preschool teacher came into view. The children emerged in a relatively orderly line, their teacher watching to check each child reached their parent or guardian. By the time little Shaunna emerged, the other two men and their kids were halfway across the playground, and the other classes were being released. Shaunna was struggling with the zip on her coat and shrugged off her teacher's offer of assistance, instead ambling aimlessly, her eyes on her zip, not on where she was going. Dan met the teacher's gaze, and both of them smiled knowingly.

"Shu?"

She reoriented so she was walking towards him, but she wasn't giving up on that zip, or not without a tantrum, and Dan didn't want to hurry her. He might not have been the most patient of people, but when it came to his daughter, he had all the time in the world. If she didn't try, she'd never learn, although it made for a very slow walk back to the car. After a further two minutes of waiting with the door open, along with a text from Adele asking if he'd forgotten her, Dan had no choice.

"Come on, baby girl, let me help." He crouched in front of her. She scowled and turned away. "We've got to get Mummy."

No joy, he scooped her up and somehow secured her into her seat whilst she continued to work on her zip. He closed the door and walked around to the driver's side, climbed in and fastened his seat belt, listening to her huff and puff behind him, followed by the slow, quiet click of the zip fastening. He started the engine and turned to grin at his daughter. "Nice one, baby girl." She grinned back.

***

At the sight of Adele and her friends emerging from the staff door of the department store, Dan slapped his hand to his forehead and sighed in undisguised and predictable despair.

"Look, Daddy. Mummy's got presents."

"So she has," he muttered, opening the door to get out and help Adele load her hoard into the boot. Or, rather, help her friends, because they weren't letting her carry any of it. "You had a good time?" he asked generally. He held the boot open for the women to pile in their multiple boxes and bags.

"Brilliant," Adele said, all smiles. The other three women nodded and smiled in agreement, taking turns to give Adele a hug and a kiss on the cheek.

"You take care."

"Look after yourself."

"Good luck for Monday."

And so on, fading out as, with a wave, the three women disappeared back inside the building. Dan adjusted the packages, shut the boot and returned to the driver's seat. Beside him, Adele groaned and fidgeted, fighting to stretch the seat belt over her bump. It clicked into place, and she flopped back in her seat with an exhausted sigh.

"You set?" Dan asked, fastening his own seat belt.

Adele nodded and glanced over her shoulder. "Hiya." She gave her daughter a smile.

"Hiya." Little Shaunna immediately picked up her school bag and rooted around inside it, the intense concentration evident in her taciturn expression—just like her dad's. She found what she was looking for—a plastic lid from an aerosol can, decorated with sequins and ribbons—and stretched to offer it to her mum, but with Shaunna's tiny arms and Adele's thirty-seven weeks of pregnancy, there wasn't much room for manoeuvre.

"Oh, this is lovely! Aren't you a clever girl!"

Little Shaunna gave an exaggerated nod. "For ear buds. Is baby coming tomorrow?"

"Not tomorrow. Monday."

"Not Saturday?"

"Nope."

"Not Saturday?"

Adele smiled. "Not Saturday, and not Sunday, but the next day."

Shaunna's brow creased in thought. Adele watched her a moment longer, decided she'd said all she was going to, and turned to face the front again. "What've you been up to today?" she asked Dan.

"Not a lot." He checked the rear-view mirror and signalled to turn right. "I sent the accounts through to Alice and finished the water-park quote. Mike's been round."

"Has he?"

"Yeah. Pricing a job in one of the apartments."

"Oh, really? Whose?"

"Err...dunno." Dan didn't try too hard to recall which number Mike had said, focusing instead on the road ahead and pondering whether to tell Adele about Rachel's mother taking Mike to court. It was a constant dilemma Dan faced; much as he loved Adele, and she wasn't malicious, she *was* a gossip. He was sure it was no more than her thoughts escaping aloud, but Mike wouldn't want everyone knowing his business. However, assuming Mike had also told Andy, Andy would tell Shaunna, and she may well mention it to Adele, who would then demand to know why Dan hadn't told her. To his shame, his usual way of dealing with it was to lie and say he knew nothing, although he was kept out of the loop more often than not—the downside of having coppers for mates.

"I was talking to Tom earlier," Adele said, effectively making—or, at least, delaying—the decision for him.

"How's he doing?"

"All right. He seemed very…chipper? Is that the word?"

"If you mean cheerful…"

"Yeah, and full of energy. It's so not like him."

Dan laughed, because she was right. He and Tom had known each other close on eighteen years, having met a few months after they both graduated from different universities with the same degree. They'd become good mates and stayed that way, until six years ago, when Tom had admitted he was in love with Adele.

At the time, she and Dan were on a long break following a particularly vicious breakup, and Adele seemed to care a lot for Tom, so Dan had given Tom his blessing, which sounded old-fashioned and sexist, but it wasn't like that. Tom wouldn't have so much as asked Adele out on a date if he'd believed he was stepping on Dan's toes. In fact, if he'd fully known the history, he would have steered well clear, but Dan and Adele's three-decade-long, on-off relationship was not something they talked about, which meant only those close enough to witness firsthand were aware of it.

When Dan and Adele got back together the last time, it had been as if the stars had aligned and created some kind of gravitational force neither could resist. Dan went from Tom's best man to top of his least-trustworthy list in a matter of a few months, and in the day-to-day scheme of things, it was easy to keep out of each other's way. However, as Tom was still the department store manager, Dan envisaged he got to see Adele rather more than he'd have liked, and she was too thick-skinned to realise the hurt she was causing. Indeed, she seemed to treat it as some kind of game.

"He's got a new girlfriend," she said.

"Oh?"

"Yep. She's called Theresa."

Dan's jaw dropped, and Adele giggled.

"I knew that'd be your reaction. Not *that* Theresa."

"I was gonna say..." Alison—the last girl Dan had dated before he and Adele got back together—had ditched him, and a couple of weeks later was dating a girl called Theresa, although as far as he could remember, Alison's girlfriend wasn't bisexual, so it was highly unlikely to be the same woman. Still, stranger things had happened...like Adele agreeing to marry Tom, for instance.

If Dan had one great regret, it was letting Tom go through with the wedding, because he'd honestly thought Adele would back out of it before the big day. As was to be expected, Adele's dad had paid for everything, and she'd handed over the planning to Eleanor, so Dan had successfully avoided contact with Adele for months. But as the day drew closer, their paths had crossed more and more frequently, and there was still such animosity between them that Adele had suggested they go out for dinner together, or whatever would give them an opportunity to escape everyone else for an evening so they could clear the air. The result of that evening was sitting in the back seat.

It was all in the past, and they were happy. They had a healthy almost-four-year-old daughter; in four days' time, they'd have a son, and it sounded as if Tom was finally moving on, too. But for all of that, Dan wished he'd stopped the wedding. If he had, then Adele might just have considered marrying him.

4: Uneasy Deals
Friday, 28th September

When Mike had told Dan he was working Saturday, it had been an excuse. He didn't need to be reminded again of how successful his brothers were. However, with the hairdressing salon quote still to do, a promise to the woman in Dovedale that her living room would be finished before Monday evening, and now an appointment with his barrister, he'd resigned himself to the fact that he'd be working Saturday, probably Sunday as well.

He hadn't exactly got up early—Bethan had been awake since three—but he'd come over to the house early, hoping to get the quote together before he left to see the barrister at ten. The quote prep was going well, thanks to Shaunna. As soon as he'd left the salon, she'd sent him a text with all the stuff her boss had said she wanted. Without that text, he'd have been lost, and he was annoyed with himself for not being on top of his game, but his head was all over the place.

"You've nicked my chair again."

Mike turned and gave Charlie a grin. He'd heard her trademark whistling as she approached, so she hadn't taken him by surprise. She was Len's...he wasn't sure what to call her. PA, accountant, marketing director, office manager—in short, she ran Len's business for him, while Len spent all his time at his car showroom, which was better than having him snarling and grunting under a heap of paperwork.

Charlie was a lot like Andy, give or take the obvious few anatomical details. From their late-night chatter when Andy was staying at the house, Mike had gleaned that they'd shared an obscene number of adventures. All that swimming with sharks and snowboarding nonsense Andy got up to, Charlie was just as bad, and when the two of them got together they turned into surfing bores. But Charlie could also be cool and professional when the need arose, and she had a point; Mike *was* sitting in her chair and using her computer. He pushed the chair back and moved to get up.

"No, no. You carry on," she said. "I'm gonna make coffee before I start work." She squinted at the screen. "What you up to?"

"Quote for Shaunna's boss."

"Ah, OK. You still not got a computer?"

"Nope. Can't afford one."

"Hm. Let me have a think on that." Charlie left again.

Mike tried to ignore the sinking sensation in his gut. Much as he appreciated people's offers of help, he didn't like owing, or relying on anyone else, and he was beginning to feel like a charity case. His van and decorating gear were bought with what little was left from settling the finance after the divorce. His furniture was the stuff Anne had said he could take from the house when she'd sold it. He only had somewhere to live because Len was doing Andy a favour. Even his daughter...

He loved her with every cell of his being, but the truth? She was born for all the wrong reasons, and she was with him because there was no-one else. Or there *had been* no-one else. After Rachel's sentencing, his brothers, his mum, Len, the lawyer... they all said he was home and dry, but he'd never shaken the fear that one day someone would take Bethan away from him. Now Jacqueline Perry wanted to challenge his fatherhood abilities, and he wasn't sure he could rise to it.

He didn't blame Rachel's mum for what her daughter had turned into; he'd met Rachel's sister and brother—Tammy and Felix, or Pez, as Len had 'christened' him—and they both seemed well-balanced, normal people. There was nothing wrong with the way they'd been brought up. There was nothing wrong with Jacqueline's parenting. She was a good mum who loved her kids—watching her fall apart in court when Rachel was found guilty had demonstrated it beyond doubt.

At the time, Mike had felt no sympathy for Rachel's family. Her mother had blamed him for her daughter's demise; her brother had aided and abetted in the sabotage of Len's cars. Her sister had refused to make a statement in court, even though she'd been as much a victim of Rachel's cruelty as the rest of them.

But six months of fatherhood was more than long enough for Mike to fully comprehend why Jacqueline Perry believed Rachel's story. When he looked at Bethan, he saw a perfect angel who could do no wrong, and he knew if he ever found himself in Jacqueline's situation, he would do the same. She was trying to protect her daughter and granddaughter, and the prospect of going up against her in court terrified Mike. He felt the power of that love, but he would fight her, if not for his rights, then for his mum's. If Jacqueline got custody of Bethan, the likelihood was his mum would never get to see her again.

"You not done yet?"

Mike shook his head. "Nearly," he lied and tried to concentrate, but Charlie was leaning against the doorpost, sipping her coffee, and watching him.

"I've had an idea. Want to hear it?"

"Sure," he agreed breezily and felt his blood pressure crank up a notch.

"I've got a computer at home. I bought it a couple of weeks before I started working for Len, and honestly, if I've switched it on twice since, I'd be surprised."

"You've been working for Len for a year, yeah?"

"Yeah, but it was top spec."

Mike laughed. "That's the opposite of what I meant. Wouldn't you be better bringing it in here?"

"I can see why you'd think that, but I actually prefer this old clockwork doodah of Len's. I've got it set up perfectly for what I do. Mine—I don't even think I got as far as connecting it to wi-fi."

"How much?"

"Ah, well, I was thinking we could trade skills. Have you met my mother?"

"Err, not that I recall." Mike had no idea where Charlie was going with this.

"She's…how to put it? Exacting. But she likes your brothers, so it's a safe bet she'll like you."

"Are you setting me up with your mother?" He hoped he sounded like he was joking, although there was a very real underlying fear that she might be doing just that. He knew very little about Charlie's family, like whether her dad was still around, for instance, although judging by Charlie's raucous laughter, he was in the clear.

"That's too funny." She was laughing so hard coffee came out of her nose and made her cough. "Setting you up, oh, God…" She shook her head. "With my mum!" She dabbed at her wet eyes and laugh-sobbed a couple of times, alternating between sighing and giggling as she tried to pull herself together. "It's too early in the day for this." She cleared her throat and continued, an occasional giggle still escaping with her words. "OK. It's like this. Our house has got six bedrooms. It's where we all grew up, and now there's only Mum, Dad, Pete and me living at home, there are three spare rooms, which Mum's been threatening to decorate since I was at uni. Then she did her back in, and Dad's rubbish at decorating, so I offered my services, except I'm not much better than my dad. And I did try. I half papered one of the rooms. Mike, it's *so bad*."

"Right. So you want me to come and decorate?"

"I want you to give me some lessons. I'm happy to do it, if you can just show me how." Charlie blinked beseechingly, still giggling a little, which made Mike laugh, too. Now he knew what the deal was, he relaxed a little, although Charlie was pretty much the only woman besides Shaunna who didn't put him on edge.

He nodded. "I'm up for that."

"You are? That's fab. Cheers, Mike. I'll bring the computer with me on Monday, unless you want to come and pick it up over the weekend?"

"Monday's fine by me."

"Great. There's no rush, by the way. Whenever you've got time. I'll leave you to finish your quote. I'll be in the gym. Give me a shout when you're done."

"Will do," Mike confirmed, but Charlie was already walking away. He got back to work on the quote, which, now he was concentrating, didn't take anywhere near as long as he'd thought it would. These days, he could calculate quantities of materials without looking them up, and all the pricing was on the merchant's website. He saved and printed the estimate, let Charlie know he was finished, and went to find his mum and Bethan. He tried the kitchen first, but it was empty, so he returned to the atrium and listened for noise upstairs.

"Mum?"

No response to that, he retraced his steps down the passageway past the kitchen and out to the conservatory, slowing to a stop to watch his mother backstepping in the pool, her palms under Bethan to support her while she floated on her back. She was loving it, too, judging by the little gurgling sounds and the way she was kicking her legs, like she was swimming for real. His mother turned his way and smiled up at him.

"You all right, lovey? Did you get your paperwork sorted?"

"Yeah. I'm gonna head off now and drop it in on my way. I'll let you know how it goes with the lawyer."

"Okey dokey. Good luck, though I'm sure it'll be fine."

"Thanks, Mum. See you later." Mike delayed, until his mum turned away, and then left for the salon.

***

47

Shaunna was opening up as he arrived, with no sign of her boss.

"It's Hayley's morning off," Shaunna explained as she opened the door. "One sec." She marched across to the counter, leaving Mike loitering in the doorway, and jabbed at the control panel on the wall. The alarm's quiet beeping stopped, and Mike assumed it was safe to enter.

"You get many break-ins here?" he asked.

Shaunna raised an eyebrow. "Just the one. I'll get the kettle on. You staying for a cup of tea?"

Mike took out his phone and checked the time. He had another forty-five minutes. "Yeah, go on, then."

Shaunna went through to the stockroom, leaving him alone in the salon.

So this was the place she vandalised—allegedly. To his mind, and everyone else's for that matter, there was no 'allegedly' about it. But Rachel Perry was too clever to leave evidence. At first, she'd admitted every charge the police brought against her, including assaulting him, though he refused to give a statement, so that charge would have been dropped anyway. By the time her case went to court, she pleaded not guilty to everything except tampering with the brakes on Elite Motors' cars. That was enough to see her go down for murder and two counts of attempted murder.

As to the rest of the charges, she claimed the police had coerced her into confessing, citing postnatal depression as the reason she'd gone along with their accusations. When the judge did the summing up at the end of the trial, he said in his mind, there was no doubt she was guilty of every single offence brought before the court, but neither he nor the jury could find her guilty 'beyond reasonable doubt'. It didn't matter. She was in prison, and Mike needed to let it go, but he felt better for knowing he wasn't the only victim, however selfish that made him.

"Here." Shaunna thrust a mug into his hand.

"Thanks."

"Welcome." She bustled away again, over to the counter, and started flipping switches. The salon came to life around him— the cash register, under-counter lights, the fish tank he hadn't noticed two days ago. There again, it was located under the giant photo of Andy and Shaunna. His brother had done well to catch her; she was absolutely stunning to look at—very curvy, gorgeous red hair—and a smashing personality, kind, generous, patient, brilliant sense of humour. He hoped one day he'd meet someone like Shaunna, that's if he ever bothered with dating again.

"What're you thinking about?" Shaunna asked, pulling him out of his drifting thoughts.

"My bad luck with women," he answered frankly.

"Yeah, you've had a run of it, haven't you?"

"Since I hit puberty."

Shaunna laughed. "It can't be that bad."

"You wanna bet? If I don't count the one-off kisses and fumbles in high school, I've had four girlfriends—that's including Anne and Rachel."

Shaunna didn't pass comment. She switched on the computer and frowned at the screen.

"Problem?"

"Hm?"

"Computer."

"Oh. No, it's always dead slow. I was thinking, if you asked your Dan or even Andy about their past relationships, they'd probably say they'd all gone badly."

Mike opened his mouth to argue, but before he could, Shaunna cut in.

"I know none of them were on a par with Rachel. What she put you through…" For a second, Shaunna's eyes blazed fury, but she got it in check. "It can take a long time to recover, but you don't need to give up living completely."

"If this is about tomorrow at Dan's…"

"It is, partly. When was the last time you went out with your mates?"

Mike laughed wryly. "Mates?"

"Or your brothers? Or anyone at all?"

He didn't answer, although he had no problem recalling the last time; it was the day Rachel was taken into custody.

Shaunna walked over to him and rested her hand on his arm. "Look, Mike, I'm not suggesting you should start dating again. Just get out of the house sometimes. Even if it's to come and watch telly with us for the evening."

"That's not fair on you. I know you and Andy got fed up with me when I stayed at yours."

"Yeah, and if you were coming round every night, then I might have something to say about it, but you haven't visited at all since you moved into the summerhouse, and you're always welcome. You know that, don't you?"

Mike smiled and nodded. "Cheers, Shaw." He saw her nostrils flare, realised why and amended. "Shaunna."

She grinned and hugged him. "I don't mind, really." She released him and went back to the counter, where the computer was stuck on the start-up screen.

"It shouldn't take that long," Mike said.

"It doesn't usually." She tapped a few keys and shrugged.

"You want me to take a look?"

"Have you got time?"

"A bit. I can come back later, if need be."

She shrugged again and moved from behind the counter so Mike could get to the computer.

"I'm coming to footy practice on Sunday," he said as he restarted the computer in safe mode.

"Are you? Awesome!"

Mike smiled. He thought it was awesome, too. "Dan asked me yesterday. Said he's looking to kick the Anchors' up the arse."

"Tell me about it. I'm kind of pleased I'm still not fit enough to play."

"From the twins?"

"Yeah, giving birth does shocking things to…well, you don't want to know, believe me."

Mike was happy to trust her on that one. The computer had finally started up. He had a quick look at the main culprits and quickly diagnosed the problem, or one of them, at least. "You've not got enough free disc space. There's a lot of stuff on here I'm pretty sure you don't need. I'm gonna delete your temporary files, which'll help a bit, but if you can manage without it for a few hours this afternoon, I'll come and sort it out properly."

"If you don't mind. We can always call in a exper…" Shaunna rolled her eyes. "Forget I said that."

Mike laughed. "No worries. My knowledge is long out of date, but I can get this sorted, no problem."

"OK. Hayley will be really happy about that."

Mike restarted the computer again and drank his tea while he waited to make sure it was working. The desktop appeared. "That's better. Right, I'll see you later." He passed his empty cup to Shaunna and moved towards the door. "Oh, I almost forgot." He backtracked and handed her the quote.

"I'll pass it on."

"Thanks. See you later."

***

Mike spotted it as soon as he got out of the van: the 1969 red Mustang parked two cars in front. He kept his eyes on his goal as he went to buy a parking ticket, returned to the van and stuck the ticket to the inside of the windscreen with considerably more force than required. Door shut, van locked, he muttered a few fucks under his breath and waited.

"Alright?" Andy acknowledged, casually strolling towards him.

"What the hell are you doing here?"

"Thought you'd appreciate the moral support."

Mike nodded, appreciating nothing. "Who told you? Dan or Mum?"

"Doesn't matter. Why didn't *you* tell me?"

"I haven't seen you."

"But you've seen Dan?"

"I went to price a job in—I don't have to explain myself to you."

"Whatever, I'm coming in with you."

"You're not."

Andy raised his arms, part shrug, part challenge, and Mike was sorely tempted to take him up on it. Short of smacking him in the teeth and causing a scene, he didn't see that he had any choice in the matter. He turned and walked up the path to the law firm's building. Andy followed him in and waited a few feet away while Mike spoke to the receptionist, who told him to take a seat. He did so. Andy sat next to him.

"Keep your mouth shut, all right?" Mike warned.

"Fine by me."

Mike stared at the wall opposite. Andy took out his phone, unlocked it, read the screen and started typing. He wasn't making any noise, but it still got up Mike's nose. He sniffed and diverted his attention to the ceiling. Andy locked his phone and put it away again.

"This is nothing to do with you," Mike said.

"Isn't it?"

"What's that mean?"

"You don't have to do this on your own."

"Oh, for fu—You know, I'm sick and bloody tired of everyone telling me what I do and don't have to do."

"Everyone as in…?"

"I don't need you to hold my hand."

Andy nodded and smirked. "Fair enough."

Mike waited, expecting him to get up and leave, but he didn't. "You're staying, then."

"I said I was."

Mike sat back and folded his arms. "What've you done with the twins?"

"With Mum."

"So it *was* her who told you."

Andy didn't comment.

"She knew you were coming here, and she didn't even mention it. Nice, that." When Andy still didn't respond, Mike glared at him. He was still smirking. "What?"

"You're being a knob."

"How's that?"

Andy picked up a magazine from the table in front of them. He turned a couple of pages. "She thinks I'm at the dentist."

"Right." Mike had nothing further to say. He knew he was being a knob, but he couldn't help it.

"Thing is, bro, this situation? It's because of me."

"No, it's not."

"Rachel—"

"Rachel nothing." The sound of a phone ringing stopped Mike from going any further. The receptionist answered it, watching him over the top of her glasses.

"Ms. Lane will see you now, Mr. Jeffries. Up the stairs, second door on your right."

"Thanks." Mike got up and set off for Ms. Lane's office, aware of Andy tailing him all the way up the stairs, but when they reached the top, Andy slowed to a stop.

"Listen, Mike. If you really don't want me in there…"

Mike shrugged. "You're here now." He knocked on the door; a female voice commanded he enter. He pushed the door open and stepped inside.

The room was smaller than he'd expected, with minimal furnishings, bland décor and no clutter. The desk positioned in the centre of the room had a slimline monitor and keyboard on top of it. There were two basic chairs on their side of the desk, behind it a vast, black leather chair, and it was empty. Mike frowned at Andy and mouthed, *Where is she?* Andy looked past him and nodded once in answer. Mike turned to find a sharply dressed woman had entered via a second door. She closed it and advanced on them with a smile.

"Mr. Jeffries," she greeted, her tone warmer now than when she'd called him in. "Michael, isn't it?" She extended a hand, and he shook it.

"That's right. Or Mike."

"Mike, and this is your brother, I presume?"

"Yeah. This is Andy."

Andy and the barrister shook hands. She gestured to the chairs on the near side of the desk, and they both moved over to them, waiting for her to sit down before they did.

"OK, Mike, I've received the paperwork from Jacqueline Perry's barrister. Mrs. Perry has stated her intention to apply for a guardianship order in respect of your daughter Bethan."

"Yes," Mike confirmed, although that was as much as he knew.

"Has she ever indicated this was her intention?"

"No, but then, I haven't seen her since Rachel's trial."

"Of course." Ms. Lane leaned back in her chair, her gaze flitting between Mike and Andy. "I've had a quick look over the information we have concerning Rachel Perry's trial. Unfortunately, she was represented by another firm. Rather, it's fortunate inasmuch as there is no conflict of interests, but it means our files pertain only to the witnesses we represented."

She was talking about Felix Perry and Len, although one of the other lawyers in the firm had represented them.

"Mike, would you mind telling me about your relationship with Rachel Perry?"

He shrugged. "We don't have one. She walked out three days after Bethan was born."

"And when was that?"

"Twenty-second of March. Bethan was born on the nineteenth."

"What was the relationship like between you and Rachel before Bethan came along?"

"Not great. We were only together because of the pregnancy."

"Were you a couple before your daughter was conceived?"

"No. We met on holiday, spent a night together. Rachel got in touch to say she was pregnant, and I told her I'd stand by her and the baby."

"Were you cohabiting?"

"We were. She moved in more or less right away—said she couldn't stay at home because her mum didn't know. But we never got on."

"Would I be right in thinking your relationship was already over before Bethan was born?"

Mike nodded. "To be honest, I don't think it ever was a relationship."

"And did Rachel make any attempts to see either you or Bethan after she left?"

"No, although when I was staying with Andy and his girlfriend, she came to the house."

"But not to see you or her daughter."

"No. She didn't even ask how Bethan was doing."

"Why do you think Rachel tracked you down?"

"I'm not sure she knew we were staying there." The questions were becoming too probing, and Mike felt under pressure. He could see the movement of Andy's hands as he latched and unlatched his fingers. He was itching to speak, but he'd promised to stay quiet.

"How many times did she visit your brother's house?"

"Once." Mike rubbed his forehead, wincing at the pain forming in his temples. Ms. Lane offered him a sympathetic smile.

"I know you're finding this distressing, but it's important I establish whether there were other occasions Rachel visited than the one mentioned in the witness statements."

Mike shook his head. "That was the only time."

"OK. Thank you, Mike. Now, before we go any further, would you like a drink?"

"No, thanks."

"Andy?"

"I'm fine, cheers."

"I won't be a second." She got up and left the same way she'd entered. Mike heard her talking quietly to someone on the other side of the door and listened in for long enough to establish the conversation was about another case. He tuned out again, instead wondering why all the questions about Rachel when he was here because of her mother. Maybe it was to see if Rachel had shown any interest in Bethan, which would probably give Jacqueline more chance of getting custody. But she hadn't. Once Mike and Bethan had played their part in Rachel's scheme, she'd deserted them. That had to count for something.

The conversation beyond the door stopped, and Mike cracked his knuckles, mentally preparing for more questions.

"You all right?" Andy asked.

He nodded.

Ms. Lane returned with a mug of coffee and resumed her seat. "OK, Mike. I'll explain why I asked about Rachel's contact with Bethan. Rachel requested a transfer to a prison with a mother-and-baby unit."

5: Possessed
Friday, 28th September

"She did fucking what?" Mike wasn't far off snarling at the lawyer, who was only the messenger when all was said and done, although she didn't seem perturbed by his outburst. Andy gave her an apologetic smile on Mike's behalf, which she acknowledged with eye contact only and continued sipping her coffee. Andy turned to his brother, not sure what to say, given he'd agreed not to say anything at all.

He'd been expecting it, or something like it, and was more surprised by Mike's reaction than he was by what Rachel had done. There again, Andy had the benefit of Josh and Sean's psychological expertise; they'd been there at the 'final showdown', when Rachel had turned up at The Blue Anchor pub and publicly humiliated herself. The start of the second half, the Lions were down by a good few goals, and Andy had a clear run...

At first, the voices had been indistinguishable from the cheers and boos—mostly boos from the home crowd—but those two words had sliced through the air like a spinning blade. *Ginger whore.* Andy had abandoned the ball to go to Shaunna, but before he'd left the pitch, George and Charlie had caught him and restrained him, the bastards.

Four months down the line, he was grateful they had. If he'd got hold of Rachel that day, it would be him doing time for murder, not her. In the aftermath, they'd gone back to Mum and

Len's, and the pieces had finally fallen into place. Kris had called George to tell him he and Ade had been in an accident. The brakes on Ade's Jag had failed, like the Corvette last Christmas, but unlike the woman in the Corvette, Kris and Ade had lived to tell the tale, or their part of it, because there was more, so much more. The break-ins at Elite Motors, the vandalism of Hayley's salon, the atrium chandelier had come crashing down just the day before the Blue Anchors match, and Rachel Perry was responsible for all of it.

Then there were her visits to the gym where Adele worked part-time, flexible hours, yet Rachel somehow always happened to be there when Adele was. Before that, Sean had spotted Rachel in the milk bar, watching him and Shaunna. Whatever he'd seen in Rachel's behaviour that day had worried him enough to warn Andy, but Andy had dismissed it as coincidence. Even when Josh mentioned he'd seen Rachel at The Red Lion—at the first Lions v Anchors match months earlier—Andy still tried to pass it off as nothing more than Josh and Sean's usual conspiracy theorising.

Ultimately, they'd both independently pre-empted Rachel's diagnosis of a personality disorder. During the trial, it had come to light that Mike wasn't the only one to suffer at Rachel's hands. She'd been physically abusive towards her younger brother and sister, although only her brother had testified while Jacqueline Perry sobbed and shook her head, refusing to believe what her son was saying, because Rachel had been clever enough to hide it from her. How many others had she hurt over the years, who, like Mike and Rachel's sister, were too frightened to take the stand?

In court, Rachel's expression had alternated between bored and gleeful. She'd thought she was going to get away with it, like she always had, except this time she'd killed someone, and the judge rejected her defence of insanity. She was a calculating, manipulative bitch with no regard for the consequences her actions had for others. In fact, she seemed to get a buzz from watching other people suffer. Now she was in prison, right where she belonged, and no doubt she'd be telling anyone who'd listen how much she was missing her daughter, or whatever other bullshit served her best.

"If she thinks I'm going to let my daughter grow up in prison…" Mike began, but the lawyer was already shaking her head.

"I think we can safely assume the request will be denied, particularly given what you say about Rachel deserting Bethan. The only reason they might consider it is post-partum depression, but there was no indication of that in her psychiatric assessment."

"She wasn't depressed," Mike said curtly.

Andy couldn't agree more. If anything she'd always seemed a bit manic, even when Andy had gone to see her in the police cells and she'd played the suicide card.

The lawyer continued, "I think perhaps the point of contention is your refusal to let Mrs. Perry see her granddaughter."

"I didn't refuse," Mike cut in and then backtracked just as quickly. "Well, I did, but she only asked once, on the way out of court. And it wasn't a polite request. She called me a few choice names and said I wasn't fit to look after a dog."

"To which you responded, 'That's no way to talk about your daughter.'"

Mike opened his mouth to protest, but Andy got in there first. "Actually, Shaunna said that."

"Shaunna being…?"

"My girlfriend."

Ms. Lane wasn't smiling as such, but she looked amused. "There's no love lost there, I take it?"

Mike sighed loudly. Andy put his head down and butted out, even though he was *desperate* to give Mike's lawyer the full lowdown on Rachel Perry. But he'd given Mike his word. And broken it.

Mike glared at Andy a moment longer before turning back to his lawyer. "It came up in the trial. When she went to Andy and Shaunna's place, it was to see Shaunna."

"For what reason? Did they know each other?"

"Only in passing. She claimed Andy was Bethan's dad, and she was trying to break them up. It's all part of her scheming. That's all she ever does."

Mike was getting agitated again, Andy knew, because he was repeatedly dislocating and relocating his right thumb. He'd always done it, even as a kid, sometimes just to make their mother squirm. But he also did it when he was pissed off or, as on this occasion, stressing out.

To her credit, his lawyer noticed, too. "We don't need to go into the nitty-gritty now. I'll go through the trial transcript again later." She sat back and clasped her hands in front of her, pausing a full minute or more before she asked, "How would you feel about offering Mrs. Perry access to Bethan?"

More minutes passed. Andy had expected Mike to say 'no' outright and looked to see why he'd delayed responding. His nod, barely discernible at first, became more definite.

"Yeah, I could agree to that, so long as she doesn't take her to see Rachel."

"We can attach conditions to your offer. That's not a problem."

"I'm not sure I'd want Bethan to stay overnight with her, either. I mean…I know Jacqueline's brought up three kids, but…" Mike shrugged, unable to justify the feeling, but Andy understood. He'd let the twins stay with his mum a couple of times, and waking up to an empty house had made him feel so wretched that he'd brought Rosie and Sorsha home again before nine o'clock the next morning. Of course, it wasn't anything like the same situation. He trusted his mum with the girls as much as he trusted Shaunna, and more than he trusted himself.

And that was the other thing: he had Shaunna. A few hours of undisturbed sexy time had been some compensation for his daughters' temporary absence. Mike had no such distraction.

Ms. Lane had been tapping away at her keyboard and continued to do so as she spoke. "I'm jotting down what we've discussed so far. What I'm proposing we do is this: I'll put together an offer that makes clear you're happy with Mrs. Perry having limited access to her granddaughter. There are several conditions we'll automatically put in place, such as not taking Bethan out of the country, ensuring any special dietary requirements or preferences are adhered to, and so on. However, you need to be aware that Mrs. Perry has already rejected the suggestion she apply for contact access rather than guardianship. Also, bear in mind she hasn't yet applied for the guardianship order, but she is legally required to inform the local authority of her intention to do so three months before submitting her application."

"But we're going to court next week."

"For the mediation information assessment meeting. The local authority received written notice on the fifteenth of August, and they'll have assessed Mrs. Perry's suitability before taking the matter further."

"That was a week after the trial. Why has it taken this long for me to hear about it?"

"That's partly why we have the assessment meeting, although it would be for the court to decide whether you should be kept informed of the progress of Mrs. Perry's application."

"How can she apply for custody of *my* daughter without anyone telling me?"

"To apply for the order, consent must be obtained from those with parental responsibility. As Bethan's mother, Rachel automatically has parental responsibility."

Mike clapped his palms to his forehead and ran them back over his hair. His hopes were dwindling fast. "She's gonna get custody, isn't she?"

The lawyer leaned across her desk and waited for Mike to look at her before she asserted, "It's absolutely not a foregone conclusion, particularly as Rachel made no attempts prior to her incarceration to arrange access to Bethan. Are you solely responsible for your daughter's care?"

"Apart from when I'm at work. Then my mum looks after her."

"So we can make a case for Bethan's primary attachment being to you and your mother. There's a possibility that Mrs. Perry will accept contact access and withdraw her application, but even if she does, I'd still recommend you attend the mediation meeting to ensure both you and Mrs. Perry are happy with any arrangements."

"And if she doesn't withdraw her application?"

Ms. Lane observed Mike in silence, as if she were weighing up how much to tell him. She had that same lawyer poker face Andy had seen on Jess many times over the years. He'd become quite good at interpreting the little signals Jess used to give off. Failing that, he'd usually been able to tickle or woo it out of her. Not so with Ms. Lane, who saved and closed the file on her computer before finally answering Mike's question.

"There's a possibility she would be granted special guardianship because of Rachel's rights."

"She's serving a life sentence in prison."

"She still has maternal rights, and you've made clear you don't want her to see Bethan. That may count against you."

***

"Alright?" Mike greeted as he stepped into the salon, heading straight for the counter and the computer.

Shaunna was midway through a cut and blow-dry and gave him a cautious smile. Hayley was organising the stockroom, but she'd be straight out as soon as she knew Mike was there, and it was clear from his demeanour that the last thing he needed today was to be hit on by a randy middle-aged hairdresser. Shaunna wondered what had happened since the morning, because he'd seemed in quite a positive frame of mind.

"OK to log out?" he asked, gesturing to the computer.

"Yep," Shaunna confirmed. She turned back to her client, separated a section of the woman's hair, combed it and snipped. "Are you all right, Mike?" she asked, with a glance in his direction.

"Hm? Oh, yeah. Fine." He nodded without looking away from the monitor.

Shaunna's client peered up at her and grimaced. Shaunna raised an eyebrow in response. "Just shout if you need anything, OK?"

"Will do."

Much as Shaunna hated to acknowledge it, Mike's presence seemed to have instantly sucked all of the joy from the salon. She reminded herself that whilst he was forever nattering her ear off, he rarely talked in company, particularly that of strangers. There was nothing odd, therefore, about his sullen silence, and yet… something wasn't right.

The stockroom door opened, and Hayley appeared, a large can of hairspray in each hand. "We haven't used this in…godda be two—oh! Mr. Jeffries. Whad a lovely surprise!" She went over to shake his hand, limp-wristed and with the back of her hand angled perfectly for a genteel kiss. It was the same move she pulled on every handsome man who came within touching distance, but it didn't work on this one.

Hayley retracted her hand and peered behind her at Shaunna, who signalled with her eyes for Hayley to go easy on him. Whether she'd take any notice was another matter. Since last Christmas, when Hayley had cajoled Andy and Dan into putting on an impromptu show for a hen party at the salon, she'd been obsessed with all things Jeffries. The only stopping block to her advertising the hen parties had been Shaunna's maternity leave, but it was only a matter of time, especially now Hayley knew for sure that there were *three of them*, and to her eye—though not to Shaunna's, of course—Mike was just as 'hod' as Andy and Dan.

For now, Hayley offered Mike a cup of tea, which he accepted and she duly delivered and then let him be, although not necessarily out of the kindness of her heart. It was a busy afternoon, and both Shaunna and Hayley had clients booked in through to five-thirty.

All the while, Mike worked away in silence. He was the most miserable Shaunna had ever seen him, and the one time she didn't have a client in front of her, he popped out to make a phone call, he said, but she was almost certain there was nobody on the other end of the line for much of the time he stood in the street with his phone to his ear. If he didn't want to talk about it, she wasn't going to drag it out of him, but for once she was wishing he would talk to her. Or talk to someone.

After her last client of the day left, Shaunna went to get the brush from the stockroom, using it as a prop to get closer to the counter.

"Almost done," Mike said, nodding at the progress bar onscreen.

Shaunna took it as permission to move closer to the computer, keeping as much distance from Mike as she could. He had his arms folded tight against his chest, the tensed tendons in his neck giving away how stressed he was. "What's happening here?" she asked.

"Updating the printer drivers. Everything was well out of date."

"Ah. That's because Hayley's terrified of accidentally downloading a virus."

"Yeah, she had plenty."

"Oh dear."

"I've got rid of them and set up the firewall and antivirus software. It was all installed on the machine already. Should run a bit better now."

"Thanks, Mike." She smiled at him, but he didn't even attempt one in response. "What are you up to tonight? Anything?"

"Working."

"On Friday evening?"

"Afraid so. I promised I'd get this woman's flat done by Monday."

"The computer would've waited, you know."

Mike sighed. "Yeah, but I need to stay…busy."

Shaunna was so close to asking the question, but Hayley had her keys in her hand, ready to leave.

"If it gives you any more trouble, text me." Mike got up and tugged his jacket free of the stool's backrest.

"Will do," Shaunna said. She watched him leave and get into his van. Hayley stopped next to her and watched him, too.

"He's nod a happy man, is he, sweedie?"

"No. He's really not."

***

"Hey," Shaunna called as she walked through the front door. Pausing to take off her coat, she sniffed, expecting a delectable aroma to fill her nostrils. Andy might not have held back in most regards, but it wasn't until she was beached with Rosie and Sorsha that he revealed his culinary talents. All those years trekking the globe had afforded him the sort of education chefs must dream of, yet amazingly, a traditional British roast was beyond him.

However, there was nothing cooking tonight. Assuming he'd had a rough day with the twins, Shaunna crept upstairs, fully expecting to find the three of them crashed out together on the bed, but the bed was made, and empty, as were both cots.

"Was the car there?" Shaunna thought aloud as she returned downstairs and opened the front door to find that no, the car wasn't there. "Weird." She shut the door again and went through to the kitchen, put the kettle on and checked her phone to see if she'd missed a call or a message. The screen wouldn't turn on. She plugged the charger in, went upstairs again to change out of her work clothes and use the bathroom, back down to the kitchen, where the kettle wasn't quite boiled, but her phone should have been charged enough to switch on. No joy. She checked the socket.

"Yeah, that'd explain it." She flicked the switch to the on position and laughed at herself. "Can't even blame hormones anymore."

Deep in thought, she put a teabag in her mug and leaned against the cupboard, wondering where they'd gone.

***

"Mummy's still not answering," Andy told the girls, who were in their seats in the back of the car. He glanced through the side window at the salon, locked, no lights apart from the small green flash on the alarm panel. She'd obviously not received his message before she left for home. He turned the ignition key and slowly pulled away, knowing he was for the high jump.

He hadn't intended staying all afternoon at his mum's, but Charlie was at a loose end, and so they'd got talking, as was their way. It was a nice distraction, not that he was bothered so much about Rachel. He didn't get worked up about stuff like that, but he was feeling for Mike. If they'd asked their family and friends a year ago, none of them would have predicted that Mike and Andy would become dads, yet they had, both in their forties and within three months of each other. It was finally something that bonded them as brothers, and Andy could imagine all too well the awful thoughts going on in Mike's head at the moment.

Shaunna was looking out of the open front door when Andy arrived back at the house, and she came to help him with the twins. Andy got out, preparing to be yelled at for worrying her, hoping a lingering kiss would tame the beast. She accepted his kiss and smiled up at him.

"Where've you been?"

"I went to meet you from work. Didn't you get my text?"

"Nope. Phone's dead."

"Ah. Well, I was only gonna suggest we went out for pizza. What d'you reckon?"

"Fine by me. I'll just go and sort my face out."

"It's beautiful, as always."

Shaunna laughed and stretched up to kiss him. "Thanks. Won't be long."

"OK. We'll wait here." Andy got back in the car; a couple of minutes later, Shaunna joined them, a waft of perfume following her in. Once she'd fastened her seat belt, Andy turned the car around—never easy in their road, given the size of the Mustang—and set off for The Pizza Place.

"Mike's been in the salon all afternoon," Shaunna said.

"Has he?"

"Yep. Fixing our computer. I'm not sure what he was playing at. He said he had a job to do before Monday."

"Did he tell you about Rachel's mum?"

Shaunna turned in her seat. "No. What about her?"

"She's applying for custody."

"Oh, my…you've got to be kidding."

Andy laughed joylessly. "I wish. We spent the morning with his lawyer."

"Did he ask you to go with him?"

"No, and he wasn't keen on me being there, but I couldn't leave him to do it on his own."

Shaunna turned to face the front again and sighed heavily. "I thought it was over."

"Yeah, so did he, but that..." The girls were too young to understand swear words, but Andy curbed his cursing anyway. The things he wanted to call Rachel were best not said aloud. "*She* gave her mum permission. Apparently, she still has parental responsibility."

Shaunna shook her head and angrily flicked her hair back. "The law really is an ass. What did the lawyer say?"

"What Mike needed to hear." Or that was Andy's impression. Ms. Lane had sounded confident enough, but he knew from Jess's work that when it involved children, the law was skewed in women's favour. All they could hope was that the law wasn't quite so much of an ass as people thought. Having Bethan been the best thing that had ever happened to Mike, and losing her would end him.

6: Coming Soon
Saturday, 29th September

"He was telling the truth, then." Dan was feeding the koi and contemplating a quick workout before the day of arguing over using the wrong cooking utensil or serving dish, not stirring thoroughly enough, being in the way, not helping, and so on, commenced in earnest.

"Uncle Mike coming?" Little Shaunna ran past and climbed onto the windowsill, pressing her face against the glass. Mike's van was parked in a space outside the next block along. Dan hadn't seen him arrive.

"He's working, Shu."

"Why?"

"So he can make pennies to buy Bethan more teddies."

"'Kay." She climbed down and raced past again, back to the sofa to continue watching TV.

"That was easy," Dan muttered under his breath. The 'why' game usually went on a lot longer, although he was wondering why himself. Saturday morning, not yet nine o'clock, and Mike was hard at it. There again, he'd need an early start if he really was planning to decorate an entire apartment in a weekend. The one-bedroom apartments in Dovedale were spacious; the two-bedroom, like theirs, were enormous. Whichever type Mike was working on, he'd be hard pushed to be done by Monday, although his sudden enthusiasm for working the weekend was about far more than buying toys for his daughter.

Dan turned and leaned against the edge of the koi pool, studying the expanse of lounge. It had taken thirty rolls of wallpaper to do the full room, and it was a while back. He knew, because Adele had helped him decide on the colour scheme—in other words, she'd chosen the paper, he'd hung it—and then they'd broken up and he'd wanted to rip it all down again. A year later, she'd married Tom. Six months after that, she'd moved back into the apartment, and they'd transformed Dan's bland spare room into little Shaunna's nursery.

Almost four years on, the rest of the apartment remained untouched. By the standards of a normal mortal who wasn't compelled to follow every new fad, it had been a long time. But there was little point in going all out on redecorating to their tastes when they *probably wouldn't* be living there much longer.

Interestingly, only Andy had passed comment on how odd it was that Adele wasn't pushing for The Great Living Room Makeover, or whatever it was Kris and Ade had dubbed it when Adele first mentioned it. No doubt it would come up again this evening, and Dan appreciated Adele taking the flak on his behalf, because the stopping block wasn't her indecision. It was his. They should have been looking at houses months ago; just that morning, Andy had emailed the details for a few more places. After Monday, Dan would give them his full attention and figure out what he wanted to do with the apartment. Until then…

"Dan?" Adele called from the kitchen.

"Yep?"

"Could you come here a sec?"

"Why?"

"Just…*come here.*"

Dan took a deep breath and did as requested. "What's up?" he asked as he reached the kitchen doorway, but he knew already. "Oh…right, err… What do you need me to do?"

"Call off the dinner party."

"Do you need to go to the—"

"*Call off the dinner party!*"

"Now? But—"

Adele nodded and inhaled through clenched teeth.

Little Shaunna pushed past Dan, gasped and put her hand over her wide-open mouth. "Mummy, s'matter?"

"The baby's coming," Dan explained, attempting to sound calm and happy because Shu looked ready to burst into tears—who wouldn't if they saw their mummy in obvious pain? He was starting to panic himself, or get excited. He wasn't really sure which.

They'd already asked the midwife what they should do if Adele went into labour before the scheduled caesarean, and she'd said to get to the hospital, so he at least had some kind of plan of action. It was everything else that was getting him in a bit of a state.

Adele was making a squeaky *hm, hm, hm* noise that would, at any other time, have been both comical and irritating. Rubbing her lower back with one hand, Dan took out his phone with the other, and for a moment stared at the screen, not sure who to call. They'd arranged for Alice to look after Shu, but that was for Monday, and Dan didn't like to impose. He didn't want to impose on his mum, either, when she'd already be looking after Bethan, but he didn't have much choice.

"What are you waiting for? Get calling!" Adele demanded and resumed squeaking.

Dan bit back a retort about her priorities being ridiculously wrong and dialled Andy and Shaunna's number, urging them to answer. It went to voicemail. He called again, same result. Adele's squeaks slowed and dropped in pitch. He gave it one last try, all set to accept he was going to have to call his mum.

"Hello?" Shaunna answered.

The squeaking stopped, and Adele blew air out of her mouth in relief. Dan did likewise, so glad to hear The Calm Voice of Reason on the other end of the line. He put the phone on speaker. "Hey, Shaunna. You OK?"

"Yep. Sorry, I was upstairs."

"Ah. Listen, we're gonna have to postpone tonight. Adele's gone into labour."

"She's…oh, wow!" Shaunna repeated the news, presumably to Andy, and then spoke into the phone again. "OK. What do you need us to do? Let everyone know about dinner?"

"Yeah, if you wouldn't mind…"

"Course not. I'm about to leave for work, but Andy could come and look after Madam, if that helps?"

"Err… I was gonna ask Mum, but…" Dan looked to Adele. She shrugged. "OK. We'll drop her off at your place, tell him."

"Will do. I'll let you go. Love to you all!"

"Cheers. I'll call later."

"Bye, and thank you!" Adele said quickly.

Shaunna made a *mwah* sound and ended the call.

Dan put his phone away. "Do we need to leave now?"

"No, we need to slow down. It's only the third contraction, Dan. I wouldn't have been worrying about the dinner party otherwise, would I?"

"OK, I'll go get—*third* contraction, did you say?"

"Yeah. I wasn't sure about the first two." Adele smiled, intending to reassure him.

He gave her a swift smile in response. "I'll get your bag. What else do you need?" He turned to leave, but she caught his arm and stopped him.

"I need for you to chill out. I'm OK, sweetie, I promise."

He nodded. "Let's get to the hospital. That'll make me feel better."

When they arrived at Andy and Shaunna's place, Dan got out of the car with Shu and carried her to the house to expedite proceedings. Andy opened the door as Dan approached, took one look at his younger brother and said, "Cacking your pants, bro?"

"You don't know the half of it," Dan admitted. "Got to keep a brave face, though, haven't I?"

Andy took Shu from Dan and glanced past him, to Adele, who was watching them from the passenger seat of Dan's convertible. She gave Andy a little wave. He waved back. "She looks like she's doing all right."

"Of course *she* is. She always does. Right, I'm off." Dan started moving away. "I left a message on Mum's phone. Dunno where she is, but she can't have gone far."

"Don't worry about it. I'm not going anywhere, and Shu loves looking after the babies, don't you?" Andy held up his hand for her to high-five.

Shu bashed his palm with hers and shouted, "Go Team Jiffies!"

"Team Jiffies!" Andy repeated with a grin.

Dan only half heard their fun interchange, still hung up on *don't worry*. He was sick of hearing it, because it was easy for everyone else to say. They hadn't been through the months of beeping machines and blood transfusions, breathing apparatus and high temperatures. They weren't the ones who discovered that losing a baby, regardless of being only a few weeks into the pregnancy, brought back not just the stress of Shu's first few months of life, but everything else that had been going on back then. That same anger flared like a flame finding oxygen, and Dan gritted his teeth. He wasn't going to take it out on Andy. Not again.

"Good luck, bro," Andy called.

Dan raised his hand in a wave as he climbed into the driver's seat once more. "You ready, babe?" he asked Adele. She giggled. "What's funny?"

"You called me babe."

"And?"

"You've never called me it before."

Dan started the car and moved off. "I'm pretty sure I have."

"No, you haven't but it doesn't matt-er-oooh-oooh-another." Adele clasped her hands to the sides of her bump and started squeaking again. Dan put his foot down.

He didn't get very far very fast. There were roadworks on the main route through the town, causing a mile-long tailback. He turned off to take a detour and got stuck behind a tractor, but at least it was still moving, unlike the lorry outside the furniture shop, the double-decker bus with its back end jutting diagonally across the road, and the idiot boy racer in a souped-up hatchback who'd spun off the roundabout, with every other driver goose-necking as they passed.

"For fuck's sake, *shift!*" Dan banged the side of his fist on the steering wheel and kept it there, horn blaring and doing nothing to reduce the chaos on the road ahead. "Right. I've had enough." He slammed into reverse, turned the wheel hard left and bumped up onto the pavement to get around the other cars. Back on clear road again, he was two minutes at most from the hospital when he spotted blue lights in his wing mirror. Anticipating it would be an ambulance, he shifted closer to the kerb and didn't pay much attention until the police car was directly behind him and indicating for him to pull over. He quickly did so—the sooner he got this cleared up the better.

The officer got out of the car, as did Dan. "Oh, bloody terrific." Of course it was going to be one of the lads who played for the Blue Anchors. He was expecting trouble.

"Dan Jeffries," the officer said, hardly trying to hide his smugness. Dan nodded. "What happened back there?" He turned his head in the direction of the roundabout, still congested with the crashed hatchback and the idiots goggling at it.

"My fiancée's in labour. We need to get to the hospital."

"Oh." The officer nodded. "Right, well, drive with more care in future, all right?"

Dan nodded. "I will, thanks."

"All the best." The police officer retreated to his patrol car.

Stunned, and, strangely, feeling much calmer, Dan got back in the car. He glanced Adele's way and shrugged. "You OK?"

"Yep. Are you?"

He reached over and took her hand. "Excited to meet our son."

Adele smiled and squeezed his hand. "Me, too."

Dan released her and fastened his seat belt, only then realising he'd driven all the way from home without it. He made it the last half mile to the hospital without further incident and parked in the dropping-off area. They walked through to the antenatal unit, where he left Adele with a midwife and went to move the car.

By the time Dan got back to the ward, the consultant had been to see Adele, confirmed she was in labour, and reassured her all was well. Adele was on the bed, propped against pillows and with a monitor attached to her belly; the fast *thump-thump* of the baby's heartbeat filled the room.

"They're doing the caesarean in the next couple of hours," she explained.

"Am I still allowed in?" Dan asked the midwife.

"Absolutely," she confirmed. "Would you like a drink, Mr. Jeffries?"

"Yeah, coffee would be great, thanks."

The midwife left and was back within a minute, with a plastic cup of coffee, which she left on the table over the end of Adele's bed. Dan thanked her, and she left again.

"God, I'm bored already," Adele grumbled once they were alone.

"Yeah, that doesn't surprise me."

Adele pouted sulkily. "Get my phone for me?"

Dan collected her bag and handed it over without complaint; she could be a princess for one day. Well, for another few weeks, and he'd be at home, hopefully with not too much happening in the way of work. Alice had offered to oversee their admin clerk, and Andy was able to do a fair bit in the evenings, once Shaunna was home from work, so Dan could look after Adele while she was post-operative, and get used to having a newborn baby all over again.

His brain was already racing ahead, thinking about the future. Strange as it would no doubt seem to anyone other than Adele, he was looking forward to sleepless nights, teething, colic, sterilising bottles... But they weren't there yet. Just a few more hours and he could finally get organised; it wasn't his style to leave things hanging. In business, he was successful because he acted fast; he took risks, and it usually paid off. In his personal life, however, the rash decisions had always come back to get him.

A nurse came into the room and wheeled a blood pressure monitor over to the bed. "How are you feeling, Adele?"

"Great."

The nurse fastened the cuff around Adele's arm. "This is your second one, is that right?"

"Yeah. We've got a little girl. She was prem."

"How early was she?"

"Thirteen weeks. Nine hundred and thirty grams."

"Wow, she was tiny. How old is she now?"

"Four next month."

"And is she doing OK?"

"She's doing brilliantly."

The blood pressure monitor beeped, and the nurse smiled again. "All fine."

"Phew! No pre-eclampsia this time."

"No, and that's a good, strong heartbeat baby's got. I think you're going into theatre next, so you're looking at about half an hour before they take you down."

"So soon?" Dan asked.

"Nothing to worry about," the nurse said and then left them alone again.

Dan stayed turned towards the door so Adele couldn't see his face. "You've not had any more contractions since we got here."

"No, but the consultant said he'd do it today anyway."

Dan swallowed hard, annoyed with himself for getting tearful.

"Come here, sweetie," Adele commanded gently. He shook his head. "Come on."

"I should be looking after you."

"We're looking after each other."

He relented and sat on the chair next to the bed, looking around the room and then homing in on the monitor screen. "Incredible. Was it like this last time?"

"Sort of. Do you remember the text you sent me?"

"Which one?"

"When I told you I was in hospital."

"Oh, that one." Dan cleared his throat, still feeling guilty for how dismissive his reply had been that day. He'd been more concerned about his dead koi than Adele's hospitalisation, convinced she was making a fuss over nothing, like she'd done throughout her pregnancy. He still didn't know what she'd been playing at, because it was attention-seeking, and it was Tom's attention she was after, not Dan's, even though she'd known from the start that the baby wasn't Tom's.

Dan wasn't proud of himself for screwing Tom over. If the boot had been on the other foot, Dan would have landed in the same place as Rachel Perry. But at least in the end he'd done the decent thing. He'd walked away so Tom and Adele could make a go of their marriage with 'their' baby. While Shu had the Jeffries colouring, she was the spitting image of Adele. Like no-one had suspected Andy was Krissi's father, no-one would have doubted Shu was Tom's if they'd stuck to the story.

So Dan had kept his mind on the koi, and the bastard who'd sold him the diseased fish that infected the rest got the full brunt of his rage, whilst Adele got a text to the effect of 'What is it this time? An ingrown hair on your bikini line?' She hadn't bothered replying. The next message he received after that was from Tom the following day, to tell him the baby had been delivered by emergency caesarean and Adele had had a stroke. All Dan could do was sit at home, nursing his broken fingers and drinking away the pain.

The week that followed was still a confused blur and probably always would be. The stabbing, the surgery, the morphine… Every time he came round, Adele was sitting at his bedside, but it had been a good few days before she'd told him she'd broken off the marriage. Then he'd met Shu for the first time, and nothing else mattered…until now, and the imminent arrival of their second child.

"All right then, Adele and Dan. Are you ready?"The midwife and a porter with a wheelchair drew to a halt at the end of the bed.

Adele smiled at Dan and took his hand. "As we'll ever be."

Dan moved away for the midwife to disconnect the monitor from Adele's belly, while the porter wheeled the chair closer for Adele to get into it. Once she was comfortable, the four of them made the journey to the lift and then down to the operating theatre. Aside from the short contraction Adele had as they left the lift, everything was low-key, no sense of urgency, which Dan found disconcerting, because it was at odds with how he was feeling. They'd left the baby heart monitor on the ward, and he was trying to stay focused on Adele rather than the ever-cycling worry that if something had gone wrong on the way down, they wouldn't know about it. He was on the brink of convincing himself that the midwife and porter were faking the calmness for precisely that reason, when Shaunna came along the corridor towards them.

"Alright?" Dan asked, once again overwhelmed by relief.

"Yep. Hayley sent me packing. Apparently, I was too distracted to be trusted with peroxide." Shaunna hugged Dan and whispered close to his ear, "Everything OK?"

"Err, yeah," he said doubtfully. Shaunna released him and quickly hugged Adele.

"Come through when you're done here," the midwife told Dan.

"OK, will do." He waited for the three of them to clear the double doors to the operating theatres before he turned back to Shaunna. "I don't know what's going on."

"What d'you mean?"

"Well, they've told us she's having the caesarean now, but…I don't know. It's all too calm, if you get me?"

Shaunna laughed and squeezed Dan's arm. "That's *good*," she said.

"It wasn't like this the last time?"

"God, no. It was panic stations. They rushed us down here, with the monitors, and Adele was still in the bed. We were straight into theatre." Shaunna blinked back tears at the memory. "It was terrifying."

Dan glanced at the theatre doors and then back at Shaunna. "Do you want to go in with her again?"

"Not unless you want me to."

"Not necessarily, but…I never thanked you for being there for her last time, and I suppose if anyone should be at Adele's side, it's you. You've earned the right, I haven't."

"Oh, Dan. That's a lovely thought. Thank you. But you should go in now. I'll be out here waiting, OK?"

Dan nodded and moved towards the theatre doors.

"Good luck!" he heard Shaunna call as he stepped into the cool, bright corridor beyond.

The anaesthetist was in the process of setting up Adele's epidural when Dan reached the room, and a healthcare assistant brought theatre scrubs for him to put on before he was allowed in. In spite of all the machines, overly bright lights, and faces hidden by green surgical masks, Adele seemed very chilled.

"D'you reckon Andy and Shaunna'll ever get married?" Dan asked. It wasn't an entirely random thought, although he hadn't intended to say it out loud.

"Course they will," Adele said in her 'I know something you don't know' voice. Dan raised an eyebrow in query and waited for her to elaborate, which she duly did. "They've talked about it. They're going to wait, though, until the twins are old enough to be part of it."

"So what'll that be, then? Wedding in a half pipe?"

Adele laughed. "Can you imagine? Mind you, they make designer skiwear."

"Yeah, I know. I've got some."

"Hm. You've had those salopettes since you were at university."

"Not true. I bought them for Calgary."

"That's still ten years ago."

"Snow doesn't go out of fashion."

Adele rolled her eyes. She looked different without her make-up and false eyelashes: younger, and beautiful as ever.

They continued their playful quarrel while the staff fitted Adele with surgical stockings and a catheter. Someone put electrodes on her chest, whilst someone else put a cannula in her hand and attached a bag of clear fluid. Injections of antibiotics and something to stop blood clots were given; the anaesthetist checked the epidural had worked its magic, and then it was time.

"Can we give him a name yet?" Adele asked.

"Almost," Dan said. He took up position at Adele's side, aware of his racing pulse and sweaty armpits. The theatre was air-conditioned, so it wasn't especially warm, but Dan was worked up enough to feel like he was in the middle of a full workout. Beyond the green screen, the surgeon and her staff toiled, talked through each step—the incision, parting muscles, cutting Adele's uterus—

"Brrr," Adele said, and the midwife laughed.

"That's your waters breaking, my love."

"It feels weird." Adele's eyes widened, and she looked at Dan. "Really weird. Kind of tickles, except I can't feel a thing."

"Completely normal," the midwife assured her.

"All right, here's baby," the surgeon said.

She lifted the baby up, high enough for Adele to see. Dan gulped and covered his face with his hand.

"Oh, you, silly…" Adele grabbed him around the head and tugged him to her.

"What a handsome son you've got here. Congratulations, both. We'll just give him a look-over."

She handed the baby to the paediatrician, and Dan watched, more curious and less frantic, as his son's breathing, reflexes and so on were tested.

"Ten," the paediatrician said with a smile and brought the baby back, placing him on Adele's chest. Dan was crying so much his face hurt.

"What's it out of?" he asked.

The paediatrician laughed. "Competitive dad, eh?" She directed the question at the baby and then looked up again, still laughing. "Ten out of ten," she confirmed.

"Get in there!" Dan grinned through his tears. He leaned in to give Adele a gentle kiss and turned his attention to his son.

"Hello, baby." Adele brushed her finger over his cheek, glancing up and repeating the action with Dan. "Can we give him a name *now*?" she asked.

Dan nodded. "Yep. What did you want to call him?"

"You first."

"Robbie."

"Robbie?" she repeated. She scowled. "Please tell me you're not naming our son after Rob Simpson-Scumbag? I mean, I know you've been mates forever, and he didn't really do anything wrong. But what about Andy?"

"You want to call him Andy?"

"No." Adele tutted and gave a huge airy sigh.

"It's nothing to do with Rob."

"Are you sure? I mean, it's a lovely name, but we might as well call him Henry if you're going to name him after a mate."

Dan shrugged. "It'd mean he'd have your dad's name, too. Is that what you want?"

"Not really. But you and Aitch are still best mates now. Why Robbie?"

"It's just... Don't laugh, but it's what I always wished my name was."

"Yours is perfect, sweetie."

"Nah. It's not."

"It is. I love it. You wanna know how much I love your name, *Daniel*?"

Dan shifted uncomfortably. He'd only ever been called 'Daniel' when he was in trouble, other than by his mum, who'd always insisted on calling all three sons by their full names.

"I wanted Robbie to have your name," Adele said.

"Dan Junior?" He laughed and shook his head, but he could feel his face getting warm. "Poor kid."

"OK. So how about Robert Daniel Jeffries?"

Dan pondered for a moment, repeating the name in his head.

"What do you think?" Adele prompted.

"I think I'm the luckiest man alive. I love you." Dan poked his little finger inside Robbie's tiny fist.

Adele sighed and placed her hand on top of Robbie's. "I love you, too."

"D'you reckon we'll ever get married?"

"Don't push it, Jeffries."

7: Niece in Need
Saturday, 29th September

With only one short wall left to paper, Mike considered the inch of paste in the bottom of the bucket and reluctantly concluded he'd need to open another packet. It was always the way, but he kept bag clips in the van for that eventuality. It was either that or waste three-quarters of a packet of paste on every job. He finished trimming the last drop on the feature wall and stepped back, leaning on the doorjamb to admire his work. He was shattered, not surprisingly, seeing as he'd been at it since eight a.m. without a break, and it was almost noon. But he'd made good progress. The lounge would definitely be done before the end of the day, probably before Dan and Adele's dinner party.

He was in a bit of a quandary, and he wasn't sure why, because yesterday, his mind had been made up. He didn't want to go to the dinner party. But with only the radio for company and four hours of thinking time, he'd been coming round to the idea. These days, he got on with his brothers, and he loved their girlfriends, or Shaunna, at any rate. Adele was nice enough, but she was too much like Anne for Mike to feel comfortable in her company.

And, of course, he adored his nieces. His family squarely laid the blame for that on Bethan's arrival, but it wasn't the case. He'd always wanted to be a dad; he'd just been too selfish to become one through choice, or maybe it was self-preservation.

Either way, he and Anne had only tried the once and were in agreement they didn't want to go through it again. If she was bitter about it, now he had Bethan, she certainly hadn't shown it. Because of his daughter, he was a better man, the man he should have been for Anne, but she'd never needed him as much as Mike needed her. *Bloody awful way of showing it.* He shook his head, ashamed. Hindsight. It was like that moment on the quiz shows where they rolled out the big prizes in front of the losers—*look at what you could've won.*

"Ah, well." He sighed philosophically and pushed off from the doorpost, stooping to collect offcuts of wallpaper on his way across the room. He shoved them down inside the almost full bin bag, compressing the rest of the offcuts to make room for more.

If he did decide within the next few hours that he was going to Dan and Adele's, he'd be taking Bethan with him. It was one of the things he'd hated as a kid—his mum working all the time—and whilst he could now appreciate the necessity, he wouldn't be following her example if he could help it. He wasn't even that bothered about losing face by changing his mind. He'd done what he'd said he was going to do, so it wasn't like he'd been lying.

Whether he was going or not, he wouldn't last out the rest of the day without eating. He picked up the key the owner had given him and left the apartment, setting off on foot for the late shop on the main road. It was a ten-minute walk, and he'd eaten the two sandwiches and half of the multipack of Penguin biscuits by the time he arrived back at Dovedale.

Taking a detour, he went to Dan and Adele's and knocked. No-one answered, and he noticed with some disappointment that Dan's parking space was empty. The company would've been nice, but it wasn't meant to be. Feeling a bit despondent, he trudged back upstairs and mixed a new batch of paste. There was enough to finish the living room and the entrance hall, and while the paste thickened, he prepped the hallway walls so he could do just that.

He finished pasting the first length of paper as his phone rang. Dan, no doubt calling to say they were back from wherever and inviting him down for a cuppa. Typical.

"Alright?" Mike answered.

"I am, as it goes. Guess what?"

"What?"

"You're an uncle again."

"You're kidding. But I thought…" Mike was gobsmacked, in a good way. "Everything all right?"

"Perfect. Just over three and a half kilograms."

"In English?"

"Seven pound twelve."

"Not bad at all, that. So what've you called him?"

"Robbie. Robert Daniel."

"Huh. No surprises there," Mike said with a chuckle.

"Why?"

"You were always on about changing your name when you were little. Drove Mum mental with it."

"Bloody hell, you remember that?"

Mike laughed. "You'd be amazed at some of the stuff I remember, like that time Andy talked you into putting that crocodile clip on your—"

"Yeah, all right, bro. You're making my eyes water here."

"Soft arse." They both continued laughing a moment longer, and then Mike said, "Congratulations, Dan. You did good."

"Cheers."

"Pass on my love to Adele, yeah?"

"Will do. Speak to you later."

"Bye." Mike moved his phone away from his ear in time to see the 'call ended' message. Decision made, then. He smiled to himself, genuinely delighted for his brother and Adele, and then eyed the length of paper on the paste table, already dry in patches. Picking up the paste brush to start over, he wondered what he was going to do with his evening now. It was incredible how a few hours of talking himself into socialising had made the idea of a night in with his sleeping daughter somewhat less appealing.

With that thought came a surge of guilt. At home caring for Bethan was where he should be, and they were already missing out on a full day together. What he needed to do was shift up a gear, get as much of the job done as he could today and leave the rest until Monday so he could spend Sunday being a dad. If footy practice was still on, he'd go, but he wouldn't play. They could watch it together.

The rest of the afternoon flew by, with an occasional text message from Andy or Shaunna and a few posts online tagging him, first photos of his new nephew, who looked like he'd inherited an even mix of his mum's and his dad's colouring. He wasn't quite as dark as the rest of the Jeffries clan—or the rest bar Rosie, who was a redhead, like her mum—although Robbie already had Dan's frown. Good-looking little lad, though. Mike locked his phone and got back to work.

By six o'clock, he'd finished the living room and the hallway, and he'd got a first coat of paint on the bedroom walls. Even taking Sunday off, he'd be done by Monday evening, all being well. Feeling a bit achy from going like the clappers, he gathered together the stuff he was finished with, left his ladders and table where they were, and locked up the apartment.

On his way downstairs, he pondered what to eat this evening. His mum would've fed Bethan, so a takeaway was in order. He had a tenner in his pocket and, until the cheque cleared, about two quid in the bank, so it was a bit irresponsible, but if he didn't get something on the way home, he'd be too tired to bother cooking and end up going to bed hungry.

"I didn't think you'd still be here!"

Mike startled out of his thoughts. Mrs. Hunter was coming up the stairs towards him.

"Alright?" he greeted.

"Yes, thanks. You?"

He nodded. "Not bad."

"Have you been here all day?"

"Yeah, pretty much," Mike confirmed, underplaying the ten hours solid he'd worked on the apartment. "Living room's done, and the hallway."

"Gillian will be pleased. I've only popped in to feed her cat."

"Oh? I didn't see a cat."

"No, you won't have done. It's a funny creature, comes back in the evening for its dinner, sleeps on her bed, and then goes out again in the morning."

"Cats are nocturnal, aren't they?"

"Quite right. Ours are never home at night. Anyway, if Gill's cat does deign you with an appearance, he's quite friendly, but he'll get in your way and pester you for fuss."

"Thanks for the warning," Mike said. He'd stopped still too long and was starting to seize up. He stepped off. "Good to see you again."

"You, too," Mrs. Hunter responded, and they passed on the stairs. As Mike reached the bottom, she called his name. He turned and peered up at her. "If you're ever working over my way, do stop in for a coffee. It would be lovely to see you again." She offered him a quick smile.

"Cheers," he said and, with a courteous but tired nod, continued on his way.

Only when he pulled up outside The Pizza Place ten minutes later did his heart rate return to normal. Mrs. Hunter's open invitation had put him on the spot, even though she was only being friendly. She knew he was a single parent with a baby, because she'd asked and he'd told her, and she probably felt sorry for him.

They had the single parenting in common, but that was about the only thing. She was well-to-do, with a high-paid professional job—he had no idea what. In fact, he didn't even know her first name. She was a customer, and a happy one at that. There was no need for first names, or not from his point of view, and she only knew his because that was how it was with the manual trades. None of the formal 'Mr. Jeffries' for him, although the same wasn't true of his brothers. He'd been around a few times when Dan and Andy were having meetings online, and most of their overseas clients called them Mr. Jeffries.

"Hey, Mike, be with you in a second." Krissi bounced past him and away down the pizza restaurant. He watched her in something of a daze as she stopped at a table to deliver the bill, bantered briefly with the table's occupants, and returned to his location. "How you doing?" she asked. Her eyes scanned his face and crinkled with concern.

"All right," he said. "Been working all day. I'm shattered."

"I bet." She didn't tell him he looked it, but he could see she was thinking it.

"I figured I deserve a pizza."

"Totally. What d'you fancy?"

"Err…dunno." He scanned the countertop, searching for a menu. She retrieved one from the nearest table and handed it to him. Mike looked over the list of pizzas, but in truth, he was too tired to make a choice. He shook his head. "What's good?"

"Andy likes the Full House."

Mike found it on the menu and read the list of toppings. "Blimey, you'd need a forklift to get it to your mouth. Yeah, OK. One of those, but no onions, peppers or garlic butter."

Krissi grinned mischievously. "Got a date?"

"Only with my daughter," Mike replied, impressed by how flippant he sounded. It was a long time since he'd dated, and he missed having a woman's company, but Rachel was his last, and the way he was feeling, she might be *the* last.

"How big do you want to go?"

"I've got ten quid. What'll it get me?"

"You hungry?"

"Starving."

"OK. I'll see what I can do." Krissi indicated to the seats at the front of the restaurant and left him to his own devices.

Mike sat in the chair farthest from the door and felt his back twinge. One of these days, he was going to get a massage from a professional masseuse. Between the stress of Jacqueline Perry and his job, his back and shoulders were giving him a fair bit of grief, but what could he do? He'd been self-employed long enough to know that when the work was there, he had to grit his teeth and bear it, because there was no way of predicting when it would dry up again.

Like, now, for instance: he had nothing after the Dovedale job, until Hayley gave him the go-ahead for the salon. Between that and the Hunter place, he'd be all right until the end of October, at a push. November, it normally picked up, with people wanting to redecorate before Christmas, so he needed a couple more jobs between now and then. He'd already resigned himself to using what he'd saved so far towards a deposit on a house to pay the lawyer, which would mean starting from scratch. Maybe wasting a tenner on a pizza wasn't such a good idea after all.

"Excuse me!"

Krissi's raised voice caught Mike's attention, although it wasn't directed at him. The group at the table she'd gone to when he arrived were on their way to the door, and they were moving at speed.

"Hey!" Krissi shouted. She was a few steps behind them. Without thinking, Mike jumped up and blocked their exit.

"Shift," the guy in front of him snarled.

Mike shook his head. "Think the manager wants a word with you."

"What the fuck's it got to do with you?" The guy tried to push past, but Mike stood firmly in front of the door. He might not have worked out the way he used to, but his job kept him fit, and he had a good six inches advantage, height-wise.

Krissi stepped past the group of four and stood next to Mike. "You need to pay your bill, sir," she said curtly.

"I told you. The food's shit."

"Yes, sir, you did—*after* your card payment was declined. Now, you can either call someone to come and pay your bill, or leave your ID here, and when you come back with the money, I'll return it to you."

"I'm not paying." The man turned to his three friends, who, for their part, looked embarrassed, but they weren't backing off.

"Then you leave me no choice, I'm afraid." Krissi lifted her hand, in which she had her mobile phone, and hit the call button. Mike saw the number onscreen; she wasn't bluffing. "Police, please. The Pizza Place, High Street. I'm Krissi Johansson, the manager. I've got a customer intending to leave without paying." Krissi's phone flew out of her hand and landed with a resounding clunk on a nearby table. She sighed loudly, her anger evident now, and shouted, "The customer knocked my phone out of my hand." The phone was screen down on the table, so there was no way of knowing if the call was still connected.

Whilst Krissi had been on the phone, the chef—Krissi's boyfriend, Wotto—had ushered the other staff and the rest of the customers out of the restaurant via the kitchen door. Unsurprisingly, they'd all made their way around to the front of the building; Mike could see in his peripheral vision the crowd gathered outside, and still the bloke in front of him wasn't giving up.

"Your restaurant's fucked." He sneered at Krissi. "I'm gonna tell the papers about this."

Krissi raised an eyebrow but refused to be drawn.

"We all saw that rat." He turned to his friends, and they looked at him in puzzlement.

Mike laughed. "Ridiculous."

As the guy turned back, he took a step closer so that he was up in Mike's face, or would've been, were it not for the height difference. Mike didn't so much as flinch, although equally, he didn't want a fight. "Wouldn't it be easier to just hand over your driving licence and get out of here?"

"No, because you're gonna move out of my way."

Mike nodded and stayed put.

"Police are here," Krissi said, unnecessarily, with flashes of blue illuminating the restaurant walls. If she'd been expecting their arrival to make her customers pay up, then she was sorely mistaken. The three lads who had tried to keep out of it were shoved aside as their ringleader made a run for the kitchen, but Wotto had locked the door.

"You can't trap us in here. It's against the law!" he yelled as he came storming back towards them.

"Good point," Krissi muttered under her breath.

Mike moved to the side, gesturing to the front door. "Off you go, then."

The guy stopped in his tracks, his eyes shifting between Mike and the door, which opened to admit two police officers. They both acknowledged Krissi.

"This joker, is it?" the taller of the two asked.

"Yeah. His card payment was declined, and he tried to leave without paying. He's with these three." She thumbed at the others.

"Listen," one of them said. "If you take me to the cashpoint, I'll get the money for the bill." He looked terrified out of his wits.

"No, you bloody won't," his mouthy mate shouted.

"Come on, man. We're already in enough bother."

The shorter police officer looked to Krissi. "What do you want to do?"

"If he's prepared to pay…" She shrugged. "They're barred, whatever."

"I wouldn't fucking come here again if you paid me."

"That's enough now, sir," the officer told him firmly and then signalled to the man who'd offered to pay. "I'll walk you to the cash machine and back. Make sure you don't get lost on the way."

The man nodded and followed the officer out of the restaurant. The other three stayed where they were. There was a bank on the opposite side of the road, so it wasn't long before he returned and gave Krissi the cash.

"I'll get you a receipt," she said, going behind the counter to do just that. Soon after, the police escorted the four men off the premises. Krissi watched them leave, shoving their way through the small horde of people outside—customers and passersby who'd stopped to see what was occurring. As the furore died down, the customers came back inside, chattering amongst themselves.

"Thanks," Krissi said to Mike.

"No worries. Are you all right?"

"Yeah. Just…peed off. We've lost half this evening's business because of that idiot." She studied the street beyond the front window and shook her head. "I'm glad you were here, Mike. Really glad."

"Me, too." He pulled out his phone to check the time. "I'd best get going."

"Your pizza?"

"Nah. I'll stop off at the chip shop."

"Don't be daft. If you can wait ten minutes, I'll get Wotto to remake it. I think the other one's still in the oven."

Mike sniffed. "Yeah, smells like it might be a bit too well done for me." He gave Krissi a wink, and she laughed. "If it's no trouble," he said.

"It's not." She came around his side of the counter and hugged him. "Be right back." Once again, she left to order his pizza.

Through the circular window in the kitchen door, Mike watched her approach Wotto, shaking her head vigorously. Wotto put his arms around her, and she buried her face in his neck. They stayed that way long enough for Mike to feel he was intruding. He shifted his attention to the customers, now being looked after by Krissi's staff, and wondered if what had happened was a frequent occurrence. It could've got nasty, and he wasn't sure he'd helped matters. He also wondered why Wotto hadn't come to Krissi's aid. There again, she was as tough as her mother, and both women could've taken on that bunch of twerps single-handed.

Even so, Mike would've done exactly the same for Shaunna. He'd acted on instinct and was glad to find that these days his instincts were to protect people from idiots who, unfortunately, reminded him of himself, and not that long ago.

"Here we go." Krissi approached him with a smile on her face and only the tiniest trace of evidence that she'd had a good cry in the kitchen. Mike reached into his back pocket for his money, but she shook her head. "On the house. Get yourself some beer."

"No, I don't...mind..." He stopped talking. He could feel the ten-pound note, but he didn't dare move a muscle with Krissi staring him down. No way was she going to let him pay. He pulled his hand out of his pocket and took the pizza. She offered him the kind of smile that said 'wise move'.

"Cheers for this," he said. She was still giving him that smile. "I, err, might get a couple of beers, then."

"You do that."

"OK. Take care, yeah?"

"You, too."

Mike waited for a final nod of reassurance that she was OK and set off for home once more, briefly stopping at the off-licence—thankfully without further incident.

8: Without Saying
Sunday, 30th September

07:30, Dan [mobile]
You up bro?

07:37, Andy [mobile]
Yep. Sup?

07:41, Dan [mobile]
Just letting you know training is still on. See you later.

"He's gotta be kidding." Andy put his phone back on the bedside table and stared up at the ceiling. His disbelief had nothing to do with Dan *not* cancelling football training. It was the fact he'd felt it necessary to send a text to confirm it, never mind asking if he was awake at half seven on a Sunday morning. What parent with a baby, or two, got to sleep in on a Sunday? OK, so technically he wasn't 'up' if he was lying on the bed and only wearing his boxers, but he'd been awake for nearly three hours.

He'd fed the twins at five, after which he'd been for a run and taken a shower. He was only here now because he'd come tearing into the room when he'd heard his phone vibrating, slipped on the rug and made a dive for the mattress. Shaunna hadn't stirred at all, which was something, but he'd have preferred not to chance it, especially when it was only his brother texting to state the bleeding obvious.

Of course Dan wouldn't cancel a training session when victory was in their sights. Seven games played, six wins and one defeat, leaving them in second place in the league…three points behind the Anchors. Their next match, on Tuesday evening, was against Comco—the local glass company—who were a decent side, but if they could beat them, the win would put them level on points with the Anchors ahead of next Sunday's grudge match. Ignoring for one moment that Dan could visit Adele and the baby any time of the day, and also that wild horses couldn't have dragged Andy away from the hospital when the twins were born, not forgetting Dan and Adele had been trying for this baby for two years, there was no reason to cancel their training session. At all.

"He's off his trolley," Andy muttered to himself.

Shaunna rolled over, lifted her head and glared at him from under her mess of hair, grunted, and flopped back onto the pillow.

"Hey, RHB," Andy whispered, brushing her hair out of her face.

"What time is it?"

Andy checked. "Ten to eight."

"Too early." She puffed her pillows and put them over her head. It made Andy smile. If there was one thing he'd learnt from the passionate week that had marked the start of their affair, aside from her being insatiable—not a complaint—it was that Shaunna was not a morning person. If she got her lie-in, like she would this morning, no problem. But if she was woken before she was ready to face the day, she'd huff and snarl at anyone brave or stupid enough to attempt interaction. He usually just pushed a cup of tea in her direction and kept his head down, but there were those, like Adele, who, in spite of knowing her for all of living memory, persisted in their efforts to engage first-thing-in-the-morning Shaunna. If they were lucky, they lived to walk away with their tail between their legs.

Which one is Adele? Brave, or stupid? He'd honestly never thought of her as stupid, though he knew she often thought it of herself, with her 'ignore me, I'm a ditzy blonde' excuse always on standby. She was ditzy, and she was blonde, but she also had Dan wrapped around her finger, and from what Andy had heard, before she went on maternity leave, Adele had, essentially, been managing the fitness suite where she worked as a beautician. Actually, that was a bit insulting. She'd been employed to run the beauty salon, and she was a highly qualified beautician, or beauty therapist, he wasn't sure which, or if they were one and the same thing. He had the same trouble with Sean and Josh. Sean was a clinical psychologist, Josh was a psychotherapist, but they'd gone to uni together, graduated with the same degree, and both talked for a living.

Maybe he'd ask Sean at footy later, not that it mattered. They were simply rambling thoughts for a Sunday morning when Andy had nothing better to think about, because his red hot baby was snoring under her pillow, and his daughters were fast asleep in the room next door.

I could get some work done.

With that thought in mind, he shuffled carefully to the side of the bed, put one foot on the floor—

"You getting up?"

"Err...yeah."

"OK."

Wrong answer, possibly. "I'll make you a cup of tea."

"Hmph."

"Or I can stay here?"

"Whatever."

With one foot still on the floor, which was putting tremendous strain on his obliques, Andy tried to figure out which was for the best. He could go downstairs, make her a cup of tea, and if she wanted him to stay when he returned, all well and good. If not, he'd go back downstairs and work. He got up and moved towards the door.

"Get back here."

Andy sighed in fake exasperation and did as he was told, sliding his boxers down along the way and kicking them across the floor. Sunday morning sex. They could've taken their time, a slow, gentle buildup, lots of kissing and teasing, but it was never like that. Andy pulled back the covers and waited for Shaunna to roll onto her back. She didn't, so he knelt on the edge of the mattress and leaned down, brushing her hair back to access her neck and kissing his way up from her shoulder. With his knees under her hip, he eased forward until she flipped over. She grinned at him and licked her lips, eyeing him like she was preparing to devour him. He quickly moved in, tugging her nightshirt up and over her head and settling between her thighs, sliding upward and thrusting lightly until his body joined with hers. She gasped and arched her back, her left forearm pressed to her mouth, a flesh mute, because—

"Ohhhh. Mm…"

—she was not a quiet lover, the perpetual salve on Andy's ego, the fuel that fired him to do as she asked and 'take' her. Her body…it had featured in his every fantasy since his school days, when in his mind, one by one, he'd slip each button out of its hole and peel back her white school blouse, baring pale round breasts, soft belly, smooth warm skin. As he'd grown older, the fantasy had matured with him, and he'd pushed her skirts up, or jeans down, buried his nose in dark fiery curls, teased and caressed and ultimately made love to her.

Funny how in all those years of imagining, the F-word had never entered his head. He loved, ravished, worshipped with his body, but he'd never fucked her, he didn't think. Even the two occasions they'd lost to alcohol, he wanted to believe he'd made love to her, like now, as he gave her what she asked for, the harder, faster, no holding back until—

"Ugh. God, yes."

She ground against him, her words and her actions combining to trip the switch. He was catching that wave and there was no stopping him. His body and mind were lost to the motion, no longer fighting to keep control but giving in to the sensation, consumed by it, and then, finally, he was coming down the other side, struggling towards the shore, his limbs useless, not a breath left in his lungs. Washed up and broken, he collapsed on top of her.

"Morning, baby." He smudged a kiss on her cheek.

"Morning, sexy." She sighed, a deep, deep sigh of purest satisfaction. With his one open eye, he caught her smile. "Shall I make us some breakfast?" she asked.

"I'll do it."

"Or…I can?"

"You work all week."

"Andy. Please let me make breakfast."

"OK. If you really want to. Don't you like my breakfast? I was thinking poached eggs, crispy bacon—"

"I love your breakfast," she interrupted, "but let me make it for once." She pushed up with her pelvis to get him to move, and he rolled onto his side of the bed. "I'm going to have to start doing more anyway. You'll be back at work soon. We should get into a routine." She got up and grabbed her dressing gown. "I need to express. What time were they up?"

"Five."

"OK. I'll just do enough to ease the pressure, then, and feed them at the pub." She collected the breast pump and returned to the bed. "Training *is* still on, isn't it?"

"Yep," he answered, distracted by her efficiency. Pump plugged in, bottle attached, breast connected, all systems go.

"Cool," she said and rested back on her pillows, closing one eye in a wince as the pump started up. "Mike's coming. Did he tell you?"

"No, he didn't mention it. To play, you mean?"

"Yeah, and a good thing it is, too. I told you, didn't I? About the day the she-devil kicked off at The Blue Anchor?"

"Yeah, I think so." He didn't have a clue, and she knew it, so she told him anyway.

"He was saying how much he missed playing, and he was planning to talk to Dan about it but didn't, so I mentioned it on Mike's behalf, although that was ages ago. I can't believe it took him this long, but better late than never, I suppose. He doesn't seem interested in anything at the moment. I think your brother gets a bit of depression."

"Dan?"

"Ha, no. You've got to be capable of feelings to get depressed."

Andy turned and looked at her, to see if she was serious. She gave him a grin and swapped the pump to her other breast. Andy watched in silence, his thought processes still stuck on the start of their conversation. He'd thought they had a great routine. Now he wasn't so sure.

"Going for a shower," Shaunna said and got up from the bed. He hadn't even heard the pump switch off, and it wasn't a quiet machine. "Then I'll make breakfast," she added, which was a threat. She left the room.

Andy stayed where he was. The cool draught from the open window wafted over his body, giving him goosebumps, but he was hardly aware of it. *You'll be back at work soon.* He supposed that was true, although, between the admin they'd brought in and Alice, they'd got it covered. Maybe Dan had mentioned something to Shaunna, or even to him, and he hadn't been listening. It wouldn't be the first time he'd been oblivious to what was going on around him, but until this morning, he'd assumed everyone was as happy with the arrangements as he was. He was a full-time dad, and he was getting in a few hours of work here and there. He was pulling his weight, or so he'd thought.

Jeffries and Associates was the perfect setup for them. It was small-scale, bespoke logistics, connecting customers with suppliers, which usually meant spending some time working with the customer to pin down their requirements. If the jobs that came in needed both of their input, he and Dan would work together. Otherwise, it was a case of first dibs for the fun jobs, or taking on those that suited them best.

Kitting out Black Hole Studios, for instance, needed both construction and technical expertise, so they'd worked on it together. Checking quantities where they were only responsible for sourcing and delivering construction materials usually fell to Andy. Pinning down the right gadgets and gizmos for a job with a high tech spec was within Dan's jurisdiction. The work was varied and steady, and the boring paperwork side of it had always been outsourced.

Shaunna returned from the bathroom with her hair wrapped up in a fluffy cream towel, which she unwound, releasing the flowery scent of her shampoo and her glorious red curls, darker for being wet. She stood at the end of the bed, rubbing her hair with the towel and studying Andy. "Are you getting up?"

"Nah." He gave her a cheeky grin. She shook her head vigorously, spraying him with droplets of cold water. He shivered for effect and sat up. "I was thinking," he said.

"What about?"

"I'm happy with the way things are."

"What d'you mean?"

"With work, and being at home with the girls. Obviously, I'll need to cover Dan over the next couple of months, but after that, I'd like to carry on as we are now."

Shaunna picked up her hairbrush and pulled it through her hair. It became tangled, and she swore under her breath.

Andy got up and took over the untangling, still stark naked, but Shaunna wasn't paying any attention. She was staring up at him while he kept his eyes on her hair.

"You're not bored yet?" she asked.

"Nope."

"OK."

"You thought I would be?"

"I hoped not, but with your track record…"

"Fair comment." Andy shifted his eyes to meet hers. "Are *you* happy?"

"Yep, totally. I want to do another course after Christmas, though."

"Another psychology course?"

"Maybe. Is that frivolous?"

"Not in my vocabulary, that. What's it mean?" Shaunna shoved him in the midriff. "No, it's not frivolous," he said.

"But isn't it a waste of money?"

"Not if it's something you want to do."

"I don't want to give up hairdressing."

Andy frowned. The brush came free, and he handed it to Shaunna. "What's doing a psychology course got to do with giving up hairdressing?"

"Well, it's…I don't know. Nothing, I suppose, but Hayley gave me a pay rise the last time, just in case I was thinking of deserting her, and even you thought it. When we were looking at this place—"

"Yeah, and you put me right. You've got a job you love. Why would you even consider giving it up? It'd be like me giving up the business to teach surfing. Mind you…" Andy peered upwards, pretending he was thinking about it. Shaunna nudged him, and they both laughed. She stood on tiptoes to kiss him, taking the opportunity to run her brush through his unruly hair, which on this occasion he'd already brushed, but he liked it, so he let her carry on.

"Thanks," she said.

"For?"

"Understanding?"

"Err, no worries, I guess." He wasn't entirely sure why she was thanking him.

"So we're fine as we are," Shaunna said.

"Yep. We're good."

***

"Right, let's get started," Dan called—loudly enough for Andy to hear from The Red Lion's car park, which was on the other side of the road to the playing fields. He and Shaunna were in the process of transforming the twins' car seats into pushchairs, and he stopped and glared at his brother.

"You go. I'll deal with this," Shaunna offered.

"No, he can damn well wait." Andy shook his head in irritation. Dan had thrown the ball onto the pitch, where the other players were now kicking it around, but his brother's attention was on him, not them. It was typical Dan behaviour; he was obviously pissed off with someone, which may or may not be Andy. Either way, he was going to get it in the neck, but that wasn't the reason he was taking his time.

"You really shouldn't wind him up," Shaunna said as they waited for a car to pass before they crossed the road. "Not today."

"I know, but it's fun. So what d'you reckon? Adele's given him his orders?" Andy affected a high-pitched voice. "You'd best be here by one o'clock, or I...I'll tell everyone about your tiny—"

"No way would she say that!" Shaunna looked scandalised.

"The truth hurts."

"It's so not true."

"Oh, yeah? How d'you know?"

Shaunna blushed. "Women talk about these things."

"You do, huh?" Andy nodded smugly. Shaunna laughed and said no more, although he was a bit curious to know if they talked about him as well. If they did, there'd better not be any of that tiny—

"About bloody time you got here." Dan stopped in front of him and looked him up and down. "Kit?"

Andy reached under Rosie's pushchair for his boots and smirked as he dangled them in front of his brother's face.

"Get 'em on, then." Dan moved off backwards, turned and jogged across the pitch. "Right, George. Can I have a word?"

Andy dropped his boots to the ground, keeping hold of the pushchair while he kicked off one of his trainers and shoved his foot into the corresponding boot. It had rained overnight, not too much, thankfully, but it would still mean playing in wet socks if he lost his balance.

Shaunna peered under the pushchairs' hoods. The twins had woken for their feed when they were about to leave the house, which was why Andy was late—only by five minutes. Now they were sound asleep again.

With both boots fastened, Andy did a few quick stretches to warm up, even though he'd had plenty of exercise already this morning. "Are you gonna stay out here?" he asked Shaunna.

"For now, yeah. We'll go and join the Sandison-Morleys." She pointed to Libby and Josh, standing near the goal so they got to see as much of George as was possible without invading the pitch. No sign of Pez, though, which was strange. Match or training session, he was always there, although perhaps it was as well he wasn't today. "Where's your Mike?" she asked.

Andy automatically looked on the pitch.

"He's not here," Shaunna said.

"Didn't you say he's supposed to be playing?"

"Yeah, but maybe something came up," Shaunna suggested. Andy raised an eyebrow. "I'll give him a call."

"OK. See you in a bit." He kissed her and jogged off to join his teammates.

***

"Oh! I was just about to call you." Shaunna put her phone away and gave Mike a brief hug around Bethan, snug and content in the baby sling strapped to his chest.

Mike peered down at his daughter. "Someone let Daddy sleep in this morning."

"Did she? That's…good?"

Mike smiled. "It's amazing. I actually feel human today. I'm going to see Robbie later. Visiting's two till three, yeah?"

"Yep. We're going this evening. Andy hasn't met him yet, either." Adele was still being stitched up during afternoon visiting the previous day, and everyone had left the evening slot clear for Barbara and Len. Apparently, it had got a bit heated when Len asked if Adele's mum had met her new grandson, but he wasn't to know that Adele's mum was a bitch and Adele had told her never to contact them again. Or rather, Len more than likely would've been present when Adele's mum had come up in conversation, but he didn't pay attention unless someone was talking directly to him.

"What's up with Dan?" Mike asked, his eyes following his youngest brother's path down the pitch to where Sean was leaning on the goalpost, arms folded, and looking bored. Dan looked like he was on the warpath.

"Just this game against the Anchors, I think," Shaunna said. "You know what he's like."

"All too well," Mike agreed. "Wish I'd brought my boots now."

"Why didn't you?"

"I'm a bit stiff from working yesterday. Plus, I've hardly seen this little lady all week." He affectionately smoothed Bethan's hair: the dark demi waves shared by all of the Jeffries clan other than Rosie. Bethan looked up and gave him a toothy grin.

"She's so beautiful," Shaunna said, taking Bethan's little hand between her finger and thumb. "Daddy's gorgeous girl, aren't you?" Bethan babbled in response, and Shaunna gasped. "Really? That's very interesting!"

Mike laughed. "I wonder what she's saying?"

"Oh, all kinds of wonderful things." Shaunna shifted her gaze up to Mike. "Andy's got another pair of boots in the car. Do you want me to go and get them?"

Mike wrinkled his nose. "I dunno. Maybe, in a minute. I want to ask you a favour, actually."

"Right?"

"The salon's shut on Wednesdays, isn't it?"

"No. Thursdays."

"Ah."

"Why?"

"Never mind." Mike turned to watch the football.

"What were you going to ask?"

"It's fine. I've got this mediation meeting at the court, but I can go on my own."

"With Rachel's mum?"

"Yeah. Did Andy tell you what's happening?"

"Yes, he did."

"My barrister reckons Rachel's mum'll change her mind, which is why we're having this meeting. I'm not sure how they work."

"I'll give Hayley a call, see if I can swap my day off."

"Thanks, but I don't want to put you out."

"You're not, Mike. I'll give her a call now, while I get those boots from the car. How about that?" Shaunna gave him a hopeful smile, and he nodded.

"Cheers, Shaw." She narrowed her eyes at him, and he grimaced out a grin. "Shaunna."

She laughed and patted his arm. "Be right back."

9: Leadership
Sunday, 30th September–
Monday, 1st October

Dan stepped to the touchline so he could watch the effect of the rejig, which brought more players forward to compensate for Charlie's absence, not that she was absent today. She was standing a few feet away from him, her back partly turned, whilst she watched the rest of the team passing the ball around, with feeble challenges from the subs—a group which included Steven, the newly ousted landlord's son. Andy more or less gifted the ball to 'the opposition', and Sean readied himself for action, pointlessly, it turned out. The ball went wide. Dan exhaled loudly and jogged off to retrieve it.

"We've got…" he heard Charlie begin to say behind him, but she killed the rest of the sentence. Yes, they had half a dozen balls, but the other five weren't far enough away, and he needed the space, or he'd only swear at her.

It wasn't Charlie's fault. Or Aitch's. They played Sunday league football. Part time, amateur, meant to be fun. Sometimes players had to miss a match because of work commitments, but why, for the love of God, did it have to be this one? And truthfully, Dan wasn't that angry with Charlie. She'd never let them down before, and she seemed genuinely gutted she'd miss the Anchors match. Ultimately, her work with the England women's under-16s was more important; Dan accepted that.

What he didn't accept was Aitch dropping them in it as well, especially because his spiel about having to work next weekend was the biggest load of bull Dan had ever heard pass his mate's lips. He didn't want to go up against his fellow coppers, that's all it was. For now, Dan had left Aitch to play out the session, mostly because they weren't talking to each other, and also to punish him for not saying anything until *after* Dan had told Steven that Mike was replacing him. But what really stung was Aitch's—and everyone else's—lack of interest in Robbie. No-one had congratulated him, or asked how Adele and the baby were doing. Nothing.

"Right," Dan shouted. Keeping hold of the ball, he beckoned the team over and looked to the far end of the pitch. "Josh, can you come here a sec?"

With a puzzled glance in Shaunna's direction, Josh walked over to where Dan had gathered the team, his expression changing as he neared their location. "Wouldn't it be better to get Sean to do this?"

"He's on the team."

"Or Charlie?"

Dan gave him what he hoped was a meek, beseeching look.

Josh sighed. "OK. Aitch, go and stand in the naughty corner."

Aitch threw his hands in the air and mouthed *what?* but Josh simply waved him away. Dan moved around so he was standing with his teammates, effectively handing over to Josh, who had assumed an air of authority. *Clever*, Dan thought. So that was why he'd shoved Aitch off the pitch.

"All right, people. What's going on out there today?"

The players all looked down at their boots, with the exception of Dan, who kept his eyes on Josh, convinced he could work some kind of psychology magic to get his team pulling together again. After all, they were the same skilled players they had been last season and, if he was fair, so far this season. So the problem was their mindset, and that was Josh's area of expertise, not his.

With still nothing from the players, Josh picked on Sean. "Is there a reason you've stayed by the goal during this session?"

"Yeah. I'm the goalie."

"Well, yes, but it's a *training* session. Shouldn't you be… training?"

"I suppose," Sean mumbled.

"There are people who are playing for the Lions for the first time today. I'm sure they'd be comforted to know their goalie was being put through his paces."

Dan peered behind him at his poor maligned goalkeeper. He could've predicted that Josh would pick on him, but Sean could handle it.

"I think that's the problem, actually," Andy said. "New players."

Josh turned his attention on Andy and observed him for a moment. "A problem to whom?"

"The team." Andy grimaced and corrected what he'd said. "Those of us who've been playing together for a season already."

"I see." Josh nodded slowly. "Do you all know each other?"

Dan slapped his hand against his forehead as it dawned on him he hadn't introduced Mike to the rest of the team.

Josh fought a smile. "Perhaps I should do the honours. Everyone, this is Mike Jeffries. Mike, this is everyone." He gave the same dismissive hand wave as before. "You can do the names later. What's important right now is that you all remember one thing. OK? And it's this. Your captain has just become a dad again, so he might be a bit off his game. Not only that, but he appears to have forgotten he forbade us all from talking about it for the past nine months." Josh stopped and grinned at Dan.

"You…" Dan started laughing.

"Bastard?" Josh offered.

"Know-it-all bastard," Dan corrected.

"I'll send you the bill," Josh said, retreating to where Shaunna was standing with the twins, Bethan and Libby. Kris and Ade had also arrived, as always in good time for the Sunday roast in The Red Lion that routinely followed training sessions and home matches.

"Aitch, mate." Dan beckoned him over. Aitch dutifully obliged. Dan hugged him and slapped him on the back. "I was out of line. I'm sorry."

"I'm sorry, too, and I'll do my best to swap my shift next Sunday."

"Don't worry about it."

"I will," Aitch said. "So when do I get to meet our newest player then?"

"Mike?"

Aitch laughed. "Robbie, you dozy…"

"Oh!" Dan's cheeks started to get a bit warm. "Err, well, there's a two-visitor maximum, and—"

"I'll wait till they get home," Mike offered.

"Me, too," Andy said.

"What about if you both come this afternoon?" Dan suggested. "That'll leave this evening clear for Aitch."

Andy and Mike nodded in agreement.

"So long as Shaunna's all right with that," Mike said.

"I'll go and check." Andy left to do that.

Dan watched his brother explaining to Shaunna, aware of Josh watching him. He met Josh's gaze.

"He's got you sussed, hasn't he?" Aitch said.

"Yep." Dan was grateful as ever for Josh's ability to see past his bullshit and nail the problem in one hit.

Josh's pep talk, such as it was, did the trick, and the rest of the session went very well. As was often the case, the problem resided with the management, not the team—a realisation Dan found strangely humbling. It wasn't news to him that he was influential; it had been both the curse and blessing of his professional life, and where it didn't involve the people he cared most about, he'd been able to use that 'Jeffries charisma' to good effect in his personal life, too. But seeing the impact he'd had on the Lions' performance was a real eye-opener.

When the training session was over, they all wandered over to the pub together and quickly placed their food orders so that Dan, Andy and Mike could get to the hospital in time for afternoon visiting. However, when their food was delivered, Mike was nowhere to be found.

"He's gone upstairs with my dad," Steven said from behind the bar, having caught the gist of their conversation.

"What for?" Dan asked.

Steven shrugged and went back to serving customers. It was as well it wasn't busy, because the poor lad was exhausted. He'd played well—better than ever, in fact—which got Dan wondering whether he should put one of the others on the bench and keep Steven in the starting lineup. He'd give it a try for Tuesday's match and make a decision then. For now, he tucked in to his roast beef, eager to get to the hospital. He'd almost finished eating by the time Mike put in an appearance.

"What've you been up to?" Dan asked as Mike took over from Ade, who had been feeding Bethan, so he could eat his now cold food.

"Just got myself another job."

"Good stuff. This place? I thought it was refitted a couple of years back."

"It was. I'm decorating the flat upstairs."

"Oh, right." Dan checked the time on his phone. "We need to leave in twenty minutes. You gonna be ready?"

"Yep." Mike picked up his fork and fed himself with his left hand whilst he fed Bethan with his right. Dan was impressed, particularly when, twenty minutes later, Bethan was all cleaned up, nappy changed, and Mike was ready to leave. Andy, on the other hand…

"I'll get a taxi," Shaunna said, repeating what she'd already told him.

"With two car seats to carry?"

"Or I'll get a lift with Ade." Shaunna glanced Ade's way, and he nodded.

"Are you taking three vehicles to the hospital?" Josh asked.

Dan, Andy and Mike looked to each other and mumbled in the affirmative.

"What about if Shaunna and the girls come back to ours?" George suggested. "Then you can all go in Dan's car."

"My husband the genius," Josh said proudly. George gave him a funny look, to which Josh just grinned.

"Aren't you staying at the hospital, bro?" Andy asked.

"No. I've got a…meeting at four," Dan said cagily. After they'd kicked him out of the hospital the previous evening, he'd gone home and spent a couple of hours browsing a property auction site, and he'd found the perfect house. Or perfect except for one small detail, and now was neither the time nor the place to be breaking the news to Andy, particularly as there was no guarantee he'd get the house anyway. "Shall we get going, then?"

Andy and Mike gave their daughters kisses, and Dan looked away while Andy disgustingly smooched Shaunna. Anyone would think he was leaving her for a month. With goodbyes said, Dan finally ushered his brothers out to the car, and they set off for the hospital.

***

"He's a decent weight, isn't he?" Andy remarked, bending slightly for effect as Mike at last handed over their nephew.

"Yeah, but then yours were tiny," Mike pointed out.

"Speak for yourself!"

"Seven pound twelve, he is," Dan boasted.

"We know," Mike and Andy said in fake-weary unison.

"Just saying."

"Again," Andy muttered, and then asked Mike at normal volume, "What did your Bethan weigh?"

"Seven thirteen."

Dan nodded smugly. "Yeah, but what did she score?"

"Score?" Andy repeated incredulously to make it clear he thought Dan was spouting gibberish.

"I think he's talking about the test they do to check the baby's vitals," Mike said.

"Oh, the Apgar scores? Err…" Andy frowned in thought. "Seven and nine, I think ours were. Rosie got nine. Sorsha wasn't screaming enough, apparently."

Mike nodded. "Yeah, Bethan got nine."

"Yes!" Dan punched the air.

Andy smirked. "Little Rob got ten, I take it?"

"Yep."

"That's *Robbie*," Adele corrected curtly.

She wasn't looking Andy's way, and he made a face at Dan. "What is this Robbie fixation of yours, by the way?"

"I like it, that's all."

"You don't need to tell me that." Andy gave Mike a knowing look.

Dan snarled but didn't retaliate or try to justify. Contrary to what Mike and Andy thought, he wasn't obsessed with the name Robbie. Nor did he hate his own name, and he'd got past wanting to change it a long time ago. But when he was a kid especially—though it had never gone away—he'd felt like he'd been given the wrong name. He couldn't explain it, and when he'd tried to, it had upset his mum, so he'd learnt to keep quiet, other than telling Josh, back when they were meeting regularly for Dan's therapy.

Josh had mentioned something called depersonalisation, and they'd talked about it, but it didn't really fit with how Dan felt. He wasn't hazy or disconnected from reality, just from the name 'Dan'. What hadn't helped was going to judo when he was younger and discovering the ranks were referred to as 'dans'. It made the name seem more alien to him than ever and was enough to put him off martial arts, even though both Mike and Andy had a go at them all, and what Andy did, Dan usually did, too.

Now he'd given 'his' name to his son, he felt more at peace than he had in his entire life, and if one day Robbie or Shu came to him and told him they felt like they had the wrong name, he'd support them one hundred percent. Unless they wanted to change their name to something awful, like Gavin, or Michelle, or any other name that belonged to someone who had pissed him off at some point, which didn't leave many names to choose from, now he thought on.

When visiting time was over, Dan drove Andy and Mike back to The Red Lion, so they could collect their car and van respectively, and then went home for a quick shower before his meeting with the agent from the auction company. The house was exceptional—five bedrooms, enormous living room, modern kitchen, dining room big enough to host dinner parties, basement gymnasium, sauna, Jacuzzi—and it wasn't just clever photography, either. He knew, because he'd overseen the technological installation.

Automatic garage doors and gates, keyless entry system, ambient underfloor heating, intelligent sound and light systems, and so on—the house had been ahead of its time. It was long before Jeffries and Associates came into being, and much of it would need updating to newer systems, particularly as the place had been vacant for almost a year, but if he could get it for the right price, he'd have plenty of money to update the technology.

The agent must have been inside already, because the gates opened as Dan approached, and he rolled through and up the drive, pleased to see that the gardens had been maintained. In fact, the house still looked like someone was living there, although it was situated in a private road that had its own security team, so it was unlikely squatters, burglars or other opportunists would have got anywhere near the place.

"Mr. Jeffries," the man said, holding out his hand for Dan to shake. "Derek Arnold."

"Mr. Arnold. Thanks for coming out on a Sunday."

"Not a problem. Every day is a working day in this job."

True as that might be, the auction company bore the same name as the man standing before him; Dan wasn't sure whether he should feel suspicious or flattered.

"Please—" Derek gestured for Dan to enter "—come in. I'll give you a tour."

Dan stepped inside and reached behind him to shut the front door, smiling as he watched it close itself. He'd forgotten about that.

"You live locally?"

"Yeah, on the other side of town."

"Ah. You're aware of why the guide price is so low, presumably?"

"I am. What happens once the place is sold? Who gets the money?"

"Half goes to the police, and half to the Home Office. But let's be honest, Angela Sharston doesn't need it where she is."

Dan chuckled. "True enough. Have there been many viewings?"

"Five, excluding yourself."

That was better than Dan had expected. The guide price was under half the market value, and he'd anticipated there would be many more people happy to ignore the house's history in favour of snapping up a bargain. He could only hope his brother and his friends would be able to see past it.

***

Adele's call came Monday lunchtime, to say she and Robbie were being discharged that afternoon, and Dan wasn't happy. He'd been hoping the hospital would keep them until at least Tuesday so he could present her with a done deal. The auction was on Thursday afternoon, and he was still making phone calls to solicitors and surveyors in an attempt to have enough information to place a pre-auction bid. He wanted the Sharston house, and once he'd set his mind to something, he couldn't rest until he'd got it.

What was particularly frustrating—and due to his own cowardice—was that he couldn't call on any of the surveyors they used for the business, because they all knew Andy and might let something slip before Dan grew a pair and told him what he was up to. He wasn't even sure Andy would care, although he would've seen the Sharston house listed on the auction sites, and he knew it was exactly the kind of property Dan was after, yet he hadn't mentioned it.

Notwithstanding that Angela Sharston and Jess had been partners in crime, Andy was taking liberties by making the decision on Dan's behalf, and he was tempted to call him and give him hell for it. However, it would also give the game away, and Dan wasn't ready, not just yet. But he owed it to his brother to tell him, rather than leaving him to find out from someone else.

With nothing further he could do, and Shu in school, Dan set about giving the apartment a good clean, leaving their bedroom until last so he could make up the cot. Robbie would be in with them for the time being. Dan stuck on some music, cranked up the volume until he could hear over the vacuum cleaner, and tried not to think about the house, though he was excited. He could finally get on with all of those things he had put off, and he was on an adrenaline kick that might just see him through to getting Adele and Robbie home.

It was only when he switched off the vacuum cleaner an hour later that he noticed all the messages on his phone. Six of them were from Andy, each one providing a link to a different house for sale—the Sharston place still remained notable by its absence—and three from Mike, which went:

I can hear your bloody racket outside. Get the kettle on.

Or is someone torturing you?

Ah well. In a bit.

"Shit," Dan cursed and then laughed at the messages. He didn't have the worst voice in the world, but there was a reason he only sang while home alone and to a vacuum-cleaner accompaniment. He called Mike's mobile.

"I didn't hear the phone, sorry."

"No bloody wonder. What the hell were you doing?"

"Cleaning. Adele and the baby are coming home this afternoon."

"Ah," Mike said knowingly, though quite what he knew, Dan wasn't sure, seeing as Anne had constantly complained that Mike didn't do a tap—a fact, by his own admission—and Rachel… To be fair to Mike, he'd come out of that relationship fully domesticated, and knowing what he did about Rachel, Dan doubted she'd employed the same gentle praise their mum did with Len, which was brilliant, because Len was oblivious. But then, as Mum said, with three adult sons and three ex-husbands, she'd had plenty of opportunity to practise.

"So are you coming down for a cuppa, or not?" Dan asked.

"I thought you just said—"

"There's time yet."

"All right, then. Be there in ten."

Dan hung up, made the coffee, and took his screwdriver back to the bedroom, to check the cot was securely together, pretending he hadn't done that at least a dozen times already. With the new sheets and blankets, and the mobile in place, Dan stood back to admire his workmanship, smiling and nodding to himself. He was ready to bring his son home now—and Adele,

DEBBIE MCGOWAN

he supposed, with a chuckle. For all their fighting, and her refusal to marry him, he still loved her and couldn't live without her, which wasn't to say living *with* her was all sunshine and rainbows.

Returning to the kitchen for his now lukewarm coffee, Dan took a couple of mouthfuls and chucked the rest down the sink. Half an hour had passed since Mike had said he'd be down in ten minutes. He'd probably got caught up in whatever he was doing. Still, it was Mike's own fault, for making rash promises about being done in three days. No doubt he *would* finish the job in time, if he didn't kill himself in the process, but he'd be cutting it fine. Nonetheless, Dan decided to call him; he got as far as bringing up his number when the knock came at the door.

"Sorry," Mike mumbled as he passed Dan by. It didn't go unnoticed that Mike was keeping his eyes averted and frowning heavily.

"No worries. Your coffee's cold, though."

"Yeah, I got held up."

"Oh?" Dan led the way back to the kitchen. "That doesn't sound good. You want me to nuke this, or make you a fresh one?"

Mike shook his head, still frowning. "I'll drink it cold." He emptied the mug in one go.

"You want another?"

"Yeah."

Dan refilled the coffee machine, paying attention to his brother rather than the coffee beans, only noticing when they started pouring onto the kitchen surface. He swore, scooped the spilled beans back into the bag, and switched on the machine.

"The woman from Park Lane's just been to the flat—again," Mike said.

"It's her mate who lives upstairs, is it?"

"Seems like. She came to drop off some shopping. The other day it was to feed the cat, she said, but I've seen no sign of a cat, and the bag of stuff she brought round today was weird random shit. You know, like you buy on the way to a party because you forgot you were supposed to bring something?"

"What, like peanuts and stuff?"

"I dunno," Mike said vaguely and then shook his head as if trying to clear his ears of water. "She's a bit…odd. I think she's finding excuses to come and check up on me, which pisses me off. She already knows what my work's like. I've just done her whole house."

"Maybe her friend asked her to keep an eye on you," Dan suggested.

"Yeah, maybe."

"Or she fancies you?" Dan was teasing, not that it was impossible, or even improbable, although this time last year he'd held a very different opinion of his eldest brother.

Mike was too quick to laugh it off and then changed the subject. "What time are they being discharged?"

"Adele didn't say. Not too early, hopefully. I've got something I need to finish before they get home."

"Yeah? Anything interesting?"

Dan figured Mike would be a good litmus test. "There's a house I want that's being auctioned on Thursday. I want to get a bid in today, but I'm still waiting for the land registry data to come back."

"Oh, right. Where's that, then? Somewhere local?"

"Other side of town. Mayhew Mews."

"Mayhew Mews…" Mike repeated, staring into the mid-distance as he tried to place it in his mind's eye. "The private road?"

"Yep."

Mike rubbed his chin, still pondering. "I've seen something about it recently. What was it?"

"It was in the papers," Dan said. "The Sharston Strang case."

"The Sharston…" Mike stopped and gawped at Dan. "The fraud ring Jess was involved in?"

Dan nodded slowly, watching his brother putting it all together.

"That's right," Mike said. "One of the partners lives in that road. Or lived, should I say. I'm guessing the property values took a bit of a beating?"

"Err, yeah," Dan confirmed cagily.

"So you'll get a lot of bang for your buck." Mike had missed the connection.

"You could say that," Dan agreed, grateful that the coffee was ready. "If the vendor accepts my offer—" he poured as he talked "—I'll be getting about double the bang for my buck."

"Nice one." Mike took the coffee cup from Dan. "And no chain if it's a repo, either."

"Well…no chain." He met Mike's gaze. "But it's not a repo."

Mike frowned. "But it's up for auction? That's unusual. Oh. Hang on. It's not the…"

"Sharston house?" Dan finished with a resigned nod.

"Fucking hell. Have you told Andy?"

"Not yet, so don't say anything, all right?"

Mike shrugged his agreement. "My lips are sealed, bro. But let me know when you're planning on telling him."

Dan raised an eyebrow, and Mike grinned.

"I want a ringside seat."

10: Done In
Monday, 1st October

Mike should've said no to the second cup of coffee. He'd only taken a mouthful when Adele called Dan to tell him she and the baby were ready to be picked up. The coffee was still too hot to down in one, so Mike had taken it with him when Dan turfed him out, with a promise to return the mug later, or 'Adele will string you up by the goolies. Goolie. Sorry, bro.'

Sometimes he wished he'd never mentioned it, but he'd thought his brothers might help him find the humour in what was a pretty humourless situation. For what it was worth, his sperm count hadn't dropped, and everything else was in good working order, but when he looked in the mirror…well, he didn't if he could help it, not down there.

There was a time when he'd admired his body in its state of arousal. Sure, it was vain and maybe a bit kinky that he could get off by watching himself getting off. He'd flex his biceps and roll his abs, tense his glutes and watch the muscles ripple, hard and defined, while he intentionally worked up a sweat, or even applied oil beforehand for lubrication and the sheen on his skin. At forty-two—when Anne had kicked him out for the final time—he'd been a decent-looking bloke, more than just good for his age, which was why he'd thought nothing of Rachel chatting him up that night, in his hotel bar in Greece.

That was what stung the most. When he was with Anne, women came on to him all the time. It was usually while he was working, and he'd flirt with them but also make it clear he was a married man, and a faithful one. He'd loved Anne—still did in many respects—and not once had he considered cheating on her. Even after the divorce had finalised, he'd felt a twinge of guilt if his attraction to anyone else surfaced unchecked.

Looking back, he realised his love for Anne was what kept him sane through all the crap with Rachel, because he remembered the guilt, and how it had stopped him from approaching a woman, or letting a woman close if she approached him. Rachel had refused to be put off by his apologetic compliments—*you're very beautiful, but I'm not looking for a holiday fling*—and from what he could remember, he'd enjoyed their night together, but she was gone by morning, and he was relieved. Remorse was no cure for a hangover.

So he knew, rationally, that Rachel had played him from the outset. She'd gone after him not because she found him attractive, but because he was Andy's brother. Later, when she'd started talking to him like he was a piece of shit, he'd kept reminding himself he hadn't led her on. He still loved Anne; the divorce made no difference, he still felt like he was cheating. Next came the physical stuff, but it didn't matter. Mike was already beating himself up over the unlucky coincidence that had put him and Rachel in the same hotel at the same time...

...Until he saw the girl from the travel agent's in the public gallery in the courtroom. She was there for Rachel, her best mate who'd landed in a bad relationship because of a one-night stand and an unplanned pregnancy. Hormones, well, they can make women do crazy things, like commit murder.

And it all came back to him, that day he'd gone into the travel agent's to ask about the cheap weekend in Amsterdam advertised in the window and come out with a week all-inclusive in Greece.

The man he was six months ago would've blamed Rachel for everything, and she was far, far from innocent. But he could've stuck to his guns and gone to Amsterdam. He could've said no to drinks in the hotel bar, stayed sober enough to make sure they'd used a condom, or even stopped it from going that far. She was a manipulative, clever woman, who had used him as bait in an attempt to catch his brother, but he wasn't exactly a helpless worm impaled on a hook. He'd been doing a perfectly good job of messing up his life before Rachel came into it, and whilst she'd put a huge dint in his self-confidence and cost him a testicle, she'd also given him Bethan. But if he could go back and do it all again, he'd make sure he never met Rachel Perry.

Maybe she fancies you. Dan's tongue-in-cheek remark about Mrs. Hunter had given Mike the heebie-jeebies. He was confident she was nothing like Rachel, and he did think she was attractive. Dan might've found the idea of being chased by a woman flattering, but Mike couldn't deal with it, not yet. Maybe when he could look at himself in the mirror again, he'd be ready. Until then, he'd rather be on his own.

Enough wallowing already, but then painting was like that. On the plus side, while he'd been away with the fairies, he'd finished the closet walls, which meant he was done. An entire apartment in just over two days. He backstepped out of the closet into the lounge and rotated on the spot, checking for bits he'd missed, on the lookout for visible seams in the wallpaper. He gave himself a pat on the back for another job well done and went to give the bedroom a once-over, on to the kitchen, and lastly the bathroom, taking a long-needed pee while he followed the newly whitened grout up, down and across each wall.

There was a noise, in the living room.

Mike's eyes widened. He was mid-stream, and the bathroom door was open.

The cat. Of course. It was going dark outside, and Mrs. Hunter had said it came in at night.

"Hello?" a female voice called.

"Shit," Mike hissed under his breath, kicking back with his heel in an attempt to close the door, but it was too far away. He coughed loudly. "Just in the bathroom. I'll be out in a—"

Behind him, the apartment's owner gasped. "Oh! Sorry." The door clicked shut.

Mike tried to pee faster, but it was impossible. He shook off, zipped up, flushed the toilet and quickly washed his hands, preparing to face his unexpected company. He'd known she was due back this evening, but she'd implied it would be later.

"Hi." Mike offered a quick smile as he emerged from the bathroom.

"I'm so sorry," she said again. She looked as embarrassed as he was.

"It's all right," he assured her.

"When you said 'in the bathroom', I thought you meant you were working in there, not… Yes, well…"

"My fault. I should've said I was using the loo. So anyway—" Mike gestured to the living room walls "—it's all done."

The owner—he still couldn't recall her name—looked around her and smiled. "Oh, this is wonderful, Mike." She moved closer to a wall and smoothed her palm over the paper. "Absolutely perfect."

"I had to fill a few holes in the bedroom."

"Ah, yes, behind the bed."

"Yeah," Mike confirmed, following her to the bedroom but remaining in the doorway while she inspected his work. "And I shifted all the stuff from under the bed to that cupboard."

"OK…thanks." She blushed, and Mike felt a bit sorry for her, but he hadn't been through what was under her bed. He knew what he'd kept under his own bed when he was single and without a child, and Charlie had told him a lot of women looked at porn. *There's a thought…* He hoped Charlie had cleaned up her computer before bringing it to the house, although…maybe they shared the same tastes? That would be an interesting turn-up, something to talk about, or not.

Using her room inspection to cover her embarrassment, the woman turned on the spot. "Thank you so much, Mike. Celia said you were a quick worker, and you've done such a fantastic job." She stopped turning and looked him over. "I thought she might be overstating things a little, what with her thinking you're a fitty, and all. Although I can see what she means."

Mike should have been blushing right back at her. Instead, he felt the blood drain from his face as his heart switched to overdrive. It was a compliment, and perhaps a hint on her friend's behalf, in case he was interested. It wasn't as if she was hitting on him, although it appeared Dan had been right about Mrs. Hunter...Celia. Mike wasn't going to be telling him that anytime soon.

Oblivious to his overreaction, the woman asked, "Has Theodor given you any trouble?"

"Theodor? The cat?"

"Yes. He goes into a sulk when I work away. Have you seen him?"

"No. He's not been near."

"Ah, he'll be fine." She took a step towards Mike, and he quickly got out of the way, returning to the living room, where—he really wished he could remember her name—she picked up her bag from the sofa. "Cash or cheque?"

"Cash, if that's all right?"

She took out her purse and extracted a thick wad of twenty-pound notes, wetting her fingers to count out his payment. Mike took the opportunity to gather together the rest of his equipment. "Here we are," she said, handing over the bundle of notes. "There's a bit extra there, to compensate for embarrassing you earlier." She winked at him, he assumed to indicate she was joking about why she was giving him extra, rather than there being a bit extra there to begin with.

"Cheers," he said, shoving the money into his pocket without counting it and then handing over her door key. "Any problems, give me a shout, and I'll pop back and sort them."

"Thank you."

With no reason to delay further, Mike left, crossing paths with the elusive Theodor on his way out the door. The cat gave him a dirty look and disappeared inside.

Mike was halfway down the stairs before he remembered the coffee cup and reluctantly retraced his steps back to—

"Gillian!" The name came to him in a flash.

"Back so soon?" she said as she opened the door—with an open tin of cat food in one hand, and her mobile phone between her chin and shoulder—and offered him an amused frown.

"Yeah, sorry. I left a mug in the kitchen."

"Ah. I wondered why I didn't recognise it." She stepped aside and let him go through to get it, all the while continuing with her phone conversation. Judging from what she was saying, Mrs. Hunter was on the other end of the line. Mike didn't like the way Gillian laughed as she said, "No, you filthy mare, I did not get a look at the package, although—" she lowered her voice "—it's kind of obvious anyway, isn't it?"

For a second time, Mike made a quick getaway, dumped his stuff in the van and went to Dan and Adele's.

"I'm not stopping," he said, holding out the cup when his brother opened the door.

"You all right?" Dan leaned closer and studied Mike's face.

"Yeah. Just…tired and in need of a long, hot shower. Everyone OK?"

"Yeah." Dan grinned. "Everyone's great."

"Good. I'll catch up with you tomorrow."

"All right, bro. Night."

"Night."

Mike returned to his van and sagged into the driver's seat, taking a couple of minutes to sit back, close his eyes, and breathe. Being ogled and talked about like he wasn't even there was not nice. If he ever reached a point where he was interested in women again, he'd keep in mind that it was more humiliating than flattering. Still, they weren't to know that his 'package' contained damaged goods.

He opened his eyes again and started the engine, elated to finally be heading for home. With no pending jobs, he was looking forward to spending a couple of days with his daughter, and, with any luck, while Bethan was sleeping, he'd have time to get Charlie's computer up and running, assuming she'd remembered to bring it.

It was quite an effort to get out of the van and open the gates to his mum's place, although Pez was on his way down the driveway and signalled to Mike that he'd shut them on his way out. Mike gave him a thumbs up. He was a nice kid, not his fault Rachel was his sister. Mike wished he was big enough to get past it and let Pez get to know his niece. Maybe in time... but would it be too late? Bethan was six months old already, and each day he was away from her, she'd learnt something new. Kids grew up so fast, and Mike was torn, between wanting to protect himself and his daughter, and doing the right thing for Pez and Jacqueline Perry.

He steered around the fountain and stopped the van, looking in his rear-view mirror. Pez was long gone. Mike dragged himself out of the van and went inside.

The faint sound of applause drifted across the atrium from the living room TV and died away, leaving the distant whirr of a treadmill belt. Wearily, Mike trudged across to the living room and peered through the open door. "Alright, Len?"

Len acknowledged him without looking away from the TV. "Mike. Your mum's taken Bethan over to your place. She wasn't settling."

"OK. See you in a bit." Mike set off again, too tired for a detour, really, but curious to know who was in the gym if it wasn't Len or his mum. "You're still here?"

Charlie pulled out an earphone and kept on running. "Did you say something?" With each step, her dark ponytail swung from side to side, and Mike was mesmerised. She clicked her fingers at him.

"Huh?" It took a second or two for Mike to remember what he'd said. Charlie was fit—in both senses—and it could be quite off-putting at times. "I said you're still here."

"So it would seem." Charlie grinned at him and powered down the treadmill. "I brought that computer. I left it in the office." She rolled her eyes. "Len offered to take it over to yours for me, and I told him to do one. I'll take it over now."

"Cheers, but don't worry. I'll deal with it."

"I'll give you a hand with the peripherals, then." She waited for Mike to nod in agreement before following him to Len's office, although Mike was perfectly capable of carrying a computer and monitor the short distance to the summerhouse. Or he would have been, if that was all there'd been…

"Bloody hell, Charlie. What's all this?" He stared in amazement at the printer, scanner and a ton of other stuff in boxes, all piled on top of Len's desk. "Is there even a computer in that lot?"

Charlie laughed. "I thought you might as well have it all. The router is probably too old now, and you can just throw out anything you don't want. Honestly, I won't be offended."

"That's a lot of kit."

"Yeah, but most of it I got for free. Kind of." Mike gave her an enquiring look, and she shrugged. "The firm I was working for went under, and the boss dropped me in it—left me to deal with the receivers—so I nicked as much of the office equipment as I could fit in my car."

Mike shook his head in disbelief, although he was chuckling. "No wonder you get on so well with Len. Right, what's—" He'd been about to ask what was heaviest but realised it didn't matter. "What do you want me to take?" he asked instead.

"Whatever. You can grab the computer if you like." Charlie shifted the stack of boxes out of the way so Mike could get to the computer and then draped the cables across his arms. "I'll follow with the rest," she said.

Mike eyed the boxes.

"Go on," Charlie prompted, giving him a gentle shove to send him on his way.

The computer wasn't that heavy at first, but by the time he'd made the twenty-yard trek to the summerhouse, every muscle in his arms was burning. He was pleased to see that Charlie was faring no better and had abandoned some of her hoard along the way. She stepped past him and opened the door, letting him go in first.

"Hey, Mum," he called and quickly dumped the computer on the kitchen counter—the nearest free surface.

"Evening, Michael," his mum replied quietly and with a finger to her lips. She got up from the sofa and came over to fill the kettle. "Goodness. What's all this?"

"Charlie's given me her computer."

"Oh." His mum gave Charlie an approving nod. It was a funny relationship the two women had. They saw each other a lot during the course of the day, and they were always civil, but they kept to their own domains as much as they could and were careful not to get in each other's way. There was a lot of respect on both sides, but they were very different.

"In return, Mike's going to teach me how to decorate," Charlie explained. She left them momentarily, to collect the rest of the stuff.

"Oh," his mum said again and peered up at him, leaning back a little so she could get his face in focus. "You know a bit about decorating, do you?"

Mike gave her a sickly grin. "Has she been a pain?" he asked, nodding towards the bedroom.

"Not really. Just grisly. She hasn't slept all day, so I thought I'd get her into bed. How did you get on with the flat?"

"All done." Mike stretched and rolled his shoulders, grimacing at the aches and pains. Charlie arrived with the last of the boxes. There was no space on the worktop, so she dumped them on the floor. Mike acknowledged her with a nod of thanks that morphed into a yawn. "Day off tomorrow, thank God."

"Ah," his mum said, matching his grimace. "Shaunna called to say her boss left money for the materials and you can start whenever you're ready."

"Ohhh." Mike rubbed his eyes. He needed a day off. All right, it wasn't really a day off, but a day at home would've been nice.

The kettle boiled, and Mike's mum made two cups of tea, pushing them towards him and Charlie. "I'll leave you to it."

"Thanks, Mum."

"No problem, love." She squeezed his arm on her way past and left.

Mike handed one of the cups to Charlie. "You need sugar?"

"No, thanks."

He put sugar in his own, picked up his cup and went over to the sofa, sitting bolt upright for fear he'd nod off if he got too comfortable.

Charlie sat at the other end. "Couldn't you leave it for tomorrow?" she asked. "Hayley won't mind, I'm sure."

"You know her?"

"Yeah. She used to cut our hair when we were little."

"Really? She doesn't look old enough."

Charlie raised her eyebrows. "I can't decide if you're saying she looks young for her age, or I look old for mine."

"Well, you're what? Mid-thirties?"

"Thirty-five, yeah."

"And Hayley can't be any older than fifty."

"Hm…a bit older. She didn't get married until she was thirty—she went on her honeymoon just before I started year four."

"How do you remember that?"

"Mate, if you'd seen the haircut Hayley's stand-in gave me, you wouldn't forget, either, believe me."

"That bad?"

"Shocking. It was, like, up here on this side—"Charlie tapped the side of her hand halfway up her left ear "—and down here on this side." She tapped her neck and nodded very seriously. Mike chuckled.

"Like a Veronica Lake?"

"Who?"

"Yeah, that's me showing *my* age. She's looking good, then, Hayley?"

"She is, and she's lovely, too. When Jess was sick, Hayley gave Shaunna loads of time off. She really looks after her. And she did Jess's hair."

"When she… At the undertaker's?"

"Yep." Charlie shook her head and chuckled ruefully. "She's a good egg, is Hayley. Can you imagine doing a job like that?"

"Hairdressing in general, or just the corpses bit?"

Charlie glanced sideways at Mike and said nothing. He laughed. "Are you squeamish, Charlie?"

"About death? Not even slightly. You don't grow up Roman Catholic without seeing more than your fair share of dead people." She slurped at her tea. "I used to have a t-shirt with that on it—*I see dead people*. My mum confiscated it. I wouldn't mind, but I'd only come home from uni for the weekend, and I didn't bring any other tops with me."

"God, I hope you weren't sweet-talking when you said she'd like me."

"Oh, you'll be fine. The rules don't apply to heathens." She grinned at him.

"Good to know."

They sat in silence, drinking their tea, and Mike's thoughts drifted back to his conversation with the woman at Dovedale, and how uneasy he'd felt, alone with her, in her apartment. Yet, sitting here with Charlie, he was perfectly relaxed. So relaxed, in fact, it was only when he turned to thank her again for the computer that he discovered she'd gone, leaving a note tucked under her washed mug.

> You fell asleep. Get an early night and take a day off! Cx

11: Losing the Tale
Tuesday, 2nd October

"We've got a bit of a problem."

Andy propped his tablet against the microwave so he could continue with folding the laundry. "What's that, bro?"

"One of us needs to fly out to the Czech Republic before the end of the week."

"And that's a problem because?"

"I can't do it."

Andy poked his fingers inside a tiny sleeve to turn it the right way out. "Again, that's a problem because?"

"Well, are you gonna do it?"

"If I have to."

Dan fell silent.

Andy checked to see if the call was still connected. It was. He held in his sigh, folded the little pink cardy and added it to the pile. "Are you gonna elaborate, or am I flying out blind?"

"It's those cylinder blocks for Len's mate. They arrived last week, and he says they're not right."

"I know all this. I talked to the engineer about it. They're remaking the cast moulds."

"But it shouldn't have happened."

"No, but it did, and they're fixing it. Why does that require one of us to pay them a visit?"

Dan frowned. In the background, Adele called his name, and his frown was replaced by a pained expression.

Andy smirked. "You're not trying to escape already?"

"No. As a matter of fact, I thought *you* might fancy a break."

"Why?" Andy had a good idea why.

"You haven't been away in ages."

"Since Mike turned up on my doorstep," Andy said, which was where Dan was heading.

"That's a long time, bro."

"Not even six months." Andy finished folding clothes, picked up his tablet and returned to the living room. The twins were asleep for the time being. "Right," he said, getting settled on the sofa, "tell me what you want me to do about the cylinder blocks."

"It's not what *I* want, it's—"

"Pack it in."

Dan shrugged and folded his arms. "Fine. If you say it's in hand…"Adele called him again, and he grunted. "Be right back." He got up and left Andy with a view of the window behind the dining table.

While Andy was waiting, he checked his email, firing off replies where needed, and then found the last message from the engineer in the Czech Republic, who was apologetic and confirmed the parts were being recast from new moulds. They'd be in the UK by the end of the following week. So, unless Dan knew something he didn't, there was no reason at all for Andy to fly out there.

Or maybe there was, and it had nothing to do with the cylinder blocks.

Dan arrived back in front of the camera. "Gotta go," he said, holding up a baby's bottle with an inch of milk in the bottom.

"No worr—" Andy was talking to a blank screen. "Catch you later, then," he muttered, disgruntled. He went back to the kitchen and grabbed the pile of clothes, rationalising his annoyance before he reached the top of the stairs. Dan was still adjusting to having a new baby, and Adele was probably laid up in bed. She'd have him running in and out of their bedroom like a man stuck in a revolving door.

And, of course, Dan would be worrying about the business. It had always been his top priority—the only occasion Andy could recall his brother taking more than a day off work was after the stabbing, and only then because they wouldn't let him have his laptop in the ICU.

So Andy understood all that, but he was still riled by Dan's bullying tactics, with his 'you haven't been away in months, thought you might fancy a break' when it had nothing to do with worrying about Andy's well-being. Dan was projecting his own stress, and there was no point telling him. He'd only get defensive.

For no reason other than his brother's peace of mind, when Andy returned downstairs, he made a few quick calls, the first to the engineer in the Czech Republic. The customer—one of Len's business acquaintances—restored pre-war and wartime vehicles, and he'd bought a job lot of transport wagons that should have gone to the scrapyard decades ago, but he already had buyers for them, and it was cheaper to get the parts custom-made overseas. Cue Jeffries and Associates: Andy had set about making contact with a guy he knew from way back, who worked at a small factory in the Mladá Boleslav district, soon discovering the factory wasn't small anymore.

Since the dissolution of Czechoslovakia, the company had expanded significantly and worked with some of the big car manufacturers. Andy figured it was still worth a shot. Don't ask, don't get, and all that. It was how he'd managed to talk Dan into coming on board with Jeffries and Associates in the first place—the gift of the gab, plus almost twenty years of travelling and making connections all over the world, which included Vít, the engineer at the Czech factory, whom he'd met while snowboarding in Slovakia, and who had systematically drunk him under the table.

Ten years on, Vít was overjoyed to hear from Andy, and they'd spent hours online, catching up and doing the whole virtual meet-the-family routine. It was in Andy's long-term plans to visit Vít, but not until both men's children were old enough to appreciate the experience, which certainly wouldn't be happening this side of next weekend.

Phone calls made, Andy sent Dan a bullet list of the status of all their current projects, rounding off with 'take a chill pill' and wishing he hadn't when, five seconds later, Dan called him back.

"I'm perfectly bloody chilled," he snapped.

Andy nodded slowly. "Course you are. Seriously, bro—"

"I was looking out for you! I mean, sooner or later those nomadic tendencies are gonna take over, and—"

"Whoa!" Andy's hair bristled. "I'm not going anywhere."

"If you say so."

"Are you deliberately winding me up?"

"How? I'm offering you a time-out. Take it."

"I don't want a fucking time-out!" Andy jabbed at the end-call button and started pacing the room, livid. First Shaunna, now Dan—if the option had existed, he'd have been in his running shoes and straight out the door.

"Ah, fuck."

Andy stopped pacing, combed his fingers through his hair and tugged in frustration. Maybe they had a point, but there was a big difference between legging it halfway across the globe and going for a quick run around the block to get his head together. He couldn't even listen to music without waking the girls.

It was going to take a lot longer than three months to convince everyone he'd changed, and he had. He'd felt it happen in the delivery suite, when he'd held Rosie for the very first time and watched Sorsha come into this world. That feeling hadn't dwindled in the slightest, and he could just look at his daughters for hour upon hour, never losing his sense of wonder at how they were so different yet so alike, and so beautiful he cried, often, and with no shame. Like Mike had said when he'd turned up with Bethan, 'kids change your life'.

More like they become your life, Andy thought with a smile as the tiniest noise came from the baby monitor. He knew their ways so well already that he was in no doubt it was Sorsha stirring. Rosie was more like her mummy and woke up complaining loudly, whereas Sorsha slowly eased into it, and she usually awoke first, giving him time to change her nappy and get the milk while Rosie got over the grumps.

Andy crept into the nursery and whispered, "Hey, you," as he peered down at Sorsha. She smiled up at him, her little legs kicking at the blanket. He scooped her out of her cot, cuddling her close on the way downstairs. "I think we'll go see Nana soon. What d'you reckon?" If they walked there, they could stop off and see Shaunna's dad on the way, not that he recognised them. Sometimes he made the connection that they were his granddaughters, although if he did, he called Sorsha 'Krissi', and when Krissi went to see him, he more often than not thought she was Shaunna.

It was always going to be hardest for Shaunna, even more so because her dad either didn't recognise her at all, or thought she was her mum, and then she'd have to remind him who she was, and that her mum was dead. He must've grieved for his wife a thousand times over by now, and it tore Shaunna apart, although she put a brave face on it. It was another of those things to which Andy had remained oblivious, until Kris pulled him to one side and suggested they took turns visiting Shaunna's dad so she didn't have to go through it as often. Jim Hennessy barely knew Andy to begin with, but if he asked, Andy repeated the explanation.

That's how it panned out for today's visit.

"Oh, aren't they lovely." Jim reached into Rosie's pushchair and tickled her cheek. "You look just like your mum, you do." He peered at Sorsha and then at Andy. "Where is she? Working?"

"Yep. She's popping in tomorrow."

"Tell her not to bother." He sat back in his chair and stared out of the window, his thoughts instantly lost.

Andy settled into the chair opposite. He wasn't planning on staying long.

"What are you doing with them?" Jim asked.

Andy felt the disconnection but explained what he was up to as if Jim had a grasp of the context. "We're going to my mum's for a bit. It's a nice day and I fancied a walk."

"You've still not got a car?"

"Yeah, I have." For the umpteenth time. It was Kris who didn't have a car. He travelled everywhere by train, or used to, before Ade. "A Mustang," Andy said.

"Hm." Jim's mind wandered again. He studied the sleeping babies. "Funny how they're so different. Both yours?"

"Yeah," Andy sighed.

"Where's erm…" Jim soundlessly clicked his fingers. "Oh, what the hell's his name? She's married to him. You know."

"Kris?"

"That's right. Kris. I haven't seen him in ages."

"Didn't he come in yesterday, Jim?"

"Oh, did he? No. I don't think he did. So you're, let me see… Geoff, isn't it?"

"Andy."

"That's right. Are you friends with our Shaunna?"

"Yeah. We're together."

"So Kris…what's happened to him?"

"Shaunna and Kris are divorced."

"When was that?"

"Few months back." Andy tried to keep the weariness out of his voice. Whether he succeeded, he couldn't tell, although after they'd circled the same conversation three more times, he could hear it for himself.

"We're off now, Jim. Do you need anything bringing in?"

"No, don't think so."

"OK. See you later."

"Bye."

Andy reversed the double pushchair out of the room and stopped to regroup. He hoped to God his own mum and dad would never have to go through this.

"You all right?" a care assistant asked.

He smiled. "Yeah, cheers. Does Jim need anything? Sweets, or hankies, or...?"

"Ooh. Yes, actually, could you pick him up a pack of underpants? He's not making it to the toilet. He forgets he needs it."

Andy's heart sank a little. It was yet another sign of Jim's deterioration, and he wasn't looking forward to telling Shaunna. "Yeah, no worries."

The twenty-minute walk from the rest home to his mum's was lost to his thoughts. Seeing Shaunna's dad had certainly put things in perspective. Andy had only met him a few times when he was younger: at the hospital when Krissi was born, at Shaunna's eighteenth, and then at Kris and Shaunna's wedding. He'd always been a nice enough bloke but a bit distant and quiet, nothing like Shaunna's mum. She'd been great fun, laughing and joking and getting along with everyone. At the house-warming, she'd had a few too many drinks and danced and flirted with them all—Shaunna was her mother's daughter, no mistake.

Siobhan Hennessy had died before Kris and Shaunna got married, and sometimes, Andy could tell Shaunna was thinking about her, wishing she'd still been around to meet the twins. She'd been an awesome grandma to Krissi, and she would have been to Rosie and Sorsha, too. But such was life. What mattered was making the most of it here and now, because there was no way of predicting the future. That was a lesson Andy had never needed to learn, but these days he acknowledged taking it to the opposite extreme could prove just as disastrous.

Pity he hadn't thought of that *before* he set off for his mum's.

"Trust you to come over today." She tugged her bathrobe around her and stopped to lift the front wheels of the pushchair over the top step.

"Were you in bed?"

"I was about to get in the bath."

"Ah. Sorry." Andy followed her in and shut the door. "You not got Bethan today?"

"No, Michael's taking a well-deserved day off."

"Good stuff. Is he out?"

"I don't think so. Is his van not there?"

"I didn't see it." Then again, Andy didn't remember opening or closing the gates, either. "You go and have your bath. I'll pester Mike for a bit."

"All right, love. See you after."

Andy continued on his way across the atrium and out through the conservatory, glancing longingly at the pool. He hadn't been for a swim in a while. Unfortunately, they had the match against Comco this evening, or he'd have come back later with his boardies. Tomorrow, maybe. He moved on, opening both doors to get the pushchair out of the conservatory, aware of the thump of a bass beat coming from the summerhouse, his steps falling in sync as he walked along the path Len—or Len's lads—had put between the house and the summerhouse a few weeks after Mike had moved in.

"Oh, God." Andy laughed as he got close enough to see his brother's terrible dancing. Bethan was in his arms, and she was giggling away, both of them having the time of their lives. Andy stopped, spun the pushchair to face the opposite direction, and went back the way he'd come.

"Andy?"

He stopped and turned back. "Alright, Mike?"

"Where're you off?"

"Well, I was coming to see you, but I didn't want to crash your party." He grinned.

Mike blushed. "I've just connected the speakers to the computer. They're really good."

"Yeah, I got that. Computer?"

"Charlie's. You coming in?"

"If I'm not gonna be in the way."

"Nah."

Andy parked the pushchair and lifted out Sorsha in her seat, taking her inside before repeating the process with Rosie.

"I'm looking forward to tonight," Mike said, but Andy was only half listening, his attention stolen by the array of technology neatly stacked on a wall unit.

"That's some setup."

"Yeah, it's pretty decent, as it goes. Charlie bought the computer, but she nabbed the rest from where she was working."

"I remember her telling me. That's gotta be about three grand's worth of equipment."

"Yep. You want a drink?"

"Just water'll do me."

Mike obliged and returned with two sports bottles filled with filtered water.

"Don't you own any glasses?"

"Yeah, but they get knocked over. Here, give me that—" he held out his hand for the bottle "—and I'll put it in a glass for you."

"It's fine. I was only asking."

"Fair enough. So you just popped round for fun?"

"Sort of. Dan's doing my head in."

"What's he up to?"

"Chasing up jobs I've already done, mostly, and trying to talk me into taking a business trip I don't need to take. If I didn't know better, I'd say he was trying to get me out of the country."

Mike swallowed his water down the wrong way and it came back, sending him into a coughing fit that woke Rosie. "Sorry," he spluttered.

Andy huffed and tried to settle Rosie back to sleep. She wasn't having it, so he took her out of her seat and sat her on his lap. When she—and Mike—finally stopped squawking and choking, Andy said, "There's something you're not telling me."

"About?"

"Dan."

"Dan? I haven't spoken to him since yesterday."

"What did you talk about?"

Mike frowned as he thought. "Whether Mrs. Hunter fancies me or not."

"Who?"

"A job I did recently. She recommended me to her friend in Dovedale and then came over twice while I was working. Dan was taking the piss when he suggested it—turned out he was right. I tell you what, it's no fun being the object of women's desires."

Andy laughed and peered upwards. "Dear God, please grant me the opportunity to prove my brother wrong."

"Ha. Like you aren't doing that every day already."

"You know what they say. If you've got it…" Andy flexed his shoulders and struck a pose, or as much of a pose as he could strike whilst holding a baby. It made Mike laugh.

"You look like one of those crappy posters from the eighties."

"So is that all you talked about?"

Mike's eyes moved from side to side, like he was trying to recall, though Andy knew he was putting it on. If it had been nothing, he'd have told Andy to mind his own business.

"Yep," Mike said finally. "Oh, and Adele coming home. And whether the woman upstairs owned a cat." He shrugged and drank some more water.

That was all Andy was getting out of him, and clear confirmation that Dan was up to something.

12: Thunderstruck
Tuesday, 2nd October

The best thing about playing Comco Glass, apart from them being a decent side who put in a good game, was the mini stadium at their HQ, complete with stands, a bar, and a pitch that was out of this world. It had been a wet September, and most of the pitches they'd played on—such as they could be called pitches to start with—were mud baths, or worse, they'd turned into miniature lakes, with as many postponements as games played. Not so at Comco, with its state-of-the-art drainage system and dedicated groundskeeper.

However, the downside to playing at Comco was that the CEO, a frustrated footballer who couldn't kick a ball to save his life, insisted on attending every match, and he'd been otherwise engaged at the weekend, which was why they were playing on a rainy Tuesday night. It meant the Jeffries contingent of the Lions was missing a few supporters, most notably Shaunna, who was at home with the twins. Alice was looking after Adele and Robbie, although Adele hardly ever came to watch anyway. Mike had offered to bring Len, to which Len had replied, 'Bugger am I standing in the rain for two hours', which presumably meant Pez had no way of getting there, either, and Kris and Ade were also fair-weather supporters. That left the old die-hards, aka Josh and Libby Sandison-Morley, huddled together under an umbrella at the front of the sparsely populated stands, and wearing their hand-knitted red scarves rather than waving them.

"Right, we're going with a three-five-two tonight," Dan said. "So I want…" At the sight of Sean shaking his head, he stopped. "What?"

"Have you forgotten how strong their forwards are? You're going to leave me wide open."

"What did I just say?" Dan asked and noticed a few people put their heads down and take a backstep. He sighed. "I was asking for real. I meant three-five-two."

"That's what you said the first time, bro," Andy pointed out.

"For fuck's sake." Dan laughed. "Five. Three. Two. Yes?"

"Yep," Andy confirmed.

"So that's George and Charlie up front. Mike, Aitch and Dave midfield. Me, Steve, Andy, Rich and Jonesy defending."

Andy glared at Mike. "You've stolen my position, you bastard."

"Enough!" Dan snapped. His brothers looked at each other and raised their eyebrows. The challenge hadn't been a serious one, he realised, but he wasn't backing down now. "Andy, I need you at the back in case they break through."

"Unlikely." It was, in fact, very likely, but two minutes before kickoff was no time for defeatist talk.

"Yeah, well, you can go prop up the other goalpost." Dan gave Sean a wan grin. Sean sent it right back at him. "Mike, unless you're dead on target with no challengers, get rid to George ASAP. Aitch…"

"Hand over my glory to Charlie," Aitch said, failing to keep the weariness out of his voice, which was exactly why Dan was telling Mike and Aitch specifically. Nine out of ten times Aitch made an attempt, he left it too long and lost possession. Mike was a better player, or used to be, and he was usually on target, but he also hogged the ball and refused to pass, thinking he could outstrike a striker. Or maybe it was just because he was the big brother.

"Listen, this is a live practice run. Comco might have flash kits and the best pitch outside the premier league—"

"Wasn't this a Jeffries and Associates acquisition?" Charlie interrupted, knowing full well it was. Briefly, Dan glared at her to show his disdain, before finishing with, "We know we can beat this lot, because they're crap."

"That's the spirit, chaps," a voice chirped up behind Dan, and he said a silent 'shit', knowing without looking it was Comco's CEO. They were well-acquainted through their business dealings and had worked on a few projects together, but that was only business. This was football. The CEO gave Dan a very hearty slap on the back and continued on his way to wish his own team good luck.

"Come on, then." Dan stepped aside and gestured for the rest of the Lions to go out onto the pitch.

"Nice one, bro," Andy said, flicking Dan's ear on his way past. Dan would've liked nothing more than to retaliate. However, now wasn't the time, and in any case, if he couldn't get Andy out of the way, he'd need to keep him sweet, or it would be more than a flick of the ear he'd be getting when his brother found out what he was up to.

The heavens opened almost as soon as they'd kicked off, and for the first forty-five minutes, the rain, accompanied by thunder and lightning, was torrential. At half-time, with the Lions leading one-nil, courtesy of a left-footer from Charlie Davenport, the Comco CEO approached Dan and asked how he'd feel about abandoning the game. It was a reasonable consideration, given the downpour and the rolling thunderstorm. But Dan really didn't want to. The Lions needed this win to go level with the Anchors ahead of Sunday. If they abandoned, their current lead would be discarded until the match could be rescheduled. On the other hand, Comco were playing far better than Dan had anticipated.

"Let's play on," he said.

Apparently, that was the right answer, which only served to worry Dan more, because it likely meant Comco had an ace up their sleeve. Dan watched the CEO march over to his team to report back to their captain, who listened, nodded, and gave Dan a thumbs up.

"They're bluffing," Sean said. "There's something not right."

"Like what? An injury?"

"They all look fit enough to me. I'm just getting a vibe from the big cheese."

"Should I have agreed to abandon the match?"

Sean pondered a moment and then shook his head. "You made the right decision."

Dan left Sean to observe their opponents and told the rest of the team what had gone on.

"Maybe he's worried about one of us getting hit by lightning," Aitch speculated. "It's a hell of a night."

"Yeah, but what are the odds, Aitch?"

"It's a possibility."

Dan rolled his eyes and said no more, even though Aitch was now recounting, at length, how a copper he used to work with got struck by lightning at a football match. The rest of the team feigned listening, well used to Aitch's stories that were always in poor taste but fortunately not always true.

The second half, Comco were off to a strong start and scored within the first two minutes, but it didn't last. No more than a minute later, the Lions were back in the lead, and it was a blinder. Andy deftly took possession from a throw-in, dribbling past the halfway line before he passed to Dan, who did a 270-degree turn to dodge the defending midfielders. Staring hard through the heavy rain, he found George, but there were too many Comco players between them.

Charlie was on the other side of the pitch, which meant a long pass could easily be intercepted. Instead, Dan passed to Mike, watching and praying that he would ignore his earlier advice and just go for it. He was in the perfect position to do a 'Mike special', whereby it would look like the shot was going over and then, at the last second, the ball would dip and skim under the crossbar.

And that was exactly what happened.

If there'd been a crowd to go wild, they would have done. What they got was cheering from the few Lions' supporters who'd braved the rain, a loud whoop and whistle from Libby, and polite applause from Josh, who could whoop as well as anybody if the right man put the ball in the net, as in, his husband. Players from both teams congratulated Mike, sensibly, leaving the real congratulations until full-time, by which point, much to Josh's delight, George had secured a three-one victory. Josh wasn't the only one delighted by that; not only did it put them level with the Anchors on points, it also put them ahead on goal difference—only by one goal, but Dan was happy to take it.

He tried not to swagger as the teams returned to their respective changing rooms. Sean had been right about the CEO's guff; Comco had played well enough, but their performance in the second half had rapidly declined. There was definitely something amiss.

"Anyone up for beer?" Aitch asked while they showered, receiving a chorus of yeses in response.

"Not tonight, mate," Dan said.

"You're on night duty with the little lad, are you?"

"I'll get up to him maybe twice, if I'm unlucky."

"*Un*lucky, you say?"

"He's a good little sleeper, is our Robbie. But Adele's still in a fair bit of pain."

"Bet she's got you under lock and key."

Dan stepped out from under the steamy water and grabbed his towel. "Nah. She's happy to get me out of the house." He didn't bother engaging Aitch any further, because, truth be told, he wasn't in the mood for chitchat or drinking. He was too psyched up about the auction in two days' time. He returned to the changing room, dressed, and waited to congratulate the rest of the team, leaving Mike until last.

"You played well tonight, bro."

Mike beamed. "Cheers. I saw the opportunity and took it. Didn't have time to think. Sorry."

"No need." Dan hauled his brother in for a hug. "Welcome to the team, Mike." He released him. "I'm off home." He glanced around the changing room, looking for Andy, but he wasn't there. "You staying for a drink?"

"Not sure. Andy gave me a lift."

"Gotcha." Dan frowned. "Ah, well. No idea where he's got to. Tell him I said good night."

"Will do."

Dan raised his hand in a general wave to anyone else who was there to see it and left the changing room, surprised to find Andy in the corridor outside, still in his kit, and talking to Eddie Leyland—Comco's CEO. As Dan neared their location, Andy spotted him, gave Eddie a pat on the shoulder and turned towards his brother. Eddie walked off in the opposite direction.

"Everything all right?" Dan asked.

"You know the company's moving down south?"

"Is it?"

"Yep. It's been on the cards for a while." Andy frowned. "I'm sure we had a conversation about it."

Dan shook his head. "Not that I recall."

"Whatever, it was confirmed this afternoon, and Ed was trying to keep it quiet until after the match, but someone strategically leaked the news."

Dan's hackles were straight up. "Are you having a laugh?" He spat the question at his brother.

"What?" Andy shrugged and raised his hands, immediately on the defensive.

"What the hell are you playing at?"

Andy stepped closer so he was in Dan's face. "It's nothing to do with me."

"Well, who else knew about it?"

"Dunno, but I swear, I said *nothing*. Jesus, Dan." Andy stormed off to the changing room, leaving Dan in the corridor, still raging.

It was bad sportsmanship, and Dan couldn't believe one of his team would pull that kind of low-down trick to get an advantage over Comco—that they thought he'd accept victory at any cost. It wasn't his style. If they won, they did so fair and square. Except at Quiz Night. He'd cheat, lie *and* steal to beat Complex Superiority. However, football was a noble sport, and if they couldn't win on their own merits, then Dan would rather they didn't win at all.

He was also angry with himself, for automatically blaming Andy when he knew his brother wouldn't stoop that low. It was one of the many things they had in common, and he owed Andy an apology. There was nothing else for it: Dan took out his phone and sent Adele a message to check she could manage without him for another half hour.

"I thought you were going home," Aitch said, emerging first from the changing room.

"I was, but…" Dan's phone vibrated—a reply from Adele, confirming she was fine. "I'll stay for one," he said, distracted. "I just need to have a word with Andy first."

"All right, mate. I'll get them in." Aitch set off for the bar, leaving Dan to return to the changing room, where everyone was dressed—bar Andy, who was on his way out of the shower and gave Dan a killer glare. The rest of the players made a quick exit, Mike last, who looked from Andy to Dan and raised an eyebrow. Dan shook his head, and it was enough to warn Mike off. He also left.

"I was out of order," Dan said quietly, peaceably—he hoped. Andy kept his back to him and continued to dry off. Dan sighed in exasperation. "I'm sorry, all right?" Still nothing from Andy. Dan watched him struggle to pull his jeans up his damp legs. "I know you wouldn't say anything."

"Whatever."

"Bro?" Dan didn't want to fight with him, not over this. He tried a sideways shift in subject. "What does Ed need from us?"

Andy exhaled loudly. "Why don't you ask him yourself?" Pulling his t-shirt over his head, he turned and sniped, "Seeing as I'm not to be trusted."

Dan got up and strode towards the door. "Are you staying for a drink?"

"No. I'm giving Mike a lift home. Might stop in at his for one."

For a brief second, Dan faltered, but then continued on his way. If that's how Andy wanted to play it, then screw him.

In the Comco bar, Aitch had bought a round for everyone—Comco players included—and Mike had followed them over.

"I'd get that down you pronto," Dan advised his brother, collecting his own pint from Aitch and nodding an acknowledgement.

"Does he want to go?"

"Apparently."

"Fair enough." Mike took a swig of his beer and put his glass down, seemingly in no hurry. "Did you get things sorted?"

"Nope."

"I take it he got the hump about…what we were discussing on Monday?"

Dan shook his head. "He doesn't know yet."

"OK." Mike picked up his pint again.

"He's being a knob, that's all."

Mike laughed. "Family trait."

"Are you calling me a knob?"

"No." Mike was still laughing.

"Yeah, well…" Dan forcibly loosened his shoulders and lifted his glass to his lips, speaking into it. "He's all yours, bro." He spotted Andy on his way across the room and took his leave, going to stand with Aitch and the other lads instead, although it was no improvement, seeing as they were talking about the relocation of Comco and the job losses associated with it. Not surprisingly, the CEO was nowhere to be seen, and Dan soon tired of the conversation. The majority of Comco's contracts were in the south, so it made sense for their HQ to be located there, but he wasn't about to point that out to the soon-to-be ex-employees. He returned to the bar, standing as far from his brothers as he could, wishing he hadn't stayed for a pint.

"What's up?" Aitch drew up next to him.

"Nothing really. I just got sick of listening to that lot." He tilted his head in the direction of the Comco players.

"Yeah, well, as I was saying to Dave earlier, they're one of the biggest employers in the area. We're gonna feel it. Unemployment's already up by—"

"Dave?" Dan asked, cutting Aitch off mid-flow. "*Our* Dave?"

"Who else?"

Dan closed his eyes in disbelief. "What exactly were you talking about?"

"Dave works for the Highways, doesn't he?"

"And?"

"Andy put in the application this afternoon for an escort to transport the stadium."

"Right?"

"And Dave was saying what a pain in the arse it was to bring it here in the first place."

"Aitch!"

"What?"

"Oh…for fuck's sake, Aitch. You're a copper. You're supposed to be good at keeping it shut." Dan downed his pint and slammed the glass on the counter. "I'll catch you later," he said and walked off, calling, "Andy? A word, please," over his shoulder.

A moment later, Andy arrived outside, still with a face like thunder. "What d'you want?"

"Why aren't you keeping me informed?"

"About?"

"Aitch has just been telling me that Dave was telling him that you put in the ESDAL for Comco this afternoon."

"Yeah, I did."

"Yet I know nothing about it. Oh, and in case you haven't figured it out, that's how the news leaked."

Andy's eyebrows rose. "On purpose?"

"No. They were gossiping, and you didn't answer my question."

"My email didn't arrive, I take it?"

"You know it did. I phoned you, remember?"

"Ah, yeah, that's right—to tell me again how I needed a time-out."

For all that Dan was physically stronger than Andy and could've taken him on, no trouble at all, Andy was still his older brother. Smug older brother, at that.

"I'm sorry," Dan said, and this time, his humility was authentic. "Maybe I am projecting a little. Adele's driving me nuts."

Andy smiled and squeezed Dan's shoulder. They were always the same—quick tempers, but they went off the boil just as quickly. "Some things don't change, eh?"

"No. I'm going home."

"All right, bro. Sleep well."

Dan pulled his car keys from his pocket and moved off. "I'll do my best. See you Sunday."

"You'll see me before then."

Dan was already at the door and turned back. "What?"

"Thursday? Auction? I mean, if you don't want my company, then no problem. Saves Mum having to look after our two as well as Bethan."

"You…" Dan stared at his brother's grinning face. "See you Thursday, then."

Andy winked. "Night, bro."

13: Mediate This
Wednesday, 3rd October

"Thanks for this, Shaw...na." Mike smiled an apology and pressed on his knees to stop them from jigging up and down. They were sitting in the waiting area outside the family court; the chairs were too hard, too low and too upright, and he was a nervous wreck.

"No thanks needed, hun." Shaunna placed her hand on top of his, temporarily stilling the shakes. He exhaled slowly. "OK. What do you need from me in there?" she asked.

"I don't know. Just moral support, I guess. Try to not let me lose my rag?"

"I can do that." As she finished speaking, the main doors opened behind her. She turned, and they both watched three women come into view: Jacqueline Perry with her barrister, Mike presumed, and his own barrister. Ms. Lane acknowledged him with a nod before taking up position behind the other two women whilst they waited to be processed, one at a time, by the security guard. Mike and Shaunna had already been through the security checks and signed in. Once Ms. Lane had done the same, she came over to them, shook Mike's hand and then Shaunna's. Jacqueline Perry and her lawyer walked past. Mike automatically offered them a smile and in response received a glimmer of a smile from Mrs. Perry.

"All right, Mike." Ms. Lane waited to make sure he was listening. "This is what's going to happen. We'll be in one of the smaller meeting rooms. There will be six of us present, including the family mediator. Her job today is to assess whether mediation is appropriate in our case, and if it is, she'll offer guidance and suggestions on how you and Mrs. Perry might move forward. Does that all make sense?"

"Yes," Mike confirmed. "What happens if we don't agree with her suggestions?"

"This is only the beginning of the process. It would be unusual—but not unheard of—for both parties to agree at this early stage. The family mediator will ask both of you questions to establish what you want to happen, and once she has all of the information she needs, she'll provide her professional judgement."

"There's no middle ground, though, is there?" Mike said. "I want to keep Bethan with me. Jacqueline wants Bethan with her."

"Which is why I asked if you'd be amenable to an access arrangement. It's a reasonable compromise. Another possibility would be a joint custody arrangement, but—"

"No." Mike shook his head. He didn't need to think about it. "No chance."

"Let's not jump the gun here, Mike. OK? Mary Simpson is a very fair mediator, and firm. She will put you through your paces this morning, but she's not here to judge the quality of your parenting." A voice called out 'Jacqueline Perry and Michael Jeffries'. "Keep that in mind," Ms. Lane added as she stepped off, expecting them to take her lead.

Mike and Shaunna got up and followed her along the wide corridor of the formidable building with its high ceilings and heavy mouldings—foot-high skirting boards, picture rails and paint-clogged ornate ceiling roses—to the last door on the right. Ms. Lane entered first and beckoned Mike and Shaunna inside, where Jacqueline and her lawyer were already seated next to each other on the far side of a rectangular conference table. A third woman, who looked to be around Mike's age, was pouring water into plain glass tumblers and paused to acknowledge him.

"Good morning, Mr. Jeffries. Please do take a seat." She finished pouring into one glass and moved on to the next, her eyes flitting briefly to Shaunna. "You're a friend of Mr. Jeffries?"

"Yes," Shaunna confirmed. "Shaunna Hennessy, Your Wor… ship?" She looked to Mike's lawyer for guidance.

"Just Mary," the woman said. "It's better if we work on a first-name basis." She smiled warmly.

Mike felt a little less uneasy for hearing that. "In that case, I'm Mike." He turned towards Jacqueline Perry and her lawyer but couldn't bring himself to look directly at them.

"I'm Jackie," Rachel's mum said.

Until that point, she'd been focused on Shaunna, but now Mike could feel her eyes boring into him, and he was stuck to the spot, trying to get his head around his shifting feelings towards Jackie. It was so much more human, approachable, than 'Jacqueline Perry', a stuffy deputy head who ignited his long-standing rebellion against authority and wanted to take his daughter away from him.

It took a gentle push on his back to get him moving again. He gave Shaunna a grateful half smile as they took their seats opposite Jackie and her lawyer. Ms. Lane sat on Mike's other side; he couldn't say he was happy being the only man in a room with five women.

"All right, let's make a start." Mary picked up a pencil and tapped it on the notepad in front of her. "I'm Mary Simpson, and I'm an authorised family mediator. My role here this morning is to gather information about your dispute and assess whether family mediation is appropriate.

"I've received and read the information from your barristers. Thank you, Ms. Lane and Mrs. Parker-Hillingdon. My understanding is this: Jackie, you wish to apply for a special guardianship order in respect of your granddaughter, Bethan."

"Yes, that's correct."

"Mike, you currently have full custody of Bethan, who is your daughter."

"Yes."

"Bethan's mother, Rachel Perry, is in prison. Is that correct?"

Both Mike and Jackie nodded.

Mary looked to the two lawyers. "Do we have any further information on Rachel's transfer application?"

"Yes," Jackie's lawyer answered. "It wasn't successful, but we have lodged an appeal."

Mike's heart was like a bouncing rubber ball in a box, the tiniest moment of relief that Rachel was once again out of the picture instantly snatched away by the chance she might win her appeal. She didn't want Bethan any more now than she had six months ago, and she probably didn't care if her mum got custody, either. But if he was honest, he'd expected it; Rachel no longer shocked him. Everything she did was designed to hurt other people, or that's how it seemed to him, as if she got a buzz out of their pain.

"Jackie and Mike." Mary's gaze settled on Mike for a second and then travelled across to Jackie. "How would you feel if Bethan were to join her mum in prison?"

Mike clamped his teeth together, grateful Mary's attention was on Jackie. He didn't trust himself to answer politely.

"Rachel is her mum," Jackie said. "Of course she wants to be with her daughter."

Mike reared in his seat. Shaunna grabbed his hand and kept hold.

Jackie lowered her eyes. "But prison is no place for a child to grow up."

Mike drew in a long, deep breath and held it.

"Mike?" Mary prompted.

It took all of his control to not use that breath to yell, or howl. He could've burst into tears. Instead, he shook his head mutely and hoped Mary got the gist.

"You don't want Bethan to be with Rachel," she said.

"No, I don't," Mike managed to push out.

"Thank you."

Mary looked away from him, and he vented the rest of the breath through tight lips. Shaunna smoothed her thumb over his hand. He was so glad she was there.

"That's our first point of agreement. It's unlikely Bethan will be placed with her mother if either or both of you are suitable guardians. It's not in Bethan's best interests, and Rachel's sentence by far exceeds eighteen months. In such circumstances, arrangements are usually made for the child to be cared for outside of prison, even if that means the child is placed in the care of the local authority. However, the law also accepts that a child has a right to both parents. Mike, you have made it very clear to Ms. Lane that you don't want Rachel to have access to your daughter. Is that still correct?"

"Yes."

"I'm aware Rachel is serving a life sentence for murder, but that does not necessarily mean she's a danger to Bethan. Do you have other reason to believe Bethan would be at risk if she was with her mother?"

How many reasons do you need? Mike thought, but didn't say. Rachel abused her brother and sister for years, never mind his own months of torture, or the loss of his testicle and with it every last drop of his self-esteem. Because of Rachel, he might never have a relationship with a woman again. Yet he knew that none of it meant she was a risk to Bethan.

"Excuse me. May I say something?" Shaunna asked. Mike turned to her in horror, certain she was going to tell them what Rachel had done to him. She made eye contact with him and gave the slightest of smiles. She was on his side. She wouldn't betray him. He nodded his consent.

"Of course, Shaunna," Mary said. Mike turned in time to catch the concern on Mary's face, directed at him.

"Thank you," Shaunna said. "I know this is probably in the files anyway, but Rachel walked out on Bethan when she was only a few days old. She didn't tell Mike she was leaving. No note or anything. They were sleeping in separate rooms, and if he hadn't noticed Rachel had gone, he might've gone to work and left Bethan on her own."

"Is that what happened?" Mary asked Mike.

"Yes. I only woke up because Bethan was crying. She was in the room Rachel had been staying in, and I only just heard her. I noticed Rachel wasn't there, obviously, but it took me a few hours to notice her stuff was gone. Lucky we were bottle-feeding or I'd have been screwed."

"You're self-employed." Mary indicated to the file in front of her.

"I'm a painter and decorator, yeah. Self-employed. Does that matter?"

"No, not at all. Were you self-employed when Rachel left?"

"Yes."

"You had a childminder, I presume?"

"Not back then, I didn't. My mum looks after Bethan now."

"And before that, how did you work and care for Bethan?"

"I didn't. I had to cancel jobs, let someone else take them."

"Did you claim any benefits?"

"No. I, err… It was all a bit of a shock, to be honest." There was a great deal more to it than that; his share of the house had been in his bank account, although it all went towards paying off his debts so he didn't have to declare bankruptcy. However, Mike was sure being divorced and in debt would count against him, so he said nothing further. He gave Mary a firm nod to indicate he'd finished.

"Thank you for answering my questions. I do have more for you in a short while, but don't worry." She turned to Rachel's mum. "Jackie, in your own words, can you tell us why you want custody of your granddaughter?"

"Of course." Jackie considered for a moment, or seemed to. Mike was pretty sure she had a whole arsenal of reasons stocked up and ready to launch, and it was a teacher ploy, to check they were paying attention. "Aside from Bethan being my granddaughter, I believe a little girl needs a female role model, which isn't to say I think Mike is a bad parent." She met Mike's gaze. "I think you're a very good parent. I really do. But in my job, I've seen how hard it is for children who don't have their mums in their lives, the long-term effects. Those who fare better are cared for by grandparents, usually grandmas."

Mary looked like she was waiting to see if Jackie had more to say, and the silence it created seemed to stretch for minutes. The ticking of a clock filled the room; Mike scanned the walls and located it. Only fifteen minutes had passed since they were called in. It felt so much longer.

At last, the silence was broken, but not by Mary.

"Excuse me for butting in again," Shaunna hedged. "I hope I'm not speaking out of turn, but...Bethan has female role models in her life."

Jackie's lawyer was straight on Shaunna's case. "Are you referring to yourself, Ms. Hennessy?"

"Partly. I'm Mike's sister-in-law. He has another sister-in-law, too, and his—"

"Forgive me for saying so, Ms. Hennessy, but not all role models are good ones."

Shaunna smiled and laughed lightly. Mike's stomach churned. He knew her well enough to know when she was riled, and she was riled.

Jackie's lawyer continued, "Would I be right in saying you were a teenage mother?"

"Yes. I was pregnant when I was fourteen."

"Do you honestly believe it makes you a good role model to your niece?"

"Mrs. P... whatever your name is. I have three daughters, the eldest—the result of my teenage pregnancy—manages a successful restaurant *and* she hasn't got a criminal record. You tell me."

Jackie glared across the table at Shaunna.

"I'm not calling your parenting skills to question, Jackie."

"That's what it sounded like to me."

"I'm sorry. I didn't mean it to. I don't believe for one second that what Rachel did is because of how you brought her up. On the other hand, my parents were teachers, so it probably doesn't help your case much when your lawyer calls me a bad role model."

Mike didn't know which he wanted more: to high-five Shaunna, or for the ground to open and swallow him. Mary interjected before either happened.

"I think perhaps we're getting away from the reason we're here today. I understand your concerns, Jackie. However, given that Mike's mum looks after Bethan while he's at work, I think we can safely conclude that Bethan has positive female role models in her life already. May I ask what your childcare arrangements would be, if you were to have custody of your granddaughter?"

"I plan to take early retirement," Jackie stated. She was still bristling a little from Shaunna's remark, but she was also noticeably upset by it. "I'm fifty-five. The financial penalty is negligible, and I own my house outright."

"Is there anything further you wish to add on this point, Jackie?"

"No, I don't think so."

"Mrs. Parker-Hillingdon?"

"My client has a guaranteed income for the rest of her life. She's in a far better position to provide for her granddaughter than is Bethan's father."

Mary turned to Ms. Lane and gestured for her to respond.

"Mike is solvent. He's made his business accounts available to the court, and his business is doing well enough that he's been able to secure a mortgage against his income."

That wasn't strictly true. Charlie had checked over his accounts and said his income was sufficient to apply for a mortgage, but there was no way he was going to get one, unless he went through one of Len's 'business acquaintances'.

"Do you currently live with your mum, Mike?" Mary asked.

"Not as such. I live…next door."

"In a single-skin chalet with one room," Jackie's barrister pointed out. "Has it been inspected by the local authority and certified as a suitable dwelling?"

Mike allowed himself a moment of smugness, but he tried to rein in his smirk. "Yes, it has," he confirmed. Having a brother who was a civil engineer certainly had its uses, and Andy had been insistent. In the end, it was easier for Len to sort it out than to put up with being nagged by his middle stepson.

"OK, thank you, everyone," Mary said. "To summarise so far, I am satisfied that both of you, Jackie and Mike, are equally able to provide a secure and stable living environment for Bethan, and you have Bethan's best interests at heart. You have both made it clear you don't want Bethan to join her mother in prison, which brings us back to the other matter of Rachel being granted access to her daughter. Jackie, if Mike agreed to Bethan visiting Rachel, do you feel we could move forward?"

"You mean, if Mike still has custody?"

"That's what I mean, yes."

Jackie's lawyer leaned closer to her, shielding her mouth while she spoke. Jackie nodded. "I need to take it under advisement."

Mary nodded slowly and turned to Mike. "Would you be prepared to consider allowing Bethan to visit Rachel?"

"No." Mike wasn't prepared to consider the question, never mind the answer.

"I realise—"

"No! It's bad enough that one day I'm going to have to tell her what her mum did. Can you imagine the hell she's gonna go through at school?"

Mary nodded sympathetically, which only made Mike madder.

"Ms. Lane, is there anything you want to add?"

"Not at this juncture."

"All right. I'm adjourning this meeting for one hour so I can review the information you've both provided. If you want to go for a coffee or perhaps something to eat, please do, and I'll see you all back here at one-thirty."

Mary rose to her feet, waited for everyone else to do likewise, and then followed them out of the room.

"Are you OK?" Shaunna asked Mike as soon as they were clear of Jackie and her lawyer.

"Yeah. I couldn't half do with a pint, though."

Shaunna smoothed his arm. "God, yes. We should pick up some beer and wine on the way home. Let's go get a coffee, shall we?"

Mike nodded and turned to his lawyer, who was standing a few feet away and squinting at her phone screen. "Would you like to join us? We're going for a coffee."

"Thanks, but no. I need to deal with something. I'll see you in an hour." Her brusque tone wasn't directed at them. "You did very well in there, Mike," she said, and then to Shaunna, "As did you." She gave Shaunna an amused smile.

Shaunna grimaced. "Sorry if I got defensive."

"Oh, you did that, all right, but you also made an excellent point. Enjoy your coffee." Ms. Lane turned away from them and put her phone to her ear.

Shaunna hooked her arm through Mike's and steered him away down the corridor, back to the security barrier. "I'm serious about the beer and wine, by the way."

Mike huffed out a small laugh. "Yeah, I'm well up for that today."

"Excellent. Do you want us to come to you, or—"

"Mike?"

The voice came from behind him, and he held his breath and kept walking, convinced he was going to throw up. Rachel and her mum sounded almost the same, and for a second, Mike's mind tricked him.

"Please can I talk to you?"

He didn't know how to answer and looked to Shaunna in a panic.

"Maybe you should see what she has to say," Shaunna whispered. "I'll step in if you need me to."

Mike slowly turned around. Jackie stood a few feet away and didn't move any closer.

"There's something else, isn't there?" she asked. "Something you're not telling us. About Rachel."

Mike swallowed against his reflux. "I...I don't want Bethan to know what her mum did."

"That's not it. I've been a teacher for thirty years. Not much gets past me."

Rachel did.

"I know when someone's hiding something."

"You're wrong." Mike turned his back on her and started to walk away.

"I need to understand. Please." Her voice was desperate and loaded with tears ready to fall. It stopped Mike in his tracks. "Please?"

Shaunna was standing directly in front of him, her expression matching the pain he was feeling, and the dilemma he faced. If he told Jackie what Rachel had done to him, she might see it as evidence of what Rachel had told her all along. Or maybe she'd believe him and finally accept the truth. Jackie was a good person. He turned back to face her.

"There's nothing else, Jackie. I'm just trying to do the best for my daughter. I'm sorry."

***

"Hello again, everyone," Mary greeted as they returned to the room and resumed their seats. "Thank you for your patience. This is quite an unusual case, and I needed to research the position of the law on several aspects. There is no provision in law regarding a young child accompanying a parent or guardian in prison, beyond specific safeguarding requirements, which also govern children's visits to prison, but I'm jumping ahead.

"Whilst the issue of whether Bethan's mother should be granted any form of access to her child presents a considerable obstacle to us reaching an agreement that satisfies both parties, it is my opinion that mediation is a suitable means of resolving the dispute. Jackie, can I ask you to confirm your intentions?"

"Yes. If Mike will agree to me having access to my granddaughter, I will not apply for a special guardianship order."

"Thank you, Jackie. Mike, do you wish to respond?"

"Err…" Mike was so astounded by Jackie's U-turn he couldn't even string words together. He looked to Ms. Lane, who took over on his behalf.

"Mike and I discussed this last week, and he indicated he would be happy to consider access arrangements with Jackie."

"That's good news, indeed. You will, of course, need to arrange a further consultation with your lawyers and each other to agree on specific details, which I trust will go smoothly. Please send copies of the necessary documentation to my office."

The two barristers nodded to confirm they would.

"As regards Bethan visiting Rachel in prison, I recommend we meet again, once the outcome of Rachel's appeal is known. In the unlikely event she is successful and Bethan joins her in prison, we will stop the mediation process. Thank you, and good day, everyone."

Mary picked up her files and left the room. The meeting was over.

14: Sweet Time
Thursday, 4th October

Shaunna put the phone down and turned to Andy, shaking her head; she was angry and upset. "This is crazy."

"Why? What's happened now?" he asked. She'd been on the phone with Mike for the past twenty minutes, which was a short call for Shaunna, but a record-breaker for his brother.

"It ended so positively yesterday as well." Shaunna reached up and removed the sprung clip, letting her hair down, seemingly just so she could flick it back over her shoulders in outrage. "Jackie Perry's lawyer has advised her to continue with her custody application. Now social services want to inspect the summerhouse."

Andy shrugged. "Let them. They won't find anything wrong with it."

"But he shares the bedroom with Bethan."

"So? She's six months old. A lot of people don't have the luxury of separate rooms for their kids. Separate rooms for anything, in fact."

"But in England—"

"Even here. There's no law against it. If Bethan was six *years* old, maybe. It's not gonna make any difference. He's a bloody good dad."

"Yeah, he is," Shaunna agreed, though she was still worrying for Mike. "That lawyer's a bitch." She got up from the table, continuing as she filled the kettle and prepared two mugs. "Mrs.

Parker…something double-barrelled. I still can't believe she went for me. How did she know so much? I mean, she didn't even know I was going to be there."

Andy briefly looked up from his tablet while Shaunna ranted, as she'd been doing on and off since she'd returned from the court the previous day. It wasn't her style to sit back and take the blows, but it sounded like she'd done a brilliant job of keeping her cool, for Mike's sake. Andy didn't say it, but it was the lawyer's job to know everything about Shaunna, and the rest of the family. With Kris's and Ade's TV careers, Shaunna had been under the media microscope plenty of times. But even without easy access to the information, the lawyer would have looked into the background of those closest to Mike. That was why she was earning the big bucks.

"She'll probably have a go at you next," Shaunna said.

"More than likely." Andy didn't care. He had nothing to hide. Not that he'd lived a squeaky clean existence, but there were no hidden secrets of his that could come back to bite his brother on the butt.

Shaunna set a cup of tea down next to his tablet and secured her hair in the clip again. "Why aren't you worried?" she asked, her tone a touch accusatory.

"Why would I be?" He peered up into her face, crinkled in a deep frown. He smiled and smoothed her cheek with his palm. "It'll be fine, RHB."

"I wish I had your confidence." She moved to leave, but he caught her around the waist and pulled her onto his lap. She put her arms around his neck, to stop herself from sliding off, and huffed. "This won't work."

"What won't?" He nuzzled into the dip above her shoulder blade and kissed his way to her mouth.

"Trying to distract me with…yeah, OK…" She kissed him back, turning to straddle him without breaking contact.

"I like this dress," he murmured against her lips.

"I know. That's why I'm wearing it."

He smiled into the kiss and reached between them to unfasten the buttons down the front.

"Well, that, and feeding babies," Shaunna qualified as he pushed the bodice open, revealing her very practical and what she considered unsexy maternity bra. He smoothed his palms over the soft white cotton fabric covering her breasts, so tempted. He wasn't banned from touching them, but for the time being, they weren't his to enjoy. They weren't his, period, but he was missing the intimacy of naked close contact, sucking and kissing her nipples, cupping her breasts, gently kneading… he should probably stop now…

Evidently, Shaunna was missing it, too. She slipped her arms out of her dress and unfastened her bra, casting it aside to tug Andy's t-shirt over his head, and then pressed her breasts to his chest. His eyes widened, and he exhaled heavily, unable to resist tightening his grip around her to increase the contact.

"Don't squeeze too hard," she warned.

Andy grinned and ran his hands down her back, around her hips to her thighs, shuffling her skirt up until his fingers touched the stretchy lace of her knickers. "D'you wanna take this upstairs?" he asked.

She got up, took off her knickers and returned to his lap. "Here's good," she said, and reached down to untie the cord on his sweatpants.

It was a bit awkward and involved a lot of wiggling to get into a workable position. Then the babies started crying, so they had to make it a quickie, with barely time to ride out their orgasms before Shaunna climbed off, both of them drenched in breast milk that was spurting, unaided, due to an epic let-down brought on by the combination of her climax and her babies' hungry cries. She went to deal with the twins, leaving Andy to marvel at nature, and how well it had equipped them to be parents, but also how fortunate they were. They had money and a roof over their heads, plus there were two of them to share the responsibility, and they got to choose how it worked best for them.

His mind drifted to Bhagwan, his friend in Nepal, who had little choice but to work away for days, sometimes weeks at a time, leaving his wife at home to care for however many kids they had by now. Andy had sent him a photo of Rosie and Sorsha, via the internet café run by one of Bhagwan's many 'cousins', and received a photo of Bhagwan's twin daughters with his reply. They were around ten years old, and gorgeous girls, but their life would be no different from their mum's: caring for a husband and a home and raising children.

In many—maybe all—respects, Bhagwan's dreams for his kids were no different than Andy's: health, happiness, and a chance to see the world. Where Andy had been lucky enough to experience those things firsthand, Bhagwan had only ever enjoyed them vicariously, through the stories of the visitors he guided through the Himalayas.

That last excursion to Kathmandu, when Dan was sick, Andy had done some serious soul-searching. Jess, his best friend, the rock that anchored him when all around him was a raging, swirling mess, had lied by omission, twice, and he couldn't make sense of it. They were friends with benefits who shared a house, not partners. They dated other people, talked about their conquests and their defeats. Yet Jess had deliberately stayed quiet, first about Kevin Callaghan, and then, more significantly, about Rob Simpson-Stone.

Malice aforethought. She'd used that phrase on him, whenever he'd turned up with a bottle of wine and a six-pack of beer, hoping for a bit of nookie. He knew the truth now, and he didn't hate Rob anymore, or not with the same venom Adele did, but he and Rob had been adversaries too long for them to ever be friends.

So it was Jess who had broken his heart, but it was Shaunna who'd filled his thoughts during those long days in Kathmandu, waiting for the monsoon to pass and for Dan to get better.

He'd loved her for a long time. At high school, she'd rebuffed him, and it had made no difference. Through her teenage pregnancy, the start of her life with Kris, and Andy's years of travel and adventure, his crush remained as strong as ever. All those close scrapes, it was Shaunna who had flashed before his eyes, and his regret that he'd never get the chance to love her had been quickly pushed aside by his certainty that she was happy and loved.

Finding out he was Krissi's dad had nearly killed him, and the fear he'd raped her had only faded, not gone away. The one and only time he'd been blind drunk since that party, the same thing happened, or they thought it had. They'd never know, but what he did know for sure was he'd never get that drunk again.

In the aftermath, she'd told him she didn't want another relationship, and he'd respected that. She'd given her life to bringing up Krissi. Who could blame her for wanting to live a little? So, he'd thrown himself into his work, and then into looking after Jess, and he'd made a silent promise to someday pay Bhagwan back for getting him through the hell of the Kathmandu trip. He'd set some money aside to send Bhagwan's way, fantasising what it would be like to send enough for Bhagwan's kids to go on a round-the-world trip. Pipe dreams… until Jess died, leaving her entire estate in his trust.

Rosie suddenly appeared in front of him.

"Oh, Daddy. Why are you all sticky?" Shaunna's mock-baby voice made Andy laugh.

"I got sidetracked. Sorry."

"Where did you go this time?"

"Nepal."

Shaunna nodded and kept hold of both girls while Andy gave himself a quick wipe down with the dishcloth. She was watching him the whole time; he could feel it. He put his t-shirt back on and put his arms around her, hugging all three of them at once.

"Mike'll be OK," he murmured close to Shaunna's ear.

"That's not what's worrying me. Well, it is, but…" She sighed and handed Rosie to him. "Do we need to talk about this travelling thing?"

"What travelling thing?"

"Your daydreaming."

Andy opened his mouth to argue that they really were nothing more than daydreams, but Shaunna continued before he could say it.

"It's not fair that I get to study for fun and you don't get to travel."

"Assuming I want to travel," he pointed out.

"It's what you've always done."

"Always *did*. I get where you're coming from, and thanks for thinking about me. But if I needed to get away, I'd tell you. As it is, I don't want to go anywhere, and when I do, these two will be old enough to come with me."

"OK. If that changes, you'll tell me?"

"Yep."

"Promise?"

Andy held up three fingers. "Scout's honour."

"You were never in the Scouts."

"I was, you know. For a full two weeks." He grinned, and Shaunna rolled her eyes.

"So, what time's this auction?" she asked.

"Three o'clock, at the hotel." Andy still couldn't quite believe Dan was going after the Sharston house, but then, he didn't know everything Andy did.

"Are you going to tell him?"

"I'll have to, though I doubt it'll make any difference. You know what he's like." Once Dan had set his sights on something, he rarely gave up until it was his. But maybe, for once, he'd listen and decide the risk was too great, even for him.

*****

"What're you doing here already?" was how Dan greeted Andy when he arrived at the apartment at a quarter to two. It was a reasonable question, seeing as the hotel where the auction was being held was a ten-minute drive away, at most.

"I didn't think you'd appreciate my tardiness today," Andy said. He followed his brother into the lounge, where Adele was lying on the sofa with Robbie asleep in her arms. Andy went over and peered down at his nephew. "He's a handsome lad. Must be in the genes." He gave Adele a cheeky wink. She laughed and then flinched in pain. Andy flinched with her. "How you doing, Adele?"

"Oh, I'm OK, thanks." She smiled brightly. "You?"

"Great." Andy nodded to back up his claim, unsure what else to say, in case she didn't know about the auction.

"Shall we get going?" Dan suggested.

"Sure." Andy was glad to be given a reprieve. "See you later," he said to Adele and followed his brother out of the apartment. "Your car or mine?"

"Mine. It's easier to park."

True, Dan's car was smaller, and it had power steering, which the Mustang did not, and it was a decent car, the A5. The four-door model was stylish rather than flash, even in Dan's favourite boring black, but it wasn't in the same league as his red hot baby…mark two.

The passenger window opened, revealing his brother's scowling face. "You getting in, or what?"

Andy stopped judging and climbed into the passenger seat. "Adele doesn't know, then?"

"No. I put in a pre-auction bid on Monday, before she came home, but they knocked it back." He started the car. "Why didn't you tell me it was up for auction? Because of Jess?"

"There's more to it than that. Can we go for coffee somewhere? I'll tell you what you need to know."

"Yeah, why not? We've got nearly an hour to kill."

They drove out to a coffee shop on the side of town closest to the hotel, ordered vanilla frappés, and sat at a table next to the window. Andy wasn't sure where to begin, and his indecision forced Dan to prompt him.

"So what, then?"

"What you asked before, about whether it's to do with Jess? It's not what you think. I'm not being sentimental, well, maybe I am, in some respects. It does strike me as unfair that all of Jess's money is being put to good use, and the Sharstons' isn't."

"I asked the bloke from the auction house. He said it goes to the police and the Home Office."

"The proceeds from this house sale, maybe," Andy said cryptically.

"You're saying there's more?"

"A hell of a lot more. I don't know how much, exactly, but I know what was in Jess's accounts, and there's got to be at least twice that much from the Sharston Strang stuff alone."

"The police seized Sharston Strang's assets," Dan argued.

"They did, but the Sharstons were in operation for years. It was Angie who brought Jess in."

"Hold on. I thought Jess was the mastermind behind the fraud ring."

"She was, but when the Sharstons' place went up for auction, we did some digging around. Angie and Charles bought that house for two hundred thousand, ten years ago. They also had other properties in their names, including a house in France, another in Brazil, and two that I know of in the UK. All told, we're looking at thirty mill- in property alone."

"Fuck me, that's a lot of money."

Andy laughed. "That's only the start of it, bro. I never told you how much Jess left behind, did I?"

"Not that much, surely?"

Andy raised his eyebrows.

"And you've given it all away?" Dan's tone made clear how horrified he was by that.

"Not quite all of it. About ten million was returned to the people who should've inherited it. Then there's the chunk in the pot for the trust funds. Steph and Dave got around a million, and the rest went to Campion Trust."

"Our kids are already millionaires?"

"So long as we don't have too many more between the eight of us."

Dan was astounded. "I had no idea it was that much. Does anyone else know?"

"Apart from Shaunna?" Andy shook his head. "And Josh, of course, as the other executor."

"Right, so basically, your problem is you don't want the government getting thirty million quid that doesn't belong to them," Dan stated.

"Like I said, that's only part of it. The Sharstons were in with people in high places, if you get me."

"The police?"

"Higher."

"Royal family?"

Andy laughed. "Lower. Christ, it's like holiday card games all over again."

"The government?"

"Almost. The judiciary. I guarantee Angie Sharston'll be out in less than five years, and I'd bet the kids' trust fund pot she won't be living in some probation hostel and wearing a snazzy anklet."

Dan sat back and sucked at the straw in his frappé, pondering what he'd heard. Andy could almost hear the cogs juddering to a halt as the question formed. Dan swallowed and put his cup down again. "OK, say you're right so far. What difference does it make whether I buy this house or not?"

Andy grinned. "Interesting you should ask." He took out his phone and brought up a document onscreen before handing it to his brother. "That's a list of properties the auctioneers have sold in the past twenty years." Dan was scrolling down the list. It was going on for a couple of hundred properties.

"And?"

"Angela Sharston handled the conveyance on all of them."

"That doesn't mean the auctioneers are bent. They might not have known what she was up to."

"They're hyperlinks. Click one."

Dan did as instructed and waited. The connection was slow. "We need to get a move on," he said.

Andy waited, confident Dan would be changing his mind any second.

"Oh, fuck." He looked up at Andy, stunned. "The fraud ring's still in action."

Andy nodded. "Which is why I didn't send you the details for the Sharston house, or any other houses listed by Derek Arnold."

"Why didn't you tell me before now?"

"Because…your mates are coppers."

"Not this again." Dan gave Andy's phone back. "And anyway, why haven't *you* reported it? There's plenty of evidence there that they're ripping off buyers."

"And sellers."

"How does that work?"

"Easy. They get the seller to drop the price, plant some spook bids—"

"It's Angela Sharston's house."

"Yeah, but she's not selling it, is she?"

Dan whistled. "Defrauding the Home Office? They've got some balls."

"Like I said, friends in high places."

"Way out of Aitch's league, then. Maybe we could get a message to Graham Farrar, or whatever he's calling himself these days."

Andy sighed, trying to hold his temper. "It's nothing to do with us, bro."

"Civic duty."

"Bollocks to civic duty. They're dangerous, or have you forgotten they killed Alistair Campion? No way am I risking our lives—our *children's* lives—on some airy-fairy sense of civic duty." Dan's phone alarm sounded. "You're still planning to go to the auction?"

"Yep."

Andy slammed his hands down on the table, hard enough to make the glasses leave the surface. "I give up. What's the point, if you're gonna ignore every—"

"Not to bid on the house, you…" Dan tutted and laughed in disbelief. "To cover our backs. You coming?"

Dan got up and walked out, leaving Andy sitting at the table and wondering if he'd just made one of the biggest, most dangerous mistakes of his life.

15: Bid to Win
Thursday, 4th–Friday, 5th October

The auction was being held in the same function room where they'd celebrated Josh and George's wedding the previous summer, although without the balloons and flowers and little round tables, it looked like a completely different space. There were already a good thirty or forty people sitting in the rows of chairs that all faced one end of the room, where there was a table, a projector and a screen. Men and women in smart business suits and wearing ID badges milled around, handing out auction brochures to newcomers and answering their questions. One of them approached Dan and Andy.

"Good afternoon, gentlemen." She offered them a demure smile.

"Afternoon," Dan said. Andy acknowledged her with a nod.

"Are you planning to bid today? If so, I can deal with your registration for you."

Dan withdrew his passport and his driving licence from his pocket and handed them over.

"Have you attended a Derek Arnold auction before?" she asked as she wrote down Dan's details.

"Yeah." It wasn't a total lie, in that he *had* attended a property auction before—when his mum and Len had bought their house—and for all he knew, it could have been a Derek Arnold auction, although maybe not, seeing as they were living in the place now. But it was Dan's one and only experience of auctions, and had he still intended to bid on anything, he might have needed a little more guidance. However, he'd have got it from his brother, not the auctioneer.

The woman handed Dan's documents back, along with a copy of the paperwork, a bidder's number and a brochure, and gave Andy an enquiring look, which he met with a shake of the head. She returned her attention to Dan. "If you have any questions, or wish to know more about any of the properties, please feel free to ask any of the Derek Arnold representatives. We can be identified by our name badges." She lifted hers in illustration.

Both Dan and Andy nodded once to confirm they'd heard and understood, and the woman moved on.

"Shall we sit?" Dan suggested, as the room was getting busy.

They employed the lessons of their youth—whereby each had learned the harder, though infinitely more fun way, that teachers kept their beady eyes on the naughty kids at the back of the class—and sat a couple of rows closer to the front, aiming to stay inconspicuous.

Dan flicked through the brochure, to the Sharston house listing, and leaned in to speak. "How should I play this?"

Andy gave the details a cursory glance. "Don't bid above the reserve price."

"And if no-one outbids me?"

Andy shrugged. "Or don't bid at all."

Dan considered Andy's suggestion. It was the option with the least financial risk, but he'd taken heed of his brother's warning. They'd seen what Sharston and her cronies were capable of, and the pre-auction bid made Dan's interest clear. If he didn't bid today, it would arouse suspicion, draw dangerous attention not just to him but to his family. His children.

"If I get caught up in the thrill of the moment…"

"I've got your back, bro."

I'll be right behind you.

Hiding, you mean? Dan met Andy's gaze and smiled, no need to say it out loud.

Andy chuckled and patted his thigh. "Looks like we have liftoff."

Sure enough, there was movement up front, and the projector start-up screen displayed, followed by the Derek Arnold logo. The man himself was in attendance, but it didn't look like he would be brandishing the gavel, as he was sitting to one side, away from the table where another man was positioned behind the central lectern and the woman who had spoken to Dan and Andy earlier was dealing with the laptop connected to the projector.

The Sharston house was the fifth of ten lots, and bidding on the first four properties was so fast Dan had no chance of following, although in his efforts to do so, he'd noticed a few familiar faces around the room, of property developers Jeffries and Associates had worked with at one time or another. Much like the auction he'd gone to with his mum and Len, the majority of the people were professionals well acquainted with auction-room etiquette, which made the novices stand out like the person who turns up to an ordinary party in fancy dress. Dan hoped his imitation of his brother's laid-back familiarity was more convincing to onlookers than it felt.

And so to the Sharston house: the bidding started well below the reserve price; in fact, it was exactly the amount Dan had offered in his pre-auction bid, and he was desperate to tell Andy but didn't dare for fear any movement might be construed as a bid. With no takers, the auctioneer dropped the starting bid by fifty thousand pounds, then by seventy-five thousand, at which point someone at the front raised their hand a fraction of an inch. A second bid followed quickly, from a woman in the same row as Dan and Andy, and a third from somewhere behind them.

A fourth bid brought the price up to Dan's offer, and he realised it was his chance to act. One bid would be enough, but he hesitated, and in that second of indecision, someone else placed a bid: Andy. Dan turned to him, horrified, but Andy wasn't looking his way. He was facing the auctioneer, yet his eyes were following the bids all around the room. The auctioneer was now calling out increments of ten thousand pounds, and bids were coming so quickly that Dan had no idea what price they were up to. In the crossfire of numbers and nodding heads, he thought Andy had placed a further two bids, both surpassed as soon as they'd been made, before finally, the bidding slowed. The auctioneer prompted several of the people who had been outbid, including Andy, all of whom declined.

"Sold." The gavel came down with a solid wooden *clack*, and one of Derek Arnold's team went over to deal with the woman who had placed the winning bid. Dan watched her covetously.

"Still under market value," he muttered through his teeth.

"Yeah, well." Andy folded his arms. "Let's wait and see if the sale goes through. You wanna stay for more?"

Dan shook his head. "I'm done."

***

It took exactly eighteen hours for Andy to be proved right. Typically, Dan had been so busy, getting Shu ready for school and making sure Adele and Robbie would manage without him for a couple of hours, that he'd forgotten to check Derek Arnold's listings. Or not forgotten, as such, but it wasn't nagging at him like it had been the previous evening. He was still gutted he'd missed out. Otherwise, he'd had a great week at home on paternity leave, although he was shattered. Adele was healing, Robbie had settled well, and Shu was enjoying looking after her mummy and baby brother so much it was a mission getting her to leave them and go to school.

Having finally prised Shu away from her duties, Dan duly delivered her to her classroom and drove over to Andy and Shaunna's place for a quick business meeting. He rang the doorbell and waited. And waited. He rang it again. The door opened.

"Why?" Andy asked, already walking away.

Dan didn't answer because Andy already knew why. Everyone else rang the bell and walked straight in, but Dan recalled all too well what happened the last time he'd done that. Once bitten…

"Did you see?" Andy shouted from the kitchen, where he was filling the kettle. He came back through. "You do want a cup of tea, I'm guessing?"

Dan shrugged. "If you like. See what?" One look at his brother's smug grinning face told him everything he needed to know, but Andy unlocked his tablet and brought up the Sharston house relisting anyway. Dan grunted. "I still can't see how they're making money out it, if the buyers are backing out."

Andy wandered back to the kitchen. "Didn't you read the paperwork?"

"Of course I did!" In reality, he'd skimmed through it closely enough to confirm he was in the clear, and to get away with winging it, providing he was talking to someone who knew nothing about property auctions.

"Do the maths, then. Ten percent deposit…"

Dan stood in the doorway, watching Andy prepare two mugs. "You never used to drink this much tea."

"I was thinking the same before. Must be part and parcel of being a house-husband. Get the milk for me, bro?"

Dan collected the milk from the fridge and handed it over. "Yeah, well, it won't be for much longer," he consoled.

"What d'you mean?" Andy asked, adding milk to the mugs.

"Once they're sleeping through, you'll get back to normal."

Andy shoved the milk back at Dan. "*This* is normal."

"You know what I mean," Dan said, aware his brother was getting annoyed, although he couldn't work out why. He tried to change the subject. "So Derek Arnold will pull the same stunt again, will he?"

"Never mind that. What's the problem?"

Dan opened his mouth—if he'd got as far as saying something, it would only have been 'huh?'—but Andy elaborated of his own accord.

"You think I'm not pulling my weight?" Andy picked up his tea, leaving Dan to collect his own. "Come on. I'll show you how many jobs we've got on the go." He was gone before Dan had a chance to respond.

They had to be talking at cross purposes. It was the only explanation for Andy's defensive behaviour, because Dan wasn't having a go. Given Robbie was almost a week old, and today was the first day since the birth that Dan was doing anything business related—ignoring for the time being his attempt to send Andy to the Czech Republic—Andy was more than pulling his weight.

Dan's phone vibrated in his pocket; he sighed and took it out, dismissing the call without looking. "All right, already." He picked up his tea and went through to join his scowling brother. "I wasn't accusing you of slacking."

"No?"

"No. Where did you get that from?"

"What did you say?"

"I've no idea."

"About getting back to normal."

"Yeah. I was talking about once you've got childcare organised."

"What childcare? I'm doing the childcare." Andy jabbed at his own chest to emphasise. "Aside from which, you didn't get a childminder for Shu until she was a year old."

"That was different," Dan argued. Being born so early meant his daughter was effectively three months younger than her actual age from a developmental point of view, which didn't matter so much now she was almost four. The other factor was Adele's rejection of every babysitter who came to meet them… before Alice. They hadn't planned on employing a childminder at all, but then Campion's burned to the ground leaving Alice without a job, and Adele was itching to return to work, so it kind of arranged itself.

"You're gonna stay at home until they start school?" Dan asked rhetorically.

"Yeah," Andy snapped. "As a matter of fact, I am." He pushed his tablet, and it spun across the table. Dan caught it as it went over the edge. He pushed it back.

"Like I said, I wasn't accusing you of slacking. I thought you were complaining about being at home with the girls."

Andy's nostrils flared.

"As long as you're happy…"

"What do you think?" Andy took his tablet back and turned off the screen. "So you were actually trying to give me a time-out?"

Dan laughed. "Nah. I was trying to avoid an arse-kicking for buying Angie Sharston's place."

"I'd still've found out, you moron. Or were you planning on never inviting me over again?"

"I thought I'd leave it to Adele to tell Shaunna."

"Sneaky, that, bro."

"Yeah, a bit." Now Andy was calmer, Dan decided it was safe to sit and start their business meeting for real, although he was having a problem shaking his obsession with the Sharston house. "You didn't answer my question, by the way."

"Which one?"

"Derek Arnold."

"Ah, yeah. The houses go back on the auction listing but usually end up selling at a reduced price before they get that far. And in case you're thinking of putting in another offer, don't bother. They'll already have a buyer lined up for it."

Dan wanted to argue the case for gazumping, especially with people as greedy as Derek Arnold, Angela Sharston and co. Everyone had their price. "There must be a way around it," he said.

"Yeah. Get the house off the seller before it goes to auction. Let it go, bro."

"OK." He'd try. "How d'you know all this? I know you said you did a bit of digging, but this is the sort of stuff Gray and Rob are trained to do. No offence, but you're just a civil engineer."

"Yeah, cheers for that."

"You know what I mean."

"I do, but you're overlooking that this civil engineer spent twenty years playing footsie with the ringleader and then inherited her ill-gotten gains."

"Jesus." It had just dawned on Dan how dangerous Andy's situation was. "Aren't you worried they'll kill you?"

Andy shrugged. "It's only dangerous if I think about it."

"That's what you say about skydiving."

"Same thing. I could've handed the money over, like I could choose not to jump, but where's the fun in that?"

Dan chose to stay quiet and drank his tea, trying to push aside his sudden overwhelming fear for his brother's safety. He and Andy were so similar, he sometimes forgot the one way in which they were starkly different. Admittedly, there were times when Dan had put himself in harm's way, which was why he'd learnt to control his anger. However, losing his temper and picking a fight with someone bigger and uglier than him was not the same as Andy's love of danger. Dan tried to avoid life-and-death situations; Andy went looking for them.

"Seriously, bro," Andy said, unlocking his tablet. "Stop worrying. Whether I'm dead or alive, they can't get at the money. Right, where are we?" He scanned the screen. "The cylinder blocks are on their way to Len's mate."

"Great," Dan responded.

"And the ESDAL's already gone through for Comco."

"Good to know."

"Also, we've taken delivery of the four hundred unicycles for the Moscow State Circus."

"OK."

"Yeah, I had to park them at Mum's for now. All around the fountain. I tell you what, considering they've only got one wheel, they take up a surp—"

"Hold up. The what? Unicycles?"

Andy laughed. "Do you want to leave this for another time?"

Dan shook his head, both in answer to the question and in dismay at himself for being so distracted. "I'm knackered," he admitted. "How do you do it?"

"Same way you work 365 days a year. Business is your thing. Being a dad's mine."

"Yet you're balancing both."

"You've been balancing both for four years, and it'll get easier once Robbie's a bit older. You're being too hard on yourself, as usual."

Disgruntled, Dan sat back and folded his arms. It didn't sit well with him that he was finding it impossible to keep up with the work and deal with his kids while Andy was sailing along, all chilled out and efficient. "Mike's managing."

"Mike's only got himself and Bethan to worry about. You've got Shu to get to school, Robbie to take care of… Why don't you see if Mum'll have Robbie for a couple of hours a day?"

"She's got Bethan. It'll be too much for her."

"Since when?"

"It's taking advantage."

"OK. What about Alice?"

"She's up to her eyes in the trust."

Andy sighed loudly. "You're a stubborn bugger when the mood takes."

For all that Andy was starting to piss Dan off, hearing their mum's words come out of his mouth made them both laugh.

"Don't forget," Andy added, "you're also looking after Adele and picking up her part of the parenting."

Dan conceded. "Fair comment. Right, so forget about my brother being a potential target for a fraud ring with friends in high places."

"Yep."

"Stop worrying about the business."

"Everything's in hand," Andy confirmed.

Dan nodded. "And what do I do about this house?"

"Nothing. Move on. There're plenty of other houses. I'll send you some links later." Dan opened his mouth to argue, but Andy raised his hand. "Forget about it."

Easy for him to say.

16: One Small Step
Friday, 5th–Saturday, 6th October

It was nearing eleven o'clock before Mike turned into the road to the salon, and there was, at most, half a parking space between the line of cars outside. He drove up and back down, hoping someone would have moved by the time he returned, and when that failed, he went around the block. He even considered parking at Andy and Shaunna's place, seeing as it was within walking distance, but short of making fifteen trips with his little trolley, he had no means of getting tiles, paint and the rest of his gear from the van to the shop.

By the end of his second circuit of the block, he was losing patience and decided to double park, unload, and then move the van to wherever he could. He pulled up alongside a brand new, white BMW convertible, switched on his hazard lights and waited for the stream of passing traffic to pause long enough to get out.

"This is bloody ridiculous," he muttered, throwing the door open in the next short gap between cars and quickly slamming it on his way to the back of the van.

"Excuse me, mate. You can't leave that there," someone shouted from across the street.

Mike was all set to reply with *where the fuck do you suggest I leave it?* But then he spotted the dark-blue uniform and quickly shut his mouth.

"Oh, you're the guy from the pizza restaurant," the police officer said. "The Good Samaritan?"

"Yeah," Mike confirmed hazily. "The manager's my niece. What else could I do?"

"You're Dan Jeffries' brother?"

"Afraid so."

"I thought you looked familiar. Not that I know Dan well. He's mates with our DI. The twins are older than you, are they?"

"Twins?"

"Dan and your other brother?"

"Ah." Mike chuckled, chuffed that someone thought he looked younger, when he had three years on Andy, and four on Dan. "No, I'm the eldest, and they're not actually twins."

"Blimey. They don't half look alike."

"I've heard it said."

The police officer hummed to himself and peered inside the back of Mike's van. "This is what you do for a living, is it?"

"Painting and decorating, yeah. I'm working on the salon."

The officer looked up and down the street and then back at Mike. "How long d'you reckon it'll take you to unload?"

"Five minutes, tops. I'll move it now, if you'd prefer."

"No, you're all right. One good turn, and all that." A bigger van turned into the road, revving as it approached. Mike glanced up in time to see the driver hit the horn and then quickly lift his hand when he noticed the police officer, resulting in a short *bip*. The officer shook his head and waved the other driver past. "Thinks he's driving an artic."

Mike laughed politely and set off for the salon with the first load of paint. It was strange being all pally with the police, not that he'd ever been on the wrong side of the law, but being a bit of a Jack the Lad, he'd had a few close scrapes and had always seen the boys in blue as the enemy. Maybe it was his age, because he was finally starting to appreciate how tough their job was. The fact that at least some of them remained decent human beings said a lot about their strength of character, although maybe it would be best to reserve judgement until after Sunday's match against the Anchors.

As promised, Hayley and Shaunna had moved the standard hairdryers out of the way and cordoned off the left side of the salon with yellow hazard tape. Hayley had offered to shut for a few days, but Mike had no problem working around them. The tiling would have to wait until next Wednesday evening so that the adhesive had Thursday—when the salon was closed—to fully go off. He planned to paint the left, front and back walls today, do the right wall—where the mirrors and shelves were—after the match on Sunday, and then come back first thing on Monday to get the mirrors up before they opened. Tuesday…he and Bethan were going to meet Jackie.

A cold sweat came over him at the thought, and he reminded himself again. She'd agreed not to take Bethan to see Rachel without his express permission—they'd be selling skis in hell before he gave it—and in any case, he'd be there, too. But he didn't need to worry about that until after the weekend.

With the paint stashed in the corner, Mike returned to the van to get a second load. A woman had followed him out of the salon and unlocked the BMW.

"Are you leaving?" Mike asked. She nodded and climbed into her car. Mike got in the van and moved it forward so she had room to pull out of the space, but instead, she got out of her car again.

"Sorry. I've left something behind." She smiled apologetically and dashed back to the salon.

Mike drummed on the steering wheel and peered along the street. The police officer was strolling on the other side and paying no attention to him. Mike glanced in his wing mirror. "Ah, crap." His spirit level was on the road behind him. He got out and went to retrieve it. As he straightened up, something hit his backside with force, knocking him into the tail-light array. He doubled over, stunned to silence by immediate and debilitating pain.

"Oh my god!" someone said, but he barely heard them over the whooshing in his ears and the agony of where he'd collided with the lights. If it didn't hurt so much, he'd have been laughing at the fact that he couldn't even say 'you got me in the balls!'

"Come over here," the same voice said—the BMW's owner. He felt a tug on his arm and allowed her to steer him onto the pavement. "I'm so sorry. I didn't see you."

Mike shook his head mutely, all but biting through his lip in an attempt to counter the pain and not freak out at the possibility he'd crushed his remaining testicle. He probably hadn't. He'd been hit in the balls a few times in his life, but the last time… The mere thought of going through that again was enough to make him vomit, which was exactly what he did next.

"Mike? Leah?" Shaunna arrived in front of him. "Oh, no. What's happened?"

"I was reversing the car, and…" The woman sounded so upset, and Mike would have liked to reassure her, but he couldn't speak.

"Mike, come inside. I'll get you a chair," Shaunna commanded. Mike shook his head and gave her a pleading look. No way could he sit.

"I'm fine," he muttered. "Give me a minute."

"OK." Shaunna stayed where she was, watching him and looking worried.

"I'll stay with him," the other woman offered.

"Oh, err…" Shaunna smiled, trying to cover her awkwardness.

"It's all right," Mike said, hoping both of them would leave him be, but they must have taken it as his agreement to what they'd just said because Shaunna went back inside and the woman stayed.

"Can I get you a drink or anything?" she asked.

"No, thanks. It'll pass soon. It really bloody hurts."

"Yeah, I know," she said.

Mike held in his snort of disbelief. She couldn't possibly know how much it hurt getting hit in the balls.

"I don't understand how it happened. I honestly didn't see you."

"I was bending down."

"Ah." She looked away.

Shaunna came back out with a bucket of water and threw it over the pavement, washing Mike's vomit down the nearest drain. She disappeared again, returned a moment later with a second bucket, repeated the process, and left.

"Everything all right?" a male voice asked from behind.

Mike turned his head only and raised an eyebrow.

The police officer drew up next to him and assessed the situation, flinching when he spotted Mike's protective stance. "I was about to tell you there's a parking space, but I can see you're incapacitated."

"Would you like me to move your van for you?" the woman offered.

"Are you insured, madam?" the police officer asked.

"Yes. Fully comp for any vehicle."

Mike nodded his consent. "The keys are still in the ignition."

The woman gave him yet another apologetic smile and went over to his van, picking up the spirit level that had put him in this predicament to begin with. She stuck it in the back before reversing the van into the space behind her car. A voice came through the police officer's radio, and he moved away to answer. The woman returned to Mike's side.

"Feeling any better?"

"Yeah," he said, and it was, but it was still throbbing. He chanced straightening up and leaned against the wall next to the salon door, slowly exhaling in relief. The pain had finally reached a tolerable level.

The police officer came back their way, giving a swift nod in acknowledgement as he strode past and away down the street.

"Do you need to get that injury checked out?" the woman asked.

"Nah, I don't think so. It's just…I lost one testicle already, so I'm a bit over-cautious about keeping the other one safe. You know what I mean?" He didn't know why he'd told her that. Other than the doctors who treated him, he'd only ever told his brothers and Aitch.

The woman handed him his van keys. "How did you lose the other one, if you don't mind my asking?"

"An injury that got infected."

"Ohhh, that must've been awful."

"Yeah, it was. I thought it was bruising, and it'd go down, but it didn't. I'll spare you the gory details." He was sparing himself, too. If the injury had been bad, the surgery that followed was a form of torture, or not the surgery itself. That was fairly quick, and the pain relief was very effective, but the bruising from where the hammer had hit him wasn't isolated to his testicle, and the whole of his groin was swollen and discoloured for weeks.

The salon door opened, and Hayley peered out. "Cup of tea, sweedie?"

"I'd love one," Mike said.

"Leah?"

"Well, I was just…" She looked at Mike. "Yes, I'll have one, too, thanks, Hayley."

"Be right back." Hayley returned inside.

Mike studied the woman for a moment, trying to figure out if he'd sent out some kind of signal that he wanted her to stay, which, bizarrely, he did.

She leaned against the wall, next to him. "I was here when you came in last week," she said.

"Were you?"

"We passed in the doorway."

"Oh, right. I don't recall, sorry."

"You looked a bit dazed, actually."

"I'd just come from a meeting with my lawyer."

"That would explain it."

Mike laughed ruefully, but he didn't want to talk about Jackie and the custody case. "I'm Mike, by the way."

"Leah. Good to meet you."

"And you, mostly." She gave him a pained frown, and he grinned. "I'm kidding, don't worry about it." He indicated to her car. "Nice motor."

"Thanks. I bought it with my divorce settlement."

"Yeah. Same here. It looks like you might've come out of it a bit better than I did."

"Financially, yes. We reached an agreement that my ex got the children and I got the proceeds from the house sale, which is a bit of an over-simplification, but it's a long story. Seeing as there's only me, I bought a one-bedroom flat and the car."

"Do your kids not come and stay with you?"

"Unfortunately, no." Leah lowered her eyes, and Mike felt bad for hitting a raw nerve, although, at the same time, he was thinking that if she hadn't got custody of her children, then maybe the courts weren't as sexist as he feared. But there was always someone who was going to lose out.

"Hey, I'm sorry," he said.

She carefully wiped a tear away and cleared her throat. "Do you have children?"

"A daughter, Bethan. She's six months old. Not from my marriage."

"What a lovely name."

"Yeah, thanks. She's beautiful, and she's all I've got."

"You're not with her mum anymore?"

"No." Mike said the word quickly and clamped his teeth together, wondering if he'd done more than take a hit between the legs. He was tempted to tell Leah all about Rachel, even though he'd only just met her. She seemed friendly and open, the sort of woman he might, if things were different, have considered dating, although she was probably out of his league.

Hayley returned with two cups of tea. "If you two want to go sid in the stockroom, you're welcome to do so."

"Thanks." Mike didn't really want to take her up on her offer.

"Maybe once Mike's up to moving," Leah suggested.

Hayley shrugged. "Whadever suits you, sweedie." She went back inside.

For a while, they stood in silence, occasionally attempting sips of their too-hot tea. Mike sensed Leah wanted to say something but looked like she wasn't sure if she should. A crease formed between her eyebrows, and he tried to figure out how old she was. Younger than him, mid-thirties, maybe. It was hard to tell with her make-up and freshly styled hair.

Eventually, she must've decided to chance it, and said, "Hayley terrifies you, doesn't she?"

He laughed. "Is it that obvious?"

Leah leaned closer and nudged him playfully with her elbow. "I don't blame you. I wouldn't want to cross her, that's for sure."

"She's good to Shaunna, though. She's my sister-in-law."

"Ah. So you're Rosie and Sorsha's uncle."

"Yep."

"She brought them into the salon a few weeks ago. They're gorgeous." Leah rolled her eyes. "Of course, now the resemblance is obvious. Andy, is it?"

"My brother? Yeah."

"Right. He's a nice guy, isn't he?" The way she said it was so animated, she seemed surprised by her own words.

"Yeah, he is."

Leah laughed at Mike's matter-of-fact confirmation. "Shaunna's been my stylist since…well, she was still living with her ex, and one of their friends had cancer?"

"That's right."

"She said Andy nursed their friend until she passed away."

"He did, yeah."

"Now he stays at home with his daughters."

"Uh-huh." Mike was amused by Leah's retelling of his brother's recent endeavours. He'd judged Andy very poorly in the past, which he regretted. He'd been way out of line, and Andy was, as Leah put it, a nice guy. One of the best. What he'd done for Jess, Mike couldn't have done it. He hadn't been the only one to think it was odd that his irresponsible younger brother, who'd spent most of his adult life spending money he didn't have on crazy adventures, had taken on looking after a dying woman. But Mike got it now. Andy hadn't really changed. He just did what he did, with no regard for whether other people thought it was the right thing to do. If he believed it was, then he followed his instinct, and his heart. Maybe that was the secret.

"Would you like to have a drink with me sometime?" Mike asked before caution got the better of him.

"I'd love to." Leah gave him a wide, genuine smile. "When do you have in mind?"

"I'll need to check with my mum, see when she's free to look after Bethan."

"OK, sure."

"I've got a couple of days off next week. Is a weekday evening OK with you? I don't like to spend all day at work and then go out and leave Bethan with her nana again."

"I can appreciate that." Leah considered a moment. "What about if I came over to your place?"

Mike's stomach flipped. It would be the first time he'd been alone with a woman since Rachel—well, he'd been alone with Shaunna and Charlie, but they were different. He should do it, if only to prove he could.

Leah backtracked. "Oh, look, if that's too forward of me…"

"No, it's not that. It's…" Mike paused, trying to make the choice in his head—*do I, don't I, do I, don't I*… He decided to go for broke. "Has Shaunna ever talked about the murder case?"

"Which one?"

"There's been a few, hasn't there?" Mike remarked wryly. "The one with the Corvette?"

"I think so. The brakes were sabotaged, I recall."

"Yeah. The woman who did it went to prison."

Leah nodded. "That's right."

"She's Bethan's mum."

"The woman who died?" Leah asked. Mike shook his head. "Oh…I… Gosh, I don't know what to say."

"It's all right, but she's the reason I only have one testicle."

"That's awful. You poor thing. All right, look. Forget what I said. Let's find a quiet pub near where you live, and if you need to run off on me…" She rolled her eyes again, which made Mike grin. She grinned back at him and then said sincerely, "Joking aside, I'll understand. What do you think?"

Mike thought about her proposal and shook his head. "No. Let's do what you said. Come over to my place. It's only a studio apartment, nothing special, and my mum's house is close by, if, you know, I need to run off on you."

Leah laughed. "Sounds great. Now, are you sure?"

"Yeah, I am."

"Do you still want to make it a weekday evening?"

"We can do tomorrow, if you like."

"If that's not too soon for you."

"Not at all." Mike smiled and nodded, confident he was telling the truth. "I'm looking forward to it."

*****

Bethan was in bed, the house was tidy. Mike lit a scented candle he'd found in the bag of cables that came with Charlie's computer and set it down in the middle of the side table, decided it wasn't in the middle, shuffled it left a bit, right a bit… He stopped faffing and took a step back to inspect his domain, wondering if it looked too much like a bachelor pad now he'd cleared everything away, including the TV remote, in his quest not to come across as a slob.

"Ouch." With a click, his thumb relocated, and he shoved his hands in his pockets. He was nervous, understandably, but nowhere near as bad as he'd thought he'd be. In fact, even with the Jackie Perry stuff, he felt better than he had in a long time. He had work coming in, which meant he also had money coming in, he was playing footy again, and while his goal in Tuesday's match might not have contributed much to their victory, it had felt good to be part of the winning side for once. Without that little boost in confidence, he probably wouldn't have got up the nerve to ask Leah on a date, and he was eager to make a good impression.

They'd exchanged phone numbers and agreed a time: seven-thirty, and it was twenty past now. With one last check that he'd moved the wine and beer to the fridge, Mike loaded the playlist he'd put together, set it playing at a low volume, and perched on the arm of the sofa to watch for Leah's arrival. He'd directed her to the side gate so she didn't disturb his mum and Len, or that was part of his reasoning. The other part was that he thought the summerhouse would be a bit of a disappointment if she saw inside the main house first. Even a standard three-bedroom semi-detached would look crap next to the mini-mansion with its twin staircases, crystal and marble everywhere, its own gym and indoor pool.

And, of course, he'd rather not have his mother, or his brothers, knowing his every move, although seeing as Shaunna was Leah's hairdresser, chances were it would get back to Andy soon enough. Mike had expected twenty questions yesterday, when he'd finally got over his minor injury and started work on the salon. But Shaunna hadn't said anything about it, and there'd been plenty of opportunities, given how many cups of tea she'd brought him during the course of the day.

The sudden illumination of the lawn brought Mike's attention back to the arrival of his guest. He pulled himself to his feet, straightened his shirt and ran his hand over his hair before he opened the door. Leah spotted him and smiled.

"Hi," she called, walking towards him. "This place is incredible."

"You found it OK, then?" Mike said. She arrived and gave him a friendly kiss on the cheek. He caught a whiff of her subtle perfume. It suited her.

"I called a taxi and gave the driver the postcode. Can't go wrong with satnav."

"True enough," Mike agreed, although he'd never used satnav himself. He beckoned Leah in and closed the door. "So this is my humble abode…"

Leah glanced around her and nodded. "It's fab."

"It used to be the summerhouse, but after what happened, my mum and her husband converted this so we had somewhere safe to live. It's comfy, but we need more space, really. I'm hoping to buy my own place in the New Year."

"Ah, yes. We were the same. We used to have a tiny flat over in Manchester."

"Yeah?" Mike walked over to the kitchen, still listening as he took out the wine and beer and raised both to silently ask what Leah wanted to drink.

"Oh, beer would be great," she said and then continued with her story. "It was in a very desirable area, once the regeneration started, and we loved it, but when we decided we wanted children, we moved out of the city."

"Is that where you're from? Manchester?"

"Lincoln originally, but I went to uni in Manchester, and I love the place, you know? It's so vibrant, thriving nightlife, not that we got to enjoy it much once we had Ginny and Benjamin."

Mike handed Leah an open bottle of beer and offered her a glass. She waved it away, and they both moved over to the sofa, sitting close, but not too close. "How old are your two?" he asked.

"Ginny's seven and Benj is almost four."

"Quite young, then."

"Yes, they are." Leah focused on the beer bottle balanced on her knee. "I miss them."

"You said your ex got custody?"

"Mm…not quite." That same frown Mike had noticed yesterday formed between Leah's eyebrows. "It's difficult to explain without telling you everything, but you've been honest with me."

Mike sensed her reluctance to share, and he had been very open with her. Maybe she felt she needed to level the playing field. "You don't have to tell me if you don't want to."

Leah took a breath, held it, and let it go again, turning slightly so she was facing him. "I'm transgender."

"Right…" Mike scratched his ear, not sure what that meant, or he knew what it meant, but not in relation to Leah, and it threw him. "So you're a man?"

"I'm a trans woman."

"Ah, gotcha. I thought you meant you were a man inside a woman's body." Mike shook his head. "That sounds awful. Sorry. All I was trying to say is…" He was just digging himself in deeper. "Sorry."

Leah laughed and reached across, lightly squeezing his hand. "Don't worry about it." Her smile was beautiful and infectious, and Mike found himself smiling back. Leah withdrew her hand again. "OK, from the top, I was born male, brought up as a little boy, tried very hard to be a little boy, then a big boy, then a man, until one day, I couldn't pretend anymore."

"Is it like being in the wrong body?"

"Sort of. It's more like…OK. Imagine getting up tomorrow and you're still you. You feel exactly the same as you always did, but everyone is suddenly treating you like you're a woman. Holding doors open for you, assuming you need help with anything that requires physical strength, insulting your driving—"

Mike's frown stopped Leah going any further.

"You getting the vibe?" she asked.

"That's got to be hell."

"Well, I was stereotyping a bit, and it's more about a feeling that what's inside and what's outside don't match up. But I could deal with that, mostly, and Tim, my ex, was very supportive."

"Oh." Mike had assumed her ex was female. "So you were always attracted to men?"

"Yes, although that's not true of every trans person. Some people are straight before and after they transition."

"I sort of get it."

"You do?" Leah asked. She didn't look like she believed him, which was as well.

"No," he admitted. "Way over my head."

She laughed. "At least you're honest. I was going to say to you yesterday, when you told me you'd lost a testicle, it's a pity we didn't meet a couple of years back, you could've had one of mine."

"It'd be awesome if they could do that," Mike said thoughtfully, for a moment completely missing that Leah was joking. He blushed. "Sorry."

"It's OK. It's probably wrong… No, it *is* wrong of me to have inferred from meeting your brother a few times that you'd be like him, although you are a lot alike."

"To look at?"

"Yes, but more the way you are. Laid back, non-judgemental."

Mike weighed it up. He'd never really thought of himself as being like Andy before, although he supposed there was some truth in it. He took people as he found them, and if Leah was talking about herself, then to his mind, she was a woman. He wouldn't have known she'd once lived as a man without her telling him.

"Do you tell everyone?" he asked.

"Only those I'm close to, or hoping to get close to. I'm lucky, really. I pass, with a lot of help from Shaunna and my beautician. Trans women risk their lives every time they leave their homes—they're not even safe there. But I felt safe telling you. It's like I already know you. Is that weird?" Before he could figure out how to answer, Leah added, "No pressure, Mike, but if we were ever considering going beyond sharing a beer…"

"To be honest, I don't know if I'm ready for anything like that yet. Rachel did a number on me. Not just my balls."

"Emotionally, you mean."

"Yep, and it's getting easier, but there are only three women who don't scare the shit out of me. Until yesterday, there were only two: Shaunna and Charlie, who works for my stepdad. Even my mum, and my other sister-in-law, because they've got that streak of…I don't know what. Vindictiveness, I guess. See, if a bloke's giving you grief, you can just smack him, but a woman?" Mike shrugged. "Charlie said she'd teach me self-defence so I could defend myself without hurting the other person, but it's more than that. I could've walked away from Rachel, packed up and left, even though it was my flat. I could've told the police, but I didn't. I just took it."

"But that's not your weakness, Mike," Leah said. "That's Rachel's manipulation."

"Yeah, I know, and that's what I'm scared of. I didn't see it happening, not even at the end. She left us, not the other way round. And it was only once she'd gone I realised what was going on."

Mike stopped talking and swigged his beer. It was the first time he'd admitted to anyone that he'd been brainwashed by Rachel's abuse to the extent that it hadn't occurred to him to leave. So, along with his fear and powerlessness, he also felt gullible, stupid. Andy hadn't fallen for it, although Rachel's mum had, and she was still being sucked in by it. At least that was one thing they had in common.

"I'm a miserable bastard," Mike said, laughing to make light.

"Not really," Leah placated. "You're good company."

"Hm, I'm not, but I'll try harder. Want another beer?"

"Please."

Mike took the empty bottles and exchanged them for full ones, making a vow to himself not to bring Rachel up for the rest of the evening, which turned out to be much easier than he'd imagined. Leah talked about her kids and her ex, who seemed a decent guy. He'd supported her every step of the way, but their relationship began to break down not long after Leah started her hormone treatment.

"It does odd things to your emotions. Made me cry a lot, and my brain didn't seem to work quite the same way. The kids made it harder. They just sort of accepted it. To them, I was the same person as before, but I wasn't stable, and we'd opted to pay for the treatment privately, which was why we sold the house. We talked about it. I needed Tim to take care of Ginny and Benj for us while I transitioned. It was all too much to cope with. After the surgery, we decided to go our separate ways, and I go to see them every other weekend. I still love him, and he still loves me, but he's a gay man, and I'm a straight woman. I've always been a straight woman, which Tim sees now. That's really what finished us. He'd never accepted who I was until the surgery, and he felt betrayed, like I'd lied to him, though I never did."

Mike thought it was tragic, but he could also sympathise with Leah's ex. "Sounds like it's all pretty amicable, then?" he asked as he got up to collect another two beers.

"Yes, very much so. We're going away together at Christmas, as a family. I need to rebuild my relationship with the kids."

As Mike came back across the room, a knock at the door made him jump and slosh beer out of the tops of the open bottles. He peered through the window. "Oh." He opened the door, smiling. "Alright, Charlie? I didn't know you were working today."

"Don't even ask." She shook her head in despair. "You know Len and his big mouth. Anyway, I'm not stopping. I need to catch the first train in the morning. I've been trying to get hold of Dan, but he's not answering his phone. Can you tell him I'll be there for the second half? Might even make it for the first half yet, but I don't want to get his hopes up." She sniffed and peered past Mike. "Oh! Sorry. Didn't know you had company." She nodded at Leah. "Alright?"

"Hi," Leah replied.

"Leah, this is Charlie, who I was telling you about. Charlie, this is Leah..." Mike trailed off, not sure what to call her. His date?

Charlie grinned. "Yeah, no need to explain. Nice candle, by the way."

"Ah, yeah. It was in the bag with the cables. I'll replace it sometime."

"Don't worry about it. Looks like you got more use out of it than I would've done. I'll leave you to it. Nice to meet you, Leah."

"You, too."

Charlie gave Mike another big cheesy grin, turned and jogged away. Mike watched her until she was back inside the main house and then shut the door. "Sorry about that." He returned to the sofa and handed over Leah's beer.

"Thanks. So that's Charlie."

"Yeah. That's Charlie. When she's not running my stepdad's business for him, she's a professional football coach."

"Cool. She seems nice."

"She is." Sometimes, Mike thought that was the only reason she talked to him, because she was too nice to tell him to push off. After all, it was Andy she was friends with, really.

"I need to make a move soon," Leah said. "I've enjoyed your company this evening."

"With all my moaning?"

"Oh, you didn't moan…much." She gave him a wink. "I gave it back, didn't I? And anyway, if you can't moan at friends, who can you moan at?" Leah raised her bottle in a toast.

"True enough. Cheers." Mike tapped his bottle against hers. "I've enjoyed this evening, too."

Leah kept glancing past him, to where he'd been standing with Charlie a few minutes ago, as if she expected her to reappear, but Charlie would be on her way home by now.

It wasn't long after that Leah called a taxi, and Mike was glad to be let off the hook in one respect. Whilst he thought she was attractive, and she seemed to think the same about him, the chemistry was definitely missing. There was no magic spark, perhaps for no other reason than the crap they were both carrying from their previous relationships. But if her sudden departure was because she thought something was going on between him and Charlie, she was mistaken.

17: Anchors Away
Sunday, 7th October

It wasn't especially loud banging, or particularly high-pitched squeaking, but it was too early on a Sunday morning for this much noise, and it had been going on long enough to get on Shaunna's nerves. She peered across the table at Barbara, who conjured a brief smile in response. They were both feeling it.

"I should've just changed the tap washer myself," Barbara said.

Rosie shoved Shaunna's nipple out of her mouth and started griping. Shaunna adjusted position and poked it back in again. "Is it difficult?" she asked.

"Changing a washer?" Barbara shook her head, her eyes never leaving Sorsha in her arms, so that she was essentially telling her granddaughter, not Shaunna. "I've done it a few times—I had to, didn't I? Yes, I did." She smiled at Sorsha and got a happy gurgle in response.

"Didn't the lads help out?" Shaunna asked.

"Oh, they were next to useless, but they were only kids. Their dad wasn't so bad, but their stepdad..." She shook her head again, this time in disdain. For a moment, her gaze became distant. She gave a rueful chuckle. "Does Andrew ever talk about him?"

"Dad the Second?" Shaunna queried innocently.

"Surely they're not still calling him that. Are they?"

"Yep, although they don't talk about him often—usually only if they're reliving naughtiness from primary school."

"Hm. It's funny. Whenever the school secretary phoned, if I answered she'd call me 'Mrs. Thurston', yet she'd call Jerry 'Mr. Jeffries'. I never understood her logic, and it drove Jerry up the wall. We even asked the lads if they'd consider changing their surname to Thurston to make it less confusing all round."

"They didn't like that idea, I'm guessing."

"Ha, you could say that. We didn't bring it up again, and by the time I met Carl, they'd all left home."

"Dad the Third," Shaunna said with a grin.

"They don't call Leonard 'Dad the...'" At Shaunna's nodded confirmation, Barbara trailed off and started to laugh. "Good Lord. Mind you, he's very fond of them—of you all." She became thoughtful again. "I might have to tell him that. He'll be tickled pink. And it didn't come from me this time."

Rosie had fallen asleep, and Shaunna put her in her chair so she could take Sorsha from Barbara. She was glad, in a way, that they'd got up early and come over to Barbara and Len's place. She loved Barbara to pieces, and it also gave Shaunna a rare chance to spend time with her daughters. That said, she couldn't say she was happy with the reason for their early morning visit. Since she'd told Andy about social services coming out to see Mike, he'd been worrying about the summerhouse, and he'd decided to give it a quick check over before the Lions v Anchors match.

"What are you thinking about?" Barbara asked.

"Mike and this social services nonsense."

"It's that flaming lawyer's doing, isn't it?"

"Yeah, I think it is. Jackie Perry seems lovely, actually."

"I imagine you're right." Barbara got up and moved to walk around Shaunna to the kettle, pausing to peer down on her two granddaughters, her hand resting on Shaunna's shoulder. "I wish Michael would find someone like you. I don't know how you did it, but Andrew's a different man since he's been with you. It's such a relief to know where he is and that he's safe."

Shaunna blushed and kept her head down, listening to the sound of the kettle filling against the backdrop of bangs and squeaks. Their conversation had been a useful distraction from the racket, but now she was aware of it again, it was quickly becoming as annoying as it had been before.

"How long does it take?" Barbara asked rhetorically, peering up in the general direction of the noise. "I've got an idea…" She left the kitchen; a moment later, she called upstairs, "Want a cuppa?"

The banging stopped immediately. Barbara returned to the kitchen and gave Shaunna a wink. "I'll pop up and finish the job in a bit."

Shaunna laughed, ever impressed by her mother-in-law's cunning. "I'd have thought Len would've known at least a dozen plumbers who owe him."

"No doubt," Barbara agreed. "But he's got Felix on the job." At the sound of nearing footsteps, she lowered her voice and added, "He's having a hell of a time."

Shaunna shrugged in query, but there was no chance to explain, as Len and Pez—Felix—came into the kitchen. Pez was carrying a metal toolbox and looked around for somewhere to put it down.

"I'll take that," Len offered. Pez handed it over, and Len left the kitchen again.

"How are you, Pez?" Shaunna asked. "I haven't seen you for a while."

"I'm good, thanks." He attempted a smile and fidgeted. "Are you OK?"

"Yeah, I am, thank you for asking." Shaunna had almost asked why he'd not been at football this past week but decided not to, in case it was because of whatever Barbara had mentioned. But then Pez brought it up anyway.

"I've missed coming to footy."

"We've missed you, too," Shaunna said meaningfully. "You're coming today, aren't you?"

Pez looked pained. "I…don't know if that's a good idea."

He was a quiet young man with little self-confidence, but he still cheered them on from the sidelines, and he was kind of family, which, Shaunna realised, was probably why he'd stayed away. "Because of Mike?"

Pez nodded.

Barbara shot a warning glance Shaunna's way, but she wasn't going to say anything that might go against Mike's case. "He knows what your mum's doing is nothing to do with you."

"It's not that. The barrister said I wasn't to talk to him."

"They probably meant about the case."

"Not just the case. With Rachel being moved to a hospital and stuff…" Pez started twitching.

"Hospital?" Shaunna met Barbara's gaze; she hadn't known, either. "What kind of hospital? Psychiatric?"

"Yeah, but not because of what she did. Sorry, I don't know anything else."

"It's OK. I could have a word with Mike, tell him not to talk to you until the case is over. Would that help?"

Pez shrugged. "I want to talk to him. I want to get to know him and Bethan better. I mean, it's great when I come here and—"

"Here you are, Felix. Tea." Barbara pushed a cup into his hand.

"Th-thanks."

Soon after, Len returned, and Pez stayed quiet, but Shaunna had got the gist. Barbara was letting him see Bethan while Mike was at work. If he found out, well, Shaunna didn't care to predict his reaction. He was still living in fear of Rachel and her family, but Pez was no threat. Nonetheless, Barbara was taking a huge risk, and it was an abuse of Mike's trust. After everything he'd been through, he'd likely never forgive her. Unfortunately, that meant Shaunna keeping it to herself until after the football, because Andy would be livid when she told him about Rachel.

Sean, on the other hand, would be smug as anything; he'd said Rachel would end up in hospital sooner or later. However much Shaunna hated Rachel—and she hated her more than any other person she'd ever met—she was mentally ill. But it was so hard to remember that when she thought about what Rachel had done to Mike—to them all. Like when Andy had gone to see her in the police cell and she'd threatened to kill herself, they'd concluded it was another of her mind games, an attempt to get Andy's sympathy. But then, Sean had pointed out that people with the kind of personality disorders Rachel displayed were more likely than the average person to attempt to take their own lives.

Shaunna didn't feel in the least bit guilty for wishing more than once that Rachel would do it. Not even now, when it sounded like she might have tried. Because if Sean was right about there being no cure, at some point in the distant future, Rachel would be released from prison, and someone else would become her unwitting victim. She might even try to track them down, and it would start all over again.

At the sound of the conservatory door opening, followed by Andy's and Mike's voices, Pez shot up from his chair.

"Thanks for the tea," he muttered, setting the three-quarters-full cup down on the table and making a run for it. "Bye."

"See you later?" Shaunna called after him. He gave her a hurried shrug, and then he was gone. A moment later, the front door slammed.

Mike and Andy stepped into the kitchen, both glancing in the direction Pez had taken. Mike moved Bethan's pushchair to one side. She was wide awake and looking around her with interest.

"Who was that?" Andy asked.

"Pez," Shaunna replied.

Andy nodded. "This his tea?" He picked up the cup and drank from it without waiting for an answer.

"Oh, Andrew." His mother sighed in exasperation. "Give it here. I'll make you a fresh cup." She reached out to take the tea from him, but he jerked his arm away. Barbara narrowed her eyes at him briefly before turning her attention on Mike. "Do you want one?"

"Have we got time?"

"Kickoff's not for another hour yet," Andy said.

"Yeah, go on then." As an afterthought, he added, "Please, Mum," and gave her a nervous smile.

She tutted and switched the kettle on again.

"Pez was just saying, Mike…" Shaunna waited for him to look her way. "Jackie's lawyer told him he's not allowed to talk to you."

"Did she? What does she think I'm gonna do?"

"God knows. But I think Pez would've liked to come to the match today."

Mike shrugged. "I'm not stopping him."

Shaunna sought out Andy's gaze, and he shook his head subtly, to tell her not to pursue it.

Out in the summerhouse, Mike had told him he was meeting up with Rachel's mum in two days' time, and while he didn't say so out loud, it was clear he was worried about it. Andy had made the offer to go with him, but Mike had rejected it, reasoning that he and Jackie were meeting on neutral territory: the shopping mall food hall, therefore, a public place. Andy was pleased about that. He'd offered because it was the right thing to do, but there was no getting away from the fact that the situation with Rachel began with him, and she'd almost succeeded in driving a wedge between him and Shaunna. If he could avoid ever having anything to do with her again—and that extended to her family—he would gladly do so.

"Guess who's coming out next Saturday," Shaunna said. She was trying to change the subject, so Andy went along with it, though it took him a few seconds to remember where Shaunna was going next Saturday.

"Who?" he asked.

"Your mum."

Andy's mouth fell open. "You're not, are you?"

"I damn well am," his mother said with notable delight.

"What's this?" Mike asked.

"You don't wanna know, bro." Andy wasn't sure it was wise to discuss it in front of Len, who was sitting at the end of the table, reading the Sunday paper. There again, they could plan a surprise party in Len's presence, and it would still be a surprise to him on the night.

Shaunna and Barbara started laughing. Mike looked more confused than ever, leaving Andy no choice but to explain. "Silhouetto?"

"What's that, then?"

"A dance troupe."

"*Naked* dance troupe," Shaunna corrected.

Mike nodded. "You like that sort of thing, do you, Mum?"

"I don't know, Michael. I've never been to see one before."

"What do you think, Len?"

He glanced up from his paper and frowned. "Yeah, it's a good idea," he said. He dampened his finger on his tongue, turned the page over and carried on reading, no clue what they were talking about.

"So what do they do?" Mike asked. "Striptease?"

Shaunna shook her head. "Dance in the dark, basically, with lights behind them. Ade's their manager."

"Ah, gotcha."

"Ade and Kris'll be there, too," she added.

"And what do you think?" Mike asked Andy.

"I don't care." It was the truth. He wouldn't even have cared if Shaunna was going for the eye candy, but he knew she was only going to support Ade. His mother, on the other hand, was definitely going for the eye candy. She'd never made any secret of enjoying an opportunity to ogle a sexy man, although some of the blokes she thought were sexy, Andy had to wonder if she wasn't getting cataracts. "I suppose we'd better make a move," he said, receiving nods of agreement from Shaunna and Mike, who both quickly finished their tea.

"You coming, Len?" Mike asked.

"Where?"

"Footy."

"Ah! Yeah. I'll come down in a bit."

Mike, Andy and Shaunna gathered their children and belongings and moved off.

"Good luck," Barbara called after them.

"Luck?" Andy said with a grin. "Three Jeffries boys in one team—who needs luck with all that talent?"

His mother waved away his boast. He wasn't really arrogant, although he was feeling confident about today's match, and part of it was simply the buzz of all three of them playing footy together again. Last Sunday's training session had been the first time in more than twenty years, and they still had it, that intuitive knowledge of each other and their strengths out on the pitch. *Team Jiffies*. Andy smiled to himself. His eldest niece was as astute as her mother. As for his youngest…it was better to forget she had a mother at all.

Outside, Andy settled the twins into their seats, catching the tail end of a hushed conversation between Shaunna and Mike.

"So you didn't set me up?" Mike asked.

"No. Like I said, I thought you meant the salon job, and I knew nothing about that, either."

"Fair enough." Mike opened his van. "See you in a bit."

"OK, hun." Shaunna climbed into the Mustang's passenger seat and shut the door.

"Everything all right?" Andy asked. He started the car and slowly drove down the gravel driveway to the gates.

"Yeah, fine." Shaunna frowned. "Mike had a date with Leah last night."

"Leah from the salon?"

"Yep."

"Does he know?"

"Hard to tell. I couldn't exactly ask without giving it away."

"True enough. Is he seeing her again?"

"Probably not, by the sounds of it. I did think on Friday, when they were outside, talking…she's a bit much for your Mike. Not because she's transgender. But she's going through her own problems with her kids."

Andy got out to open the gates, got back in and drove through, pausing to see if he needed to close them again. Mike wasn't far behind him, and he watched his brother in the rear-view mirror as he climbed out of his van and pulled the gates shut. Andy put his seat belt on, still watching Mike. "That's something they've got in common, though, isn't it?"

"Yeah, but there's no chemistry, he said."

"Ah, well. He's probably better off without the aggro, to be honest."

"Ha!" Shaunna folded her arms and scowled. Andy leaned over and slow-kissed her cheek. "That's not what I meant, RHB."

"I'm kidding," she said, still scowling. "But you're right. Leah's still hoping for a reconciliation."

Andy moved off again. "Mike didn't believe you, then? About Hayley calling him off her own bat?"

"Nope, and Adele said he reckons he only got that job at Dovedale because the last woman he worked for felt sorry for him."

"Really? He told me she fancied him."

"Either way, he's underestimating himself. He needs to get back into computing. I don't know how he did it, but the salon computer is working like a dream."

"Yeah? You wanna see the setup he's got in the summerhouse. It's Charlie's old machine, but he was doing some fancy thing on it this morning. Looked like a load of old gobbledygook to me."

"Now there's a thought," Shaunna said. Andy glanced her way, and she gave him a mischievous smile. "Oh, and he said Charlie'll be back for the second half."

"Good stuff. I wonder who Dan'll take off?"

"Your Mike, I would've thought."

"Nah. He's a bloody good player, is Mike, and versatile. Now he's had a run out, he'll be on top form today. In fact, I wouldn't be surprised if he wins the game for us."

"Listen to you, bigging up your brother," Shaunna teased. "Is that a touch of hero worship I detect?"

Andy smiled and draped his arm around Shaunna's shoulders. "Yeah, well, what can I say? It only took him forty-four years, but I think my big brother's finally getting his shit together."

***

The Red Lion's car park was packed out, and there were cars parked right along both sides of the main road. Andy was almost at the terrace where Josh, George and Sean lived before he found a space big enough for the Mustang, by which point he'd lost Mike.

On the walk back, Shaunna stared in amazement at all the cars. "These can't all be for the match, can they?"

"They probably are," Andy said. Both teams had started to gather quite a home crowd, and with the pubs only a couple of miles either side of the town centre, it was easy enough for the Anchors' supporters to get to The Red Lion, although public transport on a Sunday morning was sketchy at best, so the away supporters would have driven there. Andy hoped they'd be leaving straight after the match with their heads hanging in shame. He didn't much fancy an afternoon of listening to them bragging, because they'd stay to do just that, if they won.

As they neared the playing fields, Andy spotted his two brothers, engaged in banter and laughing, which was a good sign. With Adele still recuperating, she and Dan had missed Friday night's quiz, and in the absence of the Brawn contingent, the Brains were no match for Complex Superiority. Andy had expected Dan to be more desperate to win than ever, but he seemed in good spirits. Cheerful, almost. Maybe no-one had told him.

"That's suspicious," Shaunna said, nodding to urge Andy on. "Find out what's happening and report back."

Andy mock-saluted and jogged over to his brothers. "Alright?"

"Yep. Bloody perfect," Dan said. "Aitch and Charlie are both here. We've got our full first team." Dan slung his arms around his brothers and beamed. "We're gonna slaughter the W-Anchors. I can feel it in my bones."

18: Critical Game
Sunday, 7th October

The Lions won the toss, and they were raring to go, but Dan had warned them before kickoff that they needed to pace themselves. Five minutes in, it was clear the Anchors' captain had issued the same warning. Everyone was holding back, running slowly and making long passes which no-one bothered to intercept. Nearing the ten-minute mark, the Anchors gained possession, and the game took off. The ball rebounded off the crossbar, Sean threw it out to Andy, and off they went, down to the Anchors' goal. George clipped it in nicely, but the goalkeeper punched it away and the pace dropped again.

Play continued much the same way throughout the first half, and Dan utilised the opportunity to plan his strategies for the second half. Unfortunately, they didn't get that far. With less than three minutes until the half-time whistle, Tash Granger— Aitch's much better half—gave a whistle of her own and held up Aitch's mobile phone. He offered Dan a shrug of apology and jogged over to the touchline while the game played on. Dan tried to keep an eye on the ball and on Aitch, cursing him for taking a call in the middle of their most important match of the season, but even at a distance, he could see it was serious. Aitch handed his phone back to Tash and beckoned Dan over.

"What's up, mate?"

"We're gonna have to abandon the match."

"You've gotta be kidding."

"Critical incident. I need to pull all the lads off."

Dan glanced behind him; most of the Anchors players were watching Aitch. "Coppers' telepathy," Dan muttered. "What kind of critical incident?"

Aitch raised an eyebrow, and Dan sighed. Aitch was terrible at keeping his mouth shut until it was something Dan really wanted to know.

"I'll go tell the ref," he said, giving Aitch a parting pat on the shoulder. He wasn't happy about it, but there was nothing he could do, and if they'd been playing against any other team, it would have been to the Lions' detriment. As it was, eight of the Anchors were now crowded around Aitch, who gesticulated as he spoke. The nine of them dispersed to collect their belongings and then left in the cars closest to the playing fields without bothering to get changed out of their kits.

"What was that about?" Andy asked, staring after the departing cars.

"Critical incident. Dunno what."

"Ah, crap. And we're on good form today."

"Yeah, well. We'll just have to keep it up for the rematch, won't we?" Dan called the Lions' players over so he could tell them what he knew.

"Dan!"

He turned to see who had shouted his name and muttered, "What does he want?" under his breath as the Anchors' captain jogged to his location. "Alright?"

"You going over to the pub?"

"Probably."

"Can I buy you a pint?"

Dan was taken aback, but played it cool. "If you like." He gave his brother a sideways glance, noting Andy's bemused expression.

"I'll see you over there." The man jogged back to his team.

Dan shook his head in wonder. "Is it me, or was that a bit unexpected?"

"Definitely not you, bro," Andy confirmed. "I'm gonna go give Shaunna a hand with the girls."

Dan followed Andy's progress across the pitch, still wondering what the Anchors were up to. So long as they didn't think they were going to poach Aitch…

***

Bob, the landlord of The Red Lion, was delighted by the turn of events, though he, like everyone else, became less so when a local newsflash reported that a suspect package had been left at their local train station. After the initial report, however, there seemed to be something of a media blackout, and the pub's patrons tried to focus on doing what they normally did post-match on a Sunday.

As usual, the Lions and their friends, family and supporters ordered the Sunday roast; today, it was pork with crackling, and apple and thyme stuffing, and it was delicious enough for Dan to only refresh the news page on his phone between mouthfuls, although across the table, Josh was tapping away at his screen, trying different sources, whilst his food went cold.

"Dudes," Andy said. "Aitch will call at least one of us when it's all over."

Dan and Josh made eye contact with each other, briefly, before returning their attention to their phone screens. They weren't checking for news because they were worried; the chances of their little suburban station being the target of any kind of 'terrorist' attack were very low. No, what they were doing was competing to be the first to find out what was going down, with the additional challenge of the remaining Anchors' players, who had many more friends in the police than Dan and Josh did.

An hour later, still with no news, the Anchors' captain finally finished his dinner—Bob hadn't intentionally served him last, although he seemed quite pleased with himself for having done so accidentally—and approached Dan and Andy with his hand outstretched. Andy shook it first, and Dan was reluctant to follow his brother's example, but then the Anchors' captain said, "Business, not football."

"Fair enough." Dan shook the man's hand. "Sorry, I don't know your first name."

"Scott. And you're…Dan?"

"That's right."

"Which means you're Andy," Scott deduced. Andy nodded to confirm it. "OK to talk here?"

"Sure." Dan retrieved a free stool from the next table along. Scott nodded in thanks and sat down. "You all right for drinks?"

Dan raised his half-full glass. He was drinking lager because Aitch had given him a lift; it was looking like he'd need to make alternative arrangements to get home. Andy was on his second pint of Coke and also declined Scott's offer.

"OK." Scott adjusted his position so he could see Dan and Andy at the same time. "Before I say anything else, are you aware of what's happening with Comco?"

"Not officially." Dan couldn't say more than that without giving away what he knew.

Scott raised his hands in a gesture of understanding. "Let me try that another way. Comco are relocating. Officially, the announcement will go up on their website first thing tomorrow morning. How do I know? I manage their website."

"Should you be telling us this?"

"It's out in the open already. What isn't public knowledge is that they already have a buyer for the glassworks."

"*Just* the glassworks?" Andy asked.

"Just the glassworks," Scott confirmed. "The board tried to sell the company as a going concern, and it's got a good, steady turnover, but it's not lucrative enough to attract investment."

"The investment is their R and D," Dan said defensively.

"I know, mate," Scott agreed. "And I'm gutted. My dad worked for Comco from the age of fifteen. He's dead now, but my mum still lives in one of the workers' houses. My brothers both work for Comco, and my sister-in-law. Four hundred jobs, we're losing."

Dan didn't pass comment. He stayed up to date on local business and finance, and the impact of Comco's relocation, on top of losing Campion's a few years back, was a net loss of around eight hundred jobs. In a town the size of theirs, it was going to create a massive unemployment problem.

"My proposal, then," Scott said and paused to ensure he had both Dan's and Andy's attention. "The board have decided to deal with the site as three separate entities. The glassworks, the houses, and the plot where the stadium is. The glassworks, as I say, already has a buyer. Tenants have been given first refusal on the houses, which leaves the stadium."

"They're moving it down south," Dan asserted, aware that Andy was already shaking his head. "You told me..." He stopped when he realised Andy hadn't told him anything. Aitch had, and Aitch... "I'm gonna bloody have him," he muttered.

"Who?" Andy asked.

"Who d'you think? Happy to blab about our business to anyone who'll listen. Ask him what he's doing and it's 'sorry, mate, need to know, and all that'." Dan shook his head and decided to have words with Aitch later. "So what *was* the ESDAL for?" he asked Andy.

"Run-of-the-mill job. Gatwick?"

Comco made the reinforced high-rated STC glass used for airport terminals, and while the panes were large enough to be classed as an abnormal load, it *was* a run-of-the-mill job for

Jeffries and Associates. "Right. They're not shifting the stadium, then?"

"Not as far as I know."

"No, they're not," Scott said. "It'd be as cheap to rebuild it as transport it, I would've thought, but that's your area of expertise."

"Yeah, you're right," Andy agreed. "Why are you telling us?"

"I'm proposing we make an offer to buy it."

"Who's 'we'?" Dan asked.

"The Anchors and the Lions. Or, rather, the sponsors of the Anchors and the Lions."

Dan took a quick gander at Scott's shirt to check he got the sponsor's name right. "Bryant PLC is your company?"

"Indeed it is, and—" Scott lifted slightly off his stool and fished a business card from his pocket "—I can raise half the capital." He nodded at the card, prompting Dan to turn it over. He eyed the figure written on the back and passed the card to Andy without a word. Andy read it and sucked air through his teeth.

"We need to have a chat," he said, looking Dan in the eye. It was a substantial sum that would wipe out their company reserves.

Dan turned back to Scott. "How long till it goes on the market?"

"Comco are already making arrangements with the auctioneer."

"Ah, f—" Andy shot Dan a warning glance that stopped him from swearing aloud. He downed the rest of his pint while he absorbed the information. "You want a drink, Scott?"

"I said I'd get them."

Dan handed over his empty glass. "I'm not gonna argue."

"What you having?"

"Just lager for me, cheers."

"Andy?"

He waved his hand in refusal.

Dan watched Scott all the way to the bar. "What d'you reckon, bro?"

"I dunno." Andy sat back with his hands behind his head, pondering. "Just the investment itself is a bloody big risk."

"Yeah. But it's a risk worth taking."

"Is it? What are we gonna do with a stadium? Apart from the obvious."

"The obvious being?"

"Well, aside from training and matches—"

"We've got two amateur rugby teams, God knows how many footy teams, men's and women's, school tournaments—"

"Assuming they're interested. Apart from that, there's what? Gigs, firework displays…" Andy shrugged with his elbows to indicate he'd exhausted his list.

"Seasonal markets, fitness suite, conferencing, banqueting…" Dan gave his brother a supercilious grin.

"OK. Say we *can* turn it into something viable…" Scott was on his way back from the bar, so Andy added quickly, "We need to know who's handling the auction."

"Leave it with me," Dan said.

"Lager." Scott handed over the pint.

"Cheers." Dan took a glug and set his glass down.

"Is there anything else you need to know at this stage?"

"A few things," Dan said. "We're keeping the Anchors and the Lions separate, aren't we?"

"That was my thinking, yeah. Although you've got the start of a good youth team, I'm told."

"By…Aitch?" Dan said it like it was a wild stab in the dark.

Scott laughed. "Yeah. It was. See, we're all too long in the tooth to be taken seriously, not to undermine how good both teams are. However, that youth team has a lot of potential. This is separate to the stadium proposal, but have a think about whether we could run the youth team as a joint venture. They'd bring in money. Sponsorship, advertising, government funding…"

Dan nodded. "OK. I'll talk to George and Aitch. They manage the youth team."

"Thanks. They might have to build two separate teams—lads and girls."

Dan heard Andy's 'ha, fat chance'. "It's an under-18s side, so there's no worries on that score, but if it comes to it, Charlie and Shaunna might be up for that."

"Yeah, good luck putting it to them, bro," Andy muttered.

Scott kept his head down, figuratively, by drinking his beer and attending to his surroundings. Dan seized the moment.

"So why are Comco selling through an auction? Any idea?"

Scott swallowed his beer. "Yeah. They were approached by the auctioneer."

"Interesting. I wasn't aware auctioneers touted for business."

"I couldn't say, although it's a buyer's market, and property around here isn't selling. Chances are they'll get more through an auction than a fixed-price sale, so it was a good move on the part of the auction company."

"Fair comment. A local company, I'm guessing, if they're clued up on the local economy?" Dan tried to make the question sound casual. Judging by Scott's response, he'd succeeded.

"I imagine so. I'll see what I can find out. So, from that, should I take it you're giving it consideration?"

Dan looked at Andy, who nodded. "Yeah. Definitely. Give us a couple of days, and we should have an answer for you."

"That's quick."

"No point to sitting on a honeypot." *Not if you're gonna get stung.* He wasn't sure if Andy had said it, or he'd imagined it, but either way, Dan heeded the warning.

"I've got your number," Scott said, already rising to his feet. "I'll leave you to enjoy your Sunday afternoon. Thanks for hearing me out."

"No problem. Thanks for the heads up."

They shook hands again and parted company.

***

By seven that evening, the day was at last living up to Dan's expectations. Animated movie, couch, Robbie asleep in the crook of his left arm, and Shu snuggled against his right side. Adele was sitting at the other end of the sofa, her attention divided between them, the TV and the magazine in her hands.

"Daddy?"

"Hm?"

"Robbie sleep in my room?"

"Are you tired, baby girl?"

"Noooo." She peered up at him and slow-blinked heavy eyelids. He smiled and kissed her head, the dark curls tickling his nose. Just as he thought he'd got away without answering, she said, "Daddy?" again. He sighed.

"He needs to sleep near Mummy and me."

"Why?"

"Because he's only little, and he wakes up in the nighttime."

"I don't wake up in the nighttime."

"No. Because you're a big girl now."

"When he's ten he can sleep in my room?"

Dan frowned. "Probably." Hopefully, she'd go off the idea, but at the moment, she was besotted with her baby brother, as evidenced by the way she blindly reached out and stroked the sole of Robbie's left foot. Robbie curled his toes in his sleep, which made Dan smile. Ticklish feet. One of the lesser-known, or, rather, less frequently admitted Jeffries traits. He went back to watching the film, wondering when he'd stopped enjoying action thrillers. When he became a dad, he supposed. These days, it was way more fun watching a cartoon with his kids.

"Have you heard from Aitch yet?" Adele asked.

"Yeah. I got a text, confirming what they'd said on the news." The package at the station had turned out to be someone's forgotten sports bag, but by the time it had been dealt with, everyone had left the pub, so Aitch had gone back to the station and done whatever he was supposed to have been doing before he'd rescheduled for the match. However, Dan still hadn't heard from Scott about the auctioneer, not that he was expecting to that evening.

"She's fast asleep," Adele said, nodding at Shu.

"I'll put her to bed in a bit."

"You want me to take Robbie?" Adele braced herself, preparing to get up.

"You're all right yet. Film's not finished." In his peripheral vision, Dan caught sight of Adele's amused expression. She leaned on her arm and continued to watch him. "What?"

"Nothing, sweetie."

Dan ignored her, or tried to.

"*The Lion King* is on next."

"Is it? Excellent."

Adele started giggling.

"It's not, is it?" Dan asked, trying not to sound too disappointed.

"No idea. But I'm sure we can find some way to keep the big kids happy this evening." She extended her leg and ran her toes up and down his arm. "After the little kids go to bed."

"Six weeks, the doctor said."

"But couldn't we...do *something*?"

"For real?"

Adele smiled sweetly, followed by a squeaked *Ouch!* "Yes... but...really...carefully..."

Dan's libido remained unconvinced, although his arms were going to sleep under the weight of his children, who were already asleep, so he was making a move, whatever. Very slowly, he shifted his arm from around Shu, so that she was resting partly against his side and partly against the back of the sofa. As he slid sideways, Shu followed his movement in a controlled collapse; she didn't so much as stir. Dan got up and took Robbie to his cot, returning for Shu. She grumbled sleepily as he picked her up and shushed her.

"It's OK, baby girl. Gonna put you to bed."

She flopped against his chest with her legs crossed and hands tucked under her chin, like a pixie plucked from the top of a toadstool. She was still so tiny—not necessarily anymore because she was prem, but because Adele was petite—that calling her the 'big' sister didn't quite fit yet. She was also exhausted; no request for a story, no tears. She didn't fight him at all.

"Night-night," he whispered from her bedroom doorway. He stayed a moment longer, just to watch her sleep. She was beautiful, and so incredibly precious, he'd never have believed he could feel the same love and protectiveness for Robbie as he did for Shu. His baby girl. His princess.

"Dan? What's taking you so long?"

Of course, her mother was something of a princess, too.

19: Meeting Ground
Tuesday, 9th October

She's right, Mike thought, in reference to his mum's comment when he'd gone over to the house first thing to check for mail. Bethan was picking up on how stressed he was, which meant neither of them had slept much last night. On the plus side, it turned out that Jackie Perry's lawyer had been scaremongering. Social services were *not* coming out to inspect the summerhouse, and, according to Ms. Lane, Jackie had found herself a new lawyer, who was 'more reasonable' than whatever her name was.

Mike felt as if a ten-ton weight had been lifted from his shoulders, and the effect was immediate. Typically, seeing as it was almost midday, and they'd need to leave within the hour, Bethan was fast asleep and had been for most of the morning. He was pleased, though, because it meant he'd got the washing done *and* completed another of the tasks on his IT 'refresher course', which wasn't the most accurate name for it, or perhaps that was just his experience. Sure, the basics hadn't changed, and it wasn't as if he'd been living under an anti-technology rock all these years. But he certainly wasn't up to speed on mobile devices, considering his experience consisted of using his own mobile phone, which he'd had for a long time. It did what he needed it to, and his contract cost next to nothing, so he'd seen no reason to upgrade. Needless to say, upgrading was one of the first things he'd be doing when Hayley paid him the balance for the salon job.

He logged off the training site and swallowed the dregs of cold coffee from his cup, preparing to wake the little madam. She was grouchy if she was woken before she was ready, but the bad mood passed soon enough, and the long sleep would hopefully have put her in a lovely mood for when they met up with Jackie in an hour's time.

First things first: more coffee. He filled the kettle and doubled the coffee and sugar he'd usually have. *Don't wanna be nodding off in front of Jackie. Ha.* Tired as he was, it was about as likely as Jackie telling him Rachel was going to stop trying to fuck up his and Bethan's lives.

He cared what Jackie thought of him; why, he didn't know. With or without access arrangements, his lawyer seemed confident he wouldn't lose Bethan, and his feelings for Rachel wavered between hatred and indifference, so it certainly wasn't for her benefit. He supposed a big part of it was still about proving he was a good dad, and not just to Jackie; to himself. The other, less selfish reason was he wanted Jackie to see Bethan in the best light, to show her that something good had come out of losing her daughter. Bethan had a family already—loving grandparents, brilliant aunties and uncles, gorgeous cousins. She didn't need the Perrys in her life. But they needed her.

So, Mike was nervous and stressed out, and both Andy and Shaunna had offered to accompany him, but he'd politely refused. He was hoping Jackie would, likewise, be unaccompanied, although there was a good chance Rachel's sister or brother would come with her. As far as Jackie was concerned, Mike was the reason Rachel was in prison. He'd got her banged up and kept her away from her family, at best. Worst case, he was a rapist and a 'wife' beater. Wild guesses on his part: he had no idea what Rachel had told her mum about him, or if she'd told her anything at all. Maybe they were empty threats to guarantee his silence.

There's something else, isn't there?

What Jackie had said outside the courtroom kept coming back to him. At first, he'd thought she was fishing to see if there *was* more, and he'd tried to act cool, but then she'd pleaded with him, and he was torn. Was she hoping he'd confirm for her that Rachel was every bit the sweet, innocent daughter Jackie thought she was? Or was Rachel's poison finally wearing off?

Mike was no mind reader—he often missed the point when it was given to him bluntly and in no uncertain terms—but if he and Jackie were going to come to some kind of workable understanding, it would be without the interference, however well-meant, of other people. Like Mrs. Hunter had said, it was easy to find someone who'd big you up, but the proof that he was better than his competitors was in his work, and what he had to do today was no different. Regardless of what Rachel had or hadn't told her mum, it was down to him to convince Jackie her granddaughter was in the best place and she had no reason to worry or challenge him.

Time was ticking on, and Bethan needed her lunch before they left. He peeped around the dividing wall, chuckling quietly at the sight that greeted him, of his sleeping daughter in her cot, lying the opposite way around to when he'd put her down for her nap. It was incredible to think that three months ago, she couldn't sit up unsupported. More evidence for how fast children grow up, which his brothers had been telling him for years. They'd watched Krissi from the sidelines, reluctant teenaged 'uncles' who became doting guardians along with the rest of their crazy friends, only to discover Krissi was one of theirs. A Jeffries, in blood, if not in name. And she was a nice kid.

Kid. She was twenty-five, old enough to have her own kids. Being so new to parenting himself, Mike couldn't get his head around that, because it also meant he was old enough to be a great uncle, or a…grandad. Except he didn't feel that old. He felt the same now as when he'd left uni, although he'd felt ancient when he was with Rachel. She'd kept ramming it down his throat, the eighteen-year difference, told him her friends didn't understand why she was with him. *Is he loaded, Rach? Or has he got a big you-know-what...* She'd laughed in his face and said she'd told them he was a loser. She was only with him to make sure he paid for his mistake. It was safe to say he had, and then some.

Having Bethan was *not* his mistake, though. She was the first thing he'd got right in his life. No, his mistake, he was beginning to accept, was not fighting back. Maybe it wouldn't have made any difference in the end, other than he'd have been free of Rachel's clutches sooner. Would he have fought her for Bethan? Probably not. If he hadn't had his daughter in his life, he wouldn't know what it was like without her, and he'd have carried on as before, with his dead-end job, evenings in the pub, alone but for the occasional one-night stand. His one date since Rachel hadn't even made it to the bedroom, not that it was a possibility anyway, when he shared that room with his daughter.

Who was still asleep.

He'd hoped if he stood there long enough, she'd wake up by herself, and he felt like a big mean daddy, disturbing her. Advancing on her cot, he reached down and stroked his finger over her cheek. She blinked without opening her eyes, if that were possible, and then frowned, her little nose crinkled, ready to release a cry of anguish at being dragged away from whatever it was tiny girls dreamed of.

"Hey, baby girl," he whispered. "You want some din-dins?"

Her frown softened as her eyes opened. No squawking, no tears, she smiled up at him, melting his heart, just like every day.

"Da," she said.

Unable to shift the daft grin from his face, he scooped her up out of her cot, and her little arms stretched around his, holding tightly, her cheek snuggled against his chest. "Love you lots and lots," he murmured, kissing her hair.

"Da," she replied.

For once, her nappy had stayed leak-free, *and* he remembered to put her bib on *before* he put the bowl of banana pieces on her tray. To think how reluctant he'd been to give her finger foods, and then his mum had told him she'd been giving her toasty fingers for the past month. Bethan loved toast. It was her current favourite, although rusk dipped in yoghurt was fast taking over.

"We'll go shopping later," he told her. Whether she understood the words or not, she still listened intently. He sneaked a spoonful of potato and butternut squash in between the banana chomping, and laughed when she wrinkled her nose in disgust. His mum said she looked just like him when she did that. "Should've given you carrot, huh?"

She pushed most of the potato and squash out of her mouth with her tongue in favour of more banana, squidging the rest of the piece between her fingers and grinning in delight. Mike's belly rumbled; they were meeting Jackie for lunch, but he couldn't wait that long. Keeping one eye on his daughter, he made a jam sandwich, because it was quick and easy, and sat down again. Bethan made a grab for the sandwich. He tore a crust off, swiped some jam onto the tip, and handed it over. She sucked the jam off, threw the crust over the edge of her tray and stretched out her hand for more.

"Eat your banana," he said, holding up a piece in front of her. She homed in on it and took it from him. It also went over the edge of the tray. Mike sighed and relinquished a sizable strip of his sandwich. It was the shape of things to come.

When Bethan was sure she'd sucked every last drop of butter and jam from the bread, Mike tried her with a couple of spoonfuls of the potato and squash, but she wasn't interested, so he cleaned her up and put a jar of food in her bag, along with a bottle of water, formula, nappies, wipes, bibs, change of clothes… He always used to forget something; now it was second nature.

With everything packed, he carried Bethan out to the van. He'd left her seat in situ after the football, which saved a bit of messing around. She was alert and happy, and it was making him feel more comfortable about where they were going.

"Ready to meet your other nana?" he asked, climbing in beside her. At the word 'nana', she turned her head and frowned at him. "Maybe she's a grandma." He'd leave it to Jackie to decide. He poked the key into the ignition, and…

"Crap." Of course, it had to happen today, of all days. Len was at the showroom, and his mum had gone out. He couldn't see whether Charlie's car was there, because she parked around the side of the house. He got out of the van and went to look. Sure enough, there was Charlie's GTi, and the office window was open. "Charlie?"

The window opened a further couple of inches, and she peered out. "Yeah?"

"Can you do me a favour? I need to jump-start the van."

"No problem. I'll come now."

"Cheers." Mike returned to the van, popped the bonnet and got the jump leads out of the back, checking everything was switched off while he waited for Charlie, thereby discovering he'd left the headlights on. More likely, he'd hit the switch with his knee yesterday, and it was an old van, so no beeps to alert him. Ahead of him, Charlie's Golf swung into view, and she advanced until they were bonnet-to-bonnet. Charlie left her engine running and got out.

"Is it your battery?" she asked as she propped the Golf's bonnet open.

"Lights."

"Ah." She took the ends of the leads and connected them to the Golf's battery. "I'll give it a few revs," she said.

Mike got back in the van and waited a couple of minutes, watching Bethan's face. She was fixated on something, and he glanced up to see what. There was nothing, apart from the clouds drifting across the sky, although they were probably fascinating to a baby. He tried the van again, and it was sluggish, but it did start. He gave it some gas, wincing at the exhaust's loud backfires. The stink of black smoke reached his nostrils.

Charlie appeared next to the driver's door. "Think your van's knacked, mate."

He looked at her ruefully, hoping she was wrong.

She eyed his attire and then Bethan's. "You got another date?"

"We're going to meet Rachel's mum."

"At her place?"

"The mall." The van was still spluttering.

"Do you want a lift? I've got to go down to the showroom anyway. I could drop you off on the way, pick you up later?"

Mike revved the van again; it sounded none too healthy, and the prospect of getting stuck in the mall's car park was not one he relished. "If you wouldn't mind."

"Not at all." Charlie stepped back so Mike could get out. "If you pass me Bethan's pushchair…"

He took it out of the back of the van and gave it to Charlie to put in her boot. "They're a decent size, aren't they?" he said, indicating in the direction of the hatchback's boot space as he carried Bethan over.

"Yeah. You putting her in the front or the back?"

"Back, I guess."

Charlie opened the door and pulled the seat forward, holding it while Mike wriggled through the small gap and contorted himself to strap Bethan's seat in. He emerged panting and flustered.

"It's not really a family car," Charlie admitted apologetically.

"It doesn't need to be, does it?" Mike reasoned. Charlie was single with no kids, and the nifty little 1985 convertible, procured by Len as a perk of her job, was perfect for her. At the back end of the eighties, when Mike had passed his driving test, he'd fancied getting a GTi himself, but they were too expensive, so he'd had to settle for a Ford Escort, like the rest of the male teenage population. After uni, he'd upgraded to a Cavalier SRi and sold it soon after, when he was given his first work van. He'd been driving vans ever since, and they suited his requirements, although he'd be lying if he claimed he wasn't jealous of his brothers' flash cars.

It said a lot about the kinds of women they shared their lives with. No doubt about it, both Andy and Dan had bought their dream cars, and Dan had got his after his daughter was born, so it must've been with Adele's blessing. There again, he'd had to compromise on style and go with the four-door, but it was still a fine-looking car. As for Andy's? Well, he always was a show-off, and what better way to draw attention to himself than to drive around in a 1960s bright-red American soft-top?

Rachel had much to say about Mike's van, none of it complimentary, although she wasn't so fussy when she'd been out with her mates getting rat-arsed—while pregnant—and called him at three in the morning to pick her up. The rest of the time, she'd sneered at it and spat 'I'm not getting in *that*', but she had her own car. A little blue Fiat, part of her pretty-girl bullshit.

"Close enough?" Charlie asked.

The view of the mall's main entrance directly ahead had Mike doing a double-take. "Yeah," he answered. "Sorry. I was miles away."

Charlie gave him a concerned smile. "Are you worried?"

"I am. Though not about losing Bethan. I'm confident I won't. But…"

"It's Rachel's mum." Charlie reached over and squeezed his hand.

He'd never told her what had happened with Rachel; Andy had, and Mike was OK with that. Andy trusted Charlie, and that was good enough for Mike.

"Is her mum all right?" she asked.

"Yeah. She seems nice."

"Well, I'm sure it'll be fine, but if it isn't, call me, OK? I'm only five minutes away." She patted his hand and released him.

"Thanks." He got out and fetched the pushchair from the boot before he lifted Bethan from her car seat, leaving the seat where it was. "See you later," he said to Charlie as he moved off towards the mall. A moment later, she pulled out into the traffic, tooting her horn as she passed by. Mike followed her progress until she was out of sight and then paused at the mall's entrance to psych himself.

For a Tuesday afternoon, it was busier than he'd anticipated. Even so, he had no trouble spotting Jackie walking a short way ahead of him. He used the slight lag in their arrival at the food hall to check if she had company, which she didn't, and then went straight over to join her. She waved to indicate she'd seen him.

"Hey," he greeted her. "You OK?"

"Yes, thank you." Jackie smiled at Bethan. "Gosh, you've grown so much since…I last saw you." She'd met Bethan just the once, outside the crown court, on the first day of Rachel's trial. Now, Mike sensed she was desperate to touch, to hold her granddaughter, her outstretched fingers mere inches from Bethan's hand. With obvious reluctance, Jackie straightened again and looked Mike in the eye. "Really, thank you so much."

Mike nodded to acknowledge her words, though he hadn't felt like he'd had much choice. The mediator had suggested they come to an arrangement through their lawyers, which seemed a waste of money. They were adults, after all. Surely they could figure it out between themselves and tell the lawyers what they'd agreed afterwards? Unless they didn't agree.

"Lunch is on me, incidentally," Jackie said, and before Mike could argue, she added, "I'm a senior teacher. I can afford to buy my granddaughter's father lunch once in a while."

Mike shrugged. "Fair enough."

"What do you like to eat?" Jackie gestured to the food franchises.

"I'm easy. You've eaten here before?"

"A few times. The pasta is very good."

"Fine by me. Shall I go order for us?"

"No, I'll do it."

Relieved that he didn't have to leave Bethan with her just yet, Mike looked over at the on-the-wall menu. "I'll have a lasagne, if that's all right?"

"OK. Anything else?"

"Just a coffee, thanks."

"Cappuccino?"

"Sure."

Jackie went to order, leaving Mike to find them somewhere to sit. He aimed for the closest free table and sat down heavily. So far, so good.

Soon after, Jackie returned with their food and drinks on a tray. "I went with the lasagne, too," she explained, setting a plate and cup down in front of him. "I wasn't sure if I should get anything for Bethan."

"She'll be all right for now. She had lunch before we came out. I say she had lunch…she played with a bowl of banana and nicked—" He stopped talking. It didn't seem right to admit he'd already eaten, albeit only half a jam sandwich.

Jackie put the tray to one side and sat opposite Mike. "I need to tell you something. Talk about a small world…" She picked up her knife and fork and cut a little square chunk from the end of her lasagne, lifting it from the plate and then continuing. "It's quite an interesting aside, well, for me, at least. Your sister-in-law, Shaunna?"

"Yeah?" Mike imitated Jackie and put a minuscule morsel of lasagne in his mouth.

"I worked with her mum."

"Oh, right."

Jackie smiled and became thoughtful. Her smile grew more radiant. "She was my mentor, when I started teaching. I had to look twice when I first saw Shaunna. It could've been Siobhan."

Mike nodded, unable to comment. He'd never met Shaunna's mum, although he knew she'd died some time ago, but he didn't like to say. It made for miserable conversation, and in any case, it wasn't his business. As it was, Jackie brought it up.

"I was very sad to hear Siobhan passed away. She was one of the best teachers I ever worked with, possibly *the* best, and such a lovely person. One of the girls in my first class lost her baby sister to cot death, and Siobhan and I attended the funeral. She really looked after me that day." Jackie shook her head. "Thirty-one years, I've been a teacher, and it's still the hardest thing I've endured in my career."

"Jess." Mike's thought escaped aloud, and Jackie stared at him in astonishment.

"Jessica Lambert?" she asked. He nodded mutely to confirm it. "You know her?"

"Not well. She was my brother's girlfriend, but we weren't on speaking terms."

"They're not together anymore?"

"Err…no." It seemed their conversation was destined for talk of death. "Jess passed away last year."

"Oh, no!" Jackie set her fork down. Her eyes filled with tears.

Mike shifted his attention to Bethan, who was still wide awake and quite content, watching all of the activity around them.

"I suppose I should get all of the bad news out of the way in one go," Jackie said.

Mike glanced in her direction. She remained focused on Bethan.

"Rachel hurt herself last week, after they told her she couldn't transfer to a prison with a mother-and-baby unit." She shifted her gaze to meet his. "She's in hospital."

"Hurt herself?"

Jackie nodded and closed her eyes, confirming Mike's interpretation. Whatever his feelings for Rachel, he empathised with Jackie's obvious distress.

"I'm sorry," he said, and he meant it. A meaningless one-night stand for this bloody awful mess.

Jackie pulled a tissue from her bag, wiped her eyes and blew her nose. At the noise, Bethan looked up at her, blinking in curiosity. Jackie laughed through her tears. "I bet you're wondering what all the fuss is about."

Bethan babbled a response, her little eyebrows drawing together in a worried frown that made Mike smile, grateful his daughter didn't understand the pain of the adults in her company. He hoped she didn't, anyway. He looked back at Jackie.

"This is a daft question, but would you like to hold her?"

Jackie's face crumpled again as she cried while smiling at the same time.

Mike unfastened the pushchair straps, lifted Bethan clear, and passed her to Jackie, trying not to react to Bethan's scowl. She was like that with strangers who approached when they were watching the football, or doing the shopping, or anywhere that people thought it was OK to come over and talk to the cute baby with the single dad. He was probably being paranoid about the last part, but he felt like everyone could see it and constantly came up with their own explanations for why he was on his own that would no doubt be way off the mark.

Jackie was used to children and soon won Bethan round, using exaggerated facial expressions while she told her how beautiful she was, and what a lovely outfit she was wearing, and how lucky she was to have such a wonderful daddy who loved her very much. Mike choked up at the last part, which confirmed for him that he'd made the right decision.

"I think Grandma had better eat some of this lunch before it goes completely cold, don't you?" Jackie settled Bethan in the crook of her arm and, with her free hand, picked up her fork. She met Mike's gaze. "Thank you," she said again.

"No worries." Mike followed Jackie's lead and tucked into his lasagne, pausing after a couple of mouthfuls to ask, "How d'you want to work this access thing?"

"Hm… I was thinking we should keep it informal. I could pop over and visit you, you can come over to us. I could babysit for you. I want to be a normal grandma, if you see what I mean. What do you think?"

"Yeah. Sounds good to me."

"I wouldn't want to have Bethan without you being there, at least, not to start with. But once she gets to know me—and you get to know me…"

"OK. You work term times, yeah?"

"That's right. I'm usually home by around five on weekdays, other than when we have meetings, parents' evenings, and so on. But weekends, I'm happy to go along with whatever times suit you."

Mike nodded. "Great." He concentrated on finishing his lasagne, working up to mentioning the other request Jackie had made. He almost didn't want to bring it up, when they were getting along so well, but it needed addressing. He put his knife and fork together on the plate and rubbed his chin. He'd shaved before bed last night, but his beard grew fast. It rasped against his hand.

"What do you want to do about Rachel?" he asked.

"About her seeing Bethan, you mean?"

"Yeah."

"Nothing at the moment. I'm not going to force you to do something against your will. I wish I understood why you're so adamant—why you hate Rachel so much." Jackie held Bethan's hand and kept watching her. "I can only assume it's true—what Felix said about her in court—and perhaps you had to deal with some of that, too."

Jackie sounded so defeated Mike was confident she wasn't pushing him for information. She was beginning to accept Pez's story and building up to a compromise.

She sighed deeply. "I know Rachel can be difficult. She always has been, but I don't need you to tell me anything. I'm just glad for the chance to get to know my granddaughter." She offered Mike a reassuring smile. He nodded.

"Thanks, Jackie."

"Now, much as I'd love to make the offer..." She glanced across the food hall, and Mike followed her gaze to the toilets and changing facilities. She looked back at him and wrinkled her nose. Mike laughed and got up.

"Come on, stinker." He collected his daughter and the changing bag from the back of the pushchair. Bethan shouted 'Da!' and bashed his nose hard enough to bring tears to his eyes. "Ooh, you little monster." He tickled her, and she giggled and went to do it again, but he caught her hand and blew a raspberry on her palm.

"Be right back," he said to Jackie.

Even though Mike had a valid reason for leaving her sitting on her own, it felt rude to do so, and he made short work of changing Bethan's nappy. With solid food came more solid poos and fewer incidents of it escaping her nappy. Today was not an all-up-the-back day, thankfully, and they were done in a couple of minutes. He handed Bethan back to her grandma.

"Hello, beautiful," Jackie gushed. Bethan smiled coyly. "You're not shy?" Jackie tapped her finger on Bethan's chin, and her smile became a big toothy grin. Jackie glanced at Mike. "She looks like you."

"I've got more teeth," he pointed out.

Jackie laughed. "Very true. It's been great meeting you both today, getting to know you a little. I wasn't sure what to expect before the mediation meeting, but I got a real sense of how much you care about Bethan, and seeing you together…" Jackie became serious. "I've withdrawn my guardianship application. It was straight after the trial, and I was… I've had time to come to terms with everything now, and I won't be applying again. I want to reassure you about that, because losing your daughter…" She paused and blinked back tears. "If it isn't too much to ask, maybe it is, I don't know, but I'd be grateful if you'd give some more thought to Rachel seeing Bethan. Without her, she has nothing to live for."

Unable to bring himself to saying no outright, although he was quite sure giving it more thought wouldn't change his mind, Mike simply said, "I'll think about it."

"Thank you." Jackie seemed to relax and then peered into her cup. "Can I buy you another coffee?"

Mike got up. "I'll get them."

"I don't mind."

"Really, it's fine. Same again?"

"Please. Then we can talk about more fun things, like… I'll leave it up to you."

"Err, yeah. Weaning babies or which brand of emulsion gives the best coverage?" Mike suggested with a grin.

"Oh, emulsion, definitely," Jackie said mock-seriously.

Without reservation, Mike set off for the coffee vendor, leaving his daughter with her grandma.

20: Whoosh-Splash
Wednesday, 10th October

"Alright, bro? We've got a problem."

Andy lifted Rosie's bottom and slid the clean nappy underneath. "Can't you start a convo with 'how's it hanging' or something?"

"Alright, bro? How's it hanging? We've got a problem."

Andy gave up. "What this time? You need me to fly out to Tristan da Cunha?"

"Who?"

"Not who, what."

"You lost me."

"No surprises there." Andy fastened Rosie's nappy and put her in her bouncer so he could properly continue his conversation with Dan—once he'd stopped laughing at the view onscreen of his brother's sweaty red face. "What *are* you doing?"

"Workout." Dan grinned and hoisted Robbie a few inches up, and down, and up, and down again. "I'm at Mum's."

"I figured." Andy could hear the whirr of a treadmill belt. "So, what's up?"

"The auctioneer for the stadium—"

"Is Derek Arnold?"

"Correct. We need to warn Ed."

"By warn, you mean talk him out of the auction without telling him why," Andy said.

"Tried that. He wasn't having it."

"Dan."

"Or we go to the pol—"

"For crying out loud, don't you ever bloody listen?"

"We're just gonna sit back and watch Comco get ripped off?"

"To put it bluntly, yeah, we are."

Dan nodded. "Fair enough." He ended the call.

In fury, Andy threw his tablet at the couch, where it bounced and clattered to the floor. Cursing inwardly, he bent down and flipped it over to check the screen. "That's just the fucking icing…" His own fault for losing his rag. There was nothing for it; he needed to have it out with Dan, face-to-face. "Right, girls. Let's go see Nana."

Before they left, Andy took a detour upstairs for his board shorts and three towels, in case an opportunity presented itself, and if it didn't, he'd work it in there somehow. With the girls in their car seats, he sent Shaunna a text message to let her know what he was up to. He'd be home before she was, but he probably wouldn't get around to doing the washing up, so really, he was pre-empting his excuse for later, not that she'd complain, but he'd still feel bad.

It wasn't often he left household jobs undone. All those months of looking after Jess had provided excellent training, although sometimes they weren't done to Shaunna's standards, and *then* she'd complain. Andy had left home when he was nineteen, and he probably was a slob when he was younger because he'd shared a house with other students, all of whom were like him: slackers eager to get uni out of the way so they could get on with more interesting things.

After the others moved out, he'd kept on the lease, and for a couple of years, he'd rented out the rooms to new students, but his tolerance for their drinking and slovenliness soon ran out. The last batch moved on, and even though it was a big place for one person, he could afford the rent on his own, and there was plenty of space for his 'junk', as his mother and Jess had always referred to his snowboard, longboard, diving gear, hiking boots, tent, and so on.

Shaunna didn't think it was junk. When they'd bought the house, he'd offered to sell all his stuff, but Shaunna was having none of it. So he'd bought a metal shed to house everything, and the day they came to deliver it, Shaunna told them they had the wrong address and sent them packing. When he tried to explain his reasoning—they had three bedrooms and two daughters on the way, who would, one day, need their own rooms—Shaunna had given him 'the look' and told him in no uncertain terms that there was no way a monstrous grey shed was going in *her* garden.

Quite what he was going to do with his stuff, he didn't know, but one thing was for sure: when the girls wanted their own rooms, he would make it happen, and he'd fight their mother if he had to. He hoped he wouldn't have to—she'd win—but he had to try. Shaunna was an only child. She didn't know the torture of sharing a room with a sibling.

Fourteen years he'd shared with Dan, and they'd got on all right, most of the time, but nothing was sacred, they had no privacy, they fought over posters, music, who had which bed, how to organise their furniture, who was to blame for the mess, and when they fell out big time, there was nowhere to sulk, or to cry alone when heartbroken. Luckily, Andy didn't get dumped until *after* Mike moved out and they finally got their own rooms, and Adele dumped Dan so often he was hardened to it.

These thoughts had taken Andy all the way to his mum's house, and left him oddly nostalgic, so he was pleased to see that not only was Dan's car parked outside, Mike's van was, too. Next to that was a green and white VW Camper Van, which he didn't recognise, although with Len's business, it was quite normal to see classic cars at the house, either because Len was driving them to wear in new parts or someone was coming to pick them up. On closer inspection—Andy couldn't resist—it was a VW

Bus, with a very tasteful interior conversion to a camper. As with all of the vehicles that left the Elite Motors showroom, it was in superb condition, and Andy wondered how much trouble he'd be in if he offered to take it off Len's hands.

"We could park it in the front garden, couldn't we, girls?" he said on his way to the front door. "Mummy would be OK with that." She wouldn't. She'd kill him.

Len was on his way out as Andy reached the front door and held it open.

"Look at these two cheeky monkeys," he said, grinning at the twins, and then to Andy, "That's the full set." Len continued on his way before Andy had a chance to correct him, although he'd have made a fool of himself if he had.

"Hey, Shu," he called as she ran off down the passage at the back of the atrium.

She stopped dead, turned back and came charging full pelt, squealing, "Uncle Andeeeeeee!"

With seconds to spare, he set down Rosie and Sorsha's car seats and scooped up his niece, *om-nom-nomming* her neck, which made her giggle and shriek. "Why aren't you at school today, Terror?"

"The school closed today, Uncle Andy. They shut it cos of the water."

"Oh dear. That sounds serious."

"Whoosh-splash." Shu held her hands up high in the air and then brought them down, pitter-pattering on Andy's head with her fingertips.

Andy grinned. "Is that what it did?"

"Whoosh-splash," she repeated, nodding very seriously.

Dan emerged from the passage and acknowledged Andy with a nod.

"Alright, bro? Is that right? Shu's school's shut because of the—"

"Whoosh-splash!" she said, quite loudly, finishing Andy's sentence and leaving him temporarily deaf in one ear.

"Burst water main," Dan explained.

"Ah." Andy frowned ponderously at Shu, as if between them they had solved one of the great mysteries of humankind. "That would certainly explain the whoosh-splash."

Shu grinned at him and then wriggled in an attempt to break free. "Down, please."

He did as she requested and watched her interacting with the twins, who both giggled at her, although she was acting all serious and grown up.

"I take it you've come to give me what for?" Dan said.

"Well, I was hoping to peacefully talk some sense into you, yeah."

Dan rubbed his eyes and yawned.

"Robbie's not sleeping, is he?"

"Oh, he's sleeping all right. Just not at night." Dan blinked a few times and squinted at Andy. "What are we gonna do about Comco?"

"I dunno, bro. Let me get these two sorted and we can have a chat."

Dan came over and picked up Sorsha, carrying her across the atrium and along the passageway that led to the kitchen and conservatory. Andy picked up Rosie's chair and followed, with Shu holding his free hand.

"Uncle Andy…"

"Yeah?"

"How old is Rosie and Sorsha?"

"They're almost four months old."

"When is their birthday?"

"June the thirteenth."

"When's that?"

"When it's nearly summer again."

"In the summer holiday?"

"A little bit before."

"When the Easter bunny comes?"

"Between Easter bunny and the summer holidays."

"'Kay."

Andy smiled, waiting for the next quiz topic.

"It's my birthday soon."

"No way! How exciting!"

"You coming to my party?"

"If you're inviting me, I'll be there with bells on."

Shu frowned up at him. "You got bells on?"

Andy laughed and gave himself a mental kick. How to explain a figure of speech to an almost-four-year-old?

"The bell on the bus goes ding-ding-ding, ding-ding-ding…" Shu broke free and raced ahead of him into the kitchen, singing all the way. A second later, Andy rounded the door and came to an abrupt halt.

"Whoa!" Staggering back a step, not entirely for effect, he looked around the table in wonder. "When Len said the full set, I thought he was overlooking a couple. Alright, Krissi? Wotto?"

"Alright, mate?" Wotto greeted him with a grin. "Did you see it?"

"See what?"

"You will have done," Krissi said. "The VW?"

"Ah! That's…yours?"

"Yep." Krissi beamed.

"Are you staying?" Andy's mum asked.

"Err, yeah." He stepped further into the kitchen, which was a big room, but with three babies in carry seats, one in a high chair, a free-roaming child and six adults, it was a bit of a squeeze. He made it to the table, where Dan was in the process of extracting Sorsha from her seat, for no reason other than wanting to hold her, it seemed, because she was in a great mood. In fact, Rosie was, too, and Bethan was transfixed. And covered in some kind of food stuff.

"What you eating?" Andy asked her.

"Banana rusk," Mike answered on his daughter's behalf, wiping his palm against the edge of the high-chair tray and wrinkling his nose. "She likes it."

Andy laughed. "I have that joy ahead of me."

"They're pretty tasty, as it goes," Dan said.

Mike nodded in agreement. "But don't dip them in your tea."

"Ew. That's disgusting," Krissi said.

Dan made it obvious he was looking at Krissi as he told Mike, "I remember someone who used to tip their tea over their rusk and then gobble it all up."

Krissi turned to Andy, laughing and blushing a little. "You didn't, did you?"

"Come to think of it," his mum said, "you did."

Andy raised an eyebrow at Krissi. "Genes, huh?"

She nodded with faked resignation. "What else?"

"So what about this VW, then?" Andy asked and sat down next to her.

"Oh my god, it's amazing. It's a 1973 Type Four, but the whole thing's been totally rebuilt. Get this. It's got a two-and-a-half-litre engine."

"That's some horsepower. I thought sixteen hundred CC was the max it could take."

"You're thinking of the T2."

"Oh, right, yeah. I am." Andy grinned. He knew exactly two things about VW Camper Van engines. One: the engine compartment was insanely small. Two: the engine was air-cooled. "How much did that cost you?"

"Err, well…" Krissi leaned closer and whispered, "It's my birthday present from your mum and Len. Don't tell Kris."

Andy raised an eyebrow.

"Or Mum." She gave him a pleading look.

"Don't you think *you* should tell her?"

She shook her head. "I'm kind of hoping I can come up with a convincing story?"

Andy scratched his head. She'd created quite a dilemma for him. "You're asking me to lie to your mother?" She batted her eyelashes. "I can't do that."

"But she'll tell Kris."

"So, maybe you should get in there first."

"Yeah, or maybe I'll just leave the country."

"In your camper van?" Andy teased.

"Yeah, don't even start talking about export tax."

Andy shook his head and laughed. He didn't think Kris would be upset that his mum and Len had bought the camper van for Krissi, not if she talked to him about it. That was how he and Kris had worked through their differences. It had been Sean's suggestion, as part of Kris's therapy, that he and Andy clear the air, which was weird at first. If Andy had a problem with someone, he told them straight, but Kris had needed Sean to prompt him.

There were no shock revelations—the party, Krissi, the paternity tests, the affair—Kris had just cause to be angry with Andy, to hate him, but they'd had to get past it for Shaunna. These days, they got on pretty well, and when Kris and Ade weren't tied up with filming, the four of them spent a lot of time with one another. Kris and Shaunna had been through some tough times, brought up their daughter together—Jeffries genes jokes aside, Krissi was *theirs*—and they were still close. Andy was glad about that.

"Are you all staying for lunch?" his mum asked.

"I will," Andy said and then to Dan, "We still need to have a chat. Is Charlie in the office?"

"Yeah."

"You can use my place," Mike offered. He stood to remove his key from his pocket and threw it to Andy.

"Cheers. D'you reckon you can manage all these kids, Mum?"

Her glowering expression was her answer.

Andy got up quickly and headed for the door, pausing long enough to make sure Dan had offloaded Sorsha—to Krissi, of all people—and was following.

They walked over to the summerhouse in silence, which confirmed Andy's suspicions. Dan still wanted to go in with Scott Bryant on the Comco stadium. Andy unlocked the door, waited for Dan to step inside, and then closed the door behind them. Both stayed on their feet.

"Before you suggest it again, we can't tell Ed what we know."

"I'm with you on that, bro. I've got a couple of ideas."

Andy leaned against the kitchen worktop and gestured for Dan to continue.

"What tactics are they using to get buyers to back out?"

"I don't know. Could be physical threats. Could be killing their finance avenues."

"The finance isn't a problem."

Andy started shaking his head. He knew where this was going.

"I reckon if we offer Ed more money, he'll accept."

"We haven't got any more money to offer him."

"*We* haven't, but I have."

"Dan…"

"I've been thinking about it all morning. The apartment's fine for us for now."

"Six months down the line, you're gonna want Robbie out of your room."

"He can go in with Shu."

"It was just me who hated sharing a room, was it?"

"That was different."

"How?"

"We were too close in age. Shu and Robbie—"

"What does Adele think?" Andy interrupted before Dan got carried away with his side argument.

"She doesn't know I've been looking at houses."

"She's got a right to know what you're planning to do with her money."

"My money."

"How is it? You've lived together for the better part of ten years."

"Four years."

"On and off, it's longer, and you know it."

"And what? It's the money I've saved."

"And Adele contributed nothing, did she?"

Dan's temper flared. "Not that it's any of your damn business, but no, as a matter of fact, she didn't. Her wages go into her account. Apart from that, I don't know what she does with them, and I don't care." He was staring Andy down, ready for a fight, but Andy was too astounded to think of any comeback. He held up his hands.

"You're right," he said. "I was out of order. But I'm still not sure it's a good idea. If the stadium turns out to be a white elephant, you'll lose everything."

"Then I'll have to make sure it's a success. So, are you in?"

Andy studied the ceiling, aware of his brother watching him, waiting for his answer. He wanted to say no. It was too big a risk, and not just in financial terms. They were putting themselves in the sights of Derek Arnold and his business partners—organised criminals on an epic scale way beyond what Jess was involved in.

"Come on, bro. I thought you liked a challenge."

Andy laughed wryly. "I do, but not like this."

"OK." Dan nodded. "We'll leave the business untouched, and I'll secure the additional finance elsewhere, go in with Scott on my own." Dan moved towards the door, slowly, biding his time, knowing exactly what he'd played for and that he was going to get it. Andy could have gladly punched his face in.

"You know what, bro? I fucking hate you sometimes."

21: Wise Monkeys
Friday, 12th–Saturday, 13th October

"Student loans are far too generous," Dan muttered to himself as he made a second circuit of the university car park, that one parking space, amongst the hundreds of small-engine, low-insurance, compact hatchbacks, proving elusive. Ready to give up and risk parking illegally, Dan turned into the exit lane as a car pulled out on his left.

"That's mine." He went full-lock on the steering wheel, reversed out of the way and then edged forward so neither of the two motorists queueing behind him nicked the space. He parked and locked up, trying to figure out the quickest way to Josh's office.

"This is student parking," the driver of the closest waiting car complained.

Dan shrugged. "I'm a student."

The young man eyed him with as much disbelief as he dared. "No permit."

"Left it in my room," Dan said and strode away in what he hoped was the right direction, although any direction would do if it got him away from whining undergraduates. It turned out to be a good choice, as two minutes later, he was heading up the grey-carpeted stairs to the third floor of the Faculty of Social Sciences building, where Josh and Sean had offices next door to each other.

Dan's degree was in business and management, but he'd studied organisational psychology as part of it, which had brought him into close contact with the social scientists. He could spot them a mile off—not so much of the leather-elbow-patches stereotype these days, even if one or two certainly still fitted the mould. It was more the watchful sneer, as if the rest of humanity was only worthy of their pity or scorn, and Josh had perfected it, although they'd been friends long enough for his judgement to not smart quite like it used to. Sean wasn't as bad, or maybe he was just a better actor.

Whatever, they were smart arses, the pair of them. Never mind thinking outside the box. They could think the box out of existence. When it came to their counselling skills, they were both at the top of their game, and there was very little to choose between them. Yet Dan wouldn't have got where he was without Josh, filtering his bullshit and standing between him and Andy, Adele or anyone else he loved enough to hurt. When he needed a listening ear, a wise and honest counsellor who would tell it to him like it was, there was only one man for the job.

Dan drew up outside the door—*Josh Sandison-Morley, Senior Lecturer, Psychology, Counselling and Psychotherapy*—raised his fist to knock but then hesitated, momentarily paralysed by doubt and guilt. He'd come here believing Josh would offer him reassurance. After all, Dan was acting in Jeffries and Associates' best interests. This was a golden opportunity, not just for the business, but for the Lions, not to mention stopping Comco from getting ripped off. But somewhere along the line, Dan now realised, he had stopped caring about the costs and fixated only on the benefits. He'd played dirty with Andy, disregarded his concerns for their safety, and their children's safety, in his selfish pursuit of success.

He didn't need Josh to tell him he was an idiot. He'd got there by himself. So why couldn't he just let it go, walk away?

The door in front of him opened, and Josh stood, casually leaning on the doorpost, arms folded, ankles crossed. "Are you coming in, or shall I bring a coffee out to you?"

Dan checked the door for a spyhole and frowned in confusion.

Josh laughed but offered no explanation as he stepped back inside his room. "I was about to make coffee anyway. Do you want one?"

"Err, yeah. Please." Still perplexed, Dan shut the door and turned but stayed where he was to take in his surroundings. Josh's office, like his surgery before it, was meticulously tidy and spotlessly clean. Alphabetically organised books lined bookshelves, end to end, and the shelves covered two entire walls. The external wall was mostly taken up by a blind-covered window, with Josh's desk in front of it, while the wall behind Dan consisted of one enormous noticeboard from the bookshelf wall to the door.

"That wasn't here last time, was it?" Dan asked.

Josh had his back to him, making the coffee. "Which?"

"The noticeboard."

"No, it wasn't."

Dan nodded. "It's perfect for you, this room."

"Yes. I, erm…" Josh glanced Dan's way, faking sheepish. "I may have implied to the dean that I was considering a full-time position with the police."

Dan chuckled. "They're keen to keep you, then?"

"So it would seem." Josh carried the two cups of coffee to his desk and sat down.

Dan thought he'd better sit, too, before Josh accused him of making the place look untidy. He picked up the cup closest to him and sat back, forcing himself to relax. "Are you and George going with them tomorrow?"

"To see Silhouetto?" Josh guessed—correctly. Dan nodded. "God, no. We saw them last year, and it was an enjoyable night.

They really are very talented. Dancers, I mean. Talented dancers."
Josh's face turned pink, and he quickly deflected. "So…is this
about Comco stadium."

Dan's mouth fell open. "How…?"

"I caught bits and pieces of your conversation with the
Anchors' captain."

"Ah, yeah. Of course." Dan switched his coffee to his other
hand, playing for time, although he wasn't planning on keeping
it to himself. Whatever he told Josh would stay between the two
of them. "Did you catch the bit about the auctioneer?"

"Yes. It's Derek Arnold, isn't it?" Josh's tone was matter-of-
fact, making it clear he already knew about the auction scam.

"I wondered who Andy meant by '*we* did some digging'.
Should've guessed, really."

"Graham said he always suspected the fraud ring was part of
a much bigger organisation."

"The police know?"

Josh nodded. "Graham's old unit have it on their case list,
but it's going to take time. Angela Sharston will probably be at
liberty before they complete the investigation."

"Meanwhile, innocent people are being robbed."

"Collateral damage."

Dan's anger started to rise to the surface. It was frustrating,
infuriating. "It's wrong."

"I know, but they'll get them eventually," Josh placated.

"Yeah, it's the eventually part that bothers me."

Josh sat back in his chair, sipping his coffee and watching
Dan. More than watching…mind-reading. "You really wanted
that house, didn't you?"

"I *did* want it, yeah."

"Until you found a bigger dream to chase."

"Should I stop?"

"Dan Jeffries, asking me if he should pull back on the reins?" Josh's eyes widened dramatically. "Get out of my office, you imposter!"

Dan managed to pull up a smile, but the truth of it was, he no longer trusted his own judgement. It was one thing to risk investing in a business venture that could go tits-up at any second; he stood only to lose money and face. It was another thing entirely when it wasn't his money at stake; it was Andy's, and Adele's, too, he supposed, now he'd reconsidered his brother's dressing-down. The biggest risk, however, was whether nabbing the stadium from under the auctioneer's nose was enough to endanger his family.

"It's an extraordinary business opportunity," Josh said. "George and I were discussing it the other evening."

"Were you?"

"According to George's boss, the farmers' market is looking for a new venue."

"We'd have to beef up the turf protection," Dan thought aloud, only realising the pun when Josh chuckled. "And look into installing a roof. It's not cheap."

"I can well imagine." Josh sat forward again and eyed Dan carefully. "To all intents and purposes, you're just a couple of local businesses hoping to cut out the middle man and snatch a bargain. No-one knows *you* know. Not even your would-be business partner."

Dan rubbed his chin. The cost-benefit scales were tipping again. He shrugged. "I don't know, Josh. There's a lot at stake. But if I walk away and someone else makes a goer of the stadium, I'll regret it for the rest of my days."

"Then don't walk away. Just…be careful."

***

Dan was the first to arrive at Comco, although he was only five minutes early and had expected Andy and Scott to be there already, or Scott, at least. He was a shrewd businessman—Dan had checked his credentials the day after he'd approached them—and as far as Scott was concerned, they stood only to gain from making Eddie Leyland a direct offer. If that offer was rejected, they'd go to the auction as planned. Dan wasn't sure how he was going to break it to him that if Eddie did reject their offer, Jeffries and Associates were out. He'd cross that bridge if and when he needed to.

Whilst Scott was on board for this morning's meeting, Andy hadn't wanted to come in the first place, and he'd made no secret of that. Dan wondered what had happened to his older brother, always adventurous, prepared to risk everything for the buzz, the adrenaline junkie whose neck he'd saved more times than he cared to remember. All right, Dan had his own concerns about going in on the stadium, but how often had Andy willingly risked his life in the pursuit of the next challenge? Here was this opportunity to make a mark on their local community, and potentially make a lot of money along the way—a venture with all the kudos Andy had hankered for in the past—and he wanted no part of it.

Across the lobby, the lift door opened, and Eddie's PA emerged, smiling in Dan's direction. "Mr. Leyland is ready to see you now, Mr. Jeffries."

Not wishing to appear disinterested, Dan delayed responding by collecting his phone, keys and tablet as if he intended getting up and following her. He had nothing, beyond the desire to hunt down his brother and kick him from here to Timbuktu, and only himself to blame.

"I can tell him your associates haven't arrived, if you'd prefer?"

"Yeah, if you wouldn't mind. Thanks."

Eddie's PA nodded and stepped back into the lift. The floor indicator counted up through one, two, three; Dan kept counting in his head, although ten was nowhere near enough to reinstate his patience. He returned to anxiously watching the main entrance: the swish glass doors that opened automatically and made almost no noise at all. With less than a minute to spare, Andy and Scott came through them, both looking cool and collected, like they weren't arriving for a crucial meeting at the last second.

"What kept you?" Dan asked, maintaining a neutral tone though his simmering temper was in danger of boiling over.

"Picket line," Andy said, like it was a stupid question with an obvious answer.

Dan felt his hackles rise. "And?"

"I'm not crossing a picket line."

"How did you get in, then?"

"Back of the site."

"There's a footpath from the houses," Scott explained for Dan's benefit and then remarked to Andy, "I was surprised there was no-one manning it, actually."

Andy nodded in agreement, which irked Dan. The relocation was happening, and the glassworks had already been sold. Their meeting had no bearing on the job losses, which was why he'd had no qualms about crossing the picket line himself. Still, it had made allies of Scott and Andy, which would enhance their united front before Eddie Leyland, should they ever get in to see him.

When the lift door next opened, it was Eddie, rather than his PA, who exited and came straight over to greet them.

"Sorry for the delay, gents." He shook Dan's hand, then Andy's, and finally Scott's. It seemed Eddie wasn't aware of their tardiness, and Dan wasn't about to correct him. "As you can see, we're having a spot of trouble. Please, come through." He turned and led the way back across the lobby to the smaller of Comco's two meeting rooms. "It's a shame. I was a union man myself, and I've done the best I can for my staff." He beckoned them inside and closed the door. "Between you, me and the gatepost, this decision was out of my hands, but I don't see the rest of the board taking the flak. Have a seat, gents."

Eddie gestured to a small table surrounded by eight chairs, and the three of them went around to the far side and sat down. Dan and Andy had been in this room with Eddie countless times, but it had never felt as formal or foreboding as it did today.

Eddie remained standing with his hands in his pockets and a heavy frown on his face. "You know Bill Meyer, don't you? Took over from Al Campion?"

"Yeah," Dan confirmed. "I worked with Campion's a fair bit."

"Ah, yes, you were in the same line of work."

Dan nodded, though it wasn't strictly true.

"I saw Bill at the lodge last week, and he was saying it was the same when their firm went under. Of course, it shouldn't have happened." Eddie shook his head in notable dismay. "I credited Al and Bill with more sense. Why they didn't tell the police about the blackmail, I'll never know. They could've nipped it in the bud long before it hit crisis point."

Andy wasn't looking his way, but Dan could feel the tension coming off him. Judging by the way Eddie squared his shoulders, he'd also picked up on it, leaving Dan no choice but to address it. "I heard they were being threatened from the outset, Ed, and as we now know, it wasn't an empty threat."

"True enough," Eddie agreed ruefully. "He was a good man, was Al Campion. Lessons there for all of us."

Dan clenched his jaw and let the comment go, although he was starting to think it wouldn't be so bad if Comco did get taken for a ride after all.

"Right, then." Eddie sat down opposite and rubbed his hands together. "You have a new offer for me, I believe?"

"We do," Dan confirmed. He looked past Andy to Scott, to see if he wanted to do the talking. He gestured for Dan to continue. Dan turned back to Eddie. "Twenty percent on the guide price."

Eddie stopped rubbing his hands and frowned so deeply his eyes disappeared under his bushy eyebrows, which was an interesting effect when there wasn't a single hair on his head. "Twenty-five percent and it's yours."

Again, Dan looked to Scott, who shook his head. "Twenty's our limit, Ed."

Eddie sat back and drummed his fingers on the table, clicking his tongue against his teeth. "I need to make a call," he said. "Shouldn't take long." He got up and left the room.

Scott leaned back in his chair and hummed thoughtfully. "It's not looking good." To Dan's questioning look, he elaborated, "A couple of the directors are stubborn as anything. They wanted the glassworks to go to auction, and the buyer almost doubled their offer before the board accepted it."

"They do realise they might not get anywhere near what we're offering?"

Scott raised his hands as if to say 'what can we do?' but there was nothing more they could do.

In the few minutes it took for Eddie Leyland to make his call, they talked about the future of the glassworks site, which was destined to become yet another out-of-town retail park. Much as it was bad news for the Comco work force, all of whom were skilled manual labourers, it would be positive for the stadium, and Dan was clinging to a thin thread of hope that the board would accept. However, it was clear as soon as Eddie stepped back into the room that he wasn't going to give them the answer they wanted.

"I'm sorry. I can't accept your offer. Believe me, I want to, but it's out of my hands."

***

"Drink?" Andy asked, once Shaunna and Adele had departed with Kris and Ade. They were picking up Dan and Andy's mum on the way, and whilst it amused Andy that his mother was going to watch men dance naked, Dan was utterly appalled and doing his best to forget that Adele's evening would also be spent watching well-endowed musclemen swing their things.

"Yeah, cheers," he replied, eventually, once he'd shaken the image from his head. "Cold one?"

Andy sucked his teeth as he considered their options. "Peach squash, blackcurrant high juice, orange juice, water or red wine."

Dan raised an eyebrow and smirked. "Sounds like our fridge, that. Think I'll stick with OJ."

Andy went through to the kitchen. "How are you feeling about Comco now?"

Dan grunted. "Better than I did yesterday."

Andy returned with two full one-litre cartons; he and Dan had never used glasses for their orange juice, chugging it straight from the ripped or snipped corner of the carton, much to their mother's eternal chagrin. He handed one to Dan. "You know when he was bad-mouthing Campion? I was thinking, it'll bloody serve you right if you get stung, mate."

Dan glugged, swallowed, belched, sighed, and swiped an arc with his thumb through the condensation on the back of the carton. "Yeah, my thoughts exactly. You've gotta wonder how blokes like Al and Ed reach a point where their own board dictate what they can and can't do."

"Yep. Here's to small-scale logistics." Andy lifted his orange juice, and they bashed their cartons together in a toast.

"Go Team Jiffies," Dan said with a grin.

Andy laughed. "Maybe we should register it at Companies House."

"Maybe," Dan agreed, his thoughts drifting again to Comco. "I'm gonna go to the auction."

"I thought you might."

It wasn't in Dan's nature to let go, even when logically he knew this way was better. He could start looking for houses again without having to worry about mortgage payments, and he wouldn't have to stay on friendly terms with Scott Bryant, who seemed a decent bloke, but he was still the Anchors' sponsor and captain. Best of all, they wouldn't have to split their youth team along gender lines, although if they kept to an under-18 squad, they were still within the FA's mixed-team regs. With or without Comco's stadium and all the talk of sponsorship and government funding, The Lions youth team were heading for big things. How could they not be when they had access to the best youth coaches in the country?

"I'm still gonna talk to Charlie, see if she'll do some work with the youth team," Dan said.

"You'll have to watch you don't put Aitch's nose out of joint."

"Nah, he'll be all right, I reckon. Did you invite Mike over this evening?"

"I didn't. I will." Andy was already up off the sofa. He collected his tablet from the table and placed the call.

"Is your screen cracked there?" Dan asked. Andy either hadn't heard or he ignored the question.

"I'll call you back," Mike answered and ended the call.

Andy looked at Dan, stunned. "Well, that was bloody rude," he said as his tablet lit up with the incoming call.

"Alright, ugly?" Mike greeted with a grin.

"Video call? Since when?"

"Since this morning. New phone."

"Good stuff. Shame about the picture." Andy turned the screen towards Dan, who reared in his seat and grimaced. Mike carried on grinning. Andy turned the screen back. "Is your Bethan still up?"

"Yep." Mike flipped the camera. He was lying on the sofa; Bethan was sitting between his legs, her teary gaze on the TV. She was grisly and tired. Mike flipped the camera again.

"Fancy coming over?" Andy asked.

"To yours?"

"Yep. We're having a lads' night in."

Mike frowned and shook his head. "I dunno."

Dan held out his hand, gesturing at Andy's tablet. "Give me that." Andy obliged. "Right, get your arse in that van."

Mike smirked. "Gonna make me?"

Dan shrugged and took out his phone. "Nope. I'm gonna call Adele, get her to send photos of the action onstage." He grinned, and Mike and Andy laughed.

"See you in ten." Mike ended the call again.

Dan and Andy stared at each other in amazement.

"That was too easy," Andy said.

"Yeah," Dan agreed. "Speaking of men strutting their stuff, has Shaunna's boss ever mentioned the hen party gig again?"

Andy's eyebrows rose. "Seriously?"

Dan shrugged. "Why not? It was a laugh."

"I reckon fatherhood's gone to your head. Or it's your age."

"I'm still younger than you."

"Age is but a number."

"And mine will always be one less than yours."

"Yep. Definitely some kind of mid-life crisis." Andy ducked his head out of the way, so Dan punched him in the arm instead.

"Kris was saying Silhouetto are turning work down."

"You want to step into their jocks, do you, bro?"

Dan ignored that. "I think we should let Shaunna's boss know we're available for the festive season."

Andy got up and walked towards the kitchen, pausing briefly to study his brother.

"What?" Dan asked, fighting his smirk. He was winding Andy up, and getting away with it.

"Mental," Andy muttered and left the room.

Dan chuckled quietly to himself, quickly straightening his face when he heard Andy coming back to the accompaniment of crinkling plastic—dry-roasted peanuts, tortilla chips and pork scratchings.

Andy chucked the bags on the table and sat down. Then he got up again and switched on the light under the table.

"I like that," Dan said, already transfixed by the colour-changing glow that illuminated the circular white table in the centre of Andy and Shaunna's living room.

"Yeah, it's all right." Andy glanced around him. "Ade and Shaunna did a good job of this."

"They did." With the mini waterfall and the low-level lighting, Dan was relaxed but not sleepy, although he had a feeling it was as much about the people who lived there as it was about the fixtures and fittings. His gaze returned to the table and lost focus. *The Great Living Room Makeover*. He was well up for it. All he needed now was a living room to make over. "I'll have to get out and look at some houses this week," he said.

"Did you look at the listings I sent this morning?"

"Yeah. There're a couple that seem decent on paper." Dan opened the peanuts and tipped them into his hand. "I don't care, to be honest. Anywhere'd do." He made a couple of attempts to throw a nut into the air and catch it, failed both times and upended the contents of his hand into his mouth.

"You want me to choose one for you?" Andy offered with a grin. Dan's mouth was too full to answer, although he was tempted to take him up on it without a second thought. All of the properties Andy had sent him the details for were spot on, and knowing his brother, he'd have checked them out beforehand to make sure there were no problems, structural, legal or otherwise. Now Dan had given it a second thought, he found his answer was exactly the same.

"Go for it," he said.

"For real?"

"You know what I want, and you know what you're doing. So, yeah. For real."

There was a knock at the door, which was locked because Shu sometimes sleepwalked, and Andy got up to answer it. "You won't regret it," he called back, but there was no need to offer reassurance. Dan trusted him to make a good choice, plus, if Andy was making the decision, Adele couldn't throw it back in Dan's face in future arguments. It was a win-win situation, no cost-benefit analysis required.

22: No Pushover
Saturday, 13th–Sunday, 15th October

"Are yours all in bed?" Mike asked as he came into the living room with Bethan in her carry seat. He acknowledged Dan with a nod.

"Yep," Andy answered. "The girls are sleeping through at the minute—probably won't hear a peep from them till about five, five-thirty in the morning."

Mike curled his lip in mock resentment.

Andy laughed. "It won't last. I think their teeth are coming through."

"And Robbie'll wake for a feed soon," Dan said by way of additional consolation.

Mike set Bethan's chair down on the floor and left her in it. She seemed quite happy, even if it was coming up on nine p.m. *and she was still wide awake.* This time, though, it was nothing to do with his stress levels, which was odd, considering what had come in the post that morning.

"Want a drink, Mike?" Andy asked, already on his way to the kitchen.

"Yeah, please. Whatever you're having."

"We're on the OJ."

"That'll do me." Mike took off his jacket and settled back on the sofa, sighing as his body sagged in relaxation. Tiling the salon had turned out to be another bugger of a job, and he was aching all over, or he had been. "I'd forgotten how comfy this couch is."

"Yeah, it is," Dan agreed. "I wonder if they do it in black?"

"Bit bright for you, is it?"

"Just a bit." Dan tugged a sunshine-yellow cushion from behind him and stuck it up on the back of the fire-engine-red sofa. "It's like a kids' playroom in grown-up size." Dan folded his arms and frowned at Mike. "What colour's your sofa?"

"Grey, I think." Now Mike was frowning. He wasn't sure what colour it was. "Brown, maybe?"

"Beige," Andy said, returning with three cartons of juice. "Shaunna'll be cursing us. We only went shopping this morning." He handed his brothers a carton each and gave Bethan a wink as he sat down. She smiled coyly and hid behind her blanket. "She looks tired."

"She is," Mike confirmed. "She's into everything at the moment. And she's started crawling. Well, slithering on her belly, but she's bloody fast."

"Shu didn't crawl," Dan said. "She shuffled on her bottom."

"Yeah, I remember that," Andy said, laughing. "She shifted at a fair old rate, too, didn't she?"

Dan nodded but didn't elaborate, unfortunately, because Mike would've liked to hear more. He didn't know what to expect, or what was normal, and while he'd spent the day amazed and amused by Bethan's new mode of locomotion, he'd fretted that it might mean there was something wrong with her legs. His mum's assurance that all babies were different hadn't helped much when she'd added that all three of them had learnt to crawl. Still, if Shu hadn't crawled, then he was worrying over nothing. *Just for a change.*

Mike hadn't been around when Shu was a baby—he'd seen her once, when she first came home from hospital—and having Bethan had rammed home how hurtful his lack of interest would've been to Dan and Adele, not to mention how much

Mike had missed out, and to the detriment of his relationship with his niece. Even now, Shu was funny with him. She'd acknowledge him if he asked her a question, and she'd chatter away to Bethan, but otherwise she treated him like he was a stranger.

She adored her Uncle Andy, though, and Mike didn't begrudge him that, but it had made him determined to be the best uncle he could be for the twins and Robbie, so he was a bit disappointed they were asleep. On the plus side, it looked like the colour-change lights were hypnotising his daughter. The three of them were holding their breath, watching as Bethan's eyelids slowly closed, and her grip on her blanket relaxed. Mike gave his brothers a silent thumbs up.

"It's with me working strange hours," he explained, once he was sure she was asleep. "We've got out of our routine."

"How is the work situation?" Dan asked.

"Quiet. Hayley's salon took a day longer than expected. I finished that yesterday. Other than that, The Red Lion's the only job I've got lined up, so if you need me for anything…"

Dan was still on paternity leave and handed over to Andy, who thought for a moment and shook his head. "I'll keep an ear out."

"Cheers."

"*I'll* be needing you soon," Dan said. "Well, hopefully."

"Oh? Adele's picked her wallpaper, then?"

"To be honest, she'd picked one out ages ago, but it'll have gone out of fashion and she'll end up choosing something else. I'm looking for a house." Andy none too subtly coughed out the words *Andy is*. Dan corrected, "*Andy's* looking for a house for us."

"Oh, right." Mike nodded at Andy. "If you find one going spare, send it my way, will you?"

"Will do," Andy said with a chuckle. "Shall I stick some music on? Or will it wake Bethan?"

Mike leaned forward to check on her; she was out for the count. "Nah. I wouldn't have thought so."

Andy got up and collected two remote controls from the table, clicking both simultaneously to turn the stereo up and mute the TV. Until then, Mike hadn't noticed it was on—football highlights from the day's Premiership matches that drifted out of focus with his thoughts. Of course, the sorts of houses Dan and Andy could afford were well out of his reach, although he didn't need anything that big—a ground-floor apartment would do, so long as it had two bedrooms and access to an enclosed garden. In fact, Dan and Adele's place would've been ideal, but again, it was beyond Mike's means.

"Tomorrow's match is gonna be crap," Dan said.

"Ten-nil?" Andy suggested.

"What was it last time? Twelve?"

"Eleven. He disallowed my goal, didn't he?"

"That's right. You thought you were playing basketball."

"I was hoping the ref'd send me off. I was bored."

Dan laughed. "Maybe we should all try that one. Or ask to abandon the match, seeing as it's en vogue."

"Who are we playing?" Mike asked.

"The Bluebell. Average age of sixty-five. Nice blokes, though. We go easy on them, unlike the rest of the league."

"And still beat them ten goals to nil?"

"Yeah, well…" Dan got a bit defensive. "We've gotta keep it real."

"Sore loser," Andy muttered.

"Not at all. The Anchors don't cut them any slack, do they? They're playing them next week."

"Isn't there a veterans' league?" Mike asked.

"Yeah. There's only a handful of teams in it. Technically, half the Lions are vets—same for the Anchors and most of the teams in the league, to be fair. But as a wise monkey told me not so long ago, age is but a number."

Andy threw a packet of pork scratchings at Dan, and he headed it away, laughing and pulling his phone from his pocket at the same time. "Dad duty calls. Be right back." Dan left the room with Robbie's cries coming from his phone.

Mike frowned, bemused. "How's that work?"

"iBaby."

"Come again?"

"An app. Turns an eight-hundred-quid mobile into a walkie-talkie."

"Ah, gotcha." Mike nodded. "Clever, though, hey?"

"Yep." Andy retrieved the packet of pork scratchings and opened it. "Shaunna said it went well the other day."

Mike's heart sped up; he knew Andy meant his meeting with Jackie, and it was an unwelcome reminder. With the banter, he'd almost forgotten he'd come tonight with an ulterior motive—nothing sinister, or not on his part, but it was why he'd headed straight over to Andy's place without protest, hoping for a chance to get him on his own, and here it was. "Yeah," he said eventually. "It went very well. Jackie's nice. Did Shaunna tell you she used to teach Jess?"

"Yeah, she did, and she worked with Siobhan?"

Mike nodded. "I'm taking Bethan round there tomorrow, after the match."

"You staying with her?"

"This time, yeah, till they get to know each other a bit better." They'd exhausted all the small talk on that subject, and Dan would be back down any second. Mike swallowed hard. "I got a letter this morning. From Rachel."

Andy's eyebrows rose slightly, but he continued watching the muted football highlights, waiting for Mike to say more.

"She said…" Mike took a deep breath and braced himself. "She wants to see you."

"No way." Still, Andy didn't look away from the TV screen, although he was glaring angrily at it rather than watching it. "No fucking way."

It was the answer Mike had expected, and he wasn't planning on trying to persuade Andy, or replying to Rachel. He'd tell Jackie tomorrow and leave it at that.

"What else did she say?" Andy asked.

"Not much. Just more of her mind games."

"Such as?"

"Doesn't matter." Mike switched his attention to the TV, or pretended to. The stress was making him feel sick.

"What did she say, Mike?"

He was angry with himself for even bringing it up. It wasn't fair to drag Andy into it again. But if she meant it…

"She said if you visited her one last time, she'd give up her parental rights."

For a few minutes, nothing happened. Both kept their eyes glued to the TV, but Mike felt the movement transfer along the sofa. Andy was shaking with rage. Upstairs, a floorboard creaked. Dan was on his way back down. Andy got up, stormed over to the patio doors, slid them open with force and went outside, where he stood with his hands on his head, his elbows out to the sides, feet apart, every muscle tensed.

"What's up with him?" Dan asked, the last part of the question masked by the loud roar of 'fuck' from outside.

"Rachel."

"Ah." Dan nodded and sat down again. "That'd do it."

⁕

Andy had been bang on the money with his ten-nil prediction, although he was too angry to gloat. Mike's guilt for that was mitigated to some extent by the two goals he'd contributed to their victory over The Bluebell, who were great guys, but they *were* all getting on a bit. And he'd thought Dan had been exaggerating. Even so, their goalkeeper, just turned seventy, was a spritely geezer deserving of the man-of-the-match award for saving the dozens of attempts that had come his way.

After the match, Mike set off for Jackie's while the rest of the Lions went back to their home turf for the usual Sunday roast. Whilst he was glad for a reason to get out of Andy's way, he was gutted he couldn't go with them, and not only for the grub, but Jackie had invited him and Bethan for Sunday dinner. Mike hoped she wasn't into all that nouvelle cuisine crap Rachel had liked, little tiny portions piled up to look pretty and about as filling as fresh air. There again, Pez still lived at home, and he didn't look like he was going to starve to death anytime soon.

The Perrys lived on the outskirts of the closest town to theirs, and on the way, Mike stopped off at a supermarket to pick up a bottle of wine and some flowers. The address Jackie had given him turned out to be a sizeable detached cottage, with fields on one side and the beginning of the townhouses on the other. He pulled up outside and sat for a moment, watching Bethan play with the string of toys across her seat while he got his head together. It would be better to get the Rachel stuff out the way first, so they stood a chance of enjoying the afternoon, but he was dreading it. Every time she'd come up in conversation last Monday, Jackie had become tearful, and Mike hadn't known what to say, when he was as desperate to keep Bethan away from Rachel as Jackie was to reunite the two of them. He wasn't going to change his mind, and neither was Andy.

The only way was to say it how it was, and with that decision made, Mike scooped his daughter out of her car seat and set off, past the two brand new cars in the driveway, to the front door, which opened as he approached.

"Hi," Jackie greeted him and then gave Bethan a smile that could've lit up a town.

Mike handed Bethan over to her grandma, quite certain he'd been made redundant for the afternoon.

"Come in," Jackie invited and moved away from the door. Mike followed her inside, glancing around him, trying to take in his surroundings without judgement, but it was difficult, given his trade—or one of his trades, in which he hoped his days were numbered—and the state of the décor. Based on what he knew of Jackie and Rachel, he'd somehow expected the house to be pristine, with the usual plain walls and far too many pictures, photos, paintings, and so on, that he'd seen in other middle-class homes, including his mum and Len's. It was nothing like that, more a TV-DIY aftermath, with faded washes, bumpy walls and handwritten slogans.

Jackie led him into the sitting room, which wasn't much better, and he stifled a chuckle at the image in his mind of Kris's other half having an interior-designer hissy fit if he ever clapped eyes on Jackie's house. The scant, modern furniture was dark in colour and set against a backdrop of patterned wallpaper dominated by lime green, and yellow floral curtains. Even by Mike's unfussy standards, it was hideous. But…he wasn't here as her decorator.

"I should've checked in advance," Jackie said. "Do you like curry?"

"Yeah," Mike confirmed. He'd caught a whiff of garlic and spices before his senses got overwhelmed by the terrible wall coverings. "Smells good," he said.

"Chicken jalfrezi with pilau rice, naan bread and a couple of side dishes. Felix is making those, so we could end up with jelly and mayonnaise."

Mike screwed up his nose. "Excellent."

Jackie laughed. "He's a good boy, but he has quite a few cognitive deficits, hence—" she looked around the room "—the unusual colour scheme."

"Ah." Mike was pleased she'd told him that; he wasn't sure he was doing a good job of hiding his opinion.

"After we moved here, I gave him free reign, which probably wasn't the best idea I've ever had, but it would only take a lick of paint." Jackie gave Mike a hopeless smile.

"Nah, it's...unique." He grinned.

"Yes, it's certainly that. Now, would you like a drink? We have beer, soft drinks, coffee, tea...?"

"Coffee would be great, cheers. White, one sugar."

Jackie walked past him to leave the room, carrying Bethan on her hip. "Come through to the kitchen if you like." She peered back over her shoulder. "Sunglasses might be advisable."

Mike laughed. "I've got some in the van. Oh! That reminds me." He'd left the wine and flowers in the back. "Won't be a sec."

"OK. Leave the door off the latch," Jackie called after him.

The words stirred Mike's memories of his mum saying the same to him and his brothers when they were kids going out to play in the street and yelling 'were you born in a barn?' if they left doors open at any other time.

Mike made a promise to himself to try not to inflict the same confusion on Bethan, collected the wine and flowers, and returned to the house, quietly closing the door and holding back for a moment. Jackie was talking to Bethan, telling her about Tammy and Felix, and her grandpa, who was up in heaven with the angels. Mike was sad and somewhat astounded to hear that. Rachel had never spoken about her family, or not beyond threats to tell her mother lies about him.

At the next pause in Jackie's monologue, Mike noisily made his way to the kitchen, where Jackie took one look at the flowers and started to cry, and kept crying as she made the coffee. Mike loitered awkwardly, never sure what to do when women cried, although the ones he'd been close to over the years didn't, as a general rule. Anne, he'd seen cry just the once, when the doctor told her she couldn't safely carry another baby. His mum had cried a few times, but they'd been angry tears, where the best option was to duck and run for cover. As for Rachel...he'd seen her cry, all right—in court, when she was trying to persuade the jury she was innocent, and when that failed, that she was depressed.

"I'm sorry," Jackie stuttered out through her tears. "No-one's bought me flowers in a long, long time."

"It's all right," Mike said. He edged closer, tore a piece of paper towel from the roll on the counter and handed it to her. He'd have offered to take Bethan, but he got the impression she was the only thing holding Jackie together.

With one-handed expertise, Jackie wiped her eyes and nose, and took a vase down from a shelf. "They're lovely," she said, admiring the flowers. "You really didn't need to bring anything, though."

"I'm not doing myself any favours by telling you, but they're only from the supermarket."

"Well, as they say, it's the thought that counts. Thank you." Jackie filled the vase with water and stood the flowers in it. "I'll arrange those properly later," she said and squinted at the label on the wine bottle. "Oh, yes. I'm already looking forward to a glass." She indicated to the coffee. "Best drink that first, though. Shall we sit in the lounge?"

"Sure." Mike picked up both cups and followed Jackie back into the green and yellow room, which wasn't as much of a shock the second time around. In spite of her advance warning, he hadn't even noticed what colour the kitchen was, but then, he'd been preoccupied. Once they were both seated, Mike cut to the chase. "I got a letter off Rachel yesterday." From Jackie's expression, she'd expected it.

"She said she was going to write to you, when I went to visit her on Wednesday."

"Is she back in prison?"

"No. They're keeping her in hospital indefinitely. My lawyer— my *new* lawyer—thinks they might make it a permanent arrangement. She's very unwell, Mike."

He nodded, although eight months as Rachel's 'victim'—longer, really, because it still wasn't over—made it difficult for him to accept there was a reason for her cruelty, a reason to forgive her.

"She's full of remorse for what she did to you and Bethan."

"What she did?"

"Walking out on you. She still loves you both, very much."

"That's not what her letter said. She wants Andy to visit, but he won't. Can you tell her, please, next time you see her?"

"Of course." She shook her head in confusion. "I don't understand. I mean, I know she thinks a lot of your brother, but why would she want to see him?"

Mike clamped his teeth together. He was on the brink of telling her precisely why Rachel wanted to see Andy, and it would help no-one. Instead, he rubbed his belly, feigning a hunger he'd lost at the start of their conversation.

"Did you want to eat?" Jackie asked.

Mike nodded and put on his best smile. "Let's drink our coffee, then I'll give you a hand in the kitchen."

23: Roar
Thursday, 18th October

"Let me guess. We've got a problem?" Andy had meant it as a joke, and hoped Dan would take it as such, although his tone was far from jovial; he could hear that for himself. It wasn't like him to hold onto a bad mood. However, the five days since Mike told him about Rachel's letter had been five days of constantly churning it around in his mind, revisiting his refusal, having second thoughts, and then remembering who they were dealing with. This was the woman who had taken a life, tried to kill his friends, gaslighted and physically abused his brother, set up her own brother and had a baby, all to get Andy's attention.

She was probably cackling with delight right now, knowing Andy would be thinking about her, considering giving in to her demands. She'd played her hand as expertly as ever and was once again using his brother and niece—*her daughter*—to get to him. Bethan might have given Mike the impetus to turn his life around, but she was also his Achilles heel. If he turned his back on Rachel Perry, she'd take him down.

"Well? Are you gonna say something?"

"You talking to me?" Dan asked curtly.

"Who else?"

"You're at Campion Trust, aren't you? You could've been talking to Alice."

Andy raised an eyebrow and peered down at Alice, who was sitting at her computer with her back to him. "As if I'd dare."

“Yeah, well, don’t think you can take it out on me, either. I’ll kick your—”

“All right, sorry.” With the phone to his ear, Andy peered over Alice’s shoulder, jabbing at the screen and the new contract she was drawing up for him. “Helena Fairclough.”

Alice smacked his hand away and wiped her computer screen. “I don’t know how you expect me to know if you don’t tell me these things.”

Andy made a sad face and mouthed ‘sorry’. Alice breathed out hard through her nose and made the necessary change to the document.

“Bro?” Dan said on the other end of the phone.

“Yeah, what were you saying?”

“I said nothing.”

Andy suppressed a growl. “What did you ring for?”

“Dublin.”

“You’re sending me on another wild goose chase.”

“Wrong species, bro,” Dan joked.

“Shut the f…” Andy managed to stop before he said the F-word in front of Alice, but he was too angry to trust his mouth not to betray him. For what it was worth, Dan had got the gist and kept his mouth shut, too.

Andy had seen the email a couple of hours ago; it came in as he was pulling up outside the Campion Trust office. He’d read the message, deleted it and successfully got his phone back in his pocket without launching it across the car park. Now, Dan was chasing up his non-reply, and it would have added to his rage, had there been any going spare.

“It’s only Ireland,” Dan reasoned. “An hour there and back, if that.”

“Fifty-five minutes,” Andy corrected.

“You’ll be ba—”

“Plus getting to and from the airport, check-in times, not to mention delays.”

"D'you want me to go?"

"How?" He didn't give Dan a chance to answer. "Forget it. It's just a bloody big coincidence it's the same day, don't you think?"

"I swear, I'm not pulling a fast one. It was the only day the wildlife people could make it."

"What's wrong with video conferencing?"

"They need to check the animal's fit for transportation."

Andy had no comeback to that.

Alice beckoned him over. He checked the screen again, mouthed 'thank you' and blew her a kiss. Flustered as ever by his flirting, Alice hastily sent the contract to the printer and bustled away to collect it.

"What can I do?" Dan asked.

"Not go to the auction."

"Realistically."

Andy ran his free hand through his hair. "Not go to the auction. I know what you're like."

"What's that supposed to mean?"

"It's not *supposed* to mean anything. If I'm not there to stop you, you'll end up in a bidding war and get yourself in deep shit."

He heard Dan breathing hard and fast at the other end of the line. In spite of his anger, he was, apparently, sensible enough to not argue to the contrary.

"Right," Andy said. "We don't need to be there in person to sort out what we're doing. In any case—"

"The vet's gonna want to talk to Igor."

"Yeah, bro. There's this modern contraption called a telephone. As I was about to say, before some rude S-O-B interrupted me, I'm not getting on a plane with Igor. He's deranged."

Andy wasn't exaggerating. Igor was a hardened HGV driver who had once been part of a circus that had traversed some of the most extreme routes through Russia, Europe and Asia. He liked nothing better than to scare rookies with horrifying tales of his own near-misses as well as of those who had not been quite so fortunate.

While people assumed Igor was one of Andy's less savoury contacts, he was actually a mate of Len's and didn't ask too many questions about what he was carrying, not that it was ever an issue with Jeffries and Associates. They were fully above board. Igor was also one of the drivers they could rely on for the jobs nobody in their right mind would take on, like transporting a fully grown Bengal tiger from a private collection in Dublin to a sanctuary in Rajasthan, India.

"Was there anything else?" Andy asked.

"Nope. I still think it would be better if you—"

"I'm not fucking going!" Andy shouted. Alice's nostrils flared. With a great deal of effort, Andy put a lid on his temper and lowered his voice. "I'll email the client, see if I can move the meeting forward a couple of hours. That way—"

"He's got more jobs for us. If we—"

Andy talked over Dan's protest. "*That way* I'll be with you by half three at the latest."

"And if the stadium comes up early?"

"I'll chuck all my junk out the spare room, and you can stay with us until the council rehouse you, or you get your very own urn. In a bit." Andy ended the call, trying his best not to punch anything. *Fucking brothers. Who needs them?*

"Do you want to check this through?" Alice asked. She was keeping her distance and talking very nasally, trying to block him out, Andy realised. He forced calm thoughts into his head. *Sun breaking the horizon, empty ocean, rolling tide...*

"No, thanks, Alice. I know it'll be perfect. You're a star." Andy scrawled his signature on the bottom.

"I'll email a copy right away and make sure this goes out in this evening's post." Alice signed to witness Andy's signature, deftly folded the contract in three, poked it into a hash-ten envelope and put it with the Campion Trust outgoing mail.

Brushing her hands together in satisfaction at another job well done, she turned back and offered him a sympathetic smile. "Your colours are dreadfully chaotic today," she said.

"Ha, yeah. I'm not surprised."

"I have two excellent ears for listening, if you'd care to utilise them."

Andy combed his fingers through his hair, drumming on his scalp while he considered her offer. Alice loved a good chinwag, and she had a tendency to let things slip when put under duress. All it would take was the right prompt from Dan, and she'd report back everything Andy said, word for word. No, he was being harsh. She kept her counsel when it mattered. After all, Alice had been Alistair Campion's PA and his lover; she'd known he was being blackmailed, and she'd kept the secret for years. She knew about the fraud ring, or the stuff Jess was involved in, at least, and kept that to herself, too. She might even understand his predicament.

"Do you have any brothers or sisters, Alice?"

"One. A brother. He is ten years my senior and emigrated to Germany before I left school. We were never close, regrettably, though I sense you would rather appreciate a little distance from your brothers at times."

"Like now?" Andy sighed and shook his head. "No. I'm happy we sorted our differences, but..." He shrugged, still figuring it out as he went along. "I honestly never saw myself as the sensible one."

Alice smiled knowingly. "Ah, you're mistaking fulfilment for tedium, dear. Are you discontent?"

"With the business?"

"With your life."

"Absolutely not. My life is... It's..." It was the weirdest thing. Andy had to stop to catch his breath at the sudden surge of emotion, like a barrel closing in, and he was holding on, leaving it too long. He needed to let go...

"Alice? What the... How..."

She pursed her lips and shrugged as if she had no idea what he was talking about, but he could see she was fighting a smile.

Andy laughed, still amazed, and seriously considering the possibility Alice might be a witch. It was like a steroid-enhanced version of the anger management Josh had taught him, and his rage had disappeared into thin air.

Not a revelation, a reminder, that on the other side of the tempest he was sailing with his brothers, his daughters and their mother were awaiting his safe return. "My life is awesome," he said. "I've never told you about Shaunna, have I?"

"Not in words." Alice's eyes twinkled mischievously. Andy felt himself blush, and Alice laughed. "Let me tell you..." She held up her forefinger. "I should make us some tea first."

Before Andy could protest—not that he'd intended to— Alice trotted out of the office and across to the kitchen, from where, soon after, he heard the sounds of the kettle boiling and a teapot being prepared. He used the time to send Shaunna a text: *How are my girls? x*

Her reply—*We're good. What time ru home? x*—came as Alice returned with a tray bearing a teapot, a milk jug and two cups and saucers. Andy typed a quick response: *After tea with Alice. Love you. x*

Alice set the tray down on the desk Jason shared with whichever trustee happened to be working on any given day. Andy's phone buzzed in his hand. *We love you too. x*. He smiled and put his phone away, aware that Alice was watching him, or, rather, studying the air around his head. Once upon a time, he'd found it disconcerting, but he was well used to it by now. She was analysing his scent, and from it his state of mind.

"That's much better." She smiled and nodded her approval. "Now, where were we? Ah, yes." She paused to adjust the tea cosy and resumed her seat at her desk but still facing Andy. "Are you going to sit down, dear?"

Obediently, Andy pulled out the chair next to the other desk and sat. "Should I pour the tea, Alice?"

"Not yet, dear."

"OK."

"Tea, like all good things, takes time to reach its potential." Alice raised an eyebrow and tilted her head to indicate she meant him.

"A good thing." He nodded with fake arrogance. "I can go with that."

Alice laughed. "You are a *good man*, Andy. You very much remind me of Neil. He, too, was a free spirit, and mostly happy with his lot. Unlike you, however, he refused to drop anchor. I was a solitary port in his eternal storm."

"That's beautiful, Alice." And further confirmation that she was, indeed, a witch, or psychic, maybe.

She bowed her head graciously. "Thank you. Neil is at peace now, but he was so restless, unable to settle, and you were no different. Of course, you and Jess had your little arrangement—a homing beacon, if you will."

"More a pirate than a homing beacon," Andy contended.

Alice nodded in acquiescence. "I appreciate how difficult it has been for all of you to come to terms with what Jess did. Nonetheless, she *did* bring you home."

He supposed Alice was right about that. Jess *had* brought him home, and not just the once. She'd saved his neck plenty of times, and whilst she'd deceived everyone else, she and Andy had always known where they stood with each other. They'd shared a love of danger, a sense of daring, a drive to be the best. She'd played a game of chance and got lucky. But like all games, there were losers as well as winners, and victory had come at a cost. However, whilst Andy believed in karma, he didn't see Jess's illness as payback. In the end, she'd put things right, and she'd encouraged him to follow his heart.

"The tea should be ready now," Alice said, prompting him to do the honours, which he duly did, delivering her cup to the coaster on her desk. She thanked him, and he returned to his seat. Both picked up their cups.

"So I gave off some kind of love vibe?" Andy asked.

"A love vibe? Goodness! You were almost vibrating, dear. That's what love does to us. It makes the soul sing. Even your brother, no matter how hard he pretends otherwise.

"You know, when I first met you, there was so little to distinguish you from Dan. He always has been the more reserved of the two of you, but you shared the same restiveness, almost as if you knew where you had to be yet were reluctant to make the journey."

"Yeah." Andy nodded. "That's exactly how it felt."

"I do believe your travels have granted you wisdom your younger brother does not yet possess. You both found your way some time ago. He'll realise eventually, just as you did. I'm confident of that."

Andy smiled ruefully. "I wish I was."

"Your frustration and anger get the better of you, which is understandable. You're worried for your brothers. But don't forget, these feelings are transient. They're not part of you. It won't be long before you can go back to being plain old Andy, the handsome 'surfer dude' with the stunning girlfriend and beautiful twin daughters."

Andy's face was burning, and he bashfully covered his eyes, although he was grinning at the compliment. "Cheers, Alice. There's not many people get me blushing."

"I'm glad I could oblige. Now, drink your tea, dear, before it gets cold."

***

Andy's high spirits lasted until he walked through the front door and Shaunna collapsed against him, sobbing. He thought he'd caught a flash of white bandage, but with her arms around him, he couldn't see, and he got the impression it was secondary to whatever had her in pieces.

"Shhh, it's all right, baby." He smoothed her hair and kissed the top of her head. "It's all right." In between her sobs, he listened out for any noise from the girls, not wanting to ask the question, in part because he was terrified of the answer. His gut feeling was they were fine, and he was happy to stick with that until Shaunna had calmed down and could tell him what was wrong. Ultimately, snot got the better of her, and she pulled away, trying to sniff through completely blocked nostrils. Andy lifted the front of his t-shirt, offering it to her.

She laughed through her tears. "I'b gudda gedda dishu."

"You been taking elocution lessons from Hayley, RHB?" He followed her into the living room, where she tugged about a dozen tissues from the box and noisily blew her nose.

"Sorry," she said.

"It's OK." He hated seeing her so upset. It did weird things to his brain, turned him a bit Neanderthal. "Where are the girls?"

"Upstairs."

Andy silently vented a relieved sigh. Shaunna dabbed at her eyes, mascara everywhere, but he didn't mention it. He could see now that her left wrist was wrapped in an elasticated bandage. She noticed him looking at it and sniffed back new tears.

"It's my own stupid fault." She flopped down onto the sofa and sat hunched forward with her head down.

Andy sat next to her and put his arm around her shoulders. "What happened?"

"I went to see Dad. He... He was agitated, didn't know who I was. He kept saying Siobhan, and I tried to tell him, *I'm Shaunna*, and he was getting so frustrated. He lost his temper, screamed at me to get out, so...so I did, as quickly as I could. It was awful..."

Shaunna gulped and fell against Andy, the tears taking over again. He shushed her and kept hold, waiting for her to continue.

"I caught the pushchair on the door handle, and it whipped round, trapping my hand. My wrist…" She held it up with her other hand. "I feel such a wuss. It's only a sprain."

Andy gave her a gentle squeeze. "Sprains can hurt more than fractures. Do you know that?" She nodded tearily. "Are you hurt anywhere else?"

"No. Just my wrist and…" She trailed off, and Andy filled in the gap. Visiting her dad was always distressing, and Shaunna was a tough cookie. But this time, it had really got to her.

"Did you walk home?"

She shook her head. "I walked to the drop-in centre, then I called Kris, but he and Ade were at work, so I called Mike."

"Not Dan?"

"I thought Dan was with you."

"Nope."

"Oh. Well, Mike borrowed your mum's car and came and got us." Shaunna straightened up, blew her nose again and took a few shaky breaths, followed by one slow deep breath, in, out… She flicked her hair back over her shoulders and kissed his cheek. "Did you get all your work done?"

"Err…yeah." Andy shifted his arm and twirled her curls around his fingers. She had this way of just pulling herself together, and it triggered some kind of instinct in him to protect her, fight for her, make love to her. In other words, it made him super horny, and he was only delaying acting on it because of her injury. She was also chewing her lip—a sure sign she had something else to tell him.

"There was a call for you earlier," she said.

That wasn't it. "Was there?"

"Yeah. Somebody and Thompson? Estate agents. I wrote it down."

"Ah. Good stuff." It would be to arrange a viewing of one of the houses he'd selected for Dan and Adele.

"And Kris wants to know what we think about going on holiday together."

That wasn't it, either. "When?"

"After New Year. To Leon's chalet."

"OK? That's random."

"You don't like the idea? We don't have to."

"No. I think it's a great idea, but I'd rather wait till the girls are walking."

"Don't they do baby-skiers? You know, like baby-walkers?" Shaunna glanced his way and attempted a smile. He kissed her.

"They might," he answered as if it had been a serious question. "So, come on. Hit me with it."

"Mike's decided he's going to visit Rachel."

"With Bethan?"

"No. It's next Thursday. He asked me if I'd look after Bethan for him. He asked your mum first, but she said no."

"Bloody hell. He must've told her what Rachel did, I'm guessing."

"That's just it. He hasn't told her anything about Rachel, but he's going with Jackie. I think your mum's worried it means Jackie's going to change her mind about custody."

"She's not the only one." The anger that Alice had successfully helped him quell was returning in full force. "They're manipulating him again." Andy got up and started pacing the room. "He can't see it. Why can't he see it?"

"Andy, listen."

"He's gonna lose everything because of that bitch. Why can't she just let him be? Let *us* be."

"Hun, come and sit down."

He stopped pacing. "We need to stop him from going."

"I tried, but he said he needs to see her."

"I should've said yes."

"No, you really shouldn't. That's what she wants. You." Shaunna got up and walked over to him, her tears dried, her expression determined as she smoothed her hand over his hair and kissed him on the chin. "And she's not getting you." She flicked her tongue along the cleft, tracing it up to his lips. "Do you know why?"

Andy shook his head dumbly, his anger now battling with arousal as Shaunna looked him in the eye and smiled her wickedest smile. Her hands strayed to his pants, button popped, zip down…

"Because she's getting me instead."

24: Working it Out
Monday, 22nd October

In the dark of the passageway outside his mum and Len's home gym, Dan peered through the glass pane in the door, trying to see around the corner, to where the weights were situated. The deafeningly loud rock music almost drowned the clanging of metal and primitive grunts that confirmed Dan's instincts had been correct. Still, he couldn't blame his brother for reacting this way. He'd have done exactly the same himself.

Knowing there was a real risk of getting a dumbbell hurled at him, Dan entered the gym and took his time chalking his hands, warming up, edging closer. Andy had noticed him but had yet to acknowledge his presence, and Dan made the strategic decision to work on his abs first. Lying on the floor made him more vulnerable, but it was less threatening. He needed to time it right, when Andy was reaching exhaustion and before the adrenaline kicked in, or he wouldn't absorb what Dan told him.

His back muscles registered the thud of the barbell hitting the floor, but he kept up the ab crunches, watching Andy rotate his overworked shoulders and grit his teeth against the pain. The right one, he'd dislocated three times that Dan knew of, and probably more. Anger made the Jeffries boys do idiotic things, and extreme workouts were Dan's style, not Andy's, but he'd retired from madcap overseas adventures, which was a good thing on this occasion. At least Dan could keep tabs on him here.

"What d'you want?" Andy asked without looking Dan's way.

"A couple of things." Either Andy wasn't interested, or he was doing a great job of acting it. Dan went on. "One, I'm not going to the auction."

"Yeah, right."

Dan stopped crunching and sat up. "It's the truth."

"Scott Bryant's still gonna go. You know that, don't you?"

"Let him. We don't need any more hassle—"

"We?"

"All right. *You* don't need any more hassle, especially when it can be avoided, and I'll get over it."

Andy stopped sneering and looked like he was mulling it over. After a minute or so, he nodded and held out his hand. Dan grabbed on and allowed himself to be hoisted to his feet.

"I appreciate the gesture..." Andy began. Dan jumped in before the 'but'.

"There's too much shit going on without me chasing trouble."

"Yeah, well, you weren't to know it was the same day as the auction." Andy let out a dry laugh. "Pity we can't deliver that tiger to the secure hospital."

Dan chuckled. "Yeah, that'd solve the problem, wouldn't it?" He held Andy's gaze, willing him to stand down.

It took a while, but eventually, Andy's shoulders dropped and his scowl faded, replaced by a worried frown. "Thursday's gonna be the pits." He crouched to unscrew the end of the barbell. "I'm not even arsed about the Dublin job. How bad is that?"

"D'you want me to do the conference call?"

"Nah, it's all right. I need the distraction. What's Mike doing with Bethan? Do you know?"

"No idea."

"Mum hasn't changed her mind?"

"Not as far as I know." The music was starting to get on Dan's nerves. He glanced up at the closest speaker. "Mind if I turn this down a bit?"

"S'pose."

Dan found the remote control and dropped the volume, not by much, but enough to talk without raising their voices.

"What was the other thing you wanted?" Andy asked.

Dan's stomach plummeted. Andy was barely in control as it was, but he'd brought it on himself, even if Dan fully understood why he'd done it, and he needed to know.

"Bro?" Andy prompted.

"Jackie told Mike you'd been to see her."

Andy continued with taking the weights off the bar, returning them, one at a time, to the rack. "Where is he?"

"I don't know. He'd just got back before I came in here. Len and Charlie intercepted him at the gates."

"How'd he take it?"

"How you'd expect. I'd keep a low profile until Thursday's out the way, if I were you."

"Yeah, well, you're not." Andy dropped the bar on the rack, marched past Dan and out of the gym, slamming the door behind him. The bar bounced a couple of times and settled into its groove.

***

Wherever Charlie had gone with Mike, they were taking their time coming back. Len had returned almost an hour ago with Bethan, and he and their mother had taken the grandchildren to the living room, leaving Dan and Andy in the kitchen, awaiting Mike's return. In spite of Dan trying to reason with him, Andy wasn't shifting until they'd thrashed it out. It was going to be one hell of a ding-dong, and Dan wasn't sure which of them he'd have laid money on.

Andy's phone buzzed, and he answered it with a cool, "Yeah?" Dan stepped out to afford him some privacy, or the illusion of privacy. He wasn't letting Andy out of his sight.

"When was that?" Andy asked the person on the other end of the phone. Shaunna, Dan presumed. "No. He's not come back here." It had to be about Mike. "OK… Of course I won't… Yeah, love you, too. Bye."

Dan went back in and resumed his seat opposite Andy.

"That was Shaunna," Andy said. "Mike went to our place, looking for me."

"Was he still angry?"

"You could say that. He told her he was gonna bury me."

"Ah."

"Sean was there."

"Was he?"

"Yep. It's Monday."

"Oh, right." Dan had no idea why that was significant, but it didn't really matter, so he didn't ask.

"Sean had a chat with Mike, but it made no odds." Andy got up and left the kitchen.

"Where you going?" Dan shouted, already on his feet.

Andy peered back around the door. "For a piss. Wanna come?" He squeezed out a grin, and Dan waved him away.

"Yeah, yeah, all right. Do one."

Twenty minutes on, and with no sign of Mike, Dan took a chance and popped to the loo himself. Of course, sod's law dictated that those few minutes in the two hours they'd been sitting around were the few minutes Mike chose to get back. Dan quickly shook off, flew down the stairs, jumped the last few and skidded his way across the atrium. Slowing to normal walking pace, he approached the kitchen, ominously quiet but for the fridge door closing and a muttered interchange that he couldn't make out but sounded like no more than 'excuse me' and 'sorry'. He stepped into the doorway to survey the damage.

If tension could crackle, the room would have lit up like a Faraday cage. Andy was sitting where Dan had left him; Mike was on his feet, leaning against a cupboard at the far end of the room, a beer bottle in one hand, the other shoved deep in his jeans pocket. He made eye contact with Dan. "Did you tell him?"

Dan nodded.

Mike took a long swig of his beer, his gaze settling on Andy. "Do you have any idea what you've done?"

Andy stayed facing front, his eyelids lowered as if he were reading a newspaper.

"You're gonna talk to me."

Andy shook his head.

"It wasn't a request. What did you think it would achieve? She's heard it all before, and it makes no bloody difference. Hormone imbalance led to that woman's death. Pez has got an overactive imagination. I can't wait to see what bullshit she comes up with to justify what Rachel did to me. I thought *you*, of all people, would understand that."

"Understand what, Mike?"

"What kids do to you. God forbid any of us go through what Jackie has, but would we be any different?"

"If my daughter killed someone—"

"You'd believe whatever lies she told you to convince you she *didn't do it, Daddy*. And don't pretend otherwise. Did you tell her everything?"

Andy sat back and turned Mike's way. "I didn't give her a blow-by-blow account, if that's what you're asking, but I could've done." He got up and went to the fridge. "Laptop in the face…hammer to the balls…where did she hit you with the iron again?" Andy took out a bottle of beer and offered it to Dan. "You want?"

As the words left his mouth, Mike charged him, full force. The beer bottle flew out of Andy's hand and hit the table several feet away, shattering on impact. Mike punched Andy in the gut, his fist rising to deliver a facial blow. Andy took it, no retaliation, no blocking, and it threw Dan for a moment. He'd expected all-out war, but Andy was taking the hits and not fighting back.

Dan knew he had to intervene, but how? If he stepped between them, he'd end up getting hit instead. If he tried to pull

Mike off, he'd break free and take them both on. But if he left them to it…

What he wouldn't give to have a woman here right now—his mum, Adele, Shaunna—any one of them could've stopped the fight, and it was now a fight. They were going to kill each other. But there were no women to save them this time. There was just him and his brothers. Those Jeffries boys. Pains in the arse, always causing trouble. If they weren't scrapping with everyone else, they were scrapping with each other…or sticking up for one another…

Andy shoved Mike with his shoulder, slamming him into the open fridge door and sending the contents to the floor. Dan slipped in the resultant puddle of milk, and as he lost his footing, he grabbed Mike's sleeve, taking him down with him.

"Keep out of it," Mike snarled and tried to get up, but Andy flat-footed him in the chest and knocked him back to the floor. With both arms, Dan gripped Andy's leg, clinging to it while Andy tried to shake him off. He gave it a sharp jerk, intending to fell Andy, too, except Andy had hold of the fridge door. The fridge tilted, became top-heavy, and Dan stared up in horror as, in slow motion, it toppled forwards, closing in on him. He shut his eyes and braced—

"Whoa!"

"Got it?"

"Yep. Shove it back this way."

"That's it."

Dan opened one eye, squinting up at his brothers, who were shuffling the fridge back against the wall. He started breathing again.

"Soft bastard," Mike said, shaking his head at him. "Why didn't you roll?"

"Me? Ask *him* why he didn't fight back." Dan kicked Andy's foot. "Wanna give me a hand up?"

"Nah, you look like Cleopatra down there, bro."

Mike and Andy started laughing, leaving him to get up on his own. The air on his wet back made him shiver.

"I'm bloody drenched in milk," he moaned.

"You get used to it," Andy said with a sickly grin.

"T-M-I, bro," Mike complained, though he was still laughing at Andy's Cleopatra comment.

"Is that it, then?" Dan asked. "Only, I thought you were gonna kill him."

"So did I…" Mike shrugged at Andy; the laughter stopped. "Until I hit you and realised I'd have done the same. More than that, if it hadn't been me, it would've been you. And that wouldn't do at all. I'm your big brother." Mike rested his hand on Andy's shoulder; uncharacteristically, his eyes filled with tears. "It's my job to protect you."

Andy grabbed Mike and hauled him in for a hug. "You melon. The size of us, we can look after ourselves."

Dan turned away so he no longer had to see Mike's distress. He'd never said it to anyone, not even Josh, but there were times he'd blamed Mike for what happened with Rachel. He should've walked away the very first time she hit him. Before that. Now it was becoming clear to him why Mike had stayed and taken it. It wasn't weakness on his part, nor was it entirely down to Rachel's cruelty. He was punishing himself, like he'd always done, for what he believed was his failure to protect his younger brothers, to protect Dan from Kris's great uncle.

"It wasn't your fault, Mike." Dan turned back. "It wasn't your fault."

Whether Mike understood or not, he extended an arm, pulling Dan into a three-way hug.

"Fuck me, you really are drenched, bro," Andy muttered. "Starting to smell a bit rank, too."

"Yeah," Dan agreed, grateful to Andy for saving him from blubbing. "You get used to it."

"To be fair," Mike said, pulling away from Andy for effect, "you don't smell that great, either."

"I've been working off my anger. What's your excuse?"

"I've been running all round town looking for you."

Andy nodded. "Guess we're even, then."

"Sounds like."

"Go Team Whiffies?" Dan suggested. Mike and Andy groaned. "I know how we can fix that. Anyone fancy a skinny-dip?"

"We'd best clean up first, or Mum'll kill us." As Mike spoke, a hand cuffed him around the head, then Andy, then Dan.

"Go on with the lot of you," their mum said, trying to sound cross at the same time as smiling and blinking away tears. The three of them scuffled away, like the naughty boys they were. "And don't pee in the pool. Len put some of that dye in it. You know the stuff? Puts a red ring around the offender."

"That's not actually possible, is it?" Dan muttered under his breath.

"Don't argue with your mother, Daniel!"

Andy snorted and whispered, "I told you. She's got bat ears."

"And eyes in the back of my head."

In fits of nervous laughter that weren't far off giggles, the three of them made it to the conservatory and stripped off.

"How long d'you reckon till we get our parent superpowers?" Mike asked as he slid into the pool alongside Andy.

"When our kids are about forty?" Dan speculated, racing to get his socks off—a task made no easier by the milk they had absorbed—so he could bomb his brothers. He made it, but it was a poor victory when he knew they'd let him. Their mum brought bathrobes, towels and more beer, which she left for them before retreating to the house and away from all the splashing. After a while, they cast aside childish games in favour of drinking beer and chilling at the side of the pool, talking about football, kids, girlfriends, or the lack of them.

They hadn't forgotten that Mike still had to face Rachel, and tomorrow they'd no doubt be at each other's throats again. But for one evening, they were friends as well as brothers. Three's company.

25: Visitation
Thursday, 25th October

The waiting room wasn't much different to an ordinary hospital, if Mike ignored the fact that they'd been locked in, and they were allowed only the clothes on their backs—Shaunna had even been ordered to take the clip out of her hair and was currently in the process of braiding it.

"Thanks for this," he said. He still couldn't believe she'd offered to come with him.

Shaunna's hand wrapped around his and squeezed. "Like I said, hun, no thanks needed." She held his gaze, waiting for him to acknowledge what she'd said. He nodded and forced out a smile. He didn't want to be here, was almost certain Rachel had no better side to appeal to, but he was desperate enough to try if it meant getting her off their backs for good.

The previous Friday, when Mike had called the hospital to book their visit, the hospital staff had told him Rachel needed to approve it, and he'd expected her to refuse. Then the confirmation letter came, with approval for both him and Shaunna, and it got him thinking.

Perhaps they'd fallen into the trap and were playing their predetermined parts in Rachel's scheme. After all, Mike was a way to get to Andy, and Shaunna an obstacle she'd tried to remove. Yet, not once had Rachel attempted to cause Shaunna physical injury, and it had finally dawned on Mike why.

Rachel was clever, as he knew only too well. She'd spun a sophisticated web of lies that fooled everyone into believing she was a beautiful, innocent young woman. Her friends fell for it; Mike fell for it; even her own mother, who knew her better than anyone. Really, Jackie was the biggest victim of them all.

But there was one truth that underpinned it all: Rachel was in love with Andy. That's why she refused to sever her connection to Bethan, because whatever happened, or however long Rachel stayed locked away, Bethan was Andy's niece, a way to reach him. In Rachel's warped, twisted reality, she still believed she stood a chance of getting him to love her, and the one surefire way of destroying that chance was to hurt the woman he loved.

A door was unlocked and opened, and a member of staff looked around the visitors gathered within. "Come through, please," he ordered.

Mike and Shaunna got up and followed the others, who seemed at far greater ease with the procedure. They were led into another room, which reminded Mike of the canteen in his high school, with backless seats attached to tables that were, in turn, fixed to the floor. Mike and Shaunna held back, waiting for the other visitors to sit down before they took one of the remaining two free tables, grateful that it was closest to the door through which they had entered.

With everyone seated, members of staff opened one of the doors on the other side of the room, and several patients came through, each making their way to a different table. Mike had expected them all to be in some kind of prison overalls, but they were wearing their own clothes. Another door unlocked, more patients entered, and a young-looking woman strolled towards them. Shaunna gasped at the same time as Mike realised it was Rachel. Her hair was short and a much darker blonde than he recalled, her figure more rounded, her expression…blank.

"Hi." She sat opposite Mike, her eyes unfocused, as if she were drunk. "Thank you for coming to see me. How are you?"

"I'm good, thanks. You?"

"I'm doing OK now I'm here." She lifted her hand to indicate the room they were in and, by extension, the hospital. Her sweater sleeve slid back, revealing dressings on her wrist and arm. Mike stopped looking at them, but she'd already noticed. "I hurt myself," she said.

"Your mum told me."

"That's why they brought me here. It's a hospital. Did you know that?"

Mike nodded. Her words were slurred because of medication, he guessed, and he felt sorry for her. If this was how she would spend the rest of her life, she might as well be dead. He wouldn't want to live like that.

"How are you, Shaunna? And the babies?"

"We're all very well, thanks, Rachel."

"Felix told me you had twins."

Shaunna nodded but didn't elaborate, either because she didn't want to divulge further information or didn't know what to say. Mike was struggling, too, although he'd never really been the talkative type, which had annoyed Anne no end, and Rachel had used it against him, accusing him of ignoring her when he wasn't. He only had one thing to say to her, and now she was sitting in front of him, he wasn't sure he could say it, but not because he was afraid of her. With the hospital staff dotted around the room and her drugged-up state, she was harmless, and the words he had planned felt like a death sentence.

"Is Andy OK?" Rachel asked.

"Yes, he is," Shaunna answered.

"I'd hoped he would come and see me."

Shaunna looked at Mike as she said, "He won't."

Rachel rubbed her wrist with her thumb. "I wish I didn't love him." For a moment, she frowned and then smiled. "How's Bethan?"

That was all the confirmation Mike needed to know he'd been right. Rachel had done the social niceties and asked how they were. From there, she'd asked after Andy; Bethan was nothing more than an afterthought. "She's fine," Mike confirmed. "She won't be coming to see you, either."

"But my mum said you were thinking about it."

"That's not true, I'm afraid. You will have no part in my daughter's life. Do you understand?"

"I'm her mum."

"You gave birth to her, but you were never her mum. As far as I'm concerned, you gave up your parental rights the day you walked out on her. She doesn't even know who you are." It was fighting talk, and Mike's fear returned—better than the pity that was breaking his resolve.

Something briefly flickered in Rachel's dim, emotionless eyes, a hint of the heartless psychopath who had terrorised him for eight long months, made him fight to prove his paternity, tried to take his daughter away. Even now, when she was behind bars, she was still trying to manipulate him. She blinked, cutting her cold-as-steel glare from Mike to Shaunna and back again, and his fear dissipated, literally in the blink of an eye.

He knew her game now, and she no longer had any power over him. His mistake had been the same as Jackie's, hoping to find a trace of compassion where there was none, because he, too, had bought into the myth that a mother's love was unconditional. In Jackie's case, as with his own mum, that was the reality. But this monster before him cared for no-one but herself.

Rachel got up from the table, staring hard, not at Mike—he was no use to her anymore—but at Shaunna. "Give my love to Andy," she said. And then she turned and walked away.

"I won't," Shaunna muttered and grabbed Mike's hand. "Are you all right?" she asked.

Mike nodded. "Yeah, cheers. Are you?"

"I will be once we get out of here."

∗∗∗

Jackie had taken Bethan to a nearby pub with a play area, not that Bethan was old enough to use it, but there was nowhere else for them to go, and Jackie was still under the illusion that once Mike had spoken to Rachel, he'd let her see her daughter. It was never going to happen. No child should ever have to go through that experience, especially to see a woman who was their mother in name only.

As soon as Bethan spotted Mike walking across the pub, she shouted, "Da!" and he strode over and scooped her out of her pushchair, cuddling her close until she bashed his face with her palm.

"Hey, baby girl," he said. She grinned at him, showing off her teeth—four of them now. "Has she been all right?" he asked Jackie.

"Yes, she's been a very good girl. How did it go at the hospital?"

"OK, I guess. She's on some serious medication, isn't she?"

Jackie nodded. "Yes. It's to stop her from hurting herself again, and to control the personality disorder. It seems to me all it's done is dull her senses." She was watching Mike closely, and while he was aware of it, he kept his eyes on his daughter. "You haven't changed your mind," Jackie said.

"No. I'm sorry. I've told Rachel she won't see Bethan."

He'd expected Jackie to be devastated by his decision—even though, from his point of view, nothing had changed—and for a while, she was very quiet and thoughtful. Shaunna went to buy drinks and order food; they were remaining near the hospital so Jackie could attend the evening visiting session. Mike fussed unnecessarily over Bethan, uncomfortable with the silence but confident that reasserting his position had been the right thing to do.

Eventually, Jackie sighed and said, "I accept your decision, Mike. You have my word I won't mention it again."

After Jackie had left for the hospital, Shaunna went outside to call Andy. He and Dan had taken an overnight ferry to Dublin for a business meeting, and they'd taken the kids—all four of them, seeing as Shu was off school for half-term. Mike couldn't imagine they'd get much business done with three babies and a preschooler in tow, but what did he know? He only had Bethan to worry about, or not worry so much anymore. She was sleeping, and the pub was quiet. It was the most relaxed Mike had felt in a long time.

"I miss this," he said to Shaunna when she returned from her call.

"What's that?"

"Going out for a drink."

"Why don't you ask your brothers?"

"Yeah, I might just do that. How's their trip going? Everything all right?"

"Oh, they're fine, apart from Dan failing to mention he got seasick."

"Nice."

"And Shu now wants a pet tiger."

Mike chuckled. "They'd best look for somewhere with a big garden, then."

"You're not kidding. I think Andy found them a house, actually."

"Has Dan really handed over the decision to him?"

"Yep. Only because he doesn't want to fight Adele."

"Fair enough." Mike wouldn't want to take her on, either. She was feisty, was Adele. She knew her own mind and had Dan right where she wanted him, but not in the same way Rachel had controlled Mike. He could see the difference now, between women who were strong and independent, like Adele and Shaunna, and women who were abusive and controlling, like Rachel. Thankfully, women like Rachel were few and far between, although it wasn't so long ago he'd had trouble believing that.

"You know what I really miss?" Mike said. "Going for a drink with a woman. I don't even need the romance—definitely don't need all the crap that goes with it. The company's enough for me, and it's different from being out with the lads. No pressure to get hammered, for starters."

Shaunna nodded. "I know what you mean. It's what I like about meeting up with my male friends. I think, on the whole, the opposite sex judge you less harshly. Like, when I'm with Adele, she'll pass comment on other women, and sometimes I just know she's taking a poke at me.

"This one time we were at the beach, there was a woman there who was a bit bigger than me—not much—and she was wearing a bikini, which was really nice, gorgeous colours that complemented her complexion, and it fitted her really well, so it wasn't as if she was bulging out all over the place.

"But Adele was looking down her nose, saying how big women shouldn't wear bikinis. They should stick to swimming costumes, maybe even cover up with a sarong, which I do if I'm somewhere like that, because I don't want people like Adele thinking the same about me."

Mike shook his head, genuinely bamboozled. "But you're stunning, Shaunna. Why would anybody complain about seeing you in a bikini?" He realised what he'd said and screwed his eyes shut. "Sorry. My bad."

Shaunna laughed. "It's OK. Dan's done it a couple of times. It's a Jeffries-man thing."

Mike opened his eyes a fraction and peered at her through his lashes. She smiled and gave him a saucy wink.

"Dan flirts with you and gets away with it?" he asked, not believing it for a second.

"Not in front of Adele."

"I was gonna say."

"Anyway," Shaunna continued, "with having Krissi and everything, I heard enough bitching to last me a lifetime, and it was almost exclusively by girls, who grew up into judgemental women. I'm not saying men aren't judgemental; maybe they are when they're with each other. But if they do judge me, it's usually positive, and who doesn't love a bit of flirting? I mean, if you've got it, why not flaunt it?" Shaunna rolled her eyes. "That sounds so bigheaded, doesn't it?"

"Not if it's true." Mike knew he should look away. He was taking too much notice of the many assets Shaunna possessed—her glossy long red hair, still pulled back in a braid, a few escaped curls tumbling forward onto her face, long-lashed green eyes, plump dusky lips, large round breasts—he really needed to stop.

Shaunna laughed, her cheeks flushed bright pink. "I know what you're doing," she teased.

"Sorry." Mike was getting a little hot under the collar.

"Don't be. It's only flirting…well, maybe a bit of ogling, but it's a huge compliment. I'm not offended."

"Yeah, Andy might not be quite so understanding."

"Surprisingly, he's OK with it. He says it makes him feel victorious. Other men can look all they like, but I'm *his* woman. Ha, that makes him sound like a caveman. But he's not possessive or jealous."

Mike understood what she meant; he'd felt the same about Anne, and then he'd lost her, although not to another man, which was something. To the end, they'd had a decent sex life. It was the rest of it that fell apart. "That's the other bit I miss. The intimacy." He hadn't meant to say it out loud.

"Has it been a while?" Shaunna asked.

"Yeah. A long while. About a year, I think. I kind of blocked all memory of sex with Rachel."

"Understandable."

Mike delved briefly into the little he did recall of their relationship, such as it was one. He'd lost his attraction to Rachel almost as soon as she'd moved in, and fear was the only reason he'd got it up for her. He'd faked orgasms so she would leave him alone and was grateful she was out with her mates, and no doubt sleeping around, more than she was at home with him.

"You need a friend with benefits," Shaunna asserted.

Mike laughed and shook his head. "Do they even exist?"

"Oh, yeah. That's what Andy and Jess were."

"I thought they were together."

"Maybe on and off, but they were never exclusive."

"I didn't know that." Whether having a 'friend with benefits' was the way forward for Mike, he wasn't sure. All he knew was that he didn't want another relationship yet, but even if he did get lucky enough to form a friendship with a woman who wanted the same as he did, at some point, he'd need to tell her about his testicle, which would inevitably lead to telling her about Rachel. Still, he'd managed to tell Leah, and if the attraction had been there...

"Penny for them."

Mike realised he was smiling. "I'm finally healing, Shaw." He flinched as if expecting her to hit him, but it was all an act. "Na," he amended.

She laughed. "Yes, Mi—Ke. You are."

26: Green and Blue
Thursday, 25th October

After the previous night's sleepless voyage, the kids were all out for the count within fifteen minutes of leaving Dublin; Shu had been asleep before they'd boarded, and she hadn't stirred as Dan had settled her in her bunk. The sea was much calmer, the weather forecast was promising, and Dan wasn't looking quite so green as he had on the way over. Andy was optimistic there would be no gut-spilling, so optimistic, in fact...

"I'm gonna go the bar, bro."

"Will they let us bring drinks back to the cabin?"

"If they don't, we won't be buying any. Won't be long." Andy left his brother in charge and set off for the bar. Predictably, Igor was already propping it up.

"Alright, man?" Igor greeted him.

"Yeah, you?"

"I am now." Igor raised his tumbler of vodka—a double—and threw it down his throat like it was water. The empty glass made a resounding clunk as it hit the bar, and Igor waved money at the bartender. "Hey, mate, when you're ready, please."

"Won't be a second."

Andy glanced around the sparsely populated bar; there hadn't been many passengers waiting to board, but then, it was a Thursday night. He'd only taken the ferry to Dublin once before, on a Saturday, and it had been jam-packed with England fans travelling over for the Ireland v England friendly that was abandoned due to rioting. He'd been ashamed to call himself an England fan that day, and it was a long time before he went to another big match, which was more to do with his globetrotting than fear of getting caught up in trouble again.

The few other occasions he'd had business—or pleasure—in Ireland, he'd flown, which he'd have done this time if he'd been coming alone. Well, he wouldn't have been coming at all.

"Would you like a drink?" Igor asked.

Andy waved his offer away. "Let me get you one. It'll make up for me leaving you on your own."

"When was that?"

"In about two minutes' time."

"Oh!" Igor laughed loudly and slapped Andy on the back, making him stagger. "I see. Going back to cabin?"

"Yeah," Andy confirmed with difficulty. Igor had fairly winded him. "Kids, y'know?"

"Yes. Actually, no. I don't." A further boom of laughter filled the bar.

"What can I get you, sir?" the bartender asked Igor, who redirected to Andy.

"Two pints of Guinness and a double vodka, please."

The bartender set up the first Guinness and collected another tumbler for Igor's vodka.

"Did you find out all you needed today?" Andy asked.

Igor gave an arms-wide shrug. "Get tiger from Ireland, take to India. Easy-peasy."

Rather than offering any kind of response, Andy watched the Guinness level rising in the glass until the barman flipped the tap off.

"It is all in hand, Andy. Don't worry." The bartender delivered Igor's vodka. He drank it.

Andy gave Igor a sideways glance, receiving a wide gappy grin in return. In spite of the couldn't-care-less act, and the fact that he was as mad as a hatter, Igor knew how to do his job, and he did it very well. He was a terrifying man—heavily scarred face, crazy eyes, lots of tattoos—not a person Andy would want to cross. Yet his biggest boast was that he'd never faked his tachograph, and he looked the sort who'd have taken the chance, but as he'd told Andy, at length and in gratuitously gruesome detail, tiredness *kills*.

With both pints of Guinness poured, Andy topped up Igor's vodka—again—and returned to the cabin without spilling a drop of beer.

"The sea must be flat as glass," he said, putting Dan's drink down in front of him and sucking the foam from the top of his own.

Dan blew air out of his mouth and swallowed heavily. "Guinness? Are you sure?"

"When in Ireland…" Andy reasoned.

"Except we're not." Dan sipped the bitter, dark beer and shuddered.

"Irish Sea. Close enough for rock and roll."

"You're doing it on purpose."

"Dunno what you're talking about."

Dan took another mouthful. His cheeks ballooned, and he shoved the glass across to Andy. He'd turned a funny colour again. "Speaking of glass," he said through teeth clenched in an effort to defer the inevitable, "the auction site's still down."

"Is it?"

Dan showed Andy the 'HTTP Error 503 - Service Unavailable' message on his phone.

"Server overload?" Andy speculated.

"What are we? Ten p.m.?"

"Yeah, just gone."

"A six-hour server overload? Unlikely. It's been taken offline."

"Or they're still updating the info from today's auction."

Dan didn't look convinced. He reached over for the Guinness he'd just given to Andy, glugged at it, swallowed and put it down again.

Andy held back a smirk. He'd told Dan if he didn't think about it, his seasickness would pass. Needless to say, Dan hadn't believed him.

Swapping his pint for his phone, Dan said, "I'm gonna give Bryant a call." He tapped at the screen and put his phone to his ear. "I reckon they've been rumbled."

Andy was thinking the same thing, topped off with a huge helping of guilt. He could think of only one reason why Derek Arnold had been rumbled, and he'd rather keep the guilt and be proved wrong than discover what he feared was the case: Dan had blabbed.

Dan chucked his phone down. "No answer. Who else would know?"

"How about no-one?"

"We've got to know someone."

"Bro, just… Let it go, yeah?"

Dan folded his arms and scowled. "OK."

Andy shook his head and laughed. "That's not letting it go."

Dan opened his mouth to protest, clearly thought better of it, and asked, "Did Shaunna get home safely?"

"Sort of. She's staying over at Krissi's. Didn't want to be home alone."

"You two are as bad as Josh and George."

"Are you calling my missus clingy?"

Dan grinned. "What if I am?"

"Let's take this outside." Andy nodded at the porthole behind Dan. "To be honest, she's not coping well with her dad at the minute."

"Is he getting worse?"

"Yeah. He really went for her the other week. Not physically, although she hurt herself trying to get away from him. Your phone's ringing, by the way."

Dan leaned forward and frowned at the screen. He hit the green button and put his phone on speaker. "Alright, Josh mate? I was just talking about you."

"Were you?"

"Err, yeah." Dan cleared his throat. "What can I do you for?"

"Guess what."

"Derek Arnold's website's down?" Dan guessed.

"Yes. Guess what else."

"Dunno. What else?"

"Scott Bryant is Derek Arnold's web programmer."

Dan's jaw dropped, and he gawped at Andy, who was doing pretty much the same thing.

"Or he was, until today."

"Did they sack him?"

"Officially, yes."

"Unofficially...?"

"He said you're to leave well alone."

Dan's gawping transformed from shock to puzzlement, but Andy had already sussed it out.

"Incidentally," Josh added, "Graham sends both his regards and congratulations on the birth of your son."

"Gray—"

"I'd best go. It's past my bedtime, and George is clock-watching. See you Sunday."

"Cheers, Josh," Andy said before the line went dead.

Dan was still flabbergasted long after Josh ended the call. Eventually, he uttered, "Bryant's an undercover cop?"

"That's what the man said. Well, not in so many words."

"But how? I mean..." Dan shook his head and looked at his phone again, as if it might give him the answer. "So that sob story about his mum living there and his family losing their jobs was a pack a lies?"

"Hm…maybe not. It'd be good cover," Andy reasoned.

"What would he have done if Eddie had accepted our offer?"

"I don't think there was ever any danger of that. He was pretty certain the board were gonna reject it."

"You're saying they've got people planted at Comco?"

"It's possible."

Without thinking, Dan picked up his Guinness again and took a long drink. "Bloody undercover cops. They're like ants."

"Good analogy, that, bro." Andy tapped his glass against Dan's. "Don't go throwing boiling water over them, will you?"

"They're probably impervious."

"Probably. I'll tell you what, though. That's serious trust Bryant, or whatever his name is, has extended to us. He's basically blown his cover. Mind you, he could be leaving the area. Whatever, best not mention it to Aitch."

Dan reared and squared his shoulders. "D'you think I'm an idiot?"

"No," Andy said peaceably. "I don't. Aitch, on the other hand…"

"I won't tell him you said that. Now, shift it. I've got half a pint of stout to throw up." With no time to wait, Dan got up, pushed past Andy and made a hasty exit.

Andy settled back in his chair and supped his pint, tuning out the sound of retching coming from the en-suite. He'd thought a drink might settle Dan's stomach; in retrospect, brandy would've been a better choice. It might've knocked him out, too, stopped him thinking about the stadium auction, although even Andy had to admit it was an interesting twist.

So Scott Bryant was an undercover cop. The news didn't come as a shock to Andy. He'd thought there was something suspect about him from the off and had dismissed it in an effort to prove his brother was wrong; he hadn't lost his sense of adventure. He just didn't crave it the way he used to.

However, Dan was right about one thing: Andy *had* needed to get away from home—in order to confirm he no longer needed to get away from home. When the twins were old enough to appreciate the experience, he'd rethink his position. In the meantime, he was happy with his lot. More than happy.

He'd heard from the estate agent that Dan's house had fallen through. It was no big deal, not in the grand scheme of things— of Mike standing up to Rachel, and Dan being warned off by Gray's old unit. They could finally get back to normal. *Yeah, right,* Andy thought with a rueful chuckle. Christ only knew what trouble the pair of them would get him into next.

You're the hero, who comes swashbuckling in to save the day. That's what she said, his red hot baby, the week they shagged each other senseless on every available surface of his mum's house, and that was *a lot* of house. He was a hero, and he was OK with that, so long as there were no more dragons to slay. All he wanted was a nice quiet life, at home with his girls, maybe a chance to repeat that week at his mum's place...

The vibrating of his phone in his pocket amplified his aroused state—even more so once he tugged it free and saw who was calling.

"Hey there, RHB."

"Hey, sexy. How's it hanging?"

"Upright."

Her laughter was pure filth. "Tell me more."

"I was just thinking about you, me, mum's house..."

"Oh, God. Don't even go there."

Now he laughed. "You OK?"

"Yeah. I decided to come home."

"Oh?"

"Not for any bad reason. I wanted my own bed, and a bit of privacy, that's all. What are your plans for the evening? Well, what's left of it."

"Not much. Just having a beer. Dan's sick as a dog. He's throwing his guts up."

"He's not there?"

"In the bathroom."

"Huh." She lowered her voice to a husky whisper. "Wanna play?"

He listened for a noise from Dan: still retching. "We'll have to be quick." Somehow, he didn't think that was going to be a problem.

"Want to know what I'm wearing?" Shaunna asked.

Andy gulped. *Nope, not gonna take long at all.* He was getting too warm, but he couldn't very well strip off with Dan only a few feet away behind a flimsy door. "What you wearing?"

"Camisole and knickers."

"The red ones?"

"See-through *and* red."

Andy groaned and shuffled down his seat, popping the button on his jeans. "Should've made this a video call."

"Oh, God, yes. Shall I call you back?"

It was tempting. Very tempting. But it would waste what little time they had. "Nah, tell me what you're doing." He slid his hand under his jeans' waistband; the zip started to open.

"I'm lying on the bed, imagining you're here, kissing my neck…I love how your stubble tickles my skin, makes me shiver all over. Oh, God, I'm so turned on…" She moaned into the phone, and Andy knew she was doing exactly as he was. Her breathing was fast and shallow, and she panted between the words. "You flick your tongue over my nipple…I can feel your hot breath on my belly, going down…mmm…"

A tiny cry came from the travel cots across the room— Robbie, not that it mattered who; Andy would have got up to whichever of them it was. The crying stopped. *Probably just dreaming.* Andy kept going, hoping they had enough time. He was *so close*.

The toilet flushed, and the bolt shot back.

"Crap."

"Don't think there's anything left in me to crap," Dan muttered, keeping his eyes averted as he walked over to the cot and grinned down inanely on his son.

At the other end of the line, Shaunna was giggling. "Ah, well. It'll keep."

It would have to, but he'd been *so damn close!* "I'm gonna go. Sleep well, baby. I love you."

"Love you, too, sexy. Night."

Andy sighed heavily in frustration and threw his phone down on the table. "I remember now," he said, fastening his jeans.

"What's that, bro?" Dan asked.

"Why I hate sharing a room with you."

27: Letting Go
Friday, 26th October

Two overnight ferry voyages, no sleep and a serious case of dehydration, Dan felt like death warmed up. Adele had told him to stay in bed, but his need to find out if the auction had gone ahead was far greater than his need to avoid being yelled at. He tried Josh first, but he had no news, and reiterated what he'd said the previous night. Dan needed to leave well alone, and he *was* doing. He didn't care what had happened to Derek Arnold, nor did he have any intention of telling Aitch about Scott Bryant, although he was intrigued to know what yarn the Anchors had been spun about their sponsor's sudden disappearance. They might not even know yet.

A little surreptitious digging was in order; Dan went through a proxy server and tried Derek Arnold's site, which was now displaying 'HTTP 404 - Not found'. Next, he went to Comco's site, which was still online and, surprisingly, still had an active link in the footer to Scott Bryant's site. Dan clicked on it, fully expecting to hit another '404', but Bryant's site was still live.

With a fake stretch and yawn to cover himself—Adele was helping Shu dress up as a princess, and they probably wouldn't have noticed if he'd burst into flames—he got up from the sofa and went through to the bedroom, where he flicked through the junk in his wallet until he found the card 'Scott' had given him. From the colour scheme and logo, right down to the street address and URL, every detail on the business card matched what was on the website. Every detail bar one: the phone number.

"Bryant PLC. Rosemary speaking. How may I help you?"

"Hi, Rosemary. It's…Rob. Could I have a word with Scott? Is he free?"

"May I ask why you're calling, sir?"

"Yeah, I was hoping Scott would be able to help me with a design for my company website."

"I'll put you through to one of our designers. Please hold the line."

"I'd prefer to deal with the man at the top."

"Mr. Bryant isn't directly involved with the company, sir."

"I don't suppose you have a contact number for him, do you?"

"I'm afraid I don't, sir. Mr. Bryant was only involved in getting the company off to a good start. It's owned and managed by a group of young entrepreneurs."

Bryant's an angel investor? "Does he ever put in an appearance, Rosemary?"

"He prefers to remain anonymous, sir."

"I bet he does." Apart from giving the company his name, except, of course, it wasn't.

"Would you like to speak with our design team, sir?"

Dan had heard all he needed to and was tempted to just hang up, but he wasn't that rude. "I'll call back another time. Thanks for your help, Rosemary." He ended the call.

Bryant PLC's website was still open on his tablet, and he scrolled through the links while he considered his next move, pausing to snarl at the 'Proud sponsors of…' page and the squad photo. So it seemed the only 'sting' involved Jeffries and Associates and Comco, and Dan supposed he should feel honoured the police had chosen them. Maybe the whole thing was a scam, and the stadium wasn't even up for auction. He could safely investigate that, just ask around a few of the Comco employees…

"Daddy, Daddy, Daddy!" In a blur of shiny pink and lilac, Shu came haring into the room and was straight up on the bed. "Bouncy, bouncy, bouncy."

"Get down, Shu. You're gonna fall."

"Princess bouncy castle for my birthdayyyy." She launched herself from the bed straight into his arms and clung to him. Her silky 'princess' dress made it almost impossible to keep hold of her, and she was slipping out of his grasp. "Bounce, bounce, bounce…" Up and down she went, breathless with excitement. "Bounce, bounce, bounce, bounce…"

"Agh!" Dan doubled over and made a dive for the bed, taking his daughter with him. *Fucking princess shoes. Who puts heels on a four-year-old?*

Shu gasped and pulled back. "Daddy, s'matter?"

"Nothing," he muttered through gritted teeth. Shu blinked big dark eyes at him, her mouth forming a tiny pink 'O'. She looked so worried. He attempted a smile of reassurance. Her eyes widened further.

"You got a poorly tummy?"

"No, baby girl. You just be careful with those kicky feet, OK?"

"Oh!" Her brow crinkled in a deep, thoughtful frown. After a few seconds, she asked, "I kick your balls?"

In spite of the pain that still had him paralysed, he laughed and pinched her nose. "Yeah, you little monkey, you did. But it's OK." He pulled her closer and placed a gentle kiss on her forehead, smiling as he murmured, "I'll get over it." And he would.

It was time to call it quits.

***

"Did you get the memo?" Aitch set his pint down on the answer sheet and dragged a stool into the minuscule space between Dan's and Sean's stools.

"The what?" Dan asked.

"Shop talk. Sorry. It's been a long week. The email, I meant."

"Yeah, you're gonna have to give me a bit more to go on, Aitch."

"The rescheduled match?"

"No."

"Well, the Anchors got it."

"Well, the Lions didn't."

"Huh." Aitch picked up his pint and supped. Sean snatched away the answer sheet and wiped it dry with his sleeve.

"So, when is it?" Dan asked, seeing as Aitch didn't seem eager to volunteer the information.

"New Year's Eve."

"That's not so bad."

"Isn't it?"

"Could've been New Year's Day."

"Yeah, but, the thing is…" Aitch frowned into his beer and shrank back a little. "I'm away for New Year."

"You're not."

"Mate…"

"No, Aitch. I need you."

"But it's only—" Aitch shut his mouth, which was as well. Dan was ready to lamp him one. However, he'd also realised he was being unreasonable in expecting Aitch to change his plans for the festive season when it was *only* football.

"I'll talk to the FA," Dan said at the same time as Aitch said, "I'll talk to Tash." Dan shook his head and repeated, "I'll talk to the FA. There's a few Sundays free in the new year. Failing that, we'll hire portable floodlights and play on a weeknight." Fleetingly, Dan reflected that if they'd got the stadium, it wouldn't have been a problem. He looked over at Andy, sitting with his Complex Superiority teammates at the next table along. Andy mouthed 'let it go'. Dan nodded to confirm he had and turned back to Aitch. "You staying to kick their arses, then?"

"Me? I'm bloody crap at quizzes, but yeah. I'm staying."

"Nice one."

"Quality, not quantity, bro," Andy said, in reference to the fact that Brains and Brawn now numbered six to Complex Superiority's five.

Shaunna, who for historical reasons, was part of Dan's team, fluttered her eyelashes and leaned forward, resting her chin on her hand, her pose exposing her full cleavage. "Bigger is *always* better," she said.

Andy sat back, so he, too, was showing off his 'assets'…and his obvious appreciation of the view. Dan covered his eyes so he didn't have to witness their overtly sexual flirting. They'd always done it, and being a couple had only made them worse.

Sadly, however, it looked like Andy was going to be proved right, but he at least had the decency not to gloat when he and Dan went to get drinks during the music round halfway through the quiz, by which point Brains and Brawn were trailing twenty points. They returned to their respective tables, where Dan laid claim to Aitch's seat—he was visiting the Gents'—so he could talk strategy with Sean.

"If we play our joker on the Moving Pictures round…" Sean suggested.

"Assuming it's actually about movies."

"Have you got a better suggestion?"

"Not really." Dan's gaze settled on their opponents, huddled around their answer sheet, firing answers at Josh while he scribbled away. Again, for historical reasons, and to keep the team sizes even, whilst Sean and Kris were part of Brains and Brawn, Sophie and Ade were part of Complex Superiority: five graduates, three of them with master's degrees. Dan huffed in disdain. "It's more like University Bloody Challenge than The Red Lion Quiz. No wonder they're wiping the floor with us."

"Aye, but don't forget, we beat them three weeks on the trot," Sean pointed out.

"Back in July, and now it's October." Dan shook his head. "There's nothing else for it. We're gonna have to merge the teams." As he said it, Josh looked up from his answer sheet and gave Sean the biggest, smuggest grin Dan had ever seen. Sean snarled.

"Not a feckin' chance," he said.

Dan laughed. "Film round?"

Sean nodded, and they played on, brave and fierce in the face of tremendous adversity, where the Sport round stood as much chance of being about Australian slang as it did of being about actual sport, and the Moving Pictures round turned out to be about stolen works of art. At the end, they exchanged answer sheets, knowing this time, victory would not be theirs.

"Sorry we're gonna beat you," Andy said, not sounding sorry at all, and then added, in case there was any doubting his insincerity, "Again."

Dan was too knackered to do anything more than shrug it off. "Yeah, well, it's a bit like the ABBA rule, bro."

"ABBA rule?"

"Anyone but the bloody Anchors."

"Ha, yeah. Never thought of that."

Brains and Brawn didn't win, but they finished eight points behind Complex Superiority, who *did* win, and Dan was happy with that. When all was said and done, they were allies in the fight to beat the Crash Test Mummies—the team headed by the leader of Josh and Sean's parish council—and they'd at least achieved that goal, a small consolation prize for the lousy month they'd had. He'd missed out on both the Sharston house and the Comco stadium, and he'd witnessed his brothers being dragged halfway back to hell by Rachel Perry, but they'd all come through the other side. Then there was Robbie's arrival, of course, adding to the Jeffries boys' ranks, and Shu's birthday in two days' time.

Now he thought on, it hadn't been such a bad month after all.

***

"Why didn't you tell me you wanted that house?" Adele's question caught Dan as he teetered on the edge of sleep and startled him back to wakefulness.

"Which house?" he asked, knowing full well she meant the Sharstons'. He'd had a feeling something was up on the way back from quiz night, and he'd half considered addressing it before they got into bed. Actually, that was a lie; he'd gone straight from *she's got the hump* to *I'm knackered, it can wait till morning*. Evidently it couldn't, and he was a fool for thinking it could. A fool, and a coward.

"It was meant to be a surprise," he said. Adele responded with a short, sharp 'hm' of disapproval. "Plus, you'd just given birth."

"You should've waited."

"It was an auction. I had to act fast."

"No, Dan, you didn't."

He took the less dangerous option of not arguing back, instead waiting for her to say what she needed to, but aside from her angry nose-breathing, she was giving him the silent treatment. He was too tired for an argument, and Robbie would be awake in an hour, so he made himself comfortable again, started to drift…

"…not even an apology?"

He sat up and switched on the light. "OK. Let's have it."

"Why didn't you tell me?"

"I just explained that."

"It was a surprise, and I'd just had Robbie, yeah, whatever, Dan. You never tell me *anything*."

"That's not true."

"OK, then. What about the stadium?"

"What about it? It was a business deal."

"You were going to secure the loan against the apartment."

"*My* apartment."

Adele laughed—a high-pitched, disbelieving laugh that had him shrinking back under the duvet. "Of course!" she said with a sarcastic tut and eye roll. "I'd totally forgotten it was *your* apartment. How silly of me!"

"I wasn't gonna do that anyway. I had the money in the bank."

"Then why didn't you buy the stadium?"

"It…I changed my mind." The stress of lying to her was giving him a headache.

Adele pulled herself up the bed, casually arranging her pillows as she spoke. "If you'd *asked*, I could've given you the money."

"Given me what money?" *Stupid question. How the hell…?*

"The extra five percent Eddie wanted. I could've given it to you, or lent it to Jeffries and Associates, seeing as it was a—" vicious air quotes "—business deal."

Dan scowled and mumbled, "It wouldn't have made any difference."

"Why not?"

"Because…" He bit his tongue. If he told her about Derek Arnold, it'd be all around town before next sun down. He got out of bed. "I'm gonna make a hot chocolate. D'you want—"

"No. Thank you." She glared up at him and jabbed his side of the bed with a pointy-nailed finger.

Dan stayed where he was. Adele's eyebrows rose and her lips all but disappeared. He quickly sat—on the edge of the bed with his back to her and his head down.

"You didn't tell me because you don't trust me," she accused.

"It's not that I—"

"Stop it. I know when you're lying."

Dan shook his head. "I'm not. I *do* trust you, in all the ways that matter." He turned and offered her a humble smile, which she dismissed with a diva-style 'talk to the hand' gesture. He relented. "OK. It's because you can't keep your mouth shut."

"Ha! Listen to the pot calling the kettle black!"

Dan reared defensively, all set to argue he only passed on information that was useful—hardly the same as mindless gossip—and if it was something that would put them in danger, he kept it to himself. But could he stand to be a hypocrite *and* a liar?

No, he couldn't.

"I'm sorry, you're right. I should've told you about the Sharston place, and the stadium. I didn't, but not for the reason you think. I did it because I love you, and I want to give you the best of everything." He waited for the counter-argument, prepared to stick to his guns because it was the truth. Their relationship was difficult; they fought too often over trivial things and were both demanding and selfish. But he always loved her, and she loved him.

No counter-argument forthcoming, he chanced a glance her way, and she beckoned with her finger. He got back into bed, waiting for her to get into a cuddling position before he put his arms around her. She was still tender from the caesarean.

"I love you," he said.

"I know. I love you, too. But the thing is, sweetie, even though you think you're doing it for all the right reasons—and I love that you spoil me—we're a couple. We need to make the big decisions together." She peered up at him. "Don't we?" He nodded. "Which means you've got to trust me, OK? You've got to let me take my share of the responsibility."

"Do you trust me?" He'd never questioned it aloud before, but her rejection of his marriage proposals had left their mark. Adele's mum had cheated on her dad. Adele had cheated on Tom—with Dan. Maybe she thought if he'd done it with her, he'd do it with another woman, but there was only one for him, even if he never could figure out what she wanted.

Gingerly, and with a determined, tight-lipped expression that for once he was sure had nothing to do with him—beyond him having impregnated her in the first place—Adele shuffled up the bed and planted a lingering kiss on his lips. "Of course I trust you," she whispered and then looked him in the eye. "If I didn't, I'd have made more of a stink about living in *your* apartment, being chauffeured around in *your* car, using *your* money to pay for everything…"

"It's *ours*," he argued.

"And *my* money?" she asked. "That's ours, too?"

"If you want it to be."

Her leg slid over his as she tickled her fingernails down his belly, rendering him speechless—intentionally, he thought, but he wasn't going to grumble. "You know what we should do, sweetie? Open a joint bank account."

"I can agree to that."

"And we should look for a house *together*."

"Anything you want."

"No, Dan. It's not about what *I* want. It's what *we* want."

Her fingers nudged past the waistband of his shorts, and he let out an involuntary groan. "Do *we* want to get married yet?" he chanced bravely, given what was in her hand.

"Not yet," she said, returning her mouth to his before carefully kissing her way downwards. When she reached her destination, she murmured, "But *we're* thinking about it."

28: Paper Capers
Sunday, 28th October

After Mike left Jackie's, he didn't know what to do with himself. He had a whole Sunday free—or not quite the whole day. He needed to pick Bethan up later and head over to Dan and Adele's place for Shu's fourth birthday party. Until then, he had no work and nowhere to be. His choices, then, were to either put the day to good use and work through the rest of his IT course, or waste it on mindless hours of channel hopping. He even contemplated giving the van a bit of a service, seeing as it was still spluttering intermittently, which meant it probably needed a new fuel pump, or worse. Maybe it was better not knowing.

It was only at the last set of traffic lights on his route home, when he pulled up behind a VW Golf GTi—he sincerely hoped the driver couldn't hear the *put-put* coming from the van's engine compartment—that it dawned on him. He *did* have something to do, assuming, of course, that Charlie was free. He turned off the road and stopped outside the gates to make the call.

"Alright, Charlie? What you up to today?"

She grunted. "House-sitting. Mum and Dad are away for the weekend, and Pete's working. Seriously, it's like being under house arrest."

"You waiting on a delivery or something?" It was a daft question, given it was a Sunday; then again, some companies delivered seven days a week.

"Nope. Just my mother's paranoia about burglars. Why? Do you need me to come over? Please?"

Mike laughed. "I was gonna suggest I came over to you. This decorating thing?"

"Ah! Oh! Right, yeah. Good idea."

"You up for it?"

"Absolutely."

"What do you need me to bring?"

"Err…OK, well, I've got the paper, paste, paste brushes, wallpaper scissors…"

"So, if I bring my pasting table and—"

"Got one."

"Ladders?"

"Got those, too."

"You're very organised." No surprise there. Mike had seen the way she dealt with Len's business, which was a far more complex job than hanging wallpaper.

"Just bring you," Charlie said. "Satnav or manual?"

Mike grinned—to himself, seeing as it was a voice call, but he could've made a video call on his awesome new phone. The novelty still hadn't worn off. "Satnav," he confirmed.

"Cool. I'll text you the postcode now. It's number seventy-one."

"OK. See you in a bit." He hung up. Ten seconds later, the text message arrived, his phone auto-detected the postcode and opened the satnav app. Impressed, he set off as per the onscreen instructions and less than ten minutes later arrived at Charlie's house.

It was weird, turning up to 'a job' and not unloading all his gear. He felt kind of naked without it, but he soon got over his self-consciousness when Charlie let him in and immediately led him to the wallpaper disaster zone.

"You did this?" he asked.

"Guilty as charged." She looked like she was admitting to a bank robbery. "Can you fix it?"

"Err…" Mike nodded and then shook his head. "No, but I can strip it and we can start over."

"OK. Yes. Whatever you say." She left the room.

Mike stayed where he was, picking at the unstuck, overlapping edges of the paper which *almost* covered one wall, each subsequent length slightly more skewed than the last so that the final drop was two inches from the corner at the top and overlapping it at the bottom. But the plaster was in good shape. "You got a spirit level, Charlie?"

"Yep. I'll bring it now."

She returned with a wallpaper steamer and the spirit level. "I know how to do this bit," she said, plugging the steamer in and handing over the spirit level. "What do you need that for?"

"To mark a vertical line so we can get the paper straight."

"Ah. I just started from one end and worked across."

Mike put the level up against the nearest corner. "Yeah, look at that."

Charlie came over and peered at the off-centre bubble. "That's…not level."

"Nope." Mike moved the spirit level along the wall. Charlie handed him a pencil, and he drew a line.

"Got that. What's next?"

"Depends."

"Are you in a rush?"

"I've got to be at Dan's by four, for Shu's birthday."

"OK. Why don't you work on another wall, and when I've got rid of this effort, you can show me how to do it properly?"

"Sounds good to me."

Mike mixed the paste and cut a few lengths of paper while Charlie went to make coffee for them both. By the time she returned, the wallpaper steamer was ready to go, and she set about stripping the wall. As they worked, Mike regaled her with the tale of how he met Leah—the spirit level had reminded him, and the memory still brought tears to his eyes.

"You're not still seeing her?" Charlie asked, amused but sympathetic.

"Nah. We didn't click. You know what I mean?"

Charlie nodded. "I know what you mean." She continued with her stripping, finishing at around the same point as Mike reached the end of the wall opposite. He climbed the ladder to trim the end against the ceiling, smoothed the brush over the paper, and returned to floor level, where Charlie stood, shaking her head in wonder.

"How do you do that?" she asked. "Honestly, we've only been at it twenty minutes, and it's perfect."

Mike shrugged. "Practice, I guess. It's pretty easy, though, once you get the, err, hang of it."

"Hm…"

Mike moved the ladder around the corner. "First up, you need another plumb line."

"Do I?"

"To get the first piece on straight. Then the rest you line up against the first one."

"You'd better show me again, and I'll do it next time."

Mike talked her through what he was doing. It would've been the most boring lesson ever, except Charlie was a very attentive student, and once he'd shown her how to get a length up on the wall, straight and bubble-free, she did the next one without any assistance and finished off the wall by herself. Mike dealt with the corner, and they moved on to the next wall, on which the door was situated.

"This is gonna get tricky, isn't it?" Charlie said. "OK, sensei, show me how it's done." She took a step back and folded her arms.

Mike chuckled. "It's not that tricky. I'll do this piece, you can do the other."

Charlie nodded in agreement and moved aside so she could watch without getting in the way. It was almost second nature to Mike, and he kept forgetting to explain what he was doing, but Charlie had followed anyway, and she was ready with the next length of paper as soon as he was done.

She climbed the ladder and aligned the top of the paper against Mike's piece. "How long we got?"

Mike checked his phone. "Couple of hours yet."

"Oh, we'll be done well before then."

Mike surveyed the final wall: the fiddly one, with the window, radiator and electrical sockets. Even so, it wouldn't take them more than an hour. He left Charlie to finish the strip by the door and cut and pasted the lengths for when she was done.

"How's that?" she asked, stepping back to admire her work. Mike drew up next to her.

"Nice one." He nodded his approval. "Are you ready for the final stretch. It's a bit more challenging, but it won't take us long."

"Let's do it."

The first couple of lengths went up easily enough; the next one incorporated the start of the window recess.

"Same principle as the inside corners," Mike said. Charlie climbed the ladder and smoothed the paper down, butting it against the previous length. The window was open, and as she descended the ladder, a small gust lifted the paper away from the recess. The top started to curl away from the wall, and Mike moved to stop it, as did Charlie. His intention—to hold it so it didn't unstick further whilst Charlie went back up the ladder—was lost the instant he registered their closeness. Charlie's hip jutted into his groin and goosebumps rose along his bare arm as it brushed against hers.

"Awkward," she murmured. Still, she didn't move away.

The continued physical contact had sent signals firing around Mike's body, and if he didn't move soon, she'd know it. "Err, have you got it?" he asked.

"Which? The paper, or the message?"

"What d'you mean?"

Slowly, keeping her proximity, Charlie turned around and looked up at him. "It's mutual," she said. "The attraction."

"But…I thought you were seeing someone."

"You mean Megan?"

Mike nodded, although she could have provided any name at all, it wouldn't have mattered. His point was…well, his point was clearly way off base. "You're not a lesbian?"

Charlie's eyebrows rose and her eyes widened in annoyance. "No, I'm not," she said coolly. "I'm bisexual. I thought Andy or someone might've told you."

"Sorry. I didn't know." Her statement had thrown him a little because he'd figured part of the reason she didn't scare him was that there was no possibility of them ever being more than friends. Now he was waiting for the panic to set in and kill his arousal, except it didn't, and he wasn't sure what else to say. *I don't want a relationship* sounded like the brush-off, and right now, with his erection sandwiched between them, the very last thing he wanted to do was give her the brush-off.

"You need to make the first move, Mike."

His racing pulse filled his ears, and his stomach churned. "I don't know if I can."

Charlie offered him a smile of reassurance. "That's fine. We don't need to do anything."

"But I really want to." He swallowed, trying to lubricate his mouth, dry from heavy breathing. "Would you be upset if I told you it's only sex?"

"You mean you want a fuck buddy?"

Mike cringed. "I prefer the term friend with benefits myself."

Charlie laughed. "Whatever. We're mates already, and we're both single, so why not?"

She stretched up as he leaned down, their mouths meeting in a kiss that bypassed the peck stage and went straight to tongues and clashing teeth. His hands skimmed her back, down over her bra straps, catching in the creases of her soft jersey vest before he reached the bare strip of skin at her waist. He traced it around to the front, lightly tickling the satiny skin of her belly as he worked up the courage to unfasten her jeans. Her hands cupped his buttocks, pulling him against her and leaving little room for manoeuvre. He eased back and fumbled the button; she mimicked the action with his jeans, and he froze.

"I told you, didn't I?" he asked.

"What?"

"I've only got one ball."

Charlie stopped what she was doing, reached up and cupped his cheek, trying to keep her face straight, and failing. "So had Hitler, allegedly. Didn't hear Eva complaining." She returned to kissing him, but he was having a problem getting past his *disfigurement*. Charlie sighed into his mouth. "What difference does it make, unless you're planning on becoming an underwear model?"

"I'm not," he said.

She laughed against his lips. He wasn't trying to be funny, and he was probably coming across as a total dork, but she was still kissing and rubbing against him. His erection reinstated itself, and he returned the kiss, successfully unbuttoning her jeans and sliding them down just enough to grip her hips. Her muscles flexed to his touch, and he rutted, relaxing and finding his rhythm.

"I'm gonna go get a condom," she whispered, pulling away. "It'll give you time to make sure this is what you want. OK?"

"If it's what you want."

"Err…gonna go get a condom? That should give you a clue."
She left the room. He remained where he was, aroused enough
to ignore his second thoughts for the time being. It had been
too long since he'd felt virile, desirable. It helped that he'd had a
chance to show off something he was good at, even if it was only
hanging wallpaper. It also helped that he'd always been attracted
to Charlie, for her talents on the pitch as much as for her curvy
yet muscular physique.

She came back into the room, waved the condom at him
and then left it on the windowsill. On her travels, her jeans, still
unbuttoned, had slipped down further, revealing sculpted lower
abdominals and a glimpse of dark-brown hair peeking from the
waistband of women's grey boxers. He was staring, and probably
drooling, but he didn't care, and while he stared, she kicked off
her shoes and pushed her jeans down over her hips. Treading
out of them, she met his gaze and smiled.

"You getting your kit off, or what?"

"Scars." He pointed to his chest.

"Keep it on, then," she said, pulling her vest off and dropping
it to the floor. She reached both arms behind her to unfasten her
bra, letting it fall away. Now wearing only her boxers, Charlie
looked Mike up and down and shrugged, waiting for him to
make his move.

He advanced on her, pushing her back against the wall and
the still-wet wallpaper. He kissed her brusquely, trailing down
her chin, to her neck, to her breasts as she pushed away from
the wall, hoisting them into his face. He cupped and caressed,
squeezed, licked and sucked, needing as much contact as he
could get. As he kissed his way back to her mouth, his hands
roamed downwards, finding the coarse, dark hair with his
thumbs and circling, lower and lower.

"Take it off, please?" Charlie implored, tugging at his t-shirt.
His reluctance dwindling, he let her remove it, wriggling one
arm out at a time so he could continue working his way inside

her boxers. Now, both topless, the skin-to-skin contact had her lifting her pelvis, and his finger slid over her clitoris. For a few seconds, she stopped kissing him back, her expression giving away her pleasure as he applied light pressure and rapid strokes.

"That's so good," she said breathlessly as she grabbed at his zipper, her hands clumsy in her arousal. Shoving both his jeans and boxers down past his hips, she wrapped her fingers around him and tightened her grip. "OK?" she asked.

"Yeah." Better than. He thrust into her hand, setting the rhythm. "We might not need the condom after all," he said. He enjoyed penetrative sex, but it wasn't the be all and end all. Mutual masturbation could be just as satisfying, maybe more so, and the intimacy of the contact, of sharing an orgasm, was the same either way.

Mike pulled back so he could watch what they were doing to each other. It was pretty damn hot, and a relief that his boxers were concealing his scrotum, although he was at the point of not really caring. He sensed Charlie was more or less there with him, and as she rocked her hips, his fingertip slid back far enough to skim the ridge of her pubic bone. She squeezed him in her fist, her rhythm becoming erratic as she grabbed his head with her free hand and slammed their lips together, breathing hard through her nose. Her orgasm was enough to set his in motion, and he zoned out, riding high on the sensation, the powerful spasm that gripped him as he pumped into her hand.

"Might need to rehang that piece," he said, glancing over Charlie's shoulder as he came down, suddenly feeling self-conscious and hyper-aware of his surroundings. They'd just jacked each other off in her mum's spare room, and they hadn't even finished hanging the wallpaper first.

She looked, too, and laughed. "Yeah, well, it'll have to wait till next time. You've got a birthday party to get to."

"Shit, yeah." He looked around for something to clean up with.

"I'll get some loo roll," Charlie said and left the room, returning with a whole roll of toilet tissue.

"Cheers." Mike took it from her and tried to find the end of the roll. Charlie had already cleaned herself up and was putting her bra back on. "I was wondering," Mike said, "d'you fancy coming to a four-year-old's birthday party with me?"

"Um, not really?"

"Fair enough."

"But I will, for a mate."

Epilogue
Sunday, 28th October

"Bloody hell! Are you sure?" Mike muttered, using Bethan's car seat to nudge his way through the throng. He'd assumed all the cars outside Dan and Adele's place belonged to Dovedale residents, so he hadn't grumbled *much* about them having to park on the main road and lug Shu's present and his daughter all the way to the apartment. Judging by the filled-to-capacity— and then some—living room, he'd assumed wrong.

"Welcome to a Circle kids' party," Krissi said drolly.

"Where *are* the kids?" Charlie asked, which was a good question; it was all adults as far as the eye could see.

"Bouncy castle out back."

Mike stretched to peer over the heads of everyone else. Beyond the apartment's small patio and lawn was a bigger communal garden, where Shu and about twenty other four-year-olds were reaching bionic altitudes on an enormous, sparkly pink bouncy castle. "Where's Dan?"

"Feeding Robbie. Bedroom, I think."

"That's handy." Bethan needed a nappy change and quite possibly a nap. "You OK here?" Mike asked Charlie.

"Yep. You want me to get you a beer?"

"Yeah, cheers. See you in a bit." Mike dodged back through the crowd to his brother's bedroom and knocked on the door. "Dan? Can I come in?"

"If you must."

Mike opened the door, stepped inside, and quickly closed it again. "It's mad out there."

"You're not wrong." Dan was sitting on the bed with Robbie fast asleep in his arms. "I'm just making sure he's settled," he said with a wink.

Mike laughed. "Adele invited them all, then, did she?"

"Yeah, though most of them are Shu's classmates' parents. They'll be gone soon, and Shu's been up since…well, I don't think she slept at all, to be honest. So she'll be having an early night. Then it's just us grown-ups."

"Oh, right." Mike spread Bethan's changing mat on the bed and lifted her out of her car seat.

"I hope you're all right with that," Dan said.

"What?"

"I know you're not comfortable with social gatherings, and it's a bit underhand, but…Adele and Shaunna thought it best not to say anything."

Mike paused with a baby wipe in mid-air. "What are you prattling on about?"

"We're having a barbecue after the kids've all gone home."

Mike finished cleaning Bethan's bum—only wee—and put her clean nappy on. "And?" he prompted.

"And…we thought you'd refuse to come."

"I'm here, aren't I?"

"Yeah, for Shu's birthday party." Dan was suddenly very attentive to his son. "Which finishes at half four."

"Half four?" Mike repeated. Dan gave a regretful nod. "What time did it start?"

"Two."

Now he'd figured out what Dan was telling him, Mike was torn between calling him a knob and laughing at the ludicrous lengths they'd gone to in order to get him here. They really wanted him to come that badly? "Maybe next time, just try inviting me?"

"Thing is, bro, we did that last time."

"Yeah, and I was gonna come, but Adele went into labour."

"And the time bef—were you?"

"Yep. I went down to yours to tell you, but you'd already gone to the hospital."

"Ah." Dan looked sheepish.

Mike could see how bad Dan felt about lying, and while he was a bit pissed off about it, he could understand why they'd done it.

"Look, I'll hold my hands up. I'm not sociable like you and our Andy. I'm not sure you two would be, either, without the mates you've got. We can't all be that lucky."

"Friendship's not about luck, Mike. It's about putting yourself out there, taking a chance on other people."

"Yeah. I get that. What can I say? I'm a slow learner." He was trying to alleviate Dan's guilt, but there was an element of truth to his words. Mike hadn't put himself out there, first because he couldn't be bothered to make the effort, and then, when he finally did, he'd fallen into Rachel's trap. Slowly but surely, with the help of Shaunna and Charlie—and his brothers—he was beginning to accept that friendship *was* worth the effort. "Anyway," he said, "I've brought a mate along. Hope you don't mind."

"Not at all. Anyone I know?"

"Charlie. And she's driving, so I can have a beer."

"Good stuff." Dan shuffled to the side of the bed and carefully got up so he didn't disturb Robbie. He put him in his cot and turned back to his brother. "You know, Mike, being single's nothing to be ashamed of."

"I'm not. But it's no fun playing gooseberry. Me and Charlie were talking about it on the way over, and we're gonna be each other's plus-one as and when."

Dan nodded. "A good idea. Sort of friends with benefits, if you get me."

343

Mike felt the heat rush up his neck and tried to come up with a jokey retort to throw Dan off. There was another knock at the door.

"You decent, bro?"

"No!" Mike and Dan answered at the same time. The door opened anyway.

"Alright?" Andy asked, frowning as he looked from one to the other. They both nodded. "What you up to?"

"Settling Robbie," Dan said. Bethan had fallen asleep on her changing mat. "You want to leave her in here, Mike?"

"Yeah, if you wouldn't mind."

"No worries. I'll get the travel cot." Dan dodged past his brothers and out of the room.

Andy put his hands in his pockets and gave Mike an artificial smile.

"It's all right," Mike said. "He told me."

"Sorry."

"I'll forgive you this once."

"You came with Charlie, she was saying."

"Yeah. I was teaching her how to hang wallpaper. She agreed to come with me."

"Being single is nothing to be ashamed of."

"Oh, for fu… Dan just said exactly the same bloody thing. I'm not ashamed. I kind of like it, as it goes."

"Shame, that. You and Charlie—"

"We're mates, that's all," Mike interrupted. Andy's eyebrows rose. "Shaunna and Sean aren't screwing each other, are they?" It was a defensive low blow, and Mike regretted it the minute the words left his mouth.

"I dunno. They might be." Andy grinned, and Mike was grateful to him for letting it pass.

"Yeah, you wouldn't be grinning if they were."

"No, maybe not. But I know what you mean. Me and Charlie are mates and nothing more. It's purely platonic—except when we talk waves, then it goes a bit deeper." Judging by Andy's dreamy expression, he wasn't joking. He shook himself out of it. "Anyway…what were you saying?"

"That me and Charlie are just mates."

"That's right."

"Like…you and Jess were."

Andy turned and looked him in the eye. "Err…Mike?"

He nodded to confirm Andy's interpretation. "Don't tell Dan, though, will you?"

"No worries."

"Tell me what?" Dan passed between them and started setting up the travel cot.

"Oh, err…" Mike began, but he had nothing.

"Mike was just—" Andy circled his hand, like he was winding his brain in a bid to come up with something "—wondering… how much you're selling the apartment for." He shrugged apologetically, but there was no need. Dan had always been the same: if they could get him talking about money and his chances of making some, he'd instantly forget everything that had preceded it. It was a brilliant, well-practised diversion, and Mike would've high-fived Andy, except it would've given the game away.

"You know what?" Dan said. "That's not a bad idea." He put the mattress inside the cot and turned to Mike. "How would you feel about renting?"

"The travel cot?"

Dan laughed. "No, you plonker. The apartment."

"Oh!" Mike scratched his head, a delaying tactic so he could gauge whether Dan was serious. He certainly seemed to be. Mike nodded. "Yeah. If the rent's right."

"We've still got to find a house, but it should be this side of Christmas, and we can discuss it, negotiate a mutually acceptable rate. Deal?"

Mike took his time settling Bethan in the cot so he could mull it over. On the one hand, he didn't want to be in thrall to Dan; on the other, the apartment was exactly what he was after. He stood up straight again and held out his hand. "Deal," he said. He and Dan shook on it.

"Nice one," Andy said. "Right, shall we get back out there and join in the fun?"

Dan checked he had his phone and ushered his brothers towards the door. "You just wanna get on that bouncy castle."

"Too bloody right."

They made it outside in time to watch Shu blow out the candles on her birthday cake. It was a princess-themed, two-tiered Wotto special. On the top was a tiny princess that looked strikingly like Shu and which Adele quickly removed for safe-keeping before Krissi 'helped' Shu cut up the cake and dole it out—along with party bags—to her friends.

The children and their parents departed, leaving family and Dan and Adele's friends...The Circle. Mike knew them all, some better than others. Shaunna, for instance...

"Glad you came," she said, stopping to hug him on her way to refill her wine glass.

"Me, too." Mike followed her progress. She'd never know how grateful he was for all she'd done for him over the past few months. He honestly believed he wouldn't have made it through without her support, or Andy's.

"You need another beer, bro?"

"Yeah, cheers." Mike swigged the last inch from his bottle and gave it to Andy. All those years they hadn't got on, and it turned out it was just as their mum had always said. They were too alike, and these days, Mike was more than happy to accept the comparison—to either of his brothers, in fact. He looked around for Dan, eventually spotting him outside, with Shu in his arms, her head resting on his shoulder while he swayed her from side to side. She was loving her daddy's attention, but the poor little mite was shattered.

A bottle of beer was pushed into Mike's hand, and he snapped out his trance in time to see Andy head over to Shaunna. He gave her a lingering kiss and then whispered something in her ear that made her smile.

"Alright, mate?" Aitch said, stopping next to Mike.

"Alright, Aitch. How you doing?"

"Not too bad. Dan was telling me Rachel's been causing grief again."

"Yeah…not grief, as such. It's sorted now, anyway."

"Good to know. Listen, if she gives you any more trouble, give me a shout. I've got a couple of things on Ms. Perry that'll shut her up once and for all."

"OK." Mike didn't want to know. "Cheers, Aitch," he said, but Aitch was already on his way out to Dan.

"More fun than hanging wallpaper?" Charlie nudged him playfully.

"I'll come back to you on that one."

She nudged him again, not so playfully this time, and he grinned.

"D'you know what I've done? Left that condom on the windowsill. My mum and dad'll be home by now."

"Oops."

"Yeah, well, it's not like I'm fifteen, is it? Mind you…" She chewed her lip in thought. "That's Teddy's old room. I might just say I found it under the bed."

"Is your mum that bad?"

"No. She's that Catholic."

"My mum had a condom drawer."

"Really?"

"Really. Ask her if you don't believe me."

"Err, no."

Mike laughed. He'd had 'the talk' when he was about ten and had avoided any subsequent conversations with his mother about his sex life. At forty-four, he thought he'd probably be able to manage without lessons in the birds and the bees, although he'd thought that when he was forty-three, and he'd been wrong, but he'd never make that mistake again.

"The birthday princess is going to bed," Dan announced, carrying Shu through the living room, stopping for kisses from grandparents, aunties and uncles, biological or otherwise. When he returned, he fired up the barbecue and patio heaters, and most people went to sit outside.

"We're going home, Michael," his mum said. "Do you want us to take Bethan?" Before Mike could get a word in, she continued, "We're taking the twins, and…I know she's been with her grandma most of the day, but it'll save you having to worry about getting her to bed." She rubbed his arm and smiled up at him; she wasn't offering for his benefit.

"Yeah, that'd be great, Mum. Thanks. I'll come and give you a hand."

***

"Guess what."

Dan and Andy looked at each other and rolled their eyes. "What?" they asked in unison.

"Fine. If you're not interested…" Josh started to walk away.

"We are," Dan said quickly.

Josh turned back. He looked decidedly superior. "Someone's bought the Comco stadium."

"How d'you know?"

"I'm afraid it's confidential."

"Josh, please?" Andy said, or whined, really. Josh ignored him.

"Do *you* know who's bought it?" Dan asked.

"Yes, *I* do."

"Right."

Josh folded his arms and grinned. He was waiting for Dan to give in and ask the question, and Dan *really didn't want to*, but they knew each other of old. Josh would hold out, just for the fun of it, until Dan was begging shamelessly to know what he knew. Unless a suitable distraction came along...

George slid his hands around Josh's waist, encapsulating him from behind and murmuring close to his ear, "Adele asked if you want a coffee. She's putting the kettle on."

"Sweet nothings..." Dan muttered to Andy and averted his eyes, a little embarrassed but also highly amused by the way George could turn his husband from stubborn stoic to blushing romantic with a touch and the offer of caffeine.

"Is he winding you up?" George asked.

"No, he's been quite—" Josh started to answer but stopped when George tutted. "Oh!"

George chuckled and kissed Josh's cheek. "You're very warm," he observed, with a mischievous wink at Dan and Andy. "D'you think you should maybe move away from the barbecue?"

"I will...soon," Josh said. "I came over to tell them about the stadium."

"Uh-huh?" George released him. "Do I need to hold your coffee to ransom?"

"No." Josh smiled and batted his eyelashes. "I'll tell them now." George looked doubtful. "Promise."

Seemingly taking him at his word, George left.

Josh watched him retreat, all the way to the kitchen, and then turned to Dan with a wicked grin, but Dan was past playing games.

"Who bought it?" he asked.

"A local non-profit company."

Dan scratched his chin, fighting back a smile. There were times Josh's wind-ups really pissed him off, but he had a feeling this one was worth waiting for, so he asked, very slowly, "Which local non-profit company?"

"Are those sausages cooked yet?" Josh examined the barbecue. "Those at the back look done."

"So help me, in a minute, I'm gonna—"

Josh shifted his attention back to Dan and studied him for a moment before decreeing, "You're overdue a refresher on your anger management technique."

Dan laughed in disbelief. "You'll say that in front of my brother, but you can't tell us who told you about the Comco stadium?"

"It was a joke. I don't give refreshers, nor have I ever—"

"Josh, just bloody tell us, mate."

"Seeing as you asked so nicely. Ellie called to wish little Shaunna a happy birthday, and she happened to mention that James is coming up this way tomorrow to sign off on some trust projects."

"With you so far," Dan said to demonstrate he was.

Andy chuckled. Dan glared at him, and he busied himself with turning the sausages.

"You were saying," Dan prompted.

"Yes, James is coming up tomorrow…" Josh nodded as he said each word. Dan nodded with him and then shrugged. Andy snorted beer out of his nose. It landed in the flames, making them hiss and sizzle.

"Sleep deprivation," Josh concluded. "Or a lobotomy." He leaned closer to Dan and squinted at his forehead. "No scars, though."

"Sleep deprivation," Andy confirmed at the same time lifting his arm to block Dan's forward trajectory. "Don't hit him, bro."

"I wasn't going to." He pointed. "Your sausage is on fire."

Andy glanced down at his pants first and then at the barbecue. "Ah, crap." He quickly shoved the sausages out of the flames and tipped his beer over them. "Marinade," he said.

Josh laughed. "You two are utterly hilarious when you've had a drink."

"I'm still waiting for you to get to the point," Dan said curtly.

Josh sighed. "Andy, could you explain, please. I think I'm getting a migraine."

"No worries." He turned to Dan. "You listening?"

"I will if anyone says anything worth listening to."

"For fuck's sake." Andy picked up one of the sausages and shoved it in Dan's mouth to make sure he couldn't interrupt, or that was the plan. "OK. Comco stadium is now—"

Dan pulled the sausage from his mouth and finished Andy's sentence. "—a Campion Community Trust project."

"Well done!" Josh said.

Dan was stunned. "Jay bought—"

"—the stadium," Andy said, nodding.

"But I'm a—"

"—trustee? There're five of you. It only needs—"

"—three signatures. I know. Would you stop—"

"—interr—"

"No, really. Pack it in."

"I'm going," Josh said. "Although, actually, I was reading a very interesting study last week, which posited the theory that finishing each other's sentences and speaking at the same time are phenomena more frequently observed in monozygotic—"

"We're not twins!" Dan and Andy said in unison, followed by, "Fuck."

With a know-it-all smirk, Josh returned to George—now bearing coffee—and left them to their beer and barbecue.

"I hate it when he does that," Dan grumbled.

"Who does what?" Mike asked coming up between them and nicking a sausage. He bit the end off. "Why does it taste of lager?"

Dan thumbed in Andy's direction. "When people call us twins."

Mike frowned. "Yeah, I don't like it much, either, to be honest. Two's company, and all that. I think Shu's nailed it, actually."

Andy raised his beer bottle to his brothers and waited for them to do the same. "Here's to Team Jiffies?"

"Team Jiffies!"

They bashed their bottles together. Three arcs of frothy beer shot up into the air and landed with a *whoosh–splash*, successfully extinguishing the barbecue.

The End

About the Author

Debbie McGowan is an author and publisher based in a semi-rural corner of Lancashire, England. She writes character-driven, realist fiction, celebrating life, love and relationships. A working class girl, she 'ran away' to London at seventeen, was homeless, unemployed and then homeless again, interspersed with animal rights activism (all legal, honest ;)) and volunteer work as a mental health advocate. At twenty-five, she went back to college to study social science—tough with two toddlers, but they had a 'stay at home' dad, so it worked itself out. These days, the toddlers are young women (much to their chagrin), and Debbie teaches undergraduate students, writes novels and runs an independent publishing company, occasionally grabbing an hour of sleep where she can.

Social Media Links

Website: debbiemcgowan.co.uk
Newsletter Signup: eepurl.com/b8emHL
Blog: deb248211.blogspot.com
Facebook: facebook.com/DebbieMcGowanAuthor and facebook.com/beatentrackpublishing
Twitter: @writerdebmcg
YouTube: youtube.com/deb248211
Instagram: instagram/writerdebmcg
Google+: plus.google.com/+DebbieMcGowan
Tumblr: writerdebmcg.tumblr.com
LinkedIn: uk.linkedin.com/in/writerdebmcg
Goodreads: goodreads.com/DebbieMcGowan

By the Author

Checking Him Out Series
Checking Him Out (Book One)
Checking Him Out For the Holidays (Novella)
Hiding Out (Novella – Noah and Matty – HBTC Crossover)
Taking Him On (Book Two – Noah and Matty)
Checking In (Book Three)
The Making of Us (Book Four – Jesse and Leigh)

Seeds of Tyrone Series
~ co-written with Raine O'Tierney
Leaving Flowers (Book One)
Where the Grass is Greener (Book Two)
Christmas Craic and Mistletoe (Book Three)

Hiding Behind The Couch Series
The ongoing story of 'The Circle'…
Nine friends from high school;
Nine friends for life.

The Story So Far…
in chronological order:
novellas and short novels are 'stand-alone' stories, but tie in with the
series. Think Middle Earth—well, more Middle England, but with a
social conscience!

Beginnings (Novella)
Ruminations (Novel)
Class-A (Short Story)
Hiding Behind The Couch (Season One)
No Time Like The Present (Season Two)

354

The Harder They Fall (Season Three)
Crying in the Rain (Novel)
First Christmas (Novella)
In The Stars Part I: Capricorn–Gemini (Season Four)
Breaking Waves (Novella)
In The Stars Part II: Cancer–Sagittarius (Season Five)
A Midnight Clear (Novella)
Red Hot Christmas (Novella)
Two By Two (Season Six)
Hiding Out (Novella – CHO Crossover)
Breakfast at Cordelia's Aquarium (Short Story)
Chain of Secrets (Novella)
Those Jeffries Boys (Novel)
The WAG and The Scoundrel (Gray Fisher #1)
Reunions (Season Seven)
To Be Sure (Novella)
Tabula Rasa (Gray Fisher #2)
What A Scorcher! (Short Story)
Goth of Christmas Past (Novel)

Stand-Alone Stories

Champagne (LGBT Historical Novel)
'Time to Go' in *Story Salon Big Book of Stories (Contemporary Short Story)*
And The Walls Came Tumbling Down (Sci-fi Novel)
No Dice (Sci-fi Novel)
Double Six (Sci-fi Novel)
Sugar and Sawdust (M/M Romance Short Story)
Cherry Pop Valentine (M/M Romance Short Story)
Coming Up ~ co-written with Al Stewart (LGBT Short Story)
Of the Bauble (LGBT Fantasy Romance Novella)
So Long, Little Black Diamonds (Short (True) Story)
The Pastor's Last Drop (Historical Novel (Ongoing) – Wattpad)
When Skies Have Fallen (LGBT Historical Romance Novel)
A Snowy Ball (When Skies Have Fallen #1.5)
The Great Village Bun Fight

www.hidingbehindthecouch.com
www.debbiemcgowan.co.uk

Beaten Track Publishing

For more titles from Beaten Track Publishing,
please visit our website:

http://www.beatentrackpublishing.com

Thanks for reading!

www.ingramcontent.com/pod-product-compliance
Lightning Source LLC
Chambersburg PA
CBHW030551180626
46816CB00005B/1500